About the Authors

A charity-working, dog-walking, child-wrangling, dust-ignoring bookworm, **Jessica Gilmore** lives in the beautiful and historic city of York with one patient husband, one daughter, one very fluffy dog, two dog-loathing cats and a goldfish called Bob. As day dreaming is her very favourite hobby and she loves a good happy-ever-after Jessica can't believe she's lucky enough to write romance for a living. Say hi on Twitter at @yrosered or visit sprigmuslin.blogspot.com

RITA® Award-winning author **Leah Ashton** never expected to write books. She grew up reading everything – from pony books to cereal boxes at breakfast. One day she discovered romance novels – and one day, much later, wondered if she could write one too. Leah now writes happy ever afters for heroines who definitely don't need saving. When she's not writing, Leah loves all day breakfast, rambling conversations and laughing until she cries. She really hates cucumber. And scary movies.

Sherelle Green is a Chicago native with a dynamic imagination and a passion for reading and writing. Her love for romance developed in high school after stumbling across a hot and steamy Mills & Boon novel. She instantly became an avid romance reader and decided to pursue an education in English and Journalism. A true romantic, she believes in predestined romances, love at first sight and fairytale endings.

D0994416

Affairs of the Heart

Affairs of the Heart:
One Magical Night

JESSICA GILMORE

LEAH ASHTON

SHERELLE GREEN

MILLS & BOON

First Published in Great Britain 2021
By Mills & Boon, an imprint of HarperCollins*Publishers,* Ltd
1 London Bridge Street, London, SE1 9GF

www.harpercollins.co.uk

HarperCollins*Publishers*
1st Floor, Watermarque Building,
Ringsend Road, Dublin 4, Ireland

AFFAIRS OF THE HEART: ONE MAGICAL NIGHT © 2021 Harlequin Books S.A.

A Will, a Wish...a Proposal © 2015 Jessica Gilmore
Beware of the Boss © 2013 Leah Ashton
Red Velvet Kisses © 2014 Sherelle Green

ISBN: 978-0-263-30243-1

MIX
Paper from
responsible sources
FSC™ C007454

FSC
www.fsc.org

This book is produced from independently certified FSC™ paper to ensure responsible forest management.

For more information visit: www.harpercollins.co.uk/green

Printed and bound in Spain
by CPI, Barcelona

A WILL, A WISH...
A PROPOSAL

JESSICA GILMORE

To Jo, Rose and Sam—the best godmothers
any girl could ask for!

Thank you for all the love and support you give my
girl. She is very, very lucky to have you (as am I!).

Love you all very much,
Jessica x

CHAPTER ONE

'WHAT ON EARTH were you thinking?' Max Loveday burst into the office and shook the printed out press release in his father's direction. True to form his father's chair was turned away from the desk, allowing the occupant to face the window. Apparently the view over the city 'inspired' him.

'What on earth is DL Media going to do with a dating app?'

More pertinently, where exactly were the millions of dollars his father had apparently paid out for the app going to come from? In the last year every budget had been squeezed and slashed to accommodate his father's spending spree; there was no more give in the entire company.

Steven Loveday swivelled the black leather chair around and looked at his son, his expression as guileless as that of a three-month-old baby. It was, Max reflected, the expression he always wore when he was up to something.

And he usually was.

'Max? What a lovely surprise.'

Steven's voice was as rich as molasses and just as smooth. The kind of voice that oozed authority and paternal benevolence, as did the warm brown eyes and wide smile. It was a shame he didn't have the business acumen to match the veneer.

'When did you get back from Sydney?'

As if Max hadn't dropped him an email the second he had landed. He tightened his grip on the press release.

'Two hours ago.'

'I'm touched that you rushed over to see me but there was no need, dear boy. Take the rest of the day off.'

His father beamed at him as if he was giving Max a great treat.

'Why don't you go and visit your mother? Have you heard from her at all?'

'I can't take the day off.' Max refused to be diverted. He held up the piece of paper his PA had pressed into his hand the second he had walked into DL Media's head-quarters. 'What on earth is this? Why didn't you consult me?'

His father leaned back and stared at him, his chin propped on his steepled hands. It was a look he had probably seen in a film: the wise patriarch.

'Max.' There was steel in his voice. 'I know your grandfather gave you a lot of leeway, but can I remind you this is *my* company now?'

Just.

Max held a third outright, his father another third. But, crucially, the final third, the controlling share, was held in trust by his father until he retired. Then it would go to Max. If there was a company left by then. Or if Max didn't ask the board for a vote of no confidence first...

'Grandfather did *not* give me a lot of leeway.' He could feel the paper crumple, his grip tightening even more as he fought to control his temper. It was so typical of his father to reduce all his years of hard work and training to some sort of glorified work experience. 'He trusted me and trusted my judgement.'

As he never trusted you... The words were unsaid but hung in the air.

'Look, Dad, we have a five-year plan.' A plan his father seemed determine to ignore. 'A plan that kept us profitable through the financial crisis. We need to focus on the core business strengths, not get distracted by... by...' Max sought the right diplomatic words. *Shiny new toys* might be accurate, but they were unlikely to help the situation. 'By intriguing investments.'

Steven Loveday sighed, the deep breath resonating with regret. 'The problem with your grandfather was that he had no real vision. Oh, he was a media man through and through, and he knew publishing. But books are dead, Max. It's time for us to expand, to embrace the digital world.'

Max knew his mouth was hanging open, that he was gaping at his father with an incredulous look on his face, but his poker face was eluding him. His grandfather had had no vision? Was that truly what his father thought?

'He took DL global,' he managed after a long pause. 'Made us a household name.'

A name his father seemed determined to squander. What was it they said? One generation to found, another to expand and the third to squander? It looked as if Steven Loveday was going to prove the old adage right in record time.

Max's hands curled into fists. *Not if I have anything to do with it.*

'Everyone wanted this, Max. Have you seen the concept? It's brilliant! Bored and want to go out? Just log on and see who's free—make contact, get a reservation at a mutually convenient restaurant, book your taxi home.

And if the evening goes well you can even sort out a hotel room. It's going to revolutionise online dating.'

Possibly. But what did online dating have to do with publishing?

Max began to walk up and down the thickly carpeted office floor, unable to stay standing meekly in front of his father's desk like a schoolboy any longer.

'But we can't afford it. And, more crucially, it's not core business, Dad. It doesn't fit with the plan.'

'That was your grandfather's plan, not mine. We have to move with the times, Max.'

Max bit back a sigh. 'I know. Which is why we were the first to bring eBooks to the mainstream. Our interactive travel guides and language books are market leaders, and thanks to our subscription service our newspapers are actually in profit.'

He shouldn't need to be explaining this to his father. Max had always known that his father would inherit the controlling share of the company, even though Steven Loveday had only played at working over the last thirty years. He also knew how hard his grandfather had struggled with that decision, how close he had come to bypassing his son altogether for his grandson. But in the end even his hard-nosed grandfather hadn't been able to bring himself to humiliate his only child with a very public disinheriting.

And now the family business was paying the price.

The increasingly awkward silence was just beginning to stretch to excruciating when a loud and fast hip-hop tune blared out of the phone on his father's desk. It was the kind of ringtone Max would expect from a street-wise fifteen-year-old, not a fifty-eight-year-old man in a hand-made suit and silk tie, but his father's eyes lit up as he grabbed the telephone, his body swaying a little to the furious beat.

'Sweetie?'

Max could just make out a giggle from the caller. Not that he needed to hear the voice to know who it was. The inappropriate ringtone, the soppy expression on his father's face, the nauseating tone of his voice...

It had been six months. If his father was playing true to form he should be getting bored with his latest crush by now. But then none of this latest infatuation was running true to form. Not bringing it out in the open, not leaving Max's mother and setting up a love-nest in a Hartford penthouse... No, Steven Loveday's little affairs of the heart were usually as brief as they were intense, but they were always, *always* clandestine.

This...? This almost felt...well, *serious*.

His father looked over at Max. 'Mandy sends her love.'

Max muttered something inaudible even to himself. What was the etiquette here? Just what *did* you say to your father's mistress? Especially a mistress several years younger than yourself—and your own ex-PA. She'd giggled a lot less then.

To occupy himself while his father continued to croon sweet nothings down the phone, he pulled out his own phone and began to scroll through the long list of emails. As usual they were multiplying like the Hydra's head: ten springing forth for each one he deleted. His father's name might top the letterhead, but Max's workload seemed to have tripled in the last year no matter how many sixteen-hour days and seven-day weeks he pulled.

Delete, forward, mark for attention, delete, *definitely* delete... He paused. Another missive from Ellie Scott. What did Miss Prim and Proper want now?

Max had developed a picture of Ellie Scott over the last two months of mostly one-sided emails. She had to be of a similar age to his recently deceased great-aunt, probably wore tweed and had those horned reading glasses. In tortoiseshell. He bet that she played bridge, golfed in sturdy brogues and breakfasted on kippers and anaemic toast.

Okay, he had based her on all those old classic series featuring British spinsters of a certain age. But the bossy, imperative, clipped tone of her emails made him pretty certain he couldn't be that far off in his estimate.

And she lived to plague him. Her requests for information, agreement, input and, worst of all, his actual presence had upped from one a week to almost daily. Sure, the money his great-aunt had left to start a literary festival in a tiny village in the middle of nowhere might seem important to Miss Scott, but he had actual *real* work to do. At some point he was going to have to see if he could delegate or refuse the trustee post he had been bequeathed. *And* get somebody to sort out the house that was part of the same unwanted legacy.

There was just no time for anything that didn't involve clearing up after his father.

Max's finger didn't even pause as he pressed 'delete'. He moved on, reading another and another, and—hang on a minute. His eyes flicked back up the screen as he reread one, barely able to believe the words dancing in front of his eyes.

Irregularity...
Share of the company...
Your great-aunt...
Twenty-five per cent.

Max blinked, casting a quick glance over at his father. Did he know? Could it possibly be true that his recently deceased great-aunt had kept hold of her twenty-five per cent of DL Media even after she had walked away from her work and her family? The same great-aunt who had left her house and belongings to *him*? This could change everything.

Maybe Miss Scott's luck was in. A trip to Cornwall might be exactly what the lawyer ordered.

'Sorry about that.' His father's expression was a discomfiting mixture of slightly sheepish and sappy. 'Max, I would really appreciate it if you had a word with your mother.'

Here they went again. How many times had Max been asked to broker a rapprochement in the constant battlefield that was his parents' marriage? Every time he swore never to do it again. But someone had to be the responsible one in the family, and somehow, even when he could still measure his age in single digits, that person had had to be him.

But not this time.

'I'm sure she would rather hear from you.'

The sappy look on his dad's face faded. He was completely sheepish now, avoiding Max's eye and fiddling with the paperclips on his desk. 'My attorney has told me not to speak to her directly.'

Time stopped for one long second, the office freezing like a paused scene in a movie.

'Attorney? Dad, what on earth do you need an attorney for?'

'You're going to be a big brother.'

Max stopped in the middle of a breath. He was *what*?

'Mandy's pregnant and we're engaged. The second your mother stops being unreasonable about terms and we can get a divorce I'll be getting married. I'd like you to be my best man.'

His father beamed, as if he were conferring a huge honour on Max.

'Divorce?' Max shook his head as if he could magi-cally *un*-hear the words, pushing the whole 'big brother' situation far away into a place where he didn't have to think about it or deal with it. 'Come on, Dad. How many times have you fallen in love, only to realise it's Mum you need?'

Max could think of at least eight occasions without trying—but his dad had never mentioned attorneys be-fore.

'Max, she's demanding fifty per cent of my share of the company. And she wants it in cash if possible. DL can't afford that kind of settlement and *I* sure as hell can't. You have to talk her down. She'll listen to you.'

She wanted *what*? This was exactly what DL Media didn't need. An expensive and very public divorce. Max had two choices: help his dad, or involve the board and wrestle control of that crucial third of the company from his dad.

Either option meant public scrutiny, gossip, tearing the family apart. Everything his grandfather had trusted Max to prevent.

A pulse was throbbing in his temple, the blood thrum-ming in his veins. Talk to his mother, to the board, to his dad, go over the books yet again and try and work out how to put the company back on an even keel. There were no easy answers. Hell, right now he'd settle for *dif-ficult* answers.

Steven Loveday was still looking at him, appeal in his eyes, but Max couldn't, *wouldn't* meet his gaze. In-stead he found himself fixated on the large watercolour on the opposite wall: the only one of his grandfather's possessions to survive the recent office refurbishment. Blue skies smiled down on white-crested seas as green cliffs soared high above the curve of the harbour. Trengarth. The village his great-grandfather had left behind all those years ago. Max could almost smell the salt in the air, hear the waves crashing on the shore.

'I'm away for the next two weeks. The London office is shouting out for some guidance, and I need to sort out Great-Aunt Demelza's inheritance. You're on your own with this one, Dad. And for goodness' sake, don't throw everything away for an infatuation.'

He swivelled on his heel and walked towards the door, not flinching as his father called desperately after him. 'It's different this time, Max. I love her. I really do.'

How many times had he heard that one? His father's need to live up to their surname had caused more than enough problems in the Loveday family.

Love? No, thank you. Max had stopped believing in that long before his voice had broken, along with Father Christmas and life being fair. It was time his father grew up and accepted that family, position and the business came first. It was a lesson Max had learned years ago.

'Ellie, dear, I've been thinking about the literary festival.'

Ellie Scott turned around from the shelf she was rearranging, managing—*just*—not to roll her eyes.

It wasn't that she wanted to stifle independent thought in Trengarth. She didn't even want to stifle it in her shop—after all, part of the joy of running a bookshop was seeing people's worlds opening out, watching their horizons expanding. But every time her assistant—her hard-working, good-hearted and extremely able assistant, she reminded herself for the three billionth time—uttered those words she wanted to jump in a boat and sail as far out to sea as possible. Or possibly send Mrs Trelawney out in it, all the way across the ocean.

'That's great, Mrs Trelawney. Make sure you hold on to those thoughts. I'll need to start planning it very soon.'

Her assistant put down her duster and sniffed. 'So you say, Ellie...so you say. Oh, I've been defending you. "Yes, she's an incomer," I've said. "Yes, it's odd that old Miss Loveday left her money to Ellie and not to somebody born and bred here. But," I said, "she has the interests of Trengarth at heart."'

Ellie couldn't hold in her sigh any longer. 'Mrs Trelawney, you know as well as I do that I *can't* do anything. There are two trustees and we have to act together. My hands are tied until Miss Loveday's nephew deigns to honour us with his presence. And, *yes*,' she added as Mrs Trelawney's mouth opened. 'I have emailed, written and begged the solicitors to contact him. I am as keen to get started as you are.'

'Keen to give up a small fortune?' The older woman lifted her eyes up to the heavens, eloquently expressing just how implausible she thought that was.

Was there any point in explaining yet again that Miss Loveday hadn't actually left her fortune to Ellie personally, and that Ellie wasn't sitting on a big pile of cash, cackling from her high tower at the poverty stricken villagers below? The bequest's wording was very clear: the money had been left in trust to Ellie and the absent second trustee for the purposes of establishing an annual literary festival in the Cornish village.

Of course not every inhabitant of the small fishing village felt that a festival was the best thing to benefit the community, and most of them seemed to hold Ellie solely responsible for Demelza Loveday's edict. In vain had Ellie argued that she was powerless to spend the money elsewhere, sympathetic as she was to the competing claims of needing a new playground and refurbishing the village hall—but her hands were tied.

'Look, Mrs Trelawney. I know how keen you are to get started, and how many excellent ideas you have. I promise you that if Miss Loveday's nephew does not contact me in the next month then I will go to America myself and force him to co-operate.'

'Hmm.' The sound spoke volumes, as did the accompanying and very thorough dusting of already spotless shelves.

Ellie didn't blame Mrs Trelawney for being unconvinced. Truthfully, she had no idea how to get the elusive Max Loveday *to* co-operate. Tempting as it was to imagine herself striding into his New York penthouse and marching him over to an aeroplane, she knew full well that sending yet another strongly worded email was about as forceful as she was likely to get.

Not to mention that she didn't actually know where he lived. But if she was going to daydream she might as well make it as glamorous as possible.

Ellie stepped back and stared critically at the display shelf, temptingly filled with the perfect books to read on the wide, sandy Trengarth beach—or to curl up with if the weather was uncooperative. Just one week until the schools broke up and the season started in full. It was such a short season. Trengarth certainly needed something to keep the village on the tourism radar throughout the rest of the year. Maybe this festival was part of the answer.

If they could just get started.

Ellie stole a glance over at her assistant. Her heart was in the right place. Mrs Trelawney had lived in the village all her life. It must be heartbreaking for her to see it so empty in the winter months, with so many houses now second homes and closed from October through to Easter.

'If I can't get an answer in the next two weeks then I will look into getting him replaced. There must be *something* the solicitors can do if he simply won't take on his responsibilities. But the last thing I want to do is spend some of the bequest on legal fees. It's only been a few months. I think we just need to be a little patient a little longer.'

Besides, the elusive Max Loveday worked for DL Media, one of the big six publishing giants. Ellie had no idea if he was an editor, an accountant or the mail boy, but whatever he did he was bound to have some contacts. More than the sole proprietor of a small independent bookshop at the end of the earth.

The bell over the door jangled and Ellie turned around, grateful for the opportunity to break off the awkward conversation.

Not that the newcomer looked as if he was going to make her day any easier, judging by the firm line of his mouth and the expression of distaste as he looked around the book-lined room from his vantage position by the door.

It was a shame, because under the scowl he was really rather nice to look at. Ellie's usual clientele were families and the older villagers. It wasn't often that handsome, youngish men came her way, and he was both. Definitely under thirty, she decided, and tall, with close-cut dark hair, a roughly stubbled chin and eyes so lightly brown they were almost caramel.

But the expression in the eyes was hard and it was focussed right onto Mrs Trelawney.

What on earth had her assistant been up to now? Ellie

knew there was some kind of leadership battle on the Village in Bloom committee, but she wouldn't have expected the man at the door to be involved.

Although several young and trendy gardeners *had* recently set up in the vicinity. Maybe he was very passionate about native species and tasteful colour combinations?

'Miss Scott?'

Unease curdled Ellie's stomach at the curt tone, and she had to force herself not to take a step back. *This is your shop*, she told herself, folding her hands into tight fists. *Nobody can tell you what to do. Not any more.*

'I'm Ellie Scott.' She had to release her assistant from that gimlet glare. Not that Mrs Trelawney looked in need of help. Her own gaze was just as hard and cold. 'Can I help?'

'*You?*'

The faint tone of incredulity didn't endear him any further to Ellie, and nor did the quick glance that raked her up and down in one fast, judgemental dismissal.

'You can't be. You're just a girl.'

'Thank you, but at twenty-five I'm quite grown up.'

His voice was unmistakably American which meant, surely, that here at last was the other trustee. Tired and jetlagged, probably, which explained the attitude. Coffee and a slice of cake would soon set him to rights.

Ellie held out her hand. 'Please, call me Ellie. You must be Max. It's lovely to meet you.'

'*You're* the woman my great-aunt left half her fortune to?'

His face had whitened, all except his eyes, which were a dark, scorching gold.

'Tell me, Miss Scott…' He made no move to take her hand, just stood looking at her as if she had turned into a toad, ice frosting every syllable. 'Which do you think is worse? Seducing an older married man for his money or befriending an elderly lady for hers?'

He folded his arms and stared at her.

'Any thoughts?'

CHAPTER TWO

MAX HADN'T INTENDED to go in all guns blazing. In fact he had entered the bookshop with just two intentions: to pick up the keys to the house his great-aunt had left him and to make it very clear to the domineering Miss Scott that the next step in sorting out his great-aunt's quixotic will would be at *his* instigation and in *his* time frame.

Only he had been wrong-footed at the start. Where was the hearty spinster of his imagination? He certainly hadn't been expecting this thin, neatly dressed pale girl. She was almost mousy, although there *was* a delicate beauty in her huge brown eyes, in the neatly brushed sweep of her light brown hair that looked dull at first glance but, he noticed as the sunlight fell on it, was actually a mass of toffee and dark gold.

She didn't look like a con artist. She looked like the little match girl. Maybe that was the point. Maybe inspiring pity was her weapon. He had thought, assumed, that his co-trustee was an old friend of Great-Aunt Demelza. Not a girl younger than Max himself. Her youth was all too painfully reminiscent of his father's recent insanity, even if Ellie Scott seemed to be missing some of Mandy's more obvious attributes.

The silence stretched long, thin, almost unbearable before Ellie broke it. 'I beg your pardon?'

There was a shakiness in her voice but she stayed her ground, the large eyes fixed on him with painful intensity.

Max was shocked by a rush of guilt. It was like shooting Bambi.

'I think you heard.'

He was uneasily aware that they had an audience. The angular, tweed-clad old lady he had assumed was Ellie Scott was standing guard by the counter, a duster held threateningly in one hand, her sharp eyes darting expectantly from one to the other like a tennis umpire. He should give her some popcorn and a large soda to help her fully enjoy the show.

'I was giving you a chance to backtrack or apologise.'

Ellie Scott's voice had grown stronger, and for the first time he had a chance to notice her pointed chin and firm, straight eyebrows, both suggesting a subtle strength of character.

'But if you have no intention of doing either than I suggest you leave and come back when you find your manners.'

It was his turn to think he'd misheard. 'What?'

'You heard me. Leave. And unless you're willing to be polite don't come back.'

Max glared at her, but although there was a slight tremor in her lightly clenched hands Ellie Scott didn't move. Fine.

He walked back over to the door and wrenched it open. 'This isn't over, honey,' he warned her. 'I will find out exactly how you manoeuvred your way into my great-aunt's good graces and I will get back every penny you conned out of her.'

The jaunty bell jangled as he closed the door behind him. Firmly.

The calendar said it was July, but the Cornish weather had obviously decided to play unseasonal and Max, who had left a humid heatwave behind in Connecticut, was hit by a cold gust of wind, shooting straight through the thin cotton of his T-shirt, goose-pimpling his arms and shocking him straight to his bones.

And sweeping the anger clear out of his head.

What on earth had he been thinking? Or, as it turned out, *not* thinking. *Damn*. Somehow he had completely misfired.

Max took a deep breath, the salty tang of sea air filling his lungs. He shouldn't have gone straight into the shop after the long flight and even longer drive from Gatwick airport to this sleepy Cornish corner. Not with the adrenaline still pumping through his veins. Not with the scene with his father still playing through his head.

Who knew what folly his father would commit without Max keeping an eye on him? Where his mother's anger and sense of betrayal would drag them down to?

But that was their problem. DL Media was his sole concern now.

Max began to wander down the steep, narrow sidewalk. It felt as if he had reached the ends of the earth during the last three hours of his drive through the most western and southern parts of England. A drive that had brought him right here, to the place his great-grandfather had left behind, shaking off his family ties, the blood and memories of the Great War and England, when he had crossed the channel to start a whole new life.

And now Max had ended up back here. Funny how circular life could be...

Pivoting slowly, Max took a moment to see just where *'here'* was. The briny smell might take him back to holidays spent on the Cape, but Trengarth was as different from the flat dunes of Cape Cod as American football was from soccer.

The small bookshop was one of several higgledy-piggledy terraces on a steep narrow road winding up the cliff. At the top of the cliff, imperiously looking down onto the bay and dominating the smaller houses dotted around it, was a white circular house: his Great-Aunt Demelza's house. The house she had left to him. A house where hopefully there would be coffee, some food. A bed. A solution.

If he carried on heading down he would reach the sea-front and the narrow road running alongside the ocean. Turn left and the old harbour curved out to sea, still filled with fishing boats. All the cruisers and yachts were moored further out. Above the harbour the old fisher-men's cottages were built up the cliff: a riotous mixture of colours and styles.

Turn right and several more shops faced on to the road before it stopped abruptly at the causeway leading to the wide beach where, despite or because of the weather, surfers were bobbing up and down in the waves, look-ing like small, sleek seals.

Give him an hour and he could join them. He could take a board out...hire a boat. Forget his cares in the cold tang of the ocean.

Max smiled wryly. If only he could. Pretend he was just another American tourist retracing his roots, shrug-ging off the responsibilities he carried. But, like Atlas, he was never going to be relieved of his heavy burden.

It *was* a pretty place. And weirdly familiar—although maybe not that weird. After all, his grandfather had had several watercolours of almost exactly this view hang-ing in his study. Yes, there were definitely worse places to work out a way forward.

Only to do that he needed to get into that large white house. And according to the solicitor he had emailed from the plane, Ellie Scott was holding the keys to that very house. Which meant he was going to have to eat some humble pie. Max was normally quite a fan of pie, but that was not a flavour he enjoyed.

'Suck it up, Max,' he muttered to a low-flying seagull, which was eyeing him hopefully. 'Suck it up.'

He was going to have to go back to the bookshop and start the whole acquaintance again.

Ellie was doing her best to damp down the dismaying swirl in her stomach and get on with her day.

She hadn't caved, had she? Hadn't trembled or wept or tried to pacify him? She had stayed calm and collected and in control. On the outside, at least. Only she knew that right now she wanted nothing more than to sink into the old rocking chair in the corner of the childcare section and indulge in a pathetic bout of tears.

The sneering tone, the cold, scornful expression had triggered far more feelings than she cared to admit. She had spent three years trying to pacify that exact tone, that exact look—and the next three years trying to forget. In just five minutes Max Loveday had brought it all vividly back.

Darn him—and darn her shaky knees and trembling hands, giving away her inner turmoil. She'd thought she was further on than this. Stronger than this.

Ellie had never thought she would be quite so glad for Mrs Trelawney's presence, but right now the woman was her safety net. While she sat there, busily typing away on her phone, no doubt ensuring that every single person in Trengarth was fully updated on the morning's events, Ellie had no option but to hold things together.

Instead she switched on the coffee machine and unpacked the cakes she had picked up earlier from the Boat House café on the harbour.

Ellie had always dreamed of a huge bookshop, packed with hidden corners, secret nooks, and supplemented by a welcoming café full of tasty treats. What she had was a shop which, like all the shops in Trengarth, was daintily proportioned. Fitting in all the books she wanted to stock in the snug space was enough of a challenge. A café would be a definite step too far. She had compromised with a long counter by the till heaped with a tempting array of locally made scones and cakes and a state-of-the-art coffee machine. Buying in the cakes meant she didn't have to sacrifice precious stock space for a kitchen.

It took just a few moments to arrange the flapjacks, Cornish fairing biscuits, brightly coloured cupcakes and scones onto vintage cake stands and cover them with the glass domes she used to keep them fresh.

'We have walnut, orange and cheese scones.' She deliberately spoke aloud as she began to chalk up the varieties onto the blackboard she kept propped on the table, hoping Mrs Trelawney would take the hint, stop texting and start working. 'The cupcakes are vanilla and the big cake is...let me see...yep, carrot and orange.'

'It's a bit early for cake...'

The drawling accent made her stop and stiffen.

'But I'll take a walnut scone and a coffee. Please.'

The last word was *so* evidently an afterthought.

Ellie smiled sweetly as she swivelled round. No way was she going to give him the satisfaction of seeing how uncomfortable he'd made her.

'It's self-service and pay at the till. You, however, are barred. You'll have to get your coffee somewhere else.'

'Look…' Max Loveday looked meaningfully over at Mrs Trelawney. 'Can we talk? In private?'

Ellie's heart began to pick up speed, her pulse hammering. No way was she going anywhere alone with this man. He might be smiling now, but she wasn't fooled.

'I don't think so. You had no problem insulting me in front of my assistant. I'm sure she can't wait to hear round two.'

He closed his eyes briefly. 'Fair point.'

'Oh, good.' She hadn't expected him to capitulate so easily. It was an unexpected and unwanted point in his favour. 'Go on, then. Say whatever it is you have to say.'

'I was out of line.'

Ellie folded her arms and raised her eyebrows. If Max Loveday thought he was getting away with anything short of a full-on grovel he could think again.

'Yes…?' she prompted.

'And I'm sorry. It's no excuse, but my family is going through some stuff right now and I'm a little het-up about it.'

'Tell me, Mr Loveday…' Ellie deliberately parroted his words back to him. 'Which is worse? Seducing a family man for his money or conning an old lady out of her cash? And which are you accusing *me* of?'

As if she didn't know. Well, if she'd conned the old lady he'd been right there with her; he was joint trustee after all.

'I think they're both pretty vile.' There was a bleakness in his voice, and when his eyes rested on Ellie the hardness in them unnerved her. He hadn't come back because he was stricken with remorse. He still thought her guilty.

'So do I.' The look of surprise on his face gave her courage. 'I also think making slanderous accusations against strangers and proffering fake apologies in order to get the keys to a house and a cup of coffee is pretty out of order. What do you say to *that*, Mr Loveday?'

'I'm prepared to pay for the coffee.'

It wasn't much of a retort but it was the best he could do when he was firmly in the wrong—as far as manners were concerned—and so tired that the wooden floor was beginning to look more than a little inviting. Flying Sydney to Boston to Hartford and then on to England in just a few days had left him in a grey smog that even first-class sleep pods hadn't quite been able to dispel.

'Look, you have to admit my great-aunt's will is pretty unusual. Leaving her entire fortune in the hands of a virtual stranger.'

The large brown eyes darkened with something that looked very much like scorn. It wasn't an expression Max was used to seeing in anybody's eyes and it stung more than he expected.

'Yes, she said more than once that she wished she knew her great-nephew more. I thought this was her way of trying to include you.'

Damn her, he hadn't meant *himself*—and he would bet a much needed good night's sleep she knew that full well.

'It was her money to leave as she liked. I didn't expect to inherit a penny. Nor do I need to. If she wanted to leave it all to charity that's one thing. But this...? This is craziness. Leaving it to you...to found a festival. I didn't ask to be involved.'

He just couldn't comprehend it. What on earth had his great-aunt been thinking? What did he know or care about a little village on the edge of the ocean?

'She didn't actually leave the money to me, to you or to *us*.'

Ellie sounded completely exasperated. Max got the feeling it wasn't the first time she'd had this conversation.

'I can't touch a penny without your say-so and vice versa—and we're both completely accountable to the executors. There is no fraud here, Mr Loveday, and no coercion. Nothing at all except a slightly odd request made by a whimsical elderly lady. Didn't you read the will?'

'I read enough to know that she left you this shop.'

No coercion, indeed. Ellie Scott wasn't just a trustee she was a beneficiary: inheriting the shop and the flat above it. The flat she already currently resided in, according to the will. It was all very neat.

'Yes...' The brightness dimmed from her eyes, and it was as if the sun had gone behind a cloud. 'She was always good to me. She was my godmother. Did you know that? My grandmother's best friend, and my own good, dear friend. I will always be grateful to her. For everything.'

'Your godmother?'

Damn, he had come into the whole situation blind and it was completely unlike him. It was sloppy, led to mistakes.

'Yes. But even more importantly she was your greataunt. Which is why she wanted you involved in her legacy, why she left you the house. It was the house her father was born in, apparently. And *his* father was some kind of big deal sea captain. He would have been...what? Your great-great-grandfather?'

'Yes, although I don't know anything about him or about anything to do with the English side of the family. A sea captain?' A reluctant smile curved his lips. He had been in Cornwall all of an hour and had already discovered some unknown family history. 'My grandfather took me sailing all the time. He had a house on the

Cape. Said he always slept best when he could hear the sea. Must be in our blood.'

'You can hear the sea from every room in The Round House too. Maybe my godmother knew what she was doing when she left the house to you.'

'Maybe.'

It was a nice idea. But, *really*? A house? In Cornwall? A seven-hour flight and a tedious long drive from his home. It would have been far simpler if Great-Aunt Demelza had instructed her solicitors to liquefy the whole estate and endowed a wing at her favourite museum or hospital. *That* was how philanthropy worked. Not this messy, getting involved business.

Although it *was* kind of cool to find out about his distant Cornish heritage. A sea captain... Maybe there was a photo back at the house.

A voice broke in from the corner and Max jumped. He'd forgotten about their audience.

'This is all very entertaining. But what I want to know, Ellie, is are you planning to actually start this festival or not?'

Ellie looked at him, her face composed. 'I don't think that's up to me any more, Mrs Trelawney. Well, Mr Loveday? Are you willing to work with me? Or do we need to call the solicitors in and find a way around the trust?'

'I can't just drop everything, Miss Scott. I have a very busy job. A job in Connecticut. Across the ocean. I can't walk away to spend weeks playing benefactor by the sea.'

But even as he spoke the words a chill shivered through him. What did the next few months hold? Could he find a way to make his father toe the line—or was he going to have to force a vote at the board?

He would win. He knew many of the board members shared his misgivings. But then what?

His already fragile relationship with his father would be irrevocably shattered.

It was a price he was willing to pay. And if his great-aunt's house *did* hold the key to an easy win then the least he could do was help get her dream started while he was here. His mouth twisted. It wasn't as easy to walk away from family obligations as he'd thought, even when the family member was a stranger *and* deceased.

'I can give you two weeks. Although I'll be in London some of that time. Take it or leave it.'

Ellie's cool gaze was fixed on him. As if she could see straight into the heart of him—and see all that was missing.

'Fine.'

'So I can set up a meeting?' asked Mrs Trelawney. 'I have a lot of ideas and I know many other people do too.' Ellie's assistant had given up any pretence of working, her eyes bright as she leaned onto the counter. 'We could have a theme. Or base it on a genre? A murder mystery with actors? Or should we have it food-related. There could be baking competitions—make your favourite literary cake.'

Your favourite *what*? Max tried to avoid catching Ellie's eye but it was impossible to look away. The serious, slightly sad expression had disappeared, to be replaced by a mischievous smile lurking in the deep brown depths of her large eyes.

He could feel an answering gleam in his own eyes, and his mouth wanted to smile in response, to try and coax a grin out of her, but he kept his face as calm and sincere as he could, trying to keep all his focus on Mrs Trelawney.

But he couldn't stop his gaze sliding across to watch Ellie's reaction. She was leaning against a bookcase, her arms folded as her face sparkled in amusement.

'They are excellent ideas,' he managed, and was rewarded by the quick upturn of her full mouth and the intriguing hint of a dimple in one pale cheek. 'But we are at a very early stage. I think we need to talk to the solicitors and look at funds before we...ah...appoint a committee. I do hope you can manage to hold on to those ideas for just a little longer?'

'Well, yes.' Mrs Trelawney's cheeks were pink. 'Of course. I can make a list. I have a lot of ideas.'

'I for one can believe it.' Ellie pushed away from the shelves in one graceful movement. 'I'm expecting a delivery in an hour, Mrs Trelawney, so now would be a good time for you to take your break if that's convenient?'

'My break?' Mrs Trelawney's eyes moved from Max to Ellie and back again before she reluctantly nodded.

Ellie didn't speak again until her assistant had collected her bag and left the shop. 'Poor Mrs T. She's torn between being the first to spread the gossip and fear of missing out on any more. Still, the arrival of Demelza Loveday's mysterious American great-nephew should give her enough to be getting on with. And...' there was a tart note in her voice '...you certainly managed to stir things up when you walked into my shop.'

This was his chance to apologise. Max still wasn't entirely sure what to make of Ellie Scott, but what had his grandfather always said? It was much easier to judge from the inside rather than out in the cold. 'I had my reasons. But they didn't really have anything to do with you. I'm sorry.'

Ellie pushed back a piece of hair that had fallen out of the clip confining the long tresses. 'I can't say that's okay, because it isn't. But I'm willing to give you a second chance. It's going to be hard enough for two incomers to win the support of a place like Trengarth as it is, without being at war ourselves.'

'You're an incomer?' Max wasn't exactly an expert on British accents and Ellie sounded just as he'd expected her to: like the heroine of one of those awful films where girls wore bonnets and the men tights, all speaking with clipped vowels and clear enunciation.

'I spent most of my childhood summers here, and I've lived here for the last three years, but I'll still be an incomer in thirty.' She hesitated. 'Look, I'll be honest. I would be more than happy to see you off the premises and never have to deal with you again, but we have to work together for the next two weeks. You must be tired and jetlagged. Why don't you go and rest now and come back tomorrow? We'll start again.'

Her words were conciliatory, her voice confident, but there was a wariness in her posture. She was slightly turned away, the slim shoulders a little hunched, and her arms were protectively wrapped around her. She was afraid of something. Afraid of him? Of what he might discover? Maybe she wasn't as innocent as she appeared.

He'd been putting this off long enough, distracted by his father's extra-marital shenanigans and the all-consuming pressures of living up to the family legacy. It was time to talk to the solicitors, read the damn will properly and find out just what Ellie Scott was hiding.

'That is a very generous offer. Thank you.'

Ellie exhaled on a visible sigh of relief.

'Then I'll see you back here tomorrow. I'll telephone the solicitors and see if they can fit us in. Do you know how to get to the house?'

She walked around the counter, crouching down and disappearing from view before handing him a set of keys.

They were old-fashioned iron keys. Heavy and unwieldy. 'I'll find my way, thanks. See you later, honey.'

It was both a promise and a threat—and he was pretty sure she knew it.

CHAPTER THREE

THE SHOP HAD been busy. So busy Ellie hadn't had a moment to dwell on the morning's encounter. And even though she knew a fair few of her customers had come in to try and prise information about Max Loveday out of her—or out of the far more forthcoming Mrs Trelawney—they had all bought something, even if it was just a coffee.

Slowly Ellie began to tidy up, knowing that she was deliberately putting off the moment when she would head upstairs. She loved her flat, and normally she loved the silence, the space, the solitude. Knowing it was hers to do with as she pleased. But this evening she dreaded the time alone. She knew she would relive every cutting remark, every look, every moment of her bruising encounter with Max Loveday. And that inevitably her thoughts would turn to her ex-fiancé. It wasn't a place she wanted to go.

And tomorrow she would have to deal with Max all over again.

As always, the ritual of shutting up shop soothed her. From the day she had opened it the shop had been a sanctuary. *Her* sanctuary. She had planned and designed every feature, every reading nook and display, had painted the walls, hung the pictures, shelved each and every book. Had even chosen the temperamental diva of a coffee machine, which needed twenty minutes of cleaning and wiping before she could put it to bed, and sanded the wood she used for a counter.

She had been able to indulge her love of colour, of posters, of clutter. Nobody expected a bookshop to be tastefully minimalist.

By seven o'clock Ellie could put it off no longer. Every book was in its rightful place. Even the preschool picture books were neatly lined up in alphabetical order. A futile task—it needed just one three-year-old to return the entire rack to chaos.

The shelves were gleaming and dust-free, the cushions on sofas, chairs and benches were shaken out and plumped up, the floor was swept and the leftover cakes had been boxed away. She'd even counted the cash and reconciled the till.

There was literally nothing left to do.

Except leave.

Ellie switched the lights off and stood for a moment, admiring the neatness of the room in the evening light. 'Thank you,' she whispered. If Demelza Loveday hadn't encouraged her to follow her dreams, hadn't rented her the shop, where would Ellie be now?

And, like the fairy godmother she'd been, Miss Loveday had ensured that Ellie could always stay here, always be safe. The shop and the flat were hers. Nobody could ever take them away from her. And, no matter what Max Loveday thought, it hadn't been Ellie's idea. The legacy was a wonderful, thoughtful gift—and it had been a complete surprise. The one bright moment in the grey weeks following Miss Loveday's death and the unwelcome burden of the trust.

A rap at the closed door made her jump. The shop was evidently closed. The sign said so, the shutter was drawn, the lights dimmed right down in the two bay windows. But it wouldn't be the first time someone had needed an emergency gift. That was the thing about small towns: you were never really fully closed.

'Coming,' she called as she stepped over to the door, untwisting the lock and shooting back the two bolts before cautiously opening it…just a few centimetres. Not that there had ever been any robbery beyond the odd bit of shoplifting in Trengarth's small high street.

Ellie's hands tightened on the doorframe as she took in the lean, tall figure, the close-cut dark hair and stubbled chin.

She swallowed. Hard. 'I didn't think we were meeting until tomorrow.' She didn't open the door wider or invite him to come in.

'I wanted to apologise again.' Max held up a bottle of red wine. 'I found this in Great-Aunt Demelza's wine cellar. She had quite a collection.'

'It's your collection now.' Ellie didn't reach out and take the bottle, her hands still firmly clasping the door, keeping it just ajar.

Max pulled a face. 'I can't quite get my head around that. It seemed pretty intrusive, just walking in and showering in the guest en-suite bathroom, looking around at all her stuff. I mean, I didn't actually know her.'

Showering? Ellie immediately tried to push that particular image out of her mind but it lingered there. A fall of water, right onto a tanned, lean torso… Her fingers tightened as her stomach swooped. Her libido had been dead for years. Did it *have* to choose right this moment to resuscitate itself?

'I was planning on chocolates as well, but the shop is shut.' He gestured behind him to the small all-purpose supermarket. 'They were shut this morning as well. Do they *ever* open?'

Ellie looked over at the firmly drawn shutters, grateful for a chance to think about anything but long, steamy showers. 'They do open for longer in the school holidays, but otherwise the hours are a little limiting. It's okay if you know them, but it can be frustrating for tourists—and then Mr Whitehead complains that people drive to the next town and use the bigger supermarkets.'

There. That was a perfectly safe, inane and even dull comment. Libido back in check. She was most definitely *not* looking at the golden tan on his arms, nor noticing the muscle definition under his T-shirt. No, not at all.

'You really didn't have to,' she hurried on, forcing her eyes back up and focussing firmly on his ear. No one could have inappropriate thoughts about an ear, could they? 'Really.'

'I think I did.' His smile was rueful. 'I managed a few hours' sleep on the couch and when I woke up I felt just terrible. Not just because of the jetlag. My grandfather would have been horrified if he had heard me speak to a lady that way. He brought me up better than that.'

Grandfather? Not parents? Interesting...

'Anyway, I thought I'd make amends and get some air...have a look at this town my great-grandfather crossed an ocean to escape. I don't suppose you'd like to join me? Show me around?'

No, she most definitely would not. In fact she had a very important date with the new edition of *Anne of Green Gables* she had unpacked that very morning: hardback, illustrated and annotated. She also had a quarter-bottle of wine, a piece of salmon and some salad.

Another crazy evening in the Scott household of one.

Would anything change if she threw caution to the

wind and went out for a walk before dinner, book, bath and bed? In fact she often took an evening walk. The only real difference would be her companion.

He was her beloved godmother's nephew. Surely Demelza would have wanted her to make him welcome, no matter how bad his first impression? Hadn't she just been remembering just how much she owed her benefactress? She really should replay the debt. Besides, he was trying to make amends. She wasn't used to that.

A flutter started low down in her stomach. For so many years she had been told she was in the wrong, no matter what the reality. A man admitting his mistake was a novel experience.

Ellie swung the door open and stood back. 'Come in,' she invited him. 'I just need to change my shoes and grab my bag.'

It would have been nice to have some more notice. She was still in the grey velvet skinny jeans she had pulled on that morning, teamed with a purple flowered tunic. Her hair was neatly tucked back in a clip and she wasn't wearing any make-up. Not that she usually did for work, but she suddenly wished she had some armour…even if it was just a coat of mascara.

Ellie waited as Max stepped through the door, moving from one foot to the other in indecision. She needed to go upstairs, but she seldom invited other people into her flat. Would it be odd to leave him kicking his heels in the shop while she grabbed a cardigan and quickly brushed out her hair? At least there was plenty for him to read.

'You might as well come up.'

Not the most gracious invitation, but he didn't need asking twice, following her through the dark bookshop to the discreet wooden door at the back of the shop which marked the line between home and work.

Ellie was used to the narrow, low staircase, but she could sense Max taking it more slowly, his head brushing the ceiling as the staircase turned. He breathed an audible sigh of relief when he arrived at the top of the staircase with the top of his head still intact.

The narrow staircase curved and continued up to the third storey, where her bedroom, study and bathroom were situated, but she stepped out into the flat's main hallway. It was simply decorated in a light olive-green, with the colour picked up in the striped runner covering polished floorboards. At the far end a window overlooked the street. Next to it a row of pegs was covered with an assortment of her jackets, coats and scarves; boots and shoes were lined up beneath them.

On her right the kitchen door was slightly ajar. Her unwashed breakfast dishes were still piled on the side. Ellie fought the urge to shut the door, to hide them. In the years she had lived with her ex, Simon, she had learned quickly to tidy up all detritus straight away. Leaving dirty dishes out for a few hours was a small act of rebellion, but it made the flat hers, the kitchen hers. A sign that she was free of his control.

'Just go straight ahead.' She tried to keep her voice light, to hide what a big deal this was.

The living room ran the full length of the building, with a window at either end flooding the long room with evening light. A red velvet three-seater couch and matching loveseat were arranged at right angles at one end of the room; a small dining table with four chairs stood at the other. The walls were plain white, but she had injected colour with dozens of framed posters: her favourites from her last three years of bookselling.

Max stepped inside and looked around. 'No books?' He sounded surprised.

Ellie laughed, a little nervously. 'Oh, plenty of books. I keep them on the landing and in the study. I thought being surrounded by books all day and all night would probably turn me into a *real* hermit instead of practically being one.'

'Here.' He proffered the wine to her. 'Please, take it.'

Ellie looked at it. She needed to make her position clear before she accepted the wine...before she showed him round the village. Before she was distracted again by the evening sun on a bare arm or visions of showers. She had promised herself that she would always speak out, always be honest, never allow herself to be pushed back into being the quiet, submissive ghost she had been with Simon.

Only it wasn't quite so easy in practice.

She took a deep breath, her fingers linking, twisting as she did so. 'I'll be honest, Mr Loveday...'

His eyebrows flew up at her words but he didn't interrupt, just leaned back against the wall, arms folded as she spoke.

'You were very rude to me earlier. You don't know me, and you had no evidence for your words. If it was up to me you would be on your way back to New York right now but for one thing. Your great-aunt. It was her wish that we work together and I intend to honour that. But if you speak to me again the way you did earlier then I will be talking to the solicitors about resigning from the trust.'

She wanted to collapse as she said the words, but forced herself to remain standing and still. Although she couldn't stop her eyes searching his face for telltale signs. For narrowed eyes, a tightened mouth, flaring nostrils. Signs she knew all too well.

She clasped her hands, trying to still their slight

tremor. But Max Loveday's face didn't change—except for the dawning hint of respect in his eyes.

'Fair point—or should I say fair points? First of all, please, if we're going to work together, do call me Max. Secondly, I don't live in New York. I live in Connecticut, so if you do send me away please make sure I end up in the correct state. And third...' He paused. 'You're right. I was rude. There are reasons, and they have nothing to do with you. I can only apologise again.' He closed his eyes briefly. 'There are things going on at home that make it hard for me to believe in altruism, and my great-aunt *did* leave you this building.'

'I didn't ask her to.'

'No, but look at it from my point of view. I don't know you. I just see the cold, hard facts. She was on her own... possibly vulnerable. She left her fortune in your—in *our* hands—and bequeathed to *you* a home and livelihood. On paper, that's a little suspicious.'

Ellie hated to admit it, but he had a point—and she had been shocked by the will and her own prominent part in it. There was one thing he hadn't taken into consideration, though.

She laughed. 'You didn't know your great-aunt very well, did you? I can't see her being taken in by *anybody*. She didn't suffer fools gladly.'

'I didn't know her at all. She moved over here before I was born. I wish I'd made an effort to see her before it was too late.'

'You should have done. She was worth knowing. Right, I'm just going to...' She gestured upstairs. 'I won't be long. Make yourself at home.'

She slipped out of the room. She didn't care about impressing Max Loveday, but there was no way she was heading out without brushing her hair and powdering her face. Maybe a quick coat of mascara. To freshen up after a long day at work. That was all.

Trouble was, she wasn't even fooling herself.

So this was Ellie Scott's home. Bright, vibrant, and yet somehow bare. For all the posters on the walls, the cushions heaped on the inviting sofas, the view of the sea from the back window, there was something missing.

Photos. There were no photos. Not on the walls, not on the sideboard, nor on the mantelpiece over the cosy-looking wood-burning stove. He had never yet met a woman who didn't decorate her personal space with family portraits, pictures of friends, holidays, favourite pets, university formals. Max himself had a framed picture of his parents on his desk in his office, and a few childhood photos in his apartment. The picture of himself aged about ten on his grandfather's boat, proudly holding up a large fish, was one of his most prized possessions.

Maybe they were tucked away like her books, but somehow he doubted it. Where had she come from? What had made a young woman in her early twenties move to a tiny village miles from civilisation and stay there? Or had she walked out of the sea? A selkie doomed to spend her life in human form until she found her sealskin once more? With those huge brown eyes and long, long lashes Ellie certainly fitted the bill.

'Okay, ready when you are. I hope I didn't keep you waiting too long?'

When Ellie had said she would be a minute Max had been prepared for a twenty-minute wait. Minimum. Yet barely five minutes had passed since she had left. She had pulled a long light grey cardigan over her tunic, swapped her pumps for sneakers and brushed out her hair. That was it.

Yet she looked completely fresh, like a dryad in spring.

Anything less like the manicured, blow-dried, designer-clad women he worked with, dated and slept with was hard to imagine. But right now she was fresh iced water to their over-sugared and over-carbonated soda. Not that he was looking in any real way. It was the contrast, that was all. It wasn't that he was actually interested in wholesome girls with creamy skin. He just didn't know many. Or *any*.

'Yes. Ready.' He might be staring. He wasn't staring like some gauche teenage boy, was he? Reluctantly he pulled his gaze away. 'Come on, honey, let's go.'

The sharp breeze that had greeted him earlier in the day had died away, and despite the hour the sun still cast a warm glow over the village. The gentle warmth was a welcome contrast to the heat and humidity of home and the wet and cold of the Sydney winter—not that Sydney's worst could compare to the bone-chilling cold of a Connecticut winter, but it could still be unpleasant.

'There are more houses up there, the school and the children's playground.' Ellie pointed up the hill away from the coast. 'Useful things like the doctor's surgery and the bus stop that takes you to the nearest towns. But I don't suppose you're interested in those?'

'Not unless I was planning to move here.'

'What will you do with the house?' She turned and began to walk the other way, down the hill and towards the swell of the sea. He fell into step beside her.

'I don't know.'

The moment he had stepped into the wide hallway of The Round House, looked at the seascapes and compasses on the walls and heard the rumble of the sea through the windows he had felt a connection. But even the idea of keeping it was impractical.

'It's way too far away to be a holiday home, but now I know there's a real family link I'd hate to sell it on.'

'Trengarth has enough holiday homes. It needs young families to settle here, to put down roots. They're talking about closing down the primary school and bussing the kids over to the next town.' She paused and looked back up the hill. 'Once this was a proper high street: haberdashers, ironmongers, butchers, toy shop...the lot. Your great-aunt has some amazing photos, dating right back to Victorian times. Now it's all gift shops and art galleries, and the front is buckets and spades and surf hire.'

She sounded sad. Nostalgic for a Trengarth she couldn't ever have actually experienced.

'Is that why you moved here? To put down roots?' Was there a family in her future? A man she was hoping to settle down with? There had been no hint of anyone else in her flat. No hint of any family or partner.

'I moved here because it felt safe. Because there was someone here I loved and trusted.'

She didn't say any more, and he didn't push it as they carried on to the bottom of the hill. When they reached it she crossed over the road to a narrow sidewalk, taking the right-hand fork along the harbour wall.

On the other side of the road, houses faced out: brightly coloured terraced cottages in whites, blues, pinks and greens making a cheerful mosaic. Winding narrow streets twisted and turned behind them, with houses built higher and higher up the cliff.

'This is the old town. Most of these would have been fishermen's cottages once.'

'Once?'

'Some still are,' she admitted. 'Some are retirement

properties, and a few are owned by villagers. But probably half are holiday cottages. Which is fine when they're full. My business depends on tourists with money to spend and time to browse, and so do the cafés, the B&Bs, the art galleries and the bucket and spade shops. It's when they're empty, or they don't get rented out and are only visited two weeks a year, when it's a problem. That's why it's important that we really try and make this festival a success. It could bring so many more people here.'

She stopped and leaned on the iron railings, looking out over the curve of the old harbour.

'I love this view. The fishing boats safely moored inside the harbour, the powerboats and sailboats further out... Sometimes I wish I could sail, just set off and see where I end up.'

Her voice was unexpectedly wistful. Max stole a glance at her profile. She was in another world, almost oblivious to his presence as she stared out at the white-flecked waves.

'You don't sail? You live by the sea and don't sail? You must surf, then.'

He gave her an appraising look. She was very slim, almost to the point of thin, but there was a strength and a lithe grace in the way she moved. She would probably be a natural on a board.

She shook her head.

'Swim?'

'No.' A reluctant smile curved her mouth. 'I love the sea, but more as something to look at, listen to. I'm not so much one for venturing on to or into it.'

'Wow...' He shook his head. 'You live literally five minutes away and you just *look* at it? I was going to try and hire a boat while I'm here. I think I may have to offer to take you out for a sail. It'll change your life.'

'Maybe.'

It wasn't a refusal, and her smile didn't slip away as she resumed walking.

'Okay, if you take that road there it will lead you to the most important building in Trengarth: The Three Herrings. There *is* another pub further along, with a beer garden and a view of the harbour. It's lovely, but...' She lowered her voice. 'It's mostly used by tourists and in-comers. The *real* Trengarthians frequent The Three Herrings, even though there is no view, the chimney smokes and the grub is very much of the plain and plentiful variety.'

'Got it.'

'Do you want to see the beach?'

'Sure.'

They turned around and walked back, past the high street and onto the wider promenade. No houses here. Just shops selling ice cream, sun cream and beach toys, a couple of board shops filled with body-boards, surf-boards and wetsuits, which Max noted with keen interest, and a few cafés.

'The Boat House,' Ellie explained, when he stopped in front of a modern-looking glass and wood building on the ocean side of the road. 'Café by day, bistro by night, and a bit of a cool place to hang out. I used to have dinner with your Great-Aunt Demelza here on a Friday evening.' Her voice softened. 'I turned up as usual the Friday after she died...just automatically, you know? I didn't really take it in that she was gone until I was seated by myself.'

'I'm sorry. Sorry that you miss her and that I didn't know her. And that nobody came to the funeral—although we lost Grandfather just a few months before, and things were difficult.'

That was an understatement. His father had barely

finished the eulogy before he'd had started gathering up the reins at DL and turning the company upside down.

'It's okay. Really. I have some experience at arranging funerals.'

There was a bitter note to her voice that surprised him.

'Besides, she was very clear about what she wanted. I didn't have to do much.'

She turned away from The Boat House and headed towards the slipway that would take them on to the beach.

Max stood for one moment to take in the view. The slim figure all in grey was getting smaller as she walked along the wide golden sweep of beach. The cliffs were steeper on this side of the bay, green and yellow with gorse, and rocks and large pebbles were clustered at the bottom before the stony mass gave way to the softer sand.

The sea roared as the tide beat its inexorable way in, the swell significant enough to justify the presence of lifeguards' chairs and warning flags. Not that it seemed to deter the determined crowd of surfers bobbing about like small seals.

The breeze had risen a little. Enough for Max to feel a slight chill on his arms as he stepped on to the sand. He inhaled, enjoying the familiar tang of salt, and heard the cry of gulls overhead and the excited shrieks of a gaggle of small children who were racing a puppy along the tideline.

For the first time in a long time Max could feel the burden on his shoulders slip away, the tightness in his chest ease.

'Hey, Ellie!' he yelled. 'Wait for me.'

He took off after her, enjoying the burn in his calves as he sprinted along the resistant sand, enjoying the complete freedom of the here, the now.

'This is magnificent,' he panted as he skidded to a halt

beside her. 'What a beach. If I lived here I'd have two dogs, a boat, and I'd surf every day.'

She flushed. 'I do *walk* on the beach, even if I don't immerse myself in the sea. And I have thought about maybe getting a guinea pig.'

'A *guinea pig*? You can't walk a guinea pig.'

'Some people do. They have harnesses and everything.' But she caught his eye as she said it and a smile broke out on her face: a full-on, wide-mouthed grin.

It transformed her, lighting up the shadows of her face, bringing that elusive prettiness to the forefront. Max stood stock-still, stunned.

'Harnesses…right. I see.' He turned back as he said it, instinctively heading for the safety of the large white house just visible at the top of the cliffs.

He wasn't here to flirt, and Ellie wasn't giving off any signals that she might enjoy the kind of no-strings fun he'd be interested in. It was far better not to notice how her face lit up, not to notice the sparkle in the large eyes or the intriguing dimple in her cheek. Far, *far* better not to notice just how perfectly shaped her mouth was: not too large, not too small, but pretty damn near just right.

'Come on,' he said, bouncing on his heels. 'I'll race you back to the road. Loser buys the winner a pint. Ready? *Go!*'

CHAPTER FOUR

'THAT WASN'T FAIR. You had a head start.' Ellie pulled the long, tangled mass of hair out of her face, twisting it into a loose knot. Her heart was thumping from the unaccustomed exercise. She'd thought she was fitter than that, although she couldn't remember the last time she had run at full pelt, aware of nothing but her legs pumping, her heart beating fit to burst, the wind biting at her ears.

'If you're going to be a sore loser…'

Max looked annoyingly at ease, leaning on the railing and waiting for her, his cheeks unflushed, his chest not heaving for breath. Unlike hers.

'No, no, I concede. I'm not sure I'd have won even with a head start. Next time *I* pick the competition. Speed-reading, maybe.'

She stepped onto the causeway to join him, but as she did so she heard her name called from someone behind her and twisted round to see who it was. It wasn't often she found herself hailed in such a friendly way.

A group of wetsuit-clad surfers had left the sea and were making their way up the beach, boards tucked under their arms.

'Ellie, wait!'

She turned to meet them, all too aware of Max behind her. The surfers were all locals. Some were born and bred, and some were incomers like Ellie, lured to Trengarth by the sea, the scenery and the pace of life. Ellie often forgot just how many people her own age lived in the village, many working at The Boat House café or the hotel of the same name, others owning businesses they ran from their homes. The group in front of her included a talented chef, a website designer and an architect.

'Hi...' She wasn't sure why she was so self-conscious as she called back, but the heat in her cheeks wasn't completely down to her recent exercise.

'Are you coming to the quiz tonight?' asked Sam, the architect, as he jogged ahead of his friends to join her. 'We would never have won last week without you.'

It wasn't often she ventured out, but a week ago she had popped into the pub, completely unaware that it was the weekly hotly contested quiz night, and had been co-opted on to a team. She had felt unexpectedly welcome, and for the first time had been uneasily aware that her incomer status might be something she enforced on herself. Especially where the under-thirties in the village were concerned.

'Well, if you ever picked up a book you might have a chance. I sell quite a selection, you know. Come in and I'll make a personal recommendation.'

'Tempting...' Sam was standing a little closer, his blue eyes smiling down into hers in unmistakable invitation.

Ellie waited for that same jolt of libido she had experienced earlier. Sam was tall, handsome, he wore the tight-fitting wetsuit very well and was looking down at her with appreciation. But, no. Nothing. Not even a tiny electric shock.

Disappointing. He would be a much more suitable person to have a crush on. If only her body would agree.

She took a step back, breaking the connection. 'Besides, I was more than useless at the sports questions and I had no idea how terrible my geography was until last week. I've been paying extra attention when I shelve the travel guides to try and brush up a little.'

'So you'll come?'

The rest of the group had caught up with Sam and were waiting for her answer. She knew them all, but none of them was close enough to count as a friend.

She hadn't noticed the difference before.

'I...I might,' she said finally. 'I was about to pop down to the Herrings to introduce Max to the place so... Oh, this is Max Loveday. Miss Loveday's great-nephew. He's come over to sort out the house and help me make a start on the festival.'

She was aware of Sam's appraising gaze as she introduced the rest of the group to Max, and was glad when she could finally make her escape with the promise that she might see them later.

Max didn't speak for a few moments as they retraced their steps along the seafront, but the silence was tight, the easy camaraderie of the beach gone as if it had never been.

'Is he your boyfriend?'

Ellie felt her cheeks warm again. She didn't need to ask who he was referring to. 'No.' She was glad her voice didn't squeak. 'I'm not seeing anyone at the moment. Are you?'

What did they say? Attack was the best form of defence, and she really didn't want to be discussing her personal life with anyone. Especially not with Max Loveday.

'Me?' His voice was amused. 'Not at the moment. My last relationship ended a couple of months ago. I was always too busy to date, and it was apparent that our timetables didn't match, so I called it off.'

He sounded as detached as if he were discussing cancelling a dinner reservation, not ending an intimate relationship.

'Your *timetables*?' Had she misheard? Was that some kind of slang term for sexual compatibility? Or something really hip to do with auras?

'Stella wanted to get engaged this year, but I'm not going to get married before thirty. Ideally I would like to be around thirty-four, and I don't really want to think about kids until two years after that.' He shrugged as if that was the most natural reason to break up in the world.

'But...' She stared at his profile in fascination, looking for some hint that he was teasing her. 'Didn't you love her?'

'I liked her. We had a lot in common. She was from my world.' Max paused. 'That's what's important. That's what ensures a harmonious marriage. Love isn't enough of a bedrock to build a marriage, a family on. It's not solid enough, not real enough.'

'It isn't? Surely it's the most important thing?'

Despite her hideous three years with Simon and his warped idea of what love meant, in spite of her mother's inability to exist without it, love was still the goal. Wasn't it? Right now she might only find it in books and films, but one day, when her libido was behaving itself and she found herself attracted to the right man at the right time, she hoped she would fall in love. Properly this time. Not mistaking infatuation and fear for the real thing.

She hadn't even considered a timetable.

'My parents were madly in love.' His mouth twisted. '*Madly* being the operative word. Apart from the times when my father was in love with someone else. I don't know which was worse: the awful strained silences, the lies and the falsity when he was having an affair, or the making up afterwards. Once he bought my mother a Porsche. Red, of course. Filled it with one thousand red roses and heart-shaped balloons.'

'Oh, that sounds...' Ellie fought to find the right word and failed.

'Vulgar?' His voice was grim. 'It was. I don't want that kind of ridiculous drama in my life. Respect and mutual goals are a far tidier way to live. A lot less destructive.'

'My parents loved each other too.' The familiar lump rose in her throat at the memory. 'But there was no drama. They were just really happy.'

Max stared straight ahead. 'I spent most of my child-hood either playing peacekeeper and go-between or being ignored as they went off on yet another honeymoon. Un-less I was with my grandfather. It was all much more stable there.'

'Sounds like he wasn't so different from your Great-Aunt Demelza. She was one of the calmest people I knew.'

'Mmm...'

His mind was clearly elsewhere.

'Ellie, would you mind if I took a raincheck on the pint? I'm still pretty jetlagged and it's been a long few days. But tomorrow I'm going to start going through the house and I would really appreciate your help. You knew her best.'

'Of course.'

Ellie was relieved not to have to spend more time with him now. Especially not in the intimate setting of The Three Herrings, where the little cubicle-like snugs meant an easy drink could easily feel like a *tête-à-tête*. And it meant she could definitely get out of the pub quiz and curl up with her book, just as she had planned.

Yes, she was definitely relieved. She wasn't feeling a little flat at all...

* * *

For the longest time The Round House had been the place that Ellie loved best in all the world. It wasn't just its curious shape, like something out of a fairytale, with its high circular roof, the huge arched windows looking out to sea. Nor was it just the knowledge that in its rounded walls were rooms full of treasures. Whether your tastes ran to books, clothes, jewellery, home-baked food or collections of everything from stamps to fossils, somewhere in the various cupboards, cabinets and boxes there was bound to be something to catch your eye.

Once, at first, it had been her holiday home: the flagstone hallway liberally sprinkled with sand as she ran in straight from the beach, barely pausing to wrap a towel around her before heading to the kitchen for freshly baked scones and a glass of creamy Cornish milk. Later it had been a place for grief and contemplation, long hours huddled in the window seat on the first-floor landing, staring out to sea, wondering just where it was she belonged.

And then it had been a refuge. Literally. A place to regroup, to lick her wounds. Demelza Loveday had given her all the time, space and love in the world. It was a debt she could never repay. Making sure she helped her godmother's dream of a literary festival come true was the least she could do.

But today, watching Max open the arched front door and invite her in, a realisation hit her. One she hadn't allowed herself to articulate before.

The Round House would never be her home again. It belonged to Max Loveday. From now on it would be a second home, visited once a year, or sold on to strangers. Her last link to Demelza Loveday would be severed.

But for the moment at least nothing had changed. The

hallway was still furnished with the same aged elegance; the glass bowl on the sideboard was set in the same position. Only the hat stand was missing its usual mackintosh and scarf. Demelza's clothes had long since been gathered up and given away to charity.

'Is something wrong?'

Ellie started, aware that she had been standing immobile, staring around the hallway for far too long. 'No, sorry. It's just...' She hesitated, unsure how to articulate the strange sense of wrongness. Then it came to her. 'It smells all wrong.'

Max sniffed. 'It was a little musty when I got here, I've had all the windows open, though.'

'No, it's not that.' It wasn't what she could smell, more what she couldn't. That elusive sense that something important was missing. 'There's no smell of baking. No perfume in the air. Your great-aunt liked a very floral scent, quite heavy. It's gone now.'

Max leaned back against the wall, his casual stance and clothes incongruous against the daintily patterned wallpaper. 'The whole house was cleaned after her clothes were disposed of—she'd asked that they were given away or sold, and I guess the executors took care of that. But all her papers are here. Her books, pictures, ornaments. I have no idea what to do with it all.'

He didn't sound dismissive. Not exactly. But nor did he sound at all appreciative. He had no idea how special his gift was.

'Where do you want to start?' It wasn't his fault, Ellie reminded herself. He didn't have the links she did. What were treasured memories to her must just be so much clutter to him.

'In the library. The solicitor gave me the key to her desk. Apparently all the papers in there are mine now.

They sold off the stocks and other financial assets for the trust so it must all be family stuff.'

'More information about the sea captain?'

The pinched expression left his face. 'Maybe. That would be cool.'

In Ellie's admittedly not at all unbiased opinion, the library was the heart of the house. Demelza had turned what had been the morning room into a book-lined paradise filled with window seats and cosy nooks. In summer you could look out upon the ocean, basking in the sun through the open French windows; in winter a roaring fire warmed you as you read. The rounded walls held glassed-in bookshelves, reaching from floor to ceiling. Polished oak floorboards were covered with vibrant rugs in turquoises and emeralds. The same colours were reflected in the curtains and the geometric Art Deco wallpaper.

Would whoever bought this house keep the room this way? It was horribly unlikely.

Max had wandered over to the far side of the room, where he was examining a case of blue-bound hardbacks. 'She owned the entire catalogue...' His voice was reverential. 'That's incredible.'

'I was only allowed to touch those under strict supervision even when I was all grown up. She said they had too much sentimental value.'

Max raised an eyebrow. 'Not just sentimental; they're worth a *fortune* to collectors. These are all first edition Kerenza Press classics.' He opened the glass door and carefully slid one out. 'Just look at the quality...the illustrations. We stopped producing these years ago. I always wished we had carried on.'

'We?'

'DL Media. Kerenza was the very first imprint my

great-grandfather started. He named it after his wife, my great-grandmother.' His mouth twisted. 'It means "love" in Cornish.'

'It's a beautiful name.' No wonder Demelza had such an amazing collection of books, but why had she never mentioned that she was part of the DL Media empire? All those long talks about books, about the shop, about the festival, and she had never once let slip her literary heritage.

For the first time Ellie was conscious of a gap between her godmother and herself. Not of age, or privilege, but of secrets withheld, confidences untold.

'I knew that you worked for DL Media because of your email. I didn't know that you *were* DL.'

Ellie gave a little laugh, but it sounded false even to her own ears. Max was heir to one of the last big publishing and media companies in private hands. No wonder he wore an air of wealth and privilege like a worn-in sweatshirt: so comfortable it was almost part of him.

'She didn't mention it?'

Ellie shook her head. 'Never. She never really spoke about her life in America. Sometimes she would talk about her university days here in England. That's how she knew my grandmother. All she said about her working life was that she regretted never marrying but that in her day women could have jobs or they could have marriage, not both. She never mentioned her family or *where* she'd worked.'

'She worked for DL until my great-grandfather died. Then there was some kind of argument—about the will and the direction of the company, I think.' His face was set as he stared at the book in his hands. 'There's nothing to tear a family apart like money. Wills and family businesses must be responsible for more fractures than anything else.'

'Oh, I don't know...' That old bone-deep ache pulsed. 'Families fracture for many reasons. But sometimes we forge our own family ties. Blood doesn't always run deeper.'

'You're not close to your family?'

'I lost my father and brother in a car accident.' How could something so utterly destructive be explained in just a few words? How could the ripping apart of a family be distilled down to one sentence? 'My mother remarried.'

'I'm so sorry.' His eyes had darkened with sympathy, the expression in them touching somewhere buried deep inside her, warming, defrosting. But the barriers were there for a reason.

She stepped back, putting even more space between them. 'It was a long time ago.'

'Do you like your stepfather?'

'He makes my mother happy. She's not really the kind of person who copes well by herself. It's a relief to know that someone is taking care of her.'

It was the truth, so why did it feel as if she were lying?

'I'll definitely ship all this back, but nothing seems urgent.' Max stared at the floor of the library, now liberally covered in papers, paperclips and folders.

His great-aunt had definitely been a hoarder. And an avid family historian. There was enough here to write a biography of the entire Loveday clan—one with several volumes. But so far he hadn't found anything to indicate that she had still owned part of the company.

Ellie sat cross-legged close by, sorting through some of the newer-looking files, many of which were about village committees and his great-aunt's charitable commitments.

'This looks different. It's in a legal envelope and addressed to you, so I haven't opened it.' Ellie handed over a large manila envelope. His name was neatly typed on the label.

'Thanks...'

This could be it. His pulse began to speed as he reached for the envelope, and then accelerated as his hand brushed hers. His fingers wanted to latch on to hers, keep holding on. Her hair had fallen out of its clip while they worked and she had allowed it to flow free. Max could barely keep his eyes off the smooth flow of hair, constantly changing colour in the sunlit room, one moment dark chocolate, the next a rich bronze.

It had to be natural. He couldn't imagine Ellie sitting for hours in a hairdresser's chair. His mother had her hair cut and dyed monthly, at a salon that charged the equivalent of a month's rent for the privilege.

No wonder her alimony demands were so high.

'What is it? A treasure map for some ancient pirate Loveday's plunder?'

'Fingers crossed.' If it was what he was hoping for then it would be worth far more than any treasure chest.

Max slit the envelope open and pulled out a single sheet of paper.

'No X marks the spot.'

'Disappointing.' Ellie got to her feet in one graceful gesture. 'Shall I start tidying some of this lot up? I don't think there's any way you're going to get through this entire house in just two weeks.'

He could barely make out her words. All his attention was on the piece of paper he held. 'Read this. What does it say?'

She glanced at him, puzzled, before taking the paper. Max rocked back on his heels, his blood pumping so loudly he could barely make out her voice as she read the paper aloud.

'It says that Demelza remained a silent shareholder even after her severance from DL Media and that she's left her twenty-five per cent share of the company to you. Very nice.'

Yes! This was it. He quickly totted up the percentages in his mind.

'More than nice.' He was on his feet, his hand on hers where she held the precious paper. 'It means my grandfather only held seventy-five per cent of the company. And *that* means my father doesn't have a two-thirds majority. We're equal partners. Do you know what else, Ellie Scott? It means I can take him on and I can *win*. Thanks to my lovely Great-Aunt Demelza.'

'It does?' She was staring up at him, smiling in response, her eyes enormous, her cheeks flushed.

The breath whooshed from his chest as if he had been hit with a football at top speed. How did she do it? How did that elusive smile light her up, turn the pointed chin, big eyes and hollow cheeks into beauty?

And why didn't she smile more often?

Max took a deep breath, curling his fingers into his palms. All he wanted to do was touch her, trace the curve of her cheek, run a finger along the fullness of her bottom lip and tangle his hands in the thick length of hair. But he knew instinctively, with every bone in his body, that his touch would be unwelcome. There was a 'Keep Out' sign erected very firmly around Ellie. Trespassers were most certainly not tolerated.

She would have to invite him in. And he sensed that invitations were very rarely issued, if at all.

It was for the best. A girl like Ellie didn't know how

to play. She would need wooing and loving and protecting. All the things he had no interest in.

She stepped back, leaving the precious paper in his hands. 'You and your father are disagreeing?'

That was one way of putting it.

Max walked over to the window and stared out at the breathtaking view. The Round House was at the very top of the cliff. Just a few metres of garden seemed to separate the house from the sea stretching out to the horizon beyond.

'My grandfather was a visionary. He was an early adopter of technology, but managed to avoid the dotcom crisis, and we've weathered every financial crisis there's been. My father was always in his shadow, I guess. But since Grandfather died he's seemed determined to put his stamp on the company. He thinks anything new is worth investing in, and he's diversifying the brand into everything from jobs to dating. If there's an app for it he wants it.'

Ellie stepped forward and stood next to him, so close they were almost touching. *Almost.* 'Most media outlets have job sites and dating adverts...'

'Supported by their main publications, they can be useful income streams, yes.' He ran a hand through his hair. 'But he's not investing in the news sites at all. He's got rid of some of our most experienced journalists and is allowing bloggers and the commenting public to provide most of the content. There's a place for that, sure, but not at the expense of your main news. I came here to find a way to wrestle control of the company away from him. This—' he brandished the paper '—this means we either come to a consensus or every decision goes to the board. It's not ideal, but it's a helluva lot better than the current situation.'

'It sounds like your grandfather and your great-aunt all over again.'

He flinched at her gentle words. Was she right? Was another massive chasm about to open up in the family?

'It's not just work.' He was justifying his actions as much to himself as he was to Ellie. 'His personal life is a mess too. He's left my mother for my old PA, and just to twist the cliché has announced he wants a divorce.'

He couldn't talk about the pregnancy. Not yet.

'My mother is a mess, *he* is completely unrepentant, and DL Media is fragmenting. I have a lot of work to do.'

'Max, they're grown-ups. Isn't their marriage *their* problem? Getting sucked in too far never ends well.' There was a bitter certainty in her voice.

Max laughed, the anger in the sound startling him. 'Oh, their marriage *is* their problem. I'm not getting involved. Not any more. But I have to look after DL, whatever it takes. My mother is out for blood. She wants half the company. Can you imagine? The lawyers' fees alone could drag us down.'

'What would happen if you just walked away? They'd have to fix it then, wouldn't they?'

He shook his head. 'It's not so much them as the company. It's *my* responsibility, Ellie. I started in the distribution centre when I was fifteen. I was filing and photocopying at sixteen, writing up press releases at eighteen. I interned every year I was at Yale, and when I graduated I went straight into the New Media department. It's all I've ever known and I *won't* let them tear it apart.'

'I always wanted to work in publishing.' There was a longing in her voice. 'But I didn't go to university.'

'Why not?' It was a relief to change the subject, to focus on something else.

'My mother took a long time to get over my father's death. It was hard to leave her. And when she remarried I was...' She swallowed, her already pale cheeks whitening. 'I was engaged.'

'You were *engaged*?' He turned to look at her, shocked by her revelation. She was very pale. Even her lips were almost white.

'Yes. I was young and foolish and had no judgement.'

She smiled at him but he wasn't fooled. This smile didn't light up her face, didn't illuminate her beauty. It was only skin-deep, false.

The urge to protect her swept up, taking him completely by surprise. Somehow he knew, completely and utterly, that Ellie Scott had been badly hurt and that the scars were still not fully healed. Another reason to keep well away.

'It's not too late.'

'I'm doing a degree now, in the evenings. And at least I'm surrounded by books. It's not all bad. But what would you do if you weren't part of DL? If you weren't one of *those* Lovedays?'

But he *was* one of 'those' Lovedays. His identity was burnt into him like a brand. He couldn't escape his family history and nor did he want to.

'All I ever wanted was to make my grandfather proud and take DL to the next level.' It didn't sound like much, but it was everything. 'I can't let my father stop that.'

'Can't you work *with* him? Compromise?'

'He won't let me in, Ellie. I've tried, goodness knows. He wants me to knuckle down and accept him as head of the family. To tamely agree with every decision he makes, to meet the woman he's left my mother for and make her part of my family. We can't even be in the same room right now.'

'Then it's a good thing you're on the other side of the Atlantic.'

Max caught sight of his reflection in the mirror on the wall opposite, jaw set, eyes hard. He barely recognised himself.

'Maybe.' He made an effort to shake off the anger coiling around his soul like a malevolent snake. 'I need to get this faxed over to the company lawyers before I go to London. I can plan my next move from there. I'll get someone in to clear the rest of the house before I instruct the solicitors to sell.'

'You're not thinking of keeping the house?' Disappointment flickered over her face. 'Your Great-Aunt Demelza would have wanted you to.'

'My life's in Connecticut. When I'm in the UK I'm London-based. I have no use for it.'

Looking around, he felt a hint of regret. His family's history was soaked into the rounded walls. His eyes fell on a gilt-edged card as he spoke. It looked familiar and, curious, he picked it up.

'What's this?'

Ellie flushed and reached for it. Max held it a little longer, trying to read the curled writing, until with a pull she tugged it out of his fingers. 'Oh, that's mine. It must have fallen out of my bag. It's just some industry black tie thing. I've been nominated for Independent Bookseller of the Year. Nonsense, really, but quite sweet.'

'Are you going?'

'Oh, no. It's in London. The season starts this week. I couldn't leave the shop. Besides, I wouldn't know anyone.'

Max reached over and plucked the card out of her hand. Why was it striking a chord?

'DL have a table.'

That was it. The London office had asked him to attend and it would be the perfect opportunity for him to quell some of the rumours about the company's viability.

'You could come with me. That way you wouldn't be going alone.'

Her face turned even redder. 'That's very kind of you...'

'Not at all. I hate these things. It would be more bearable if I was with someone I knew. Especially if that someone was up for an award.'

'There's still the shop...'

'Mrs Trelawney is quite capable, surely? Look, Ellie, I was planning on going anyway. It would make me very happy if you came with me.'

Max didn't know why it mattered. She was a grown woman...she could do as she pleased. But although black tie dinners and awards ceremonies were a dime a dozen to him, he sensed they didn't really figure in Ellie's life. Besides, his great-aunt had loved Ellie, cared for her. It would be fitting thanks if he took her under his wing a little.

In fact he was being very altruistic.

'I appreciate the thought...'

'I'm not doing this to be kind,' he reassured her. 'My motives are completely selfish.'

'I really wasn't planning on going.'

'If we are going to be setting up a literary festival then this is the best thing you can do. I'll introduce you to some of the best publicists in the business. And who knows, Ellie? We might even have fun while we're there.'

CHAPTER FIVE

ELLIE DIDN'T ACTUALLY remember agreeing to *any* of this.

Not to going to the awards ceremony and certainly not to spending two nights in London with someone she barely knew.

She'd spent far too long allowing her wishes to be overridden, doing things she didn't want to in order to placate someone else: three years indulging her mother's grief, three years trying to turn herself into the perfect wife for Simon. Both had been impossible tasks.

She'd sworn she'd never allow herself to be pushed out of her comfort zone. Not ever again.

So why was she now sitting in the passenger seat of Max Loveday's hire car, watching the miles disappear as London grew ever closer?

The thing was, she couldn't deny a certain fizz in her veins, a delicious anticipation. It was mixed with fear and dread, yes, but it was anticipation nonetheless.

After three years of living very much within her comfort zone she was ready to be stretched, just a little. And if she must be stretched then a champagne reception seemed like a reasonable place to start. It wasn't as if she was going to *win* the award. All she had to do was smile and applaud the winner.

And start to make contacts for the festival. That was a

little more daunting. But Max must know the right people. He could take care of that, surely?

'Penny for them?'

'I'm sorry?'

'For your thoughts. You've been pretty quiet the whole journey. I can hear the wheels turning.'

Ellie sank back in the admittedly plush seat and stared out at the countryside. The harsh beauty of the Cornish moors had given way first to rolling hills and now to pastoral scenes fit for a movie. Sheep grazed in fields dotted by small lines of trees; copses dominated the skyline in the distance. At any moment she expected to pass through idyllic villages full of thatched cottages and maypoles.

Ellie bit her lip. It was odd, this new companionship. She'd spent more time in the last few days with Max Loveday than she had with any other person in the entire last three years—other than Demelza Loveday, of course. That must be why, despite his complete and utter lack of suitability, she found herself wanting to confide in him.

Besides, a little voice whispered, he had confided in *her*. She'd seen a crack in his façade—and she'd liked what she'd seen. Someone who wasn't *quite* so certain of his place in the world. Someone with questions. He was ruthless, sure, and ready to sacrifice his father if need be—not for personal gain, but because he genuinely believed it would be for the best. That took a lot of strength.

'This is the first time I've left Trengarth in three years.'

He darted a look over at her. 'Seriously?'

Ellie nodded.

Max let out a low whistle. 'What are you? Twenty-five? Trengarth is pretty, but that's kinda young to be burying yourself away.'

'I didn't even realise that was what I was doing. I

feel…' She hesitated, searching for the right word, not wanting to reveal too much. '*Safe* there.'

'You haven't even visited your mom?'

There was a particular ache that squeezed Ellie's chest whenever she thought about her mother: a toxic mixture of hurt and regret and a deep sense of loss.

'She's so busy, and she and my stepfather travel a great deal. Not to Cornwall, though,' she couldn't help adding, wincing at the acidity in her voice. 'But it's good to get away. Even for a couple of days. When we drove out of the village I felt as if I was leaving a cage—a little scared, but free.'

Whoa! That was far too revealing. She peeped over at Max, but his face was smoothly bland.

'Sometimes we need the perspective we get just by being in a new place.'

'I think maybe this festival is what I need. Perhaps I have got a little…' She paused, searching for the right word. 'Comfortable. After all, I host signings and launches, book clubs and children's activities. It's just a case of combining them all.'

'You'll be great.'

Would she? It was so long since she'd struck out, dared to dream of anything but safety, a bolthole of her own.

That was what Simon had taken from her. Not just her confidence and her self-esteem but also her time. Three years with him. Three years recovering from him. Time she could never get back.

Maybe all this was a sign. Max, the bequest, the award nomination. A big neon sign, telling her she needed to stop being afraid. That she had to go out there and live.

'Once I thought I'd live in London. That I'd have a flat, go to plays in the evenings, wander around exhibitions at lunchtime. Sometimes I feel like I skipped a stage in my life. Headed right for settling down and forgot to have the fun bit first.'

Ellie risked a look over at Max.

His face was bleak. 'You and me both.'

The traffic thickened as they got closer to London, the green fields giving way to buildings and warehouses. 'Why?'

She started, the one-word question rousing her from her thoughts. 'Why what?'

'Why did you hide away?'

His words hit her with an almost physical force, winding her so that for one never-ending moment she was breathless. *Why?* Because she had allowed herself to be used and manipulated for so long that she hadn't known who she was any more. But how could she say those words out loud even to herself—let alone to the confident, successful man beside her?

He might understand a little how she had been trapped by her mother's need and grief, forced to grow up too soon, to make sure that bills were paid and food was on the table and that somehow the half of her family that was left survived. Yes, he would understand that.

But would he understand her later weakness—or despise her for it? Heaven knew she despised herself. Max Loveday had made it quite clear that he thought love was a lie, an emotional trap. What would he think of a lonely girl so desperate for affection and for someone to take care of her that she'd fallen prey to a controlling relationship, allowed her soul to be stripped bare until she had no idea who she was, what she wanted?

How could he understand it when she didn't understand it herself? It was her shame, her burden.

'I don't want to talk about Trengarth. I haven't been to London for ages. What shall we do there?'

He shot her an amused smile. 'Work, go to a party... the usual.'

She seized on the statement, glad of the change of topic. 'You've been in Cornwall for four days and in that time you've spent half the day on paperwork and the rest of the day and evening working. You make noises about sailing and surfing, but you haven't left the house long enough to do either.'

Irritation scratched through his voice. 'This isn't a holiday, Ellie.'

'No,' she said sweetly. 'It *is* the weekend, though. And as you have somehow talked me into a few days away I, for one, am planning to do some sightseeing. I'll take photos for you, shall I?'

'Okay.'

'Okay to photos?'

He sighed. 'No. Okay to the rest of the weekend off. You're right. I'm nearly halfway through this trip and I haven't stopped. We should have fun in London. Let's be tourists. For today at least.'

We? A warmth stole over her. Ellie had spent so long keeping people at arm's length that although she had plenty of cordial acquaintances she wasn't at the top of very many people's 'going out' lists.

But Max Loveday wanted to go out and have fun. With her.

'Be tourists?' she echoed. 'Like the Houses of Parliament and Buckingham Palace?'

'Like all the big sights. No work and no cares this afternoon or this evening, Heck. I might even take tomorrow off too, before we have to dress up for this award nonsense. But for today we forget about bequests and festivals and DL Media. We're just two people out and about. Just two people in the city. What do you think?'

What did she think? He wanted to spend time with her, he wanted to know what her opinion was, he wanted just to hang out. With her. To have a day of carefree, irresponsible, forget-your-worries fun.

When had Ellie *ever* had a day like that? Goodness, she was pathetic. Max was right. Didn't she deserve a day out of time?

Before she forgot how to let go at all.

'I think we should do it. Where do you want to go?' She pulled her phone out, ready to search the internet.

'Let's not plan. Let's just go for it and see where we end up.'

Ellie took in a deep breath, damping down the knot of worry forming in her stomach. She could do this. She didn't need to plan everything. Spontaneous. Fun. Those adjectives *could* describe her.

They had once described the little girl running barefoot through the sand at Trengarth, living completely and utterly in the moment. She was still in there somewhere. Wasn't she?

'Perfect. We'll see where we end up. Absolutely.'

Max seemed to take the hotel completely in his stride, but although Ellie wanted to look like the kind of girl who stayed in sumptuous five-star hotels every day of her life she was aware she was failing miserably, gaping at everything from the uniformed doorman to the gilt-edged baroque decorations.

'I don't think this is within my budget,' she whispered to Max as the doorman took her case, not betraying with so much as a flicker of his eyebrow that her old tattered holdall was easily the cheapest item in the entire hotel.

She'd known they were going to stay somewhere nice, had justified the extravagance as a business expense, but this? This was the difference between high street chocolate and hand-made truffles.

It wasn't just nice, and *luxurious* didn't come close. It was the *haute couture* of the hotel world. And Ellie was very much a high street girl.

She cast a surreptitious look around, trying to find some clue as to the tariff. But there was nothing. *If you have to ask the price you can't afford it...* Wasn't that what they said?

What if you were terrified to ask the price? That meant you absolutely couldn't afford so much as a sandwich in the lavishly decorated bar.

It wasn't as if she spent much, but one night in this hotel might severely deplete her carefully hoarded savings. Her nails bit into her palms as she fought for breath. She didn't have to stay. She could go and find a more affordable room right now.

Only the doorman had shepherded them into the lift and the doors were beginning to close. Would it be too late when he opened the door to her room? It might be okay… If she bought sandwiches from a shop down the road and didn't go anywhere near the mini-bar…

And there was always her emergency credit card. Her breath hitched. She should be glad that an emergency had been downgraded from an escape plan to paying for a luxury hotel room.

'Relax, this is on DL Media,' Max whispered back.

How had he done that? Read her mood so effortlessly?

Relief warred with panic. She *always* paid her way. Money had been just one of the ways Simon had liked to control her. One of the ways she had allowed him to control her.

'Don't be silly. Of course I'll pay my own bill.'

Max leaned in closer and his eyes held hers for a long

moment before hers fell under his scrutiny. But that was no better, because now she was staring intently at the grey cotton of his T-shirt where it moulded to his chest.

It was fair to say, Ellie had conceded in the sleepless depths of the night before, that Max Loveday was a reasonably attractive male. He was young, fit, intelligent, and he had that certain air of unconscious arrogance. Infuriating and yet with a certain charm.

But had she *really* noticed? Had she taken the time before now to appreciate the toned strength of him, the long muscled legs, today casually clad in worn jeans, the flat stomach and broad chest? Of course they had never been in quite such close proximity before. She hadn't allowed him within real touching distance.

They weren't touching now, but there were mere millimetres between their bodies. His breath was cool on her cheek and his outdoorsy scent of salt air and pine was enfolding her as every inch of her began to sense every inch of him. An ache began to pulse low in the very centre of her.

He leaned in a millimetre further. 'DL Media pays for the hotel. You get dinner tonight. Deal?'

A compromise. Sensible, fair; no games, no coercion. The ache intensified, spreading upwards, downwards, everywhere. Her pulse speeded up. She wanted to lean in, to allow herself to feel him, touch him.

'Deal.' Ellie could hardly form the word. Her throat was dry. There was no air in this lift, no air at all.

At which point had she begun to notice him? Learned the way his hair curled despite its short cut trying to subdue it into businesslike submission? Learned the line of his jaw and the way his mouth curled sometimes in impatience, sometimes in disdain. sometimes in humour? Learned the gleam in the light brown eyes and the way they could focus on a person as if seeing right into their core?

How had she learned him by heart when she had been trying so hard not to see him at all?

Ellie took a step back, perspiration beading her forehead as the temperature in the suddenly too small lift rocketed. Could he tell? Could he tell that she was horrifyingly, intensely burning up with unwanted attraction? Not that it had that much to do with him *per se*. It had everything to do with three years of celibacy, emotional as well as physical.

She wasn't superficial enough to fall for a lazy smile and an air of entitlement. Oh, no. She had been blinded by charm once. She was just ready to move on, that was all. And he was a temporary fixture in her life. Safe. A two-week stop-gap. That was why he was the perfect person to hack through the forest and reawaken those long-dormant feelings.

Only he didn't feel quite so safe now.

'This way please, sir…madam.'

Thank goodness. The lift doors were open and there was her escape. A hotel room came with a bathroom, which meant one thing: a long and very cold shower. And forget all those good intentions regarding the mini-bar, Ellie needed a large glass of wine and chocolate and she didn't much care which came first.

And then she would give herself a very stern talking-to indeed.

Max stood back to let Ellie precede him out of the lift and she resisted the urge—barely—to press herself against the opposite side of the door and keep as much space between them as possible. He fell in behind her and she stiffened, all too aware of his step matching hers.

Cold shower, wine, chocolate, stern words.

Or maybe stern words, wine, cold shower, chocolate.

And a plan. A plan to start dating. There were single men in Trengarth. Sam was interested, she was almost sure of that, and there were more eligible bachelors. She would find them. She would track them down and she would have coffee and conversation just like any girl of twenty-five ought to.

Maybe even a stroll on a beach, if she was feeling daring.

'Madam, sir...this way, please.' The doorman opened a door and stood aside, an expectant look on his face.

Only it was one door.

One. Door.

Ellie stopped still.

'Madam?' There was a puzzled note in the smooth tones. 'The Presidential Suite...'

Ellie tried to speak. 'I...' Nope, that was more of a squeak. She coughed. 'Suite?' Still a squeak, but a discernible one.

There was a smothered sound from behind her and she narrowed her eyes. If Max Loveday was laughing at her then he was in for a very painful sobering up.

'Yes, madam, our very best suite. As requested.'

Ellie swivelled and fixed the openly grinning Max with her best gimlet glare. 'Suite?'

'My very efficient PA. She must have assumed...' He trailed off, but didn't seem in the least bit repentant. 'Chill, honey. I'm sure that the suite is plenty big enough, and if not I'll find you a broom cupboard somewhere.'

'I'm afraid the hotel is fully booked, sir.' The doorman didn't sound in the least bit sorry. 'If you would like to follow me?'

Stay in the corridor and sulk? Retrieve her bag from the doorman and head out into London to find a new hotel within her budget? Or walk into the suite like an aristocrat headed for the guillotine?

The tumbril it was.

On the one hand it was pretty demoralising to see just how much Ellie Scott *didn't* want to share a hotel suite with him. It wasn't that Max had expected or particularly wanted to share a room with her, but he hadn't faced the prospect with all the icy despair of one prepared to Meet Her Doom.

Plus, he wasn't *that* terrible a prospect. All his own hair, heir to one of the biggest family businesses in the world, reasonably fit and able to string a few sentences together. In some quarters he was quite the catch. But Ellie's ill-hidden horror burst any ego bubble with a resounding bang.

Although it *was* amusing to watch her torn between her obvious dismay at his proximity and her even more obvious open-mouthed appreciation of the lavishly appointed suite.

Goodness knew what Lydia, his PA, was thinking. She usually booked him into business hotels. More than comfortable, certainly, equipped with twenty-four-hour gyms, generous desk space and the kind of comprehensive room service menu that a man heading from meeting to meeting required. A world away from *this* boutique luxury.

This suite took comfort to a whole new level. It didn't say *business*, instead it screamed *honeymoon*—or *dirty weekend*. From the huge bath, more than big enough for two, to the fine linen sheets on the massive bed the suite was all about staying in.

Luckily for Ellie's blood pressure, it also came with a second bedroom. The bed there was a mere super-king-size, and the bathroom came with a walk in shower and a normal-sized bath—but the large sitting and dining area separated the two, and Ellie had claimed the smaller of the two rooms in a way that had made it very clear that trespassers were most definitely not allowed.

And in the hour since they had first entered the suite she had clammed up in a way that showed just how discombobulated she was. Even now, walking down the wide bustling street, she was pale and silent. And it didn't matter, it shouldn't matter, but Max had quite liked the way she had opened up earlier.

The way *he* had opened up.

It had almost been as if they were friends. And it was only with the resounding sound of her silence that he'd realised just how few of those he had. Buddies? Sure. Lovers? Absolutely. Colleagues, teammates, old school and college alumni, relatives, people he'd grown up with—his life was filled with people.

But how many of them were real *friends*? He hadn't discussed his parents' bitter divorce, his doubts about his father's helming of the company with anyone. Not with a single soul.

And yet he'd unburdened himself to this slim, serious English girl.

If she froze him out now then he would be back to where he had started. Dealing with feelings that were seared into his soul, struggling to keep them under control.

Besides, it would be a long two days if she was going to make monosyllabic seem chatty.

Which tactic? Normally he would try and make her laugh. Keep up a flow of light-hearted jokes until she smiled. It was the way he had always dealt with frowns and stony silences.

And if that didn't work then he would walk away without a backward glance. After all, life was too short for emotional manipulation, wasn't it?

But somehow he didn't think that she was trying to manipulate him—nor that a quip would work here. And he was honour-bound to stay. It might be time to dig out honesty...

'I didn't plan to share a suite with you. I hope you know that?'

Ellie stopped abruptly, ignoring the muttered curses of the tourists and business folk who had to skirt around her. 'I *don't* know that. I don't know you well enough.'

'I hope you know me well enough to acknowledge that I would never be sleazy enough to go for the "accidentally booked one room" trick. I don't use tricks, Ellie. If I wanted you to share my bed I'd tell you—and you would have every opportunity to turn me down with no hard feelings.'

She looked hard at him, as if she were trying to learn his every flaw, as if she were burrowing deep into the heart of him. He tried not to squirm—what would she find there? A hollowness? A shallowness?

'Okay.' She started walking again.

'Okay?' *That was all?*

'I'm sorry I doubted you.' Her voice quietened and she looked straight ahead. He got the feeling she was avoiding his eye. 'My...my ex was all about tricks. It's all I know. I don't—' Her voice broke and his hands curled into fists at the hitch in her voice. 'I don't trust what's real. I don't trust myself to see it.'

'Well...' Maybe it was time to bring in light-hearted Max. He sensed she was already telling him more than she was comfortable with. He didn't want the distance to be permanent. After all, they were together for the next forty-eight hours. It might as well be fun.

It went no further than that.

'The joke would be on me if I *was* pulling a sleazy trick. The room between our bedrooms is the size of an average hotel foyer. I think we can both sleep safely tonight.'

'Your virtue was always safe with me,' she said, but she still didn't look at him, and Max noted a flash of red high on her cheekbones. Embarrassment—or something more primal?

The hotel was centrally located, right in the heart of London. Max had travelled to the UK on business many times and was familiar with the hotels, high-end clubs and restaurants of the buzzing city—but he had never wandered aimlessly through the wide city streets, never used the Tube or hopped on a bus. It was freeing. Being part of the city, not observing it through a cab window.

They had wandered south, moving towards the river as if led by a dousing stick, and were now on a wide open street. St James's Park opened out on one side, a city oasis of green and trees in stark contrast to the golden silhouette of Big Ben dominating the skyline in front of them.

'Looks like you got your wish.' Ellie seemed to have recovered her equilibrium. 'We're in tourist central. Shall I buy you a policeman's helmet or a red phone box pencil sharpener?'

'I think I want a Big Ben keychain,' he decided. 'And possibly a shirt that says "You came to London but all you bought me was this lousy T-shirt".'

'As long as you wear it tomorrow night. So what now? We could go into Westminster Abbey? Visit the park? I think I'm allowed in the Houses of Parliament, but I might have needed to arrange it with my MP first.'

'That would be cool. I'd like to watch all your politicians yell at each other. Are you allowed to bring popcorn?'

'Nope, only jellied eels.'

'Only *what*?' She had to be kidding, right?

'They're a London delicacy. All the English love them. We just keep it hidden so the rest of the world doesn't steal our national dish. We usually wash them down with some whelks and a pint of stout.'

'Very funny.'

She laughed. 'It's true. I bet I can find you a place that sells them—if you're man enough to try them.'

'I'll take the slur on my masculinity, thanks.' He shuddered at just the thought of the slimy fish.

'Coward. Right…what would tourists do? The palace is that way.' She pointed to the park. 'And we could take your photo with one of the guards at Horse Guards. That's always popular.'

'If only I was eight… Will we get invited to have tea with the Queen?'

'Now that you've dissed the national dish it's very unlikely. You don't graduate to cucumber sandwiches until you've mastered the jellied eels.'

'Just an unworthy Yank? Another dream shattered.'

Ellie ignored him. 'So, what will it be? Trafalgar Square? Covent Garden? Or we could see a show?'

'You know, I'm pretty much enjoying just walking. Is that okay?'

Surprise flashed across her face. 'Of course.'

Their route continued riverwards to a busy intersection. Cars were such an integral part of all US cities that Max never noticed their noisy intrusion, but they seemed wrong in this ancient city, beeping and revving in front of the old riverside palaces. The road bisected the great houses from the riverfront, with pedestrians crowded onto the grey pavements.

Ellie stopped on the tip of the pavement and directed an enquiring look across the bridge. 'Shall we cross over?'

Max raised an eyebrow. 'To the dark side?'

'It *is* south of the river, but I think we'll be safe.'

'I'll hold you personally responsible for my safety.'

If Max had truly been a tourist, and if he'd had his camera, then he would have stopped halfway across the bridge and, ignoring the mutters of the tourist hordes, photographed the iconic clock tower. But all he had was his phone.

'Come here.' He pulled it out of his pocket and wrapped an arm around Ellie. He felt her stiffen. 'Obligatory Big Ben selfie,' he explained. 'Smile!'

She relaxed, just an iota, but it was enough for her to lean a little further in, for him to notice that there was softness under that slenderness, that her hair smelt of sunshine and the colours were even more diverse close up: coffee and cinnamon, toffee and treacle, shot through with gold and honey.

It took every ounce of self-control he owned not to tighten his arm around her slim shoulders, not to pull her in a little closer, to test just how well they'd fit. Every ounce not to spin her round, not to tilt that pointed chin and claim her mouth. He ached to know how she would taste, to know how she would feel pressed against him.

'Smile!'

Was that his voice? So strained? So unnaturally hearty? But Ellie didn't seem to notice, pulling an exaggerated pout as he pressed the button on the camera.

'One more for luck.' Really he wasn't quite ready to let her go. Not just yet.

CHAPTER SIX

'I'VE GOT IT!'

It was a little exhausting being a tour guide, especially in a city you didn't know that well. Ellie had grown up just thirty miles away from the capital, but her family seldom ventured into the big, bad city.

And when her friends had begun to travel in alone for gigs and shopping, and to find the kind of excitement missing from their little market town, Ellie had been stuck at home, unable to leave her grieving mother.

She still didn't know how her mother had been able just to shut down. To leave her daughter to make every decision, to take responsibility at such a young age for cooking and cleaning and hiding the fact that Ellie was basically raising herself from their neighbours and her teachers.

But Ellie had had no choice. If they had found out then what would have happened? What if she'd been put into care, the remains of her family shattered?

She had never allowed herself to resent her lonely teen years—at least not until she'd been unceremoniously swept aside when Bill had entered her mother's life. But now, as they wandered towards the South Bank, she couldn't help noticing the gangs of teenage girls dressed to the max, a little too loud, a little too consciously unselfconscious. Young, vibrant, free.

What would she have been if she had ever had the chance to find out who she was? If she hadn't been the dutiful daughter, the besotted young girlfriend too scared to open her mouth for fear of showing her lack of worldliness? And then later the terrified fiancée, softly spoken, anticipatory, as nervous as a doe in hunting season.

But today was her chance. Carefree, no agenda, no expectations—and did it matter if they did get lost?

'Got what?'

'Tourist activity number one.'

Ellie tucked a hand through Max's arm. It should have been a natural gesture. Friendly. He didn't know that she rarely touched another human being. That the protective cloud she kept swirled around her was physical as well as emotional.

Carefree Ellie wouldn't mind tugging Max down the steps off Westminster Bridge.

Carefree Ellie might be thinking of how it had felt when he'd pulled her in for that selfie. How strong he'd felt. How safe.

Might want him to touch her some more.

Max didn't resist as she pulled him down the steps. It was nice that he made no attempt to take control, to assert himself as the dominant force.

'Okay, don't keep me in suspense.' Max laughed as they came to a stop. 'Where are we headed?'

Ellie put her hands on her hips and shook her head. 'You've got eyes, haven't you? Use them.'

He looked around slowly. London's South Bank was as busy as always, crammed with tourists snapping pictures, kids on skateboards heading towards the famous skate park, people strolling on their way to Tate Modern, to the Globe, to the Royal Festival Hall. Others had stopped to browse at one of the many kiosks selling a myriad of snacks. Behind them a queue snaked out of the open doors of the London Aquarium.

The atmosphere was heated with expectation, with excitement, and yet it was inclusive and friendly, completely different from the fevered, crowded rush of Covent Garden or Oxford Street, more welcoming than the moneyed exclusivity of Knightsbridge.

I could like it here, Ellie realised with a sense of shock. It couldn't be more different from her seaside sanctuary, but there was a warm friendliness and acceptance that pulled at her.

'Um…' Max's eyes were narrowed in thought. 'Are we going to get a boat?'

'No. At least not yet. That might be fun tomorrow, though.'

'Go see some penguins?'

'Oh, I *love* penguins. We should definitely do that. But, no. I gave you a clue when I said to use your eyes.'

Ellie shifted from foot to foot, impatient with his slowness. How could he not see? The dammed thing had to be over one hundred metres high. It wasn't exactly inconspicuous!

She stared at him suspiciously. Was that a smile crinkling the caramel eyes?

'Isn't the Globe along here? Got a hankering for some Shakespeare?'

Every single suggestion sounded perfect, but she shook her head. 'Last guess.'

'Or…? What's the forfeit?' His smile widened. 'There has to be a forfeit or there's no fun…'

Ellie could feel her heart speeding up. A forfeit. Thoughts of kisses sprang unbidden into her mind, thoughts of a winner's claim. Could she suggest it? *Dare* she?

She could see it so clearly... Standing on tiptoe and pulling that dark head down to hers. That moment that felt as if it would last for ever when two mouths hovered, so close and yet not touching, and the *knowing*. The delicious anticipation of knowing that at any second they would meet.

Her stomach dipped. It had been so, *so* long since she had had a first kiss.

'Ellie?'

The teasing note in his voice flustered her, as if he had read her thoughts. Her cheeks flamed red-hot and she took a step back, all the daring seeping out of her.

'The loser has to buy the winner a souvenir that sums up the day. But it can't cost more than a fiver,' she added. 'That makes it more of a challenge.'

He just looked at her levelly, that same smile lurking in his eyes. 'You never did play dare as a kid, did you, Ellie? Okay, challenge accepted.'

'So? It's not penguins, at least not yet, it's not Shakespeare, and it's not a boat-ride. What's your final answer?'

He grinned wickedly. Damn him, he had been playing her.

'It's a good thing I'm not scared of heights, now... isn't it, honey?'

It soon became obvious that Max Loveday wasn't used to playing the ordinary tourist. Not that surprising, considering his background. From what he had let slip, his holidays were usually spent either in luxurious condos in the Bahamas or in the family home on Cape Cod. His was a life of private jets and town cars, VIP passes and prestige, and Ellie suspected that queueing hadn't played a huge role in his formative years.

It showed. He couldn't keep still, jiggling from foot to foot like an impatient child.

'How long is this going to take?' He craned his neck to look at the queue. 'Why is it so slow?'

'Because each pod only takes a certain amount of people.' Ellie smiled at an excited small girl standing in front of them, holding her mother's hand tightly. 'Be patient.'

'I could have hired out a whole pod just for us. Priority boarding, no standing in line, no sharing. Did you see that you can even have a champagne pod?'

Ellie shook her head at him, although it was hard to keep her mouth from smiling at his wistful tone. 'Yes, but that's not what tourists *do*. Tourists queue. Patiently. Take a selfie of yourself in the queue, and if you're good we'll play I Spy.'

He groaned at the pun and a flutter of happiness lifted her. It was a silly little joke but she had thought of it, shared it. With Simon she had been too busy trying to be informed and appreciative to find the courage to joke around.

She was only twenty-five. It wasn't too late. She looked down the queue: excited families, groups of friends chattering loudly, orderly tour groups patiently waiting. And couples. Everywhere. Arms slung around waists, around shoulders, leaning in, leaning on, whispering, kissing, together.

An ache pulsed in her chest. She had been so glad to get away from Simon, so relieved to be on her own, that the very thought of togetherness had repulsed her. But they had never been 'together' in that way. Not even in the beginning. Simon would never have queued, never have whispered affectionately in her ear, never sneaked a kiss or pulled her in for a longer and very public display of affection.

What must it be like? To be so wrapped up in somebody who was so wrapped up in you? Ellie stole a look at Max. He was leaning against the metal barrier, staring up at the iconic wheel. What would it be like to be wrapped up in Max Loveday?

All those first kisses, all those long walks with no idea about their destination, all those awkward first dates, all those long meals not even noticing the restaurant emptying around them—how many of those simple, necessary, life-affirming things had she been cheated of? How many had she allowed herself to be cheated of?

Maybe she'd licked her wounds in Cornwall long enough.

Ellie didn't say much as they waited—and waited—to board a pod. There was a thoughtful expression on her face that Max was reluctant to disturb, but she perked up when they were finally guided into the slowly moving pod—along with what seemed like hundreds of small uniformed children and two harassed-looking adults.

'I was definitely really bad in a past life,' he whispered to her as the kids crowded in, each of them yelling at what must be several decibels louder than legal limits.

Ellie raised her eyebrows. 'Just in a past life?'

'Believe me, a few student pranks and some adolescent attitude were not bad enough sins for *this* kind of cruel and unusual punishment.'

'They're having fun, though.' Her lips curved into a smile as she watched the children explore every inch of the pod.

'Yes,' he conceded as he steered her towards a corner. '*Noisy* fun. I vote we stand our ground here.'

'There's plenty of room.' But she put both hands on

the window and looked out. 'It's pretty slow, isn't it? I hardly feel like I'm moving.'

'Disappointed? I didn't peg you as a speed queen.'

She just smiled, and they stood in silence for a long moment as the wheel continued its stately turn, lifting them high above the city. The children quietened a merciful amount as their teachers started pointing out places of interest, and filled in the questionnaires they had all been issued with in great concentration.

The pod itself was spacious, its curved glass rising up overhead, providing panoramic three-hundred-and-sixty-degree views.

'I'm glad it's not see-through under our feet. I'm not sure I want to see the ground falling away.' Ellie shuddered.

'This was *your* idea,' he reminded her as he looked out at the incredible view. 'It's funny, you think of London as an old city, but there's so many skyscrapers. It's completely different to other European capitals, like Paris or Rome. Did you know there's see-through glass on the floor of the Eiffel Tower? Do you think you would be able to stand on that?'

'Possibly...I've never been to Paris, or to Rome.' Her voice was wistful and she continued to stare out at the skyline, her finger tracing it against the glass.

Max opened his mouth to make a flippant promise, but something in her eyes stopped him. If he ever made Ellie Scott a promise he'd need to keep it. And this was one he wasn't sure he could.

A day and a half of fun? An evening of black tie glamour? A joint project? None of them was a heavy or binding commitment. Not together or separately. So why did they feel so important? As if they meant more...as if they could mean everything... There was no way he could or *should* saddle himself with any other responsibilities towards this woman. He'd be back home in a week, and Trengarth nothing but a memory. And that was how it should be.

He had more than enough on his shoulders, thank you very much.

He kept his tone light, teasing, adding much needed distance with his flippancy, 'At the advanced old age of twenty-five you should get booking.'

She didn't respond to the lightness. 'I bet you've been everywhere. Business class and top hotels.'

He grinned at her. 'Totally unlike the hovel we're staying in tonight? DL Media have offices all over the globe. I've been to most.'

She turned then, looked at him with curiosity. 'So you only travel on business? What about for fun? For culture?'

There was a shocked undertone in her voice. It put him on edge, made him feel wanting in some way. As if he'd failed some test. 'I'll have you know there's a lot of culture in your average regional boardroom. And there's nothing as cultural as a red-eye flight and dinner at a five-star restaurant. What?'

She had started to say something and then stopped, as if she'd thought better of it.

She shook her head.

He eyed her narrowly. 'Go on.'

'It's just...' She hesitated again, biting down on her lip, her eyes not meeting his.

'Just...?' he prompted, resisting the urge to fold his arms and stare her down.

'It sounds a little lonely. I mean, you travel all over the world, and I don't really leave Trengarth, but in some ways we're both a little...' She paused, the big dark eyes fluttering up to meet his. 'A little trapped.'

Max couldn't hold back an incredulous laugh. *Trapped?* He was heir to one of the biggest companies in the world. He'd visited most of the major cities in the world. His life was golden—at least it had been.

'Honey, we are *nothing* alike. You choose to hide yourself away in your pretty little seaside village and let your life be lived through the books that you read. *My* life is about responsibilities you'll never understand. Family and employees and a heritage I need to be worthy of.'

She glared at him. 'I understand about family and I understand about responsibility. Scale isn't everything, Max. And if this is the first day you have really allowed yourself to get out of the business district and into the heart of a city then, yes, you are as trapped as I am. You may have set foot in Rome and Paris, but did you *see* them?'

Of course he had seen them! Through glass, mainly. Not like today, obviously, but there wasn't always time, and it wasn't *necessary.* His justifications sounded hollow, even as he thought them.

'The highlights, yes. But I was there to *work*, Ellie.'

'I see.' She turned away and stared out of the window. 'When *I* travel, finally, I want to see it all. Not just the bits the guidebooks show me. I want to walk through the alleyways and eat in the neighbourhood restaurants. I want to find the beating heart of the city and lose myself in it.'

'Then why haven't you?'

It took a while for her to respond, and when she did her voice was low, as if she were reluctant to admit the truth out loud.

'I was afraid. Afraid I'd be disappointed, afraid I'd get it wrong, afraid it wouldn't live up to my expectations. When you know how it feels to watch your dreams shatter it can be hard to trust in your dreams again.'

'What are your dreams now, Ellie?' His voice lowered as he moved closer to her, the pod all but disappeared, the children forgotten. There was just her and the hopelessness in her voice.

'Once they were the usual, I suppose. University, then a good job, and to fall in love and have children. Lots of children…' Her voice softened. 'I always wished I was part of a big family, and after we lost Dad and Phil I felt even more alone. That's why I loved books, I think. They were the only way I could escape, travel, try new things. I wanted to be Hermione or Lyra or Anne Shirley. Lonely children who forged their own path. Now…? I don't know, Max. I haven't dared dream in such a long time.'

'I've never thought about escape…' He hesitated. That was true, but was it the whole truth? 'I'm under pressure, sure, to be a Loveday is a pretty big responsibility. But it's a privilege too.'

'Do you still feel that way?'

He shook his head slowly. 'You're right. Now I just feel trapped,' he admitted, realising the truth of the words as he said them out loud. 'My dad wants my approval, my mom wants me onside, and the business needs me to do something clever—soon. It's like everything I grew up thinking I knew was a lie.'

'How so?'

He tried to make sense of his jumbled thoughts. 'We were picture-perfect, you know? Gorgeous house, plenty of money but not showy, members of the right clubs, giving to the right causes…and Grandfather in the centre of it, the benevolent tyrant. I thought he could do no wrong.'

He blew out a breath, some of the weight on his chest lightening as he finally spoke the heretical thoughts aloud.

'But underneath it all Dad was always resentful. I

think Grandfather kept him on a tight leash. *And* my mother. In public they were this affectionate couple, but now he's met Mandy I can't help wondering…' His voice trailed off.

'If any of it was real?'

Damn, she was perceptive. 'Oh, he had affairs. I always knew that. All the weekends Dad was working, the extravagant gifts he'd bring back. The hushed rows and then the insistence on putting on a good face in public. But underneath it all I was sure they really loved each other. Now it's all corroded—Mom is so bitter all she can think of is punishing him, no matter that it could bankrupt the company.'

Ellie drew in a deep breath, her eyes searching his face. 'That bad?'

'It's possible,' he admitted. 'And if lawyers get involved it could be a hundred times worse. That's why Dad wants me to negotiate with her. Meanwhile she wants me to promise not to ever engage with Dad's new girlfriend.' He could feel his mouth twist into the kind of cynical smile he'd never worn before this year. 'I guess I've always had to be the sensible one, the adult. I just never resented it before now.'

Her hand fluttered up and for one moment he thought she was going to touch his face. His chest tightened with anticipation, only for disappointment to flood through his veins as she lowered it again, tucking it behind her with a self-conscious gesture.

He leaned in, one arm on the glass beside her, his eyes fixed on hers. Not touching her, not even invading her space—not really—although the temptation to move that little bit further in was pushing at him…the need to move his hands from the glass to her shoulderblades. To allow them to slide down her narrow back. To feel her shiver under his touch, reining in the urge to rush, making them both wait.

But he couldn't.

Her eyes had widened, her breathing shallow and he didn't know if it was attraction or fear—he'd bet that *she* didn't really know either. There were times when he could swear that she was attracted to him: the way she smiled, ran a hand through her hair, peeped from under her lashes. Even in the line for the London Eye he had caught her looking at him with a speculation that had made his blood heat.

But the next moment she would shut off totally. She was as skittish as an unbroken colt. Part of him needed to know why, wanted to help her, protect her. But he had known her for what...? A few days? Who was he to walk into her life and arrogantly assume he could put it right?

He rocked back on his feet, casually letting his arm fall back, giving her the space she needed. He smiled at her, slow and sweet and as unthreatening as an ice cream sundae.

'Ellie Scott, I do believe we are breaking the rules.'

She was still frozen in place. 'We are?'

'We said we were going to have fun and, believe me, talking about my family is anything but. So, I am going to ask one of those nice teachers for one of their quizzes, and I am going to see if I can beat you and every single one of these ten-year-olds.'

'You don't know what the quiz is actually on.' The colour had come back into her cheeks and her shoulders had relaxed.

'I don't care. Honey, in my family we play to win. Monopoly, Clue, Mario Kart, Singstar—whatever it is, we do whatever it takes to win. And if that means bribing a ten-year-old for the answers, then watch me go.'

* * *

What would have happened if she'd smiled at him instead of standing there like a faun frozen in place by the White Witch? Would he have moved in closer? Would he have touched her? Kissed her?

What must he think? Whether he was just being friendly or was attracted to her he must think her gauche at best, ridiculous at worst.

Not that you would know, because within two minutes he had charmed two quiz sheets out of the bemused teachers and proceeded to barter, beg and bribe answers from the excited group of children, high-fiving them all when they finally exited the pod, the kids to go into the attached museum, Ellie and Max to begin a late-afternoon stroll along the side of the Thames.

'What now? Penguins?' he asked.

She looked at the queue, still snaking around the block, and pulled a face. 'It's a bit late. I don't think we'd get to the front before it shuts. Raincheck?'

'Look.' He stopped beside a poster. 'You can have afternoon tea with them. How cool! Do you think we have to eat raw fish too? I mean, I like sushi as much as the next guy, but I'm not sure I could manage a whole fish, bones and all.'

'Maybe the penguins like scones.' Her eyes flicked over the dates. 'The next one isn't till next month...the twenty-second.'

'Diary it in.' He flashed a grin at her. 'Penguins, sushi, and scones for two.'

'I wouldn't miss it for the world!'

'You still owe me a souvenir,' he reminded her. 'In fact two. I aced that quiz.'

'You cheated at that quiz.'

'The destination is all that matters. How you get there
is irrelevant.' He began to stroll along, quite unrepentant.

'Do you really believe that?' Lots of people did, obviously. But she'd expected more of him.

He slid her a sidelong grin. 'Sure I do. Don't worry
about who you kick on the way up, 'cause you have no
intention of ever coming back down again. Survival of
the fittest. Family mottoes, all of them. I bet Great-Aunt
Demelza grew up cross-stitching them into samplers so
we could hang them on our bedroom walls.'

'Oh, ha-ha.' But she didn't mind the teasing.

A glow spread through her as she watched him from
the corner of her eye. Sauntering along, dark hair ever so
slightly ruffled, the morning's stubble on his chin. Just
another American tourist enjoying the London summer
evening.

But not every tourist attracted admiring glances from
the groups of girls they passed, and not everyone exuded
such happy vibes. Which was a little bizarre, because
when they'd first met she hadn't pegged him as the relaxed type. Arrogant? Sure. Rude? Most definitely. It
was funny to think that if someone had told her just a
few days ago that she would be spending time away with
him, that he would make her laugh, make her heart beat
faster, she would have laughed—and prescribed a course
of wholesome children's books and some early nights.

And yet here she was.

And here *he* was.

She couldn't stop looking at him, fixating on the way
the late-afternoon sun glinted on his bare tanned arms,
highlighting every play of muscle. How it lingered on his
strong, capable hands. Her eyes followed the sun's playful
light as it danced over his wrists and along his fingers.
What would it be like to hold them? To slide her finger

over one knuckle? Could she? Would she dare? All she had to do was reach out.

She swung her hand a little closer in a pathetic experiment, snatching it back in a panic before allowing it to swing again. A jolt shot through her as her knuckles grazed his. It was all she could do not to cling on and never, ever let go.

'Ellie.'

He stopped and turned to face her. There was a simmering heat in his eyes…a heat that mirrored the liquid fire slipping through her veins, setting every nerve alight. Nerves that had spent so long dormant sprang to fiery life.

'If you want to hold my hand, honey, then all you have to do is take it.'

She gaped, trying to formulate some response, to deny it. But she was mute.

'But, Ellie…?'

There was a roughness to his voice, as if he was trying very hard to stay measured, to sound calm. She held his gaze despite the weakness in her knees, the tremors shivering through her. Despite the fear that she was making a mistake, the urge to retreat that was almost as strong as the urge to surge forward.

'Yes?'

'If you do then I *will* kiss you. Maybe not here, in front of all these people, and maybe not as we walk, but some time, at some point, I will kiss you. And you…' his eyes dropped to her mouth in an almost physical caress '…you'll kiss me back. Are you ready for that, Ellie?'

It wasn't the heat. Not in the end. And it wasn't the rough edge to his voice that spoke of want and passion. It wasn't his words and the arrogant assumption implicit in them. It was the tone. It was the look in his eyes. A look that said he needed her. That if she turned away he would accept it—and regret it.

And she? Would she regret it too? Just as she was beginning to regret the years she had spent hidden away, as safe as a nun in her convent and as chaste—not through vocation but through fear.

Ellie lifted her chin. She was done hiding and she was done living her life in the shadows. She was going to live. She was going to risk.

Slowly, hating the giveaway trembling of her fingers, she extended her arm and slipped her hand into his. His fingers closed around her, one at a time, softly, as if he knew not to spook her. His hand was warm, comforting, strong—and just the sense of skin against skin sent sparks dancing throughout her body. A line connected her fingertips to the pit of her stomach.

'Shall we?'

Max took a step forward and Ellie watched her arm move with him, feeling the tug on her body to fall into step behind him. And as if in a dream she followed, her stride matching his, their bodies working together. Fitting together.

She didn't know where they were headed, and right now she didn't much care. As long as her hand was in his they could walk for ever while she remembered what it felt like to yearn, to want to touch.

It felt good.

CHAPTER SEVEN

HE STILL HADN'T kissed her.

What kind of man promised a girl that he would kiss her and didn't deliver? He hadn't even come tantalisingly close. Not so much as an intimate smile all evening.

Not in their stroll along the South Bank, even though their hands had been entwined the whole time. Not as they'd perused the secondhand book stalls, nor as they'd bought milkshakes from one of the many vendors. Not over a glass of wine in a quaintly half-timbered pub, nor over dinner in a tiny Italian restaurant where the pasta had tasted the way Ellie had always imagined real Italian food would.

She'd closed her eyes and listened to the shouting from the kitchen, breathed in the mingled smells of tomato, basil and wine, and had almost imagined that she was in Rome at last.

And now they were returning to the hotel, retracing their steps along the riverside path, lit up and vibrant with the evening crowd. They were holding hands once again and he still hadn't made one single move towards her.

If she burst with anticipation it would be more than a little messy—and it would totally serve him right.

He shouldn't make promises he wasn't prepared to follow through.

'Are you tired? We could get a cab? Or,' he added a little doubtfully, 'as we're being tourists we could try buses. But I have to warn you they confuse the hell out of me.'

'Do they really confuse you or have you just never been on one?'

She was pretty sure it was the latter. He might be dressed down, but he was designer all the way at heart. She simply couldn't imagine him on a bus.

He grinned. 'Both.'

'I'm fine walking. I ate so much pasta I could do with the exercise.' *Very, very cool, Ellie.* That was definitely not in the 'Things to Say on a First Date' guide.

Not that this was. A first *or* a date. Obviously.

'I don't know what you're thinking, but I can tell there's a lot of wheels turning in that head of yours. Anything you want to share?'

How could he sound so relaxed? So amused?

Because this wasn't a first date. Holding hands with someone you'd known for a less than a week and only occasionally liked was probably completely normal to him.

'No.' She wasn't lying. She didn't want to share a single thought about dates or kisses with him. 'I'm not really thinking about anything. Just that it's nice to be out and about.'

'What shall we do tomorrow? The car is coming to pick us up at six and you'll probably need a good hour and a half to get ready...'

Ellie was about to interrupt. To tell him she only needed half an hour. A quick shower, brush her hair, slick on some mascara and lipstick and decide between her not that little black dress or her slightly longer black dress, put on her black almost-heels. It was hardly the routine of a diva.

Although she *could* visit the hotel spa and get her nails

done. It would probably wipe out her entire savings, but a little bit of pampering would be nice.

Ellie watched a group of girls totter past, only just balancing on their high strappy shoes. They were like a flock of exotic birds as they trilled and giggled in tiny, sheer summer dresses in emerald and cobalt blue, silver and sunshine-yellow.

Young, vibrant and alive.

She looked down. Skinny grey jeans. Again. High-top trainers. Again. Another short-sleeved tunic, black this time. Her hair was still twisted in the loose knot she had put it into that morning; her face was make-up free. The brightest colour in her wardrobe was a deep purple. She had switched the taupes and beiges that Simon had approved of for another colourless uniform. Another way to blend in.

The knowledge that she had chosen her own uniform didn't make it feel any better. Or any less constraining.

'Actually...' She spoke quickly before she changed her mind. 'I'll need longer than that. I might need the whole afternoon.'

Max's mouth quirked. 'Of course. *Just* the whole afternoon?'

Guilt pulled at her. 'I know we were supposed to be having fun. I'll be around in the morning to do something.'

'No, it's fine.' He pulled a face. 'I always planned to be in the office tomorrow anyway. I can't really play hooky on a Monday, and there's still so much to do in Trengarth even if I employ someone to empty the house, I might not get back to London this trip. Take as long as you need.'

He didn't tell her that she didn't need the afternoon, didn't waste time on fake compliments or try and talk her out of it. He respected her decision. That was great.

Or, more honestly, it was a little disappointing. But that was okay. She'd prove to Max Loveday that she could scrub up as well as any of his high-maintenance, trust fund, well-bred, moneyed usual dates.

And she'd prove to herself that it wasn't too late to take a chance.

He still hadn't kissed her. He knew that she wanted him to. Hell, she'd given him her hand, hadn't she? Had stared at him with those Bambi eyes and slipped those slender fingers through his, trembling as if she were abseiling over a cliff and he was her lifeline. It was a little terrifying.

It was intoxicating.

And he wanted to kiss her.

Wanted to so much he was almost trembling with it too. *Almost*.

And that was partly why he was holding back. This was a short trip and anything—anyone—he got entangled with had to be on a strictly short-term basis. Right now, what with all the crazy in his life, that was fine by him.

Besides, this was exactly what he didn't need long-term. This kind of messy emotion. Sure it felt right *now*, but what about next week? Next year? With an ocean between them and completely separate lives? It would be insanity.

Once he'd kissed Ellie would he remember that? Or would he be drawn in too far? Into something he didn't have the time or the head space to handle?

That was only partly it, though. Because it was all very well thinking about the future, but when all was said and done it would only be one kiss. But over the last two hours he'd sensed that it would be so much more to Ellie. Skittish, wide-eyed, and more vulnerable than she knew. It would be so easy to hurt her without even trying, and he didn't want to be that guy.

He shouldn't have offered…should have known better. But the words were said now. He couldn't take them back.

And honestly…? He wasn't sure he would if he could.

But he hadn't kissed her. Not yet.

Their walk was over in the blink of an eye. He must have found his way back to the hotel by luck rather than judgement, because all he'd been aware of was the feel of her hand in his. The knowledge that at any second he could pull her closer and she wouldn't stop him.

How could he not?

How *could* he?

Suddenly the shared suite didn't seem quite so funny, and the sitting-room separating their rooms seemed far too small. He wanted locks, corridors, possibly a couple of floors between them.

The hotel lobby was brightly lit, with the crystals in the chandeliers dancing rainbows, casting light onto the ornate gilt walls. Ellie seemed to have shaken off her earlier nervousness and walked confidently over to the reception desk, where a perfectly groomed woman sat. Heads together, voices low, they shared a long conversation before Ellie swivelled and walked back over to him.

'All set.' She had a mysterious expression on her face, like a child on Christmas Eve, ripe with secrets. 'Ready?'

'Absolutely.' *Not.*

Her didn't take her hand, stayed a safe distance away as they took the lift up to their floor, as they walked the few short metres to their suite. He stood gallantly back, allowing her into the sitting-room before him. But his promise was hanging in the air between them. It was in every questioning glance, every rise of her chest, every nervous flutter of her hands.

'Nightcap?' He shouldn't have made the suggestion, should simply say goodnight and get out of there. But his common sense had been overridden by his need to extend the evening even by just a few minutes.

Ellie was standing in the middle of the sitting-room, her slim, casually clad figure incongruous amongst the deep purples and gold luxury of the opulent suite. She looked as fresh as a wildflower set amidst hothouse blooms.

'No, thank you.' She turned slowly. 'I don't think I fully took this in earlier. It's very...'

'Gold?' he offered.

Her mouth tilted. 'It is that. It's all very imposing, isn't it? I'm not sure it's exactly homely, though. I can't imagine myself sprawling out on that sofa, for instance.'

Max took a deep breath. Ellie. *Sprawled. Sofa.*

His mind was full of images. Tousled hair, swollen lips, languid eyes, creamy skin...

'I would like to see that.' His voice was low, a rough rasp.

Time stopped. Her eyes flickered to his and stayed there. Neither of them able to look away as his words reverberated around the room.

It was no use. What was it they said about good intentions? And if his feet were already set on the path to hell then he might as well enjoy the journey.

'Max?'

He didn't know if she had said his name or just mouthed it, but it was too late. He was past the point of thought. Of common sense.

It took him just two strides to stand before her.

The blood was rushing through his veins, boiling hot, and his pulse was beating louder, harder than it had ever beat before. There was a deep ache in his chest that could only be assuaged by one thing. By her.

He stepped closer and waited, a bare millimetre between them. He needed her to make the final move, to show that she was in on this. Whatever 'this' was. Whatever 'in' meant.

'Ellie?' Not a command, not even a question. More a query.

Her eyes were huge, dark, desire mingling with doubt. He could overcome that doubt, kiss it out of her. But he waited. Waited for her to come to him. This had to be her decision.

His hands tingled, desperate to touch her, but he kept them at his sides.

She swallowed, a convulsive movement. Then she stepped forward.

They stood there for one second. It was an eternity. He could feel the full softness of her breasts against his chest, her legs just brushing his, her hands soft on his shoulders. Her face was tilted up towards his.

Max didn't know who made the next move. Whether or not she stood on tiptoe just as he bent forward. But their lips met, found each other as if of their own volition. And he was lost.

Lost in her scent, in her taste. Lost in the grip of her hands on his shoulders. Lost in the curve of her waist, the slenderness of her back as his arms encircled her to pull her closer.

He hadn't meant this. He had meant a soft kiss, a teasing kiss, a flirtatious kiss. But this...? This was hot and greedy and needy and all-encompassing.

He pulled her in closer, crushing her body against his, needing to feel her moulded to him. And she pressed closer yet, wrapped herself round him as if a millimetre gap was too much. And it was.

His hands moved up her back, learning her curves as

they went, until finally they were buried in the glorious weight of her silky hair. It was everything he had hoped for: fine, soft, wound around his hands.

All promises of not going too fast disappeared. He needed to see her clad in nothing but that hair...needed to explore every inch of her, touch every inch. And Ellie was with him every step, her soft hands burning a trail as they slid beneath his T-shirt, roaming across his back, across his chest, and then slowly, tantalisingly, but so very surely, moving lower, across his abdomen, and then lower still.

Max sucked in a deep breath as she reached his belt. Her hands were trembling but sure as she unbuckled his belt, moving her fingers to the first button on his jeans.

He caught her busy hands in his. 'Slow down, honey. We have all night.'

He allowed his voice to linger suggestively on the last two words and heard her gasp as his hands slid over hers, then moved slowly, oh, so slowly, his fingers caressing the soft skin of her wrists, her delicate inner elbow and up to her shoulders. He held her loosely for one moment, his lips travelling down, across her pointed chin, down her neck to feast briefly on her throat.

She was utterly still, her head thrown back to allow him access, the only sign of life her rapidly beating pulse, its overheated beat marching in step with the rapid thump of his heart. And then he moved, scooping her up in his arms, his mouth back on hers, needing, demanding, wanting as he carried her across the room and through the door. Her arms were wrapped around his neck, holding on tight, holding *him* tight.

There was no letting go. There was no going back. There was only this. Darkness, touch, moans and need. Only them. Clothes were pulled off with no care for little things like buttons. Impatient, greedy hands pushed barriers aside. Until there were no barriers left...

She should have been thinking, *What have I done?*

Instead all she could think was, *Can we do that again?*

Ellie had never had a morning after the night before. She had never done a walk of shame in last night's dress, with smeared make-up, shoes in hand, tiptoeing out through the door in the grey dawn light. Never woken up next to someone alive with the possibility of a new beginning.

She'd dated Simon for several months before they'd first slept together, and by then she'd been so besotted and so terrified of disappointing him that she had been unable to think or dream about anything but him. Her first thought on waking then hadn't been excitement or happiness but worry—the familiar gnaw of panic. Had she passed muster? Had her youth and inexperience been too obvious? Had she disgusted him?

She couldn't remember enjoying it. It had all been about *him*.

Now she could see that was exactly what Simon had wanted. Could see how he had fed on her toxic mixture of inexperience, loneliness and need. Had encouraged it until she had been exactly what he'd wanted her to be: compliant, dependent and afraid.

So waking up alone, sated, in a strange bed, naked and with every muscle aching in a curiously pleasant way was far too much of a novelty for a previously engaged woman of twenty-five. But there it was.

Alone. Ellie wasn't sure whether relief or indignation was at the forefront of her mind when she rolled over to pat nothing but cold sheets.

Relief that she didn't have to worry about her hair, her

breath, the etiquette—should she go in for a kiss or sit up primly and pretend that she *hadn't* nibbled her way over his entire body in lieu of dessert?

Or indignation that she was waking up alone with just a note to remind her that she hadn't dreamt the previous night? *A note!*

There it was on the bedside table, crisp and white like in a scene from a film.

> *Dear Ellie*
> *You looked so peaceful I didn't like to wake you. I should never have agreed to go in to the office— they called a meeting for nine a.m.*
>   *Hope your day is a lot more fun than mine. I'll pick you up at six. Enjoy.*
> *Max*
> *PS Room Service is on DL Media, so go wild. One of us should.*

Hmm... She read it through again. It wasn't a love letter—there were no declarations of undying devotion— but neither was it a 'Dear John'. It was something in between.

Which was about right, she supposed.

Ellie rolled over and stretched, enjoying the sheer space of the enormous bed. She could lie lengthways, diagonally, horizontally and still sprawl out in comfort. In fact, now she was thinking about it, she had covered pretty much every inch of the bed last night.

Heat returned to her cheeks as images flashed through her mind, her nerves tingling in sensory recognition. She sat up and looked at the rumpled pillows, the dishevelled sheets. At the clothing still distributed across the room.

Her jeans, her tunic. Oh, goodness! Was that her comfortable yet eminently sensible bra?

She covered her face with her hands. Her first ever night of red-hot seduction and she had been wearing underwear as alluring as a nice cup of tea and a custard cream.

At least she hadn't been wearing it for too long. And Max hadn't seemed to have had any complaints. Not judging by the intake of breath when he'd pulled her tunic over her head, and not judging by the heat in his eyes when he had looked at her as if she were the most desirable thing he had ever seen.

Had that been *her*? Prim Ellie Scott? So wanton, so demanding, so knowing? And now that she had allowed that side of her to surface could she lock herself away again? Slide back into her hermit ways and keep this side of herself hidden?

The thing was, she didn't want to explore it with just anyone.

Ellie slumped back onto the bed, the twist of desire in her stomach knotting into dread.

'It's a crush,' she said aloud, emphasising every word slowly and clearly. 'You can't fall in love with someone after a week. Not because they quite fancy you and make you laugh. You are *not* going to become besotted with someone you barely know. Not again.'

It was as if cold water had been thrown over her. All the fire, all the sparks at her nerve-endings extinguished by reality. Ellie shivered, pulling the quilt back over her body, wanting to be warm, to be comforted. To be hidden away.

I won't let the memory of Simon spoil this, she told herself fiercely, blinking hard, refusing to let the threatening tears fall. *I am older, I am most definitely wiser, and I am not the naïve little girl I was back then. I know what this is and I can handle it. He'll be flying back home in just over a week. Enjoy it.*

She pulled the quilt tighter still, letting its warmth permeate her goosebumped body. This was supposed to be fun, not a trip down Memories I Would Much Rather Forget Lane.

She had plans today. Big, scary and long overdue plans. What was she going to do? Hide in this bed until six or get up, get dressed and follow through? She had allowed Simon to control the last three years of her life just as much as he had controlled the three years they had spent together. She might have plucked up the courage to leave and start afresh, but she hadn't moved on... not really.

And now Max. Offering her the opportunity to explore a new side of herself. A more adventurous side. To be the Ellie she'd always intended to be before her life had been so brutally derailed.

She could take the opportunity he was offering—or she could pack up and go home. Hide away with her books for the rest of her life.

Ellie sat up again and pushed the quilt away. She was going to get up, she was going to order the most decadent breakfast on the room service menu, and she was going to follow every single part of her tentative plan.

And today was the very last day she was going to allow Simon to cast a shadow over her life. He wasn't going to taint a single second of her future. She was finally going to be free.

Meetings, meetings, meetings... Normally Max's head would be spinning with the day he had spent. The London office was the most important after their New York headquarters, and on Max's last visit eighteen months ago it had been a vibrant place full of enthusiasm and talent. Now it was full of fear, with people clinging on to their jobs determinedly or leaving, like rats jumping from a ship before they were pushed.

His father hadn't even been over, having sent in management consultants instead to shake things up. They had certainly managed that—the MD Max had worked so successfully with was long gone and in his place a board full of yes-men with no ideas of their own.

It had put the present state of DL Media into stark perspective. Max might have no appetite for a family rift, but he didn't have much choice. There was far too much at stake: jobs, the company's reputation. His grandfather's legacy.

It should be weighing on his mind, his mood should be murkier than a classic London peasouper, and yet all he had wanted all day was to stride out of that infernal boardroom, find Ellie and take her right back to bed. And stay there. The awards ceremony be damned.

He curled his hands into loose fists and took in a deep, shuddering breath. He could have made his excuses and gone. But he had stayed. Because when the chips were down he was a Loveday. Old school. Bred in his grandfather's image. So he had stayed, listened, learned and reassured.

He had ordered his dinner suit to be brought to the building, the car to pick him up straight from there. Had put the business first and his own desires second.

Like a Loveday should.

But it all felt so hollow. No thrill of business. Just the sense of another day wasted. Thank goodness for tonight.

Only Ellie wasn't waiting in the foyer. The car had

pulled up outside the hotel and for ten minutes Max waited, his phone in his hand, sending email after email to his long-suffering PA. She had been expecting a quiet week or two. Well, this was going to put paid to any plans she might have had of stepping up her flirtation with Eduardo in Accounts.

Another minute, another email.

Max checked the time. Ellie was fifteen minutes late.

Had she got his note? Had he not been clear? Had she taken offence and hightailed it back to Cornwall? He'd meant to call. He *should* have called.

But for once in his glib life he had been unsure what to say. *Thank you? That was incredible? All I can think about is touching you?*

He bit back a laugh. Absolutely pathetic. But he still couldn't think of anything better.

He checked his watch again, aware of the chauffeur's eyes on him, the engine idling. He could call.

Or he could go and get her. A gentleman always did. What would his grandfather say if he could see him sitting in a car waiting for her to come to him? He would be horrified.

It only took him a couple of minutes to walk up to their suite, but Max's heart was hammering as if he had climbed to the top of a skyscraper. He was convinced that he would open the door and be confronted by an empty suite. That he had blown it.

He had never worried before. Never waited, never chased. The second it got demanding or difficult he was out of there. He knew all too well where tears, tantrums and demands led. Had grown up with their devastation.

The door handle was slippery in his hand, reluctant to turn, but finally he had swung the door open and he strode into the opulent sitting-room.

'Ellie?'

'I'm in here.' There was nervousness to her voice, a hint of panic. 'Sorry… It all took a little longer than I thought. High-maintenance really is a full-time job. Are we late?'

Max didn't know just how deep a breath he was holding until he heard her voice. The relief hit him with an almost physical force.

'No, my grandfather told me to always pick a time half an hour in advance. It's never steered me wrong yet.'

'Then I've been panicking for nothing?' Her voice had switched from nervous to indignant. 'Honestly, Max, that was mean.'

He was going to reply. He was. But then she appeared at the door and he couldn't say anything at all. All he could do was stare. He was aware in some dim corner of his mind that his mouth was hanging open, and with some effort he snapped it shut.

And then he stared some more.

Gone was the elusively pretty girl. Here instead was a stunningly beautiful woman.

'Ellie? Wow. You look…' It wasn't the smoothest line, but it was all he could manage. Then, 'You cut your hair.'

That shimmering mass was gone. In its place was an edgy bob, cut in sharp layers. It framed her face, emphasising her eyes, her chin, her defined cheekbones.

'Yes.' Her hand reached up to touch the ends, tentative, as if she couldn't quite believe it. 'I thought it was time.'

'You look incredible.' His voice was hoarse and he couldn't stop staring.

From the tips of her newly styled hair and her heavily kohled eyes to the scarlet dress, bare at her shoulders, tight-fitting down her torso, then flaring out to mid-thigh, this was a new, dangerous, deeply desirable Ellie.

'Is it too much?' The expectant expression on her face had been replaced with panic. 'Am I overdressed? Have I gone a bit over the top? I can change.'

Yes. She was. Simultaneously over and underdressed. Overdressed because he wanted to tear that dress off her right now. And underdressed because he wasn't sure he wanted his colleagues to see quite so much of her creamy skin. He knew just what long, perfect legs she had. He just didn't want anyone else to appreciate them. Maybe she had a shawl? And some leggings?

He shook his head. What was happening to him? He was thinking like a Neanderthal. His last ex had spent most of the spring in tightfitting yoga pants and a crop top and he had never once cared.

'Max?'

He held out his hand. 'No, don't change a thing. You are absolutely perfect.'

CHAPTER EIGHT

ELLIE HAD ALWAYS thought that she hated small talk.

Standing at Simon's side, her role had been to agree with him. It had been the easiest and the safest thing to do. He wouldn't retreat into one of his terrifying sulks if she didn't say anything wrong.

Of course she couldn't be too mute—then he would accuse of her being dull, of not trying hard enough. No, it had been easier to agree with him at all times.

Tonight was as different from a night out with Simon as a glass of vintage champagne was from cheap lemonade.

Max had made no attempt to keep her near him. But his eyes sought her out as she moved from group to group, catching her gaze with an intimate smile that heated her through. And he'd made sure she was introduced to his companions, supplied with a drink. If she found herself alone even for a second then he was there, as if by magic, ready to introduce her to another key contact.

He would whisk her away, off into a corner, every now and then. She usually had to slip into the cloakroom afterwards and reapply her lipstick. Every time she did she would stop and look at the girl in the mirror. The girl with the emphasised eyes, the choppy hair. The girl in the red dress.

She couldn't hide. Not like this. Her dress was so

bright, the cut exposing far more of her arms and legs than she ever usually showed, her hair left her face and her shoulders bare, and her make-up was dramatic.

She was so used to hiding behind her hair she felt exposed without it. But she also felt free, reinvented. It had been long for so many years: one length for her ballet dancing youth, uncut in her teens because her father had loved it so, and her mother would have been devastated if it was cut.

And Simon had liked long hair on women.

She had thought about changing it, in the three years she had spent in Trengarth, but had clung on to the security blanket it offered.

There was no blanket now.

This girl had to mingle, to talk.

And people wanted to talk to *her*, to know her, to discuss her shop, the tentative festival plans. They were interested in her thoughts, in her perspective.

It was a heady experience. For so long she had listened to the voices in her head telling her she was too young, too inexperienced, that she was hampered by her lack of a degree, unable to follow her dreams—and yet at some point in the last three years she had accumulated huge amounts of industry knowledge.

She was on the front line. She knew what people wanted to read, how they wanted to purchase it, what made them angry, excited—and what left them cold. Her best book club meetings were always those where the participants were polarised. And here she was, surrounded by people who spoke her language, people who knew the prefix to most ISBN numbers, got excited by new covers and new releases. People who openly admitted to sniffing the crisp new pages of a paperback book. She was in her element.

And Max allowed her the freedom to fly.

He didn't look as if he were having quite so good a time. Oh, sure, to the casual observer he probably looked as if he was enjoying himself, standing in a group, his stance relaxed, a smile on his face. But there was a tension in his shoulders, a crinkle around his eyes that gave Ellie an inkling that he was hiding his true feelings.

Not surprisingly, here in a room full of industry professionals, rumours about DL Media were running rife. And there was no escape for him in the endlessly moving, speculating, keen-eyed crowd. He wouldn't even be able to relax over dinner. There were no formal tables nor a sit-down meal. Instead endless trays of canapés circulated. It was like dinner in miniature: teeny tarts, quiches, curls of lettuce hiding a quail's egg in their leaves, delicate slivers of cheese and quince.

Normally the very word 'circulate' would bring Ellie out in a cold sweat, but tonight she was managing it effortlessly...despite the pinch of her new and alarmingly high shoes. She had a glass of wine in one hand, something delicious swiped off a passing tray in the other, and interesting conversation.

It beat The Three Herrings pub quiz. Well, apart from the night she had helped win it. That had been pretty spectacular.

'So, DL Media are sponsoring your festival?'

Ellie had to pinch herself as she remembered that she was talking to an agent: a real, live literary agent whose clients included several of her favourite authors.

He tilted his head to one side, his eyes sharp. 'Does that mean you'll only be working with their writers?'

'No!' It wasn't the first time she had heard this. News obviously spread through the publishing world at the same speed with which it rushed through Trengarth—

and with the same accuracy. 'The sponsorship comes from Demelza Loveday's personal estate. Max is festival director, but as a family member, not a representative of DL Media.'

'A good thing, if half the rumours I've heard are true.' The agent's eyes were still fastened on her questioningly. 'Is it true their book publishing division is being sold off?'

'I heard they were going digital only.' Another person had joined the group, her face avid with the desire for information.

'Either way, I would be *very* concerned about placing a client with them,' said the agent.

'All rumours of DL Media's demise are very much exaggerated.'

Max's drawl broke into the conversation, much to Ellie's relief.

'It is possible to be both cutting edge *and* traditional, you know. Ellie, I believe the awards are about to start, and they want nominees to be near the front. Just in case your name gets called. Excuse us, please...duty calls. Here's my card. Call me. I am more than happy to continue this conversation with you later.'

His voice was calm, with that slightly arrogant edge, but the hand that held Ellie's arm was gripping tightly.

'Vultures,' he muttered.

'They're just trying to pry.'

'They're not *trying*. They're doing a fine job.' He shook his head. 'Just a hint of this kind of instability and the whole company could crumble faster than a sandcastle at low tide. You heard Tom Edgar then. If he isn't going to consider our bids then we could lose out on new authors, or on re-signing profitable ones. He has a lot of clout.'

'So what are you going to do?'

'Right now? Smile, deny, and make sure you have a great evening. Tomorrow…? Tomorrow I make some serious plans. Right, no more looking so downcast. This isn't my night. It's yours. We need to be ready to toast your success as Independent Bookseller of the Year.'

She laughed, the embarrassed heat flooding her cheeks. 'Shush, this is England. We don't boast. We shuffle in a self-deprecating way and mutter that every other competitor is far more deserving and we didn't expect to win anyway.'

'Ah, but you're with an ignorant Yank, and *we* shout our successes loud and proud.'

'I haven't actually won,' she pointed out.

'Yet.' He was looking more relaxed, the lines of strain around his mouth evening out. 'I for one am ready to cheer very loudly indeed.'

'Shh!' But she was smiling. 'It's about to start.'

It was a very long ceremony. It seemed as if there was no aspect of the book trade, from industry blogs to conferences, supply chains to sales reps, that wasn't being honoured. Ellie shifted from aching foot to aching foot, wishing she had actually tried walking in her shoes before buying them.

'You're on.'

Max's breath skimmed over her ear as he whispered, the warmth penetrating her skin, and the desire to lean back warred with the nerves jumping in her stomach like a basket of naughty kittens.

'I wish we hadn't come,' she murmured, and he chuckled, low and deep, a hand at her back. To reassure her or to keep her there? Not that she could run away in these shoes…

Best Chain Bookstore, Best Bookshop Manager, Best

Event Organiser… On and on the awards went, and the pain in her feet competed with the increasing nausea gnawing away at her.

'Ellie Scott!'

The sound of her name echoed around the room as applause and a couple of cheers greeted it. She stood rooted to the spot in disbelief and embarrassment as, true to his word, Max whooped.

'Me?'

'Go on.' He gave her a gentle push. 'They're waiting for you.'

Ellie hadn't lied when she'd said she didn't expect to win—she worked alone, in a small shop miles away from the capital. Who *knew* her? Of course a quirky city independent would win, she hadn't even bothered to prepare a speech.

The sound of Max's continuing whoops rang in her ears as she stumbled in her unaccustomed heels to the podium. The glare of the lights, the people—so many people—all staring at her, smiling at her. Waiting for her.

Waiting for her to speak.

She was alone under the spotlight of their gaze. Once, long ago, she had enjoyed drama lessons, even taken part in school plays. Now she could barely recognise that girl who had soaked up the audience's attention, but there must be some residual atom of her left, because her shoulders straightened, her voice strengthened.

'When I opened a bookshop people said I was crazy…' A ripple of amusement passed through the crowd and, emboldened by their response, she carried on. 'They thought I should open a coffee shop and have a few books dotted around. Well, I do have a temperamental coffee machine. But it's not the main attraction. The books are.'

She paused, trying to formulate her thoughts.

'It's not easy, and if I had a pound for every time someone has told me the book trade is dead my cash flow would be incredible. I can't compete with the internet giants. I can't stop people browsing and buying the eBook later. But I can—I can and I *do*—offer a tailored service. I can make book-buying fun, informative and easy. I can *recommend*. Of course I have to diversify, and not just with coffee. I run book groups for all ages, knitting groups, craft groups. I go into local schools and playgroups and to WI meetings. I open seven days a week and I stay open late.'

She looked out over the anonymous sea of people and swallowed, panic beginning to twist her chest. Who was *she* to think that she could tell one single person in this room how to sell books? Who did she think she was?

She was twenty-five, and she had run her own business for three years. She wasn't rich, but the shop was in the black and they had chosen *her* to win this award. That was who she was.

'Next year I'll diversify even further, when I curate the first Trengarth Literary Festival. But at the heart of all this diversification is one very simple mission. To get the great stories around out there, into people's hands. That's what they want. Great stories. You keep producing them and I'll keep selling them. Thank you.'

'That was pretty amazing.' Max sat back in the taxi. Amazing for Ellie, a battle for him. But he wasn't going to ruin her triumph by telling her so.

'I know!'

Ellie was glowing, the streetlamps spotlighting her in gold as the car drove them through the well-lit streets. Her hair shone, her dress glittered, but the most luminous thing of all was her smile, stretched wide across her face.

'I spoke to so many lovely people and they were so kind. Loads of them want to be part of the literary festival. I have so many business cards I don't know where to start. I thought the first year would be a really small affair, but it really looks like we might attract some big names.'

'And thanks to Great-Aunt Demelza you can actually *pay* your participants,' he reminded her. 'From what I hear that's by no means usual...especially for start-up festivals. Many of them rely on goodwill alone. A pay cheque will definitely pull people in. But I wasn't talking about the festival. I was talking about *you*. About your speech.'

'Oh...' She flushed, her cheeks coming close to matching the vibrant colour of her dress. 'That wasn't a speech. It was...'

'A call to arms?'

'No! A few panicked words, that's all.'

He inched a little closer on the seat so their legs were touching, his knee firmly pressed against hers like a high school boy on a first date, sharing a booth. 'You inspired me.'

'Really?'

'Oh, yes. In fact you have been inspiring me all evening.'

'Inspiring you to concentrate on the books side of the business?'

He slid his hand up her leg. Her stockings were a flimsy barrier. How much further was the hotel?

'Amongst other things.'

Her eyebrows rose as she leaned a little closer, her body heating him wherever they touched.

'We *do* have a day of missed fun to make up for. You spent it in meetings and, although some women might find spas and boutiques relaxing, I was terrified the whole time. We could both do with some relaxing.'

'Is that so? And did you have anything in particular in mind?'

Ellie put her hand over his, the pressure moulding his fingers around her leg. 'I'm sure we can work together to think of something.'

Her hand was warm, her fingers wound through his. Was this really the same girl who had jumped like a skittish kitten whenever he touched her? Had the dress and radical haircut given her a new confidence? Or had she been there all the time? Hidden behind the layers and the no-nonsense demeanour?

If only there was more time to explore her, to explore *them*.

'It's our last night in London. We should make it memorable.'

It did no harm to remind her—to remind himself—that this trip was finite. That although he would be returning to Cornwall with her in the morning his holiday was nearly at an end.

'Real life again tomorrow.' She sounded wistful. 'I didn't even want to come here and I've had such an amazing time. I'm not quite ready for it to end—and we didn't get to see the penguins.'

Was she talking about not wanting the trip to end— or not wanting to stop spending time with Max himself? His hand stilled under hers.

'The penguins aren't going anywhere. We could see them in the morning.'

'No, I need a reason to make sure I come back. Besides, now I know I can have scones with them I won't settle for anything less.'

'Of course you'll come back. *We'll* come back.'

We? Where had *that* come from? Max didn't usually like to make plans too far in advance. Previous relationships had begun to fracture when he had refused to commit to a wedding or a family party several months in advance.

Here he was making promises for an unspecified future date.

And it didn't make him want to run.

It was because they had barely begun. He might not be the king of long-term relationships, but neither was he a one-night stand kind of guy. He liked a relationship to run its course.

That was why he was feeling odd about knowing he would have to leave in the next few days. She would be unfinished business, that was all.

'Max?'

She was sitting there, her hand still in his, as lost in her own thoughts as he was in his.

'Yeah?'

'Thank you.'

'Honey, you don't have to thank me for anything.'

'No, I *do*.' She paused, pulling her hand away from his and shifting in her seat so that she was looking directly at him. 'I didn't want to admit it, especially not to myself, but I *was* hiding in Trengarth. I'm twenty-five and the highlight of my week is the pub quiz at The Three Herrings. And I only turn up to that once every few months.'

His body tensed. 'Why were you hiding?'

She didn't answer for a moment, her hands twisting in her lap. 'I didn't trust myself.' Her voice was low, as if she were in the confessional. 'I made a couple of bad choices. I think it made me afraid to try again. After Dad and Phil died Mum clung to me. I let that be my excuse for putting off university, for not starting my own life. But I think I was just too scared. Losing them was like losing a part of myself, losing my identity, and I just couldn't pick myself up again.'

He couldn't imagine it…having your life ripped apart before it had fully begun. 'You were very young.'

Her mouth turned up in a sad approximation of a smile. 'I suppose. But at home I had to be the adult and I allowed it. I allowed Mum to rely on me…allowed her neediness to define me. So when she met Bill and didn't need me any more it was like…like…'

'Like you'd lost everything?'

'Yes. It was exactly like that. And then there was Simon. I was so vulnerable, so lonely when I met him. I guess he sensed that. I thought he was my knight in shining armour. He was ten years older than me and so sure of himself. I was blinded by him, by what he wanted from me I didn't have to figure myself out.'

She had barely mentioned her past, and her fiancé had been no more than a name, but Max's jaw clenched at the sorrow and hurt in her voice. It hadn't been just a relationship gone wrong. She had been badly wounded and her scars evidently still ran deep.

His hands curled into fists. How could anyone hurt her? Strip away her confidence?

'I was so proud of myself for getting away. I thought it was enough…thought that I was finally living the life I wanted. I live in a place I love, doing something I feel passionately about. And those are *good* choices. They *do* make me happy. But as a human being I am still a complete mess. I don't have many friends, and I don't leave my comfort zone. Not ever. I didn't dare dream of anything else, anything more. Especially not romance. Especially not love.'

Her voice broke a little on the last word.

Max was frozen. What was she saying? Was she saying that she was falling in love with him?

Surely not? Not after a week?

Sure, last night had been utterly incredible, but that wasn't love. Was it? It was passion. It was mutual understanding. It was compatibility. And, yes, he liked the way her smile lit up her whole face, turned mere prettiness into true beauty. He liked the way she was so cool and poised on the outside and yet fire and heat inside. He liked the way she stood up for what she believed in, even when it scared her to stand up and be counted.

But that wasn't love either, was it?

Love was messy and painful and loud and selfish. Love meant to hell with the rest of the world. Love meant operating on your terms, your way, no matter who got hurt. And when it went wrong you were left defenceless, revenge your only weapon.

He couldn't risk that. Couldn't be that vulnerable. There were other ways, better ways. It might sound cold: a timetable, a wish list and a criteria. But it was the key. The key to a quiet, successful life.

Although the truth was he had never met anyone who'd tempted him to more than a nice time. Anyone who'd made him want to make plans months in advance. Never met any woman he couldn't walk away from the moment things got difficult or messy.

Did that mean he was no better than his dad?

Maybe he was just a coward.

The silence had stretched wafer-thin. He needed to say something. He had no idea what to say.

'And how do you feel now?'

He held his breath. Would she make some kind of declaration? It was fine if she did. He knew it wasn't real. It would be the adrenaline from the evening, hormones still racing around after last night. If she had really been single, hadn't so much as dated in the last three years, then no wonder she was turned upside down by the attraction raging between them. It had discombobulated *him* after all.

He just needed to handle the situation with tact, with gentle skill.

Ellie leaned back in her seat. Her hands stilled. 'I feel ready to start living again. I am completely buzzed about the festival, about the work that lies ahead. And I'm not going to hide away any more. I'm going to go out there, start living, start dating again. Last night…yesterday… the whole week…' She trailed off. 'It's made me think. Think about who I want to be, *what* I want to be. And a lot of that is down to you. So, thank you.'

'You're welcome.'

Not a declaration. Not a grand passion. She wasn't in love with him. She was already thinking ahead. Thinking past him.

Which was great.

Wasn't it?

So why did he feel…well, *deflated*? Like a hot air balloon failing to lift off into the sky?

'No, I mean it. Last night was amazing. I didn't know I could feel like that, act like that. I'd never…'

She laughed. A low sound that penetrated deep into his bones, into his blood.

'I didn't think I would ever feel that free, that wanted. You showed me how it could be…how it *should* be.'

'It wasn't just me.' Max was uncomfortable cast in the role of Professor Higgins, and Ellie was certainly no Eliza Doolittle, ready for him to pluck, mould and shape. 'I think you were ready. I just provided the opportunity. Your hair, that dress…that's all you.'

The car had pulled up in front of the hotel. This was it. He would lead her back up to their suite and hopefully unzip that tight-fitting bodice, learn her body just a little bit more. Then tomorrow they would return to Cornwall and say their goodbyes. No hard feelings. Just warm memories. He would be free to sort out all the problems with DL Media and his parents; she would be free to start her new and more exciting life. A life he had helped her to kick start.

How very altruistic of him.

He couldn't have planned it better.

And he might feel a little hollow inside *now*, but give him a week and Cornwall, London and Ellie Scott would all be distant memories. His life was complicated enough without adding long-distance relationships to it.

Besides, she didn't even want a relationship. Not with him. And that was absolutely fine.

Had she said something wrong?

Max's hand was around her waist, his fingers absent-mindedly caressing the silky material of her dress, every touch sending sparks fizzing along her nerve-endings. The shock of winning, the champagne, the buzz of the whole evening and the last twenty minutes in such close proximity to Max had combined to create a perfect maelstrom of excitement—and she knew just the perfect way to work it out.

She tapped her foot, willing the lift on. As far as Ellie was concerned they couldn't get back to the privacy of their room soon enough.

But Max was distant, mentally if not physically, and had been for most of the journey. Was he thinking about work? Planning his next step? The room tonight had twittered with gossip over DL Media's crisis. It had to be weighing on him.

She'd miss him. It had only been a week, but he had made such an impact on her life, crashing into it like a meteorite and shaking up everything she'd thought she knew, thought she wanted, thought she was. He'd challenged her, excited her, pushed her.

It was only natural that she would miss him. But his life was far, far away…a whole ocean away. And she hadn't even started to live hers yet.

It was time she did.

His arm remained around her waist as they walked the few short steps from the lift to the suite door, stayed there as he unlocked it and ushered her in.

The velvet cushions, gilt trimmings, opulent colours and brocade hangings hit her again with their over-the-top luxury. Ellie had somehow grown fond of their ridiculous suite. She had been reborn there. In less than forty-eight hours had made some huge changes. She just hoped that back in her own home she could keep the clarity and confidence she had gained here.

'Congratulations again. I thought we should celebrate.'

Max steered her over to the glass table. A complicated arrangement of lilies, roses and orchids dominated its surface, flanked by a bottle of vintage champagne chilling in an ice bucket, a lavish box of chocolates and a small purple tub.

'Champagne?'

Max followed her gaze. 'This is the hotel's Romance Package,' he murmured, his mouth close to her ear, his breath warm on her neck. 'Champagne, chocolate and massage oil.'

His eyes caught hers, full of meaning. Wherever he had been he was back. Back with clear intent.

He reached out and plucked the tub from the table. 'Sensual Jasmine with deep chocolate and sandalwood undertones. Feeling tense, Ellie?'

The promise in his voice shot straight through her.

Ellie shivered. 'A little.' It wasn't a lie.

'That's good. We can do something about that.'

Ellie swallowed, her eyes fixed on the small purple tub as he casually twisted it round and round in those oh, so capable fingers. 'We can?'

'Oh, yes. But you may want to disrobe first. I believe these oils can get rather...' His smile was pure wicked intent. 'Messy.'

'Messy?' Had she just squeaked?

'Oh, yeah. If you do it right, that is.'

She'd bet a year's takings that Max Loveday would do it right.

She stood there dry-mouthed as he picked up the bottle of champagne, deftly turning the wire and easing out the cork with practised ease.

'Well?' He poured champagne into one of the two flutes waiting by the bottle. 'What are you waiting for?'

Did he mean...? 'You want me to take my dress off?'

'Honey, I want you to take *everything* off. I have plans involving this...' He held up the champagne bottle. 'This...' He held up the massage oil. 'And your naked body. So come on: strip.'

Her breathing shallow, Ellie reached for the zip at the side of her dress. Her hands were clumsy, struggling to find the fastener, to draw it down the closely fitting bodice. Finally, *finally*, she pulled it down and let the dress fall away, standing in front of him in just her underwear.

At least it wasn't sensible this time. Tiny, silky wisps of black and red exposed far more than they concealed. It had taken all her resolve to put them on earlier, but hearing his sharp intake of breath, watching his eyes darken, filled her with a sensual power she had never felt before.

He might be issuing the demands, but she was the one in command.

She looked him clearly in the eye, didn't flinch or look away. 'Your turn. You said yourself things could get messy.'

Appreciation filled his face. 'You're playing with fire,' he warned as his hands moved to his tie. 'Be careful you don't get burned.'

'Oh, I'm counting on it.'

Ellie turned and walked into the master bedroom, head high, step confident even in those heels. She didn't need to turn around to see if he was following her. She knew he would be right behind her.

CHAPTER NINE

WHAT WAS THAT NOISE? An insistent buzz, as if an angry mosquito was trying to wake them up. An extremely loud, extremely angry mosquito.

Ellie reluctantly opened her eyes but it made no difference. The room was still dark. She put out her hand and encountered flesh; firm, warm flesh. Mmm… She ran her fingers appreciatively over Max's chest, learning him by heart once again.

Buzzzzz…

The mosquito had returned. Only it was no insect. Judging by the furiously flashing lights and the way it was dancing all over the bedside cabinet it was Ellie's phone making the racket.

Who on earth…?

Was it the shop?

Her heart began to speed up, skittering as frantically as her continuously buzzing phone as she pulled herself up, hands slipping on the rumpled sheets.

The buzzing stopped for one never-ending second, only to start up again almost immediately.

'What's that?' Max turned over, his voice thick with sleep.

'My phone. I don't know. It must be a wrong number.'

Please let it be a wrong number. Terrifying images

ran through her mind in Technicolor glory: fire; flood, theft. All three…

Finally she got one trembling hand to the phone and pulled it over, pulling out the charging cable as she did so. Turning it over, she stared in disbelief at the name flashing up on the screen.

Mum.

What on earth…? She accepted the call with fingers too clumsy in their haste. 'Mum? Is everything all right?'

There was a pause, and then Ellie heard it. It was like being catapulted back in time. A painful, breathtaking blow as the years rolled back to the moment a policeman had knocked on the door and their lives had been irrevocably altered. That low keening, like an animal in severe distress.

She had hoped never to hear that noise again.

'Mum?'

'Ellie? Ellie? Oh, thank goodness, darling. It's Bill.' The words were garbled, breathless, but discernible.

Not now…please not now.

But even as her mind framed the words she pushed the thought away, shame swamping her. How could she be so selfish when catastrophe had torpedoed her mother's happiness once again?

And what *of* Bill? Big, blustering Bill? She barely knew him, not really, but he had supported her mother, loved her, given her a new life, a new beginning.

And if it was easier for her mother to cope without Ellie, the spitting image of her dad and so similar to her brother, a constant reminder of all that Marissa Scott had lost, then how could Ellie really blame her? Didn't she herself shy away from anything that reminded her of what she only now appreciated had been an extraordinarily perfect childhood?

'Mum, what's happened? Is he...?' She couldn't bring herself to utter the last word.

'He's had a heart attack. He's in Theatre now.'

Oh, thank God...thank God. 'Where are you? In Spain?'

She looked up, but Max was already firing up his laptop, phone at the ready. His poor PA was probably on hand to take his instructions. Relief shot through her. She knew instinctively that this time she wouldn't have to do it all alone. That he would sort out a flight, at least; probably cars, hotels...

'No, we're in Oakwood. Bill's daughter had a baby, so we came back for a visit.'

They were back in England, in close proximity to London. But they hadn't told her, hadn't suggested a trip to Cornwall, asked to see her. It wasn't the time for selfishness but Ellie couldn't help the sore thud of disappointment. Couldn't stop her mouth working as she swallowed back the huge, painful lump.

Knowing and understanding her mother's need for distance didn't stop it hurting.

But she had called now. She was in pain and she needed her daughter.

'I'm on my way. Give me a couple of hours. Do you need anything? Food? Clothes?'

'No, no. I'm okay. But, Ellie? *Hurry*, darling.'

Her face was pale and set, but there was strength in the pointed chin, in the dark, deeply shadowed eyes. A feeling of indomitability. Max had the sense Ellie had been here before, travelling through the night to support her mother.

'What about our things? Your hire car? You don't need to come with me.' They were the first words she had said since the town car had pulled up outside the hotel and they had exited the ornate lobby to find themselves in the strange, other-worldly pre-dawn of London.

Not quiet, London could never be completely still, but emptier, greyer, ghostlier. The chauffeur drove them at practised speed through the city streets, soon hitting suburbs as foreign and anonymous as every city's outskirts. Warehouses and concrete gave way to residential streets and then to fields and motorways.

'It's fine. Lydia will take care of it all.' He had already fired off several emails to his PA, and even though it was late night back in Hartford she had replied, was seamlessly sorting everything out. 'Our clothes will be packed up and sent back to Cornwall, and the car is getting picked up by the hire company.'

She nodded, but her attention was only half on him as she stared out of the window at the rapidly passing countryside. She was back in her usual grey. The scarlet dress was still lying on the floor of the sitting-room, a bright red puddle of silk. Make-up free, her hair pushed back behind her ears, the only hint that the evening had happened was the faint scent of jasmine on her skin; on his skin.

He shut his eyes, images of her passing through his mind like scenes from a film. Her body, long, slender, slick with oil, as his hands moved firmly over silken skin.

'What about work? DL needs you.' Her voice was toneless.

He opened his eyes, the last remnants of the night before fading away. *Not the time or place,* he scolded himself. 'It's fine. Let's see what your mother needs and I can worry about DL later. The hospital will have WiFi, won't it?'

She nodded. 'I guess. It's a long time since I've been there. Not since Dad and Phil...' Her voice trailed off.

'Your mom's back in your old home town?'

No wonder she looked so haunted.

'For fourteen years I thought it was the most perfect place in the world.' Her voice was wistful. 'I danced. Did you know that?'

'No, but I should have guessed.' Of course she had danced. That long, toned slenderness was a dancer's legacy.

'I danced, played in the orchestra and was a member of the drama society. Phil played rugby and swam. We were like a family from an advertisement, with the golden Labrador to match.'

She turned towards him, her chin propped in her hand, her eyes far away.

'At weekends we'd all bike out for picnics in the countryside and then we'd pile on the sofa for family film and pizza night. I guess Mum and Dad must have argued, and I know Phil and I did, but when I look back it's like it's painted in soft gold. Always summer, always laughter. And then it all went wrong...' Her voice trailed off.

'The car accident.'

She nodded. 'Mum blamed herself. Dad had been travelling and was jetlagged, but she hated driving on ice so she persuaded him to pick Phil up from a swim meet. It was a drunk driver. The police said there was nothing Dad could have done. But Mum always thought if he hadn't been so tired...' She blinked, and there was a shimmering behind the long lashes.

Max's chest ached with the need to make it all right. But how could he? How could anybody?

'It must have been terrible.'

'I think that's why Mum had a breakdown. So she

didn't have to face the guilt. But I had to face it all: insurance, funeral-arranging, keeping the house going. I gave up dance, drama, friends, my dreams. There was school, there was Mum and there were books—the only escape from how grey my life had become.'

'But you got away.'

A new town, a new life. The loneliness of that life was beginning to make a twisted kind of sense to him. Could he say the same for his own choices?

Ellie nodded. 'It took a while. When I finished school I was supposed to go to university, but I couldn't see how she would cope without me and I was too proud to ask for help. Then Mum met Bill at her support group and suddenly she didn't need me any more. Worse, it was as if she couldn't bear to see me...like I made her feel guilty. She went from not being able to cope without me to not wanting to be near me. I lost everything all over again.'

Max didn't know what to say. Was there anything he *could* say? Anything that could wipe away over ten years of loneliness and grief?

He reached out instead, took her cold, still hand in his.

Ellie clung on, glad of the tactile comfort. His hands were warm, anchoring her to the here and now.

'What did you do then? Is that when you got engaged?'

The chill enveloping her deepened. *Engaged.* It was such happy word. It conjured up roses and diamonds and champagne. She hadn't experienced any of those things. Just an ornate ring that had belonged to Simon's grandmother: an ugly Victorian emerald that she had never dared tell him she disliked.

Simon was her secret shame, her weakness. She had never been able to tell anyone the whole story before. But there was a strength in Max's touch, in his voice, that made her want to lean in, to rest her burden on his broad shoulders. Just for a while.

She took a deep breath. She had said so much already...would a little more hurt? 'I hadn't seen much of my friends out of school, but it was still a shock when they went to university. So I got a job at the solicitors where my father had worked, just to get out of the house. Everyone there was a lot older, and I knew, of course, that they had only employed me to be kind.'

'Simon...'

She waited for the usual thump in her chest, the twist of dread to strike her as she said his name. But there was nothing. It was just a word, an old ghost with no way to harm her. Not if she didn't allow it.

Ellie carried on, her voice stronger. 'Simon was the only person there who didn't talk to me like I was a child. After the first couple of weeks I had a huge crush on him.' She shook her head, a bitter taste coating her mouth at the memory of her naïve younger self. 'He knew, of course. Enjoyed it and encouraged it, I think.'

She fell silent for a moment, the memory hitting her hard. Her mother's happiness—one she couldn't share. The resentment she hadn't been able to bring herself to acknowledge because it was so petty and mean; resentment that she had given up her childhood and future for her mother and now *she* was the one being left behind. And the coldness of her isolation. The dawning knowledge that her mother not only no longer needed her but somehow no longer wanted her.

Ellie shivered and Max put an arm around her, pulling her in close, holding her against his warm strength.

She turned into his comforting embrace, her arms slipping around him, allowing herself the luxury of leaning on him, *into* him, just this once. She inhaled deep, that smell of pine and salt, of sea and fresh air that clung to him even after two days in London.

'Looking back now, I can see that I was just desperate to feel loved, cared for. Simon sensed it, I think... my indecision, my loneliness...and he made his move.'

Her mouth twisted.

'He was very clever. One moment he would flatter me, make me feel like the most desirable woman alive. The next he would tease me, treat me like a silly schoolgirl. He'd stand me up and then turn up to whisk me away on an impossibly romantic date. I never knew where I stood. As he intended.'

She swallowed.

'And right from the start I tried to be what he wanted. To wear my hair the way he liked, dress in a way he approved of. He never actually said anything—but he would get this *look*, you know? This terribly disappointed look. Sometimes he would stop speaking to me altogether, not contact me if I really displeased him, and I would never know why. I'd have to figure it out. I used to sit alone in the empty house and cry, stare at my phone willing him to text me. When he finally spoke to me I'd be so relieved I would promise myself I would never upset him again. I learned what was expected of me, what would make him smile in approval. My food, my clothes, the books I read, the films I watched—all guided by him. I thought I was in love. That he protected me, cared for me.'

Max's whole body was rigid, and when she peeped over she saw a muscle beating in his cheek. His fingers gripped hers tightly, almost painful in their intensity.

'When Mum told me she was moving to Spain with Bill, selling the house, Simon came to the rescue; my knight in shining armour. He asked why didn't I move in, and I couldn't think of a single reason not to.'

She laced her fingers through Max's.

'It all happened so slowly. First he suggested I give up my job so that I could study. But then he found a hundred reasons for me to delay starting a course and I agreed. Because, you see, I thought he was protecting me.'

She swallowed again.

'I don't know when it dawned on me that I didn't have a single thing to call my own. Not for a long time. I forgot that it wasn't normal to be terrified in case you said the wrong thing, in case the house wasn't neat enough, the dishes tidied away, the bed made perfectly, my hair and clothes perfect. I didn't realise for a long time that I could barely breathe, that I was terrified of his displeasure, that just one frown could crush me.

'Because the worst thing of all,' her voice was low now, as she admitted the part that shamed her most. 'The worst thing of all is that when he smiled, when I got it right, I was elated. So that's what I strived for. I looked right, said the right things. When he was happy I was happy. I thought I was so very happy.'

She blinked, almost shocked to feel the wetness on her eyelashes.

'I don't know when I first realised that living in fear wasn't normal. Never relaxing, always worrying, never knowing what would set him off. He told me time and time again how worthless I was, how lucky I was to have him, and after a while I believed him.'

Because how could a girl with nothing be worth anything? Even her own mother had discarded her like an unwanted toy.

'When he wanted to he could be the sweetest, most tender person in the world. And I craved it. I thought it must be my fault that he was angry so often. He told me it was my fault.'

Max swallowed, his voice thick as he spoke. 'So what happened?'

'It wasn't one argument or one incident. It just crept up on me that I was desperately unhappy, and that every time someone mentioned the wedding I felt as if I was being bricked up alive. And as I got more and more scared he got more and more controlling. He wanted to know where I was every hour, would be angry if he phoned home and I didn't answer. He went through my receipts, looking for goodness knows what. One day I realised that I was afraid. I think it was the first time I'd allowed myself to think like that. But once I had it was as if a door had opened and I couldn't shut it again. So I just left. Jumped on a train to Cornwall. For six months I looked over my shoulder all the time, dreading seeing him there—and yet hoping he loved me enough to track me down. To find me.'

It was out. Every last sordid detail.

Would Max judge her? He couldn't judge her any more than she'd judged herself.

Ellie turned apprehensive eyes to him, dreading the judgement she expected to see in his face. His hands tightened on hers as he looked down at her, his mouth set, his eyes hard. But not with anger directed at her, no. Compassion softened the grim lines of his face.

'Look at you now, Ellie. Just look what you've become. You didn't let the jerk stop you. Delay you, maybe, but not stop you. You're strong, independent, successful, compassionate. You should be so proud of yourself.'

Proud? Not ashamed? Strong? Not weak? Was that really, truly what he saw?

Ellie didn't move for one long moment but then she fell against him with a gulp, tears spilling down her face, her chest heaving with the sobs she had held back for far too long.

Slipping an arm around her, Max pulled her in close, let her lean on him, let his shirt absorb her tears, his shoulders absorb her pain. He held her close, rubbed her back and kissed the top of her head as the car continued to drive through the gloom and Ellie cried it all out.

Her head ached, her throat ached, her eyes ached. In fact there wasn't a part of her that didn't hurt in one way or another. Not in the languorous way she had ached yesterday morning, with that sated, sensual feeling, but a much more painful sensation, as if she had been ripped apart and clumsily glued back together, cracks and dents and all.

Max's hand was still on hers, tethering her to the here and now, keeping her grounded. When had she ever cried like that before? She didn't think she ever had. At first she had been too numb and then? Then she had had to keep it together. One of them had to.

'Are you angry with her?' Max's voice stirred the silence.

'Sorry?'

'Your mother.' He shook his head. 'I mean, I'm pretty furious with *my* mother, for being so greedy and stubborn, and I am absolutely filled with rage against my dad for—well, for pretty much everything. But none of it is about me. I could walk away tomorrow, I guess, and leave them to it. Heck, maybe I should. Difference is I'm an adult. But you? You were just a kid. She made you be the grown-up, and then when you needed her she wasn't there.'

Ellie opened her mouth, ready to defend her mother—and herself. But the words wouldn't come. 'I...'

'It's okay, you know. You're allowed to be angry. It doesn't make you bad. It just makes you human.'

Anger? Was that what she felt? That tightening in her chest, the way her fingernails bit into her palms whenever she got a breezy, brief email from her mother?

Brief, breezy. The bare minimum of contact.

And when Ellie had fled, needing somewhere to hide out and recover, her mother hadn't been there for her. Hadn't wanted her. Hadn't known or cared that her daughter was trapped in a vicious relationship. What kind of woman left her eighteen-year-old daughter alone with a much older man she hardly knew?

'I *am* angry. So angry.' The words were almost a whisper. 'That she left me to deal with it all. That she made me be the grown-up when I wasn't ready. That she let me give up university for her. That she just left me...' Her voice was rising in volume and intensity and she stopped, shocked by the shaking fury in it.

His hand tightened on hers. 'How did you feel then?'

Ellie tried never to think about that particular time, that last betrayal. No wonder, when dragging it all up cut deeply all over again. 'Lost,' she admitted. 'I think, I wonder if she hadn't gone just then, if things might have been different. If I might have gone to university, not got engaged.'

She stopped.

'But I was an adult by then,' she said instead. 'I made my choices just as she made hers. I can't blame her. I can't blame anyone but myself.'

'No, you were still a child. You have nothing to regret, Ellie. Nothing at all.'

Neither of them spoke then, but Max continued to hold her hand, his thumb caressing the back of her hand with sure movements as the car took them through increasingly familiar countryside, finally entering the outskirts of the town where Ellie had been born.

She was finding it increasingly hard to get her breath, and her stomach was clenching as they entered the hospital car park.

'Hey.' Max gave her a reassuring smile. 'It's fine. You're not alone. Not this time.'

Ellie tried to smile back but she couldn't make her muscles obey. Right now she wasn't alone—but next week he would be gone, and she would be back to square one. On her own.

Somehow Max Loveday had slipped through all her defences and shown her just what a sham her life was. Safe? Sure. Protected? Absolutely. Hardworking and honest? Maybe. But true? No. Hiding away, not having fun, trusting no one... That wasn't true to the legacy of love and happiness her father and brother had left her, that Demelza Loveday had bequeathed to her.

Max or no Max, Ellie had to find a way to start living again.

If she could only work out where to start.

CHAPTER TEN

THE CORRIDORS WERE the same off-white, the floor the same hard-wearing highly polished tiles, the smell the same: antiseptic crossed with boiled vegetables. She might be fourteen again, hurrying down the corridor, following in her mother's frantic footsteps.

But this time Max's hand was on her arm: a quiet, tacit support. Five days ago she hadn't been able to wait to see the back of Max Loveday. Today she was grateful he was here at all.

It was as if her godmother was still looking out for her, even after her death.

'Here we are. Ward Six.'

Max would have walked straight in, but Ellie came to an abrupt halt.

'I just need a moment.'

'Sure. Take as long as you need.' He was wearing jeans with the tuxedo shirt from the night before: an incongruous mix that he somehow managed to carry off. Maybe the early-morning stubble and ruffled hair helped. Or maybe it was his innate confidence.

Or it could be the surroundings. These corridors must have seen people turn up in everything from pyjamas to ballgowns. Last time she had pulled on grey tracksuit bottoms and an old football shirt of her brother's. She could see it as if it were yesterday, feel the smooth nylon of the shirt, hear the slopping of the flip-flops she had grabbed, forgetting about the snow outside.

Ellie inhaled, a long, slow breath, filling her chest with air, with oxygen, with courage. And then she pushed open the door and walked into the ward's waiting room.

Again memories assailed her. Could they be the same industrial padded chairs? The same leaflets on the notice-board? The same water-cooler with no cups anywhere to be seen? The same tired potted plant?

Only the people were different.

She half recognised Bill's family from the pitifully few occasions when they had met; his daughter, a few years older than Ellie, now cradling a baby. His brother, as tall and thickset as Bill, his sister, red-eyed and star-ing into space.

And pacing up and down like a caged wild animal, just as she had the last time, was her mother. A little older, her skin far more tanned, her hair blonder, a little plumper, but still recognisably, indisputably Marissa Scott.

She turned as Ellie pushed the door open and Ellie stood still for a moment, wary, as if they were strangers. She had to speak, to break the silence.

'Hi, Mum.'

It wasn't enough, and yet it was all she had. But as her mother broke into a trot and ran across the room to enfold her in her arms Ellie realised that maybe, just maybe, it was enough after all.

'What a day.' Max sat back in the uncomfortable cafete-ria chair and looked down at the plate of pale fried food in front of him. He poked suspiciously at the peas, soggy and a nasty yellowish green. 'Do you think there is actu-ally *any* nutritional value in this?'

'Not an iota.' Ellie had wisely eschewed the fish and chips and gone for a salad. 'Hospital food is like school food: something to be endured.'

Max tried not to think too longingly of the food at his expensive private school. 'We should have gone out.'

'Maybe I should have insisted you leave earlier. You didn't have to stay all day. Did you get any work done?'

'Some,' Max admitted.

He knew Ellie had had an agonising day, waiting with her overwrought mother for Bill to come out of surgery, and that his day couldn't compare—but it had been no walk in the park. He had spent the day delving deeply into DL Media's accounts and his excavations hadn't uncovered any gold. All he had found was a big pit that was getting deeper by the day.

'There are some difficult decisions to make when I get back.'

His last four words seemed to hang in the air.

'I do appreciate you taking so much time out of your schedule for me. I know you were hoping to spend more time in London.' Ellie's head was bent and she was poking unenthusiastically at her salad.

'Ellie, it's nothing. And it's not as if I'm not in contact with the London office every day.' For once Max didn't want to talk about work—or dwell on how little time he had left in the UK. 'How's Bill?'

'Out of surgery. And the doctors seem pleased.'

'And your mother?'

'Surprisingly okay.' Her cheeks flushed. 'Well enough to ask who you are.'

He raised an eyebrow. 'What did you tell her?'

Her eyes lowered. 'That we work together.'

'Okay.'

He speared a soggy chip and then laid his fork down.

He wasn't hungry after all. He looked around. The room was half full: a few patients well enough to get up and walk about, harassed-looking staff shovelling food in as quickly and efficiently as engines refuelling. And friends and relatives, many with shell-shocked faces.

He really didn't want to spend much more time here, and neither should Ellie. Her eyes were deeply shadowed, her face white with tiredness.

'What do you want to do? Are you planning to stay with your mother for a few days?'

He was surprised at how much he wanted her to say no. If she didn't return to Trengarth with him today would he see her again this trip?

Or at all.

She shook her head and unexpected relief flooded through him.

'Part of me feels like I should, but there's nowhere for me to stay and Bill's family are looking after Mum. If there was any suggestion he was still in danger of course I would... No, I need to get back to the shop. There's no reason for me to hang around. Thanks for bringing me, Max.' Her eyes met his. 'For everything.'

'Any time.' He meant it too. There had been no thought in the early morning of walking away, of putting her into a car and returning to his own world. 'Do you want to find a hotel for the night or get straight off? I could get us a car in an hour, although we wouldn't get back to Cornwall until the early morning.'

She chewed her lip, her eyes flickering as she thought. 'Is it bad that I just want to go home?'

'Not at all. It's been a long day. I'll get one ordered. We can sleep in the car if we need to. Although...' He looked at his untouched plate and then at hers. 'We may want to stop for some real food first.'

'That sounds good. I'll go and sit with Mum for a bit longer.'

'I'll fetch you when the car gets here.'

She didn't move straight away. She just sat, looking as if there was something she wanted to say. Max waited, but she didn't speak, just gave him a tremulous smile as she pushed her chair back and walked slowly out of the cafeteria.

The car rolled smoothly through the night-dark moor. Clouds blocked the stars, and as Max stared out of the window all he could see was his own reflection. Unsmiling, contemplative. Angry.

Max Loveday wasn't a violent man. His battles were in the boardroom, in sales figures and profits. But tonight his blood ran hot. All he could think about was asking the driver to turn back to Oakwood, so that he could find Ellie's ex and make him wish he had never set eyes on her.

And he'd ask her mother just exactly what she had been thinking when she had allowed her teenage daughter to become the adult. When she had left that daughter alone with nowhere to turn except to an emotionally abusive and controlling man.

Only Ellie didn't want or need him to fight her battles, even though all he wanted was to ride into the lists for her, to pull on a helmet and grab a sword and rush into battle for her honour.

And to teach that scoundrel a lesson.

His lips tightened. He hadn't felt this out of control, this primal, in years. His instincts were screaming at him to protect, to avenge.

This was exactly what he wanted to avoid. This kind of messy, hot-headed emotion, pulling and pushing him away from his goals, from his plans. Love—violent, needy love—was to blame for it all. Grieving love, causing Ellie's mother's breakdown. Twisted love, creating a hellish trap for Ellie.

His hands curled into fists. It wasn't love affecting his judgement right now. It was lust and liking, respect and admiration. But it was still dangerous.

Thank goodness he would be on his way home in just a few days.

Just a few days...

It wasn't long enough.

It was far too long. A dangerously long time.

He glanced over at Ellie. She was curled up on the seat next to him, sleeping as the car wound its way through the tiny lanes that would take them back to Trengarth. Visibly yawning as they'd finished their excellent pub dinner, Ellie hadn't taken long to fall asleep once they'd returned to the car. Max wasn't surprised; she'd exorcised all her ghosts in one day. There was bound to be a price, both physically and mentally. Better she sleep it off.

What about him? Would he be able to exorcise his own ghosts?

Max shifted in his seat, wishing he could get comfortable. He supposed the question was did he even want to? After all, hadn't they kept him safe? But he had to admit his careful planning, his definition of a suitable partner, didn't fill him with the same quiet satisfaction it had used to.

He sighed, changing position once again. The whole point of getting a driver to take them all the way back to Trengarth had been so they could rest, but Max was unable to switch off. He envied the slow, even sound of Ellie's breath.

It would have been better for him to have driven himself, forced to concentrate on the road ahead rather than sit here in the dark with the same thoughts running through his mind over and over on a loop.

'Where now, sir?'

The driver was turning down the coastal road that led directly to the village.

'Should I drop the lady off first?'

They were back.

London, the suite, playing at tourists—it was all over. He should see Ellie home and that would be an end to it, *should* be an end to it. Only she was so tired. And so alone.

'No.' Max made a sudden decision. Ellie would be tired, emotionally wrung out when she came to. She might need him. And after all he had bedrooms to spare. 'Both of us to The Round House, please.'

It was less than five minutes before the car pulled in through the gates and came to a smooth stop on the circular driveway. The outside light came on as they passed it, and the orange glow cast an otherworldly light over the still slumbering Ellie.

Max eyed her. She was thin, sure, and couldn't weigh too much. How easy would it be to get her out of the car and upstairs without waking her?

Not that easy.

But she looked so peaceful he didn't want to disturb her.

He opened the car door as quietly as he could, hoping to give her just a few seconds more, but she stirred as the door clicked open.

'Where are we?' Her voice was groggy.

Max glanced over. Her hair was mussed, her eyes still half shut.

'At The Round House. It's so late I thought we could both stay here tonight. I can make up a bed for you, if you prefer.'

'No need. I don't mind sharing.' She yawned: an impossibly long sound. 'I should walk home. It's not far, but I don't think I'd make it. I'd probably fall asleep by the side of the road and have to trust that the local rabbits and sparrows would cover me with leaves.'

'Very picturesque, but if you could make do with sheets and a mattress it might be easier.'

'Okay, if you insist.' She yawned again and allowed him to help her out of the car, leaning against him as she staggered upright.

'Come on, Sleeping Beauty, let's go in.'

Max had only stayed a few nights in The Round House, occupied it for less than a week, and yet somehow it felt like coming home.

Walking in, dropping his wallet and keys in the glass bowl on the hallway table, kicking his shoes off by the hat stand: they all felt like actions honed by years of automatic practice. And the house welcomed him back. A sigh seemed to ripple through it, one of contentment. All was right in its world.

He didn't have this sense of rightness in his own apartment. All glass and chrome and space, city views, personal gym, residents' pool on site, it was the perfect bachelor pad. But when he was there he didn't fall asleep listening to the waves crashing on the beach below. His apartment was luxurious, convenient, easy—but it didn't have family history steeped into every cornice. Sure, he could move some of the old family possessions, the pictures, the barometer, over to Hartford. But they wouldn't belong there.

They belonged here.

'Do you need anything?'

The question was automatic but he wasn't sure he could help if she did. The kitchen had been bare when he'd arrived, and he'd stocked it with little more than coffee, milk and some nachos.

Luckily Ellie shook her head. 'Just bed.'

'I'm in the guest suite.' He started to lead the way up the wide staircase. 'It didn't feel right, moving into my great-aunt's rooms.'

'That's understandable. Besides, I can't see you as a rose wallpaper kind of guy.'

'It *is* very floral,' he agreed. 'But I'm secure enough in my masculinity to cope with pink roses.'

She raised her eyebrows. '*There's* a claim.'

Max slid his arm around her waist, his steps matching hers as they trod wearily up the stairs. Yet some of that weariness fell away as he touched her.

'I don't make claims. I make statements.'

Ellie had reached the landing half a step ahead. She turned to him, stepping into his embrace, her own arms encircling his waist, warm hands burrowing underneath his T-shirt. His skin tingled where she touched: a million tiny explosions as his nerve-endings reacted to the skin-on-skin contact.

'I may need you to verify that statement.'

She looked up at him, her face serious except for that dimple tugging at the corner of her mouth. He bent his head, needing to taste the little dip in her skin. He felt her shiver against him as his tongue dipped out and sampled her.

'I'm at your service.' He kissed the dimple again, inhaling her sweet, drowsy scent as he did so. 'How exactly would you like me to verify it?' He kissed his way down her jawline, pausing at her neck. 'Any requests?'

Her hands clenched at his waist. 'Anything.'

'Anything?' He slid his hands up under her top, over her ribs to the soft fullness above.

Ellie gasped. 'Anything. Just don't stop.'

'Oh, I won't, honey. Not until you ask me to.'

He walked her backwards towards the bedroom door, his hands continuing to move upwards millimetre by millimetre.

'It's only three in the morning. We've got the rest of the night.'

He couldn't, *wouldn't* think beyond that. Not now. Not when his hands were caressing her, his lips tasting her. When the scent of her was all around him.

There were decisions to be made, places to go and a world to conquer. But it could wait until the morning.

The sun would be up in just a couple of hours, but they still had tonight and Max was going to make the most of every single second.

The sun was shining in through the half-opened curtains, casting a warm golden glow onto the bed. Ellie sighed and pulled at the sheet as she turned into the gentle heat, gloriously aware that at that very second everything was all right with the world.

Except... Except was she waking up alone again? Like some Greek nymph fated never to see her lover in the light of day?

Ellie pulled herself upright and tried to work out the time. There was no clock in the room, and her phone was dead, but judging by the brightness of the sun it had to be late morning if not afternoon.

She should really get up. Check on her shop. Head back to reality. Only she was so comfortable. Reality could wait just a little longer.

'Morning, sleepyhead. Or should that be afternoon?'

Max was lounging against the door, holding something that Ellie devoutly hoped was a cup of coffee.

'I thought you were going to sleep the day away.'

'How long have you been up?' She held her hand out for the coffee and inhaled greedily, wrapping her hands around the hot mug. 'I missed you.' She allowed her hand to fall invitingly to the empty space by her side, the sheet to slip a little lower.

'No rest for the wicked. Duty called.'

He wasn't meeting her eye, and he didn't sit by her or even slide his gaze appreciatively over her body.

The message was clear. Playtime was over. Well, she had known the deal from the start. Any disappointment was simply her due payment for the unexpected fun. Back to reality with the proverbial bump.

No wonder it stung a little.

'My solicitor wants to look at the share papers in detail. He doesn't trust the scan I sent him, so it looks like I might be heading back earlier than I expected. Don't worry about the festival, though. I've asked our marketing guys to give you a hand, and my PA can do whatever you need her to do. I've emailed you all the details.'

Max sounded offhand: more like the business partner she had been expecting him to be than the understanding companion of the last few days.

'Very efficient,' Ellie said drily. 'You *have* been busy. In that case I'd better get off. I don't want to hold you up. When are you flying out?'

That was good. Her voice was level, with no outward sign that she felt as if she'd been kicked in the stomach.

Of course she'd known this wasn't for ever...hadn't been expecting more than a few more days. Only she had been looking forward to those few more days. Looking forward to discovering more about him, discovering more about herself, about who she could be with a little support and an absence of fear.

Well, she would have to carry on that discovery alone.

'Tomorrow. I've a car booked for ten tomorrow morning.'

His eyes caught hers then, and there was a hint of an apology in the caramel depths, along with something else. A barrier. He was moving on, moving away. Oh, so politely, but oh, so steadily.

Ellie knew that she should try and get up, but she was suddenly and overwhelmingly self-conscious. Her clothes were heaped on a chair at the other side of the room and she couldn't, absolutely *couldn't* get up and walk across there stark naked. Maybe she could have if the other Max had been here. The Max who couldn't keep his eyes off her. The Max who made her feel infinitely precious and yet incredibly strong, like a rare stone ready to be polished into something unique.

But this Max was a stranger, and she didn't want him to see her in all her vulnerability.

'Thanks for the coffee but, really, don't let me keep you. We both have heaps to do. Maybe I'll see you before you leave. Come down to the shop if you have a chance. I'll find you a book for the plane.'

She could be polite and businesslike too.

'Thanks, that would be good.' Max stepped back towards the door. 'Not that I'll have a chance to read for pleasure. I'll be...'

'Busy,' she finished for him. 'Back to all work and no play, Max?'

He flushed, a hint of red high on the tanned cheekbones. 'Yes.'

Shame shot through her at his quiet acceptance. 'I'm sorry. I know you have to go. I know how difficult things are.' She smiled. 'I guess I've got used to you being around.'

The colour had left his cheeks and he smiled back, the familiar warmth creeping back into his eyes. 'I've got used to *being* around. I'll miss it here.'

And me? she wanted to ask. *Will you miss me?* But her mouth wouldn't form the words; she wasn't entirely sure what she wanted the answer to be.

He was watching her now with his old intentness, the expression that made her simultaneously want to pull the sheet right up to her chin and let it fall all the way down.

'I guess I *could* take a few hours off today. I never did get round to taking a boat out. Do you have to get back to the shop, Ellie?'

Yes. No. Things were confusing enough already. Maybe she would be better off saying her goodbyes now and putting some much needed distance between them. But what could a few more hours hurt? The end line was firmly drawn in the sand. The countdown to the final hour had begun.

'They're not expecting me back till this evening. Mrs T has the shop well in hand, I'm sure.'

'Good.' He pushed away from the doorway and advanced on her, intent clear and hot in his eyes. 'In a couple of hours we should get a picnic, and then I'll show you that the sea is for more than watching. Ready to try something new, Ellie?'

He *was* talking about sailing, wasn't he? Shivers ran hot down her body.

'In a couple of hours?'

The sheet fell a little more and this time he noticed, his eyes scorching gold as they traced their way down her body.

'A couple of hours,' he agreed. 'I haven't said good morning to you properly yet, or good afternoon. In fact I may need to work my way right through to good evening...'

'Well,' she said, as primly as it was possible to be when lying barely covered by a sheet, her body trembling with anticipation, 'we wouldn't want to forget our manners, now, would we?'

'Absolutely not.' He was by her side, his eyes fixed on hers as he began to slowly unbutton his shirt. 'Manners are very important. Want me to show you?'

She nodded, her gaze skimming the defined hardness of his chest, moving lower down to where he was just beginning to unfasten his jeans.

'Yes. Yes, please, Max. Show me everything.'

CHAPTER ELEVEN

'ARE YOU SURE you've got everything?'

Ellie hadn't intended to come and see Max off. She hadn't intended to stay with him all last night, or to wake up in his arms this morning. She had intended a civilised kiss on the cheek before turning away, as if she didn't much care whether he stayed or went.

And yet here she was. She hated goodbyes as a matter of course, but this one was proving particularly unbearable. The problem with never dating, never having had a casual relationship in her life, was that she had no idea how to act now their time was coming to an end.

Should she hug him? Kiss his cheek? Kiss him properly? Shake his hand? High-five him? All of the above? Grab him and never let him go?

That wasn't in their unwritten agreement.

Max picked up his small holdall, hefting the weight experimentally. 'I think so. I didn't actually buy much while I was here, and I packed light anyway.'

'You nearly bought a boat.'

'But I wasn't planning to check that in as hand luggage. Even first class might have had something to say about that.'

'They probably wouldn't have been best pleased.' Ellie rummaged in her bag and pulled out a gold-embossed paper bag. 'Have you got room for this? I owe you a souvenir, remember?'

He eyed the bag nervously. 'It's not a trick snake, is it?'

'No.' She bit her lip, keeping back her smile with some difficulty. 'Open it when you get home.'

'That bad, huh?'

'You have no idea.'

She handed him another bag: one of the striped paper bags she used at the shop.

'Here. I know you're planning to work solidly for the next twenty-four hours, but just in case your eyes tire of spreadsheets...'

He opened the bag and slid the hardback book out. '*Tales of Cornwall*? It's lovely. Thanks, Ellie.'

'I figured you should know a little about your ancestral folk.'

He was flicking through it, pausing at some of the full-colour illustrations. 'It's a very thoughtful gift.' He looked at her, his brow crinkled. 'I don't have anything for you. I'm sorry.'

'That's okay. I wasn't expecting anything.' She swallowed, her throat unexpectedly full. 'Just promise me you won't sell the house to anyone who doesn't love it.'

'I'd keep it if I could, but you said it yourself, Ellie. The village doesn't need any more absentee owners, jetting in for two weeks in the summer. I'll make sure I only sell it to a family who want to live here all year round.'

'A book-loving family?'

'Of course. What about you, Ellie? Are you going to be okay?'

His face was serious and the concern in his voice made her hands clench a little. It wasn't that she didn't appreciate it; it was nice that someone cared even a little. But she didn't want that kind of concern from Max.

Her preference would be for the scorching looks that turned her knees to melting chocolate—made her whole body liquefy. But she'd even take his scornful mistrust. That at least had treated her as an equal, not like something fragile.

'Yes. I have your PA's email, and I promise to call DL's London office if I need advice or help.'

'That's not what I meant. Are you sure this is what you want?'

Ellie's heart thumped painfully. What did he mean? Was he offering to stay? For her to go with him? For some kind of tomorrow beyond these two weeks? Her palms felt clammy as her pulse began to race. What would she say? What *did* she want?

'Am I sure about what?'

'This…' He swept his arm dismissively in an arc, pushing away Trengarth, the sea, the view. 'It's pretty, Ellie. But is it enough? One shop? One festival? You were amazing at the weekend: passionate, knowledgeable, brilliant. You told me you dreamt once of a life in London, in publishing. Are you really content to settle for *this*?'

It was the hint of contempt in his voice as he said 'this' that really hit her. Was that what he thought? Of her? Of Trengarth? Of everything she valued? That they weren't big enough? Not important enough?

'It's okay, Max. You can head back to your important job in the big city without worrying about me. I *am* happy and *I am fine*.'

The last three words came out slightly more vehemently than she'd meant them to and Max took a step back, his eyes widened in surprise.

'Whoa, what does *that* mean?'

'It means you don't have to add me to the list of things that Max Loveday has to sort out. I like my life, Max.

I like my shop. I love my village. We don't all need to be at the very top. We don't all need to save the world.'

Confusion warred with anger in his eyes. 'I'm not trying to save the world.'

'No?'

She put her hands on her hips and glared at him. She wanted him to look as if he might miss her, darn it. To look as if not holding her, kissing her, touching her might actually cause him some discomfort. As if he wanted to pull her into bed—not tell her everything that was wrong with her life, according to the gospel of Max Loveday.

'No.'

Good intentions be damned. She was going to have to say something.

'When you came here you accused me of being some kind of con artist. Now you tell me I'm wasting my life. Things aren't that black and white, Max. Life is richer and more complicated than your narrow definition of success. Look at your dad and his girlfriend. Have you considered that maybe, just maybe, they really are in love?'

His mouth tightened. 'I don't doubt that they *believe* that.'

'How will you know if you don't give them a chance? You carry responsibility for your parents, for the whole of DL, for your grandfather's dreams. What about you, Max? What do *you* want?'

'You know what I want.'

Yes, she did. And she wasn't anywhere on that list.

'For DL Media to work like clockwork, your parents to behave, and to find your perfect wife at the perfect time? I have news for you, Max. Life isn't that simple. Life is emotional and messy and demanding, and you can't hide behind spreadsheets for ever. When you find her, this right woman at the right time to make the perfect life with, she's going to have her own chips and flaws. Her own desires and needs.'

'I know that.' His face was white under the tan, his eyes hard.

'*Do* you?'

Ellie stepped forward and put her hand on his arm, relieved when he didn't try and shake her off.

'You have helped me so much this last week. Helped me confront the past, helped me move on. I feel free, reborn. But it's down to me now. It's always been down to me. To move on or to lock myself away. *My* choice. Just like your parents can make their own choices. And you. *You* can choose too, you know.'

'I have chosen, Ellie. I choose to honour my commitments. I choose to live and dream big, to keep pushing. There's nothing wrong with that.'

'I thought I was the one who was too scared to reach out.' She looked at him, *really* at him, trying to see through to the closely guarded heart of him. 'But you're just as bad. I hope you find what you're looking for, Max. I hope it's worth it.'

He covered her hand with his and squeezed, the rigid look fading from his face. 'It will be. Same to you. Dream big, Ellie.'

'I'll try.'

His hand was warm, comforting over hers. She might not need him but the uncomfortable truth was that she did *want* him. Her bed was going to feel larger than it had used to, her walks on the beach a little more solitary. But that was fine. She had the festival to plan. A social life to start.

She stood on her tiptoes and kissed his lightly stubbled cheek, breathing him in one last time. 'You'd better get going. Safe flight, Max.'

'See you around, honey.'

'Yes.' She paused, then stepped closer, tiptoeing up towards him again. This time she touched her lips to his...a brief caress. 'Bye.'

And she turned and walked away, ignoring the whisper in her heart telling her to turn round and ask him to stay.

What could she offer him here in Cornwall? Only herself. And that would never be enough.

When had Max's office become so confining? Oh, he still had views over downtown Hartford, still had room to pace, a huge desk, a comfortable yet imposing chair. But somehow his horizons felt strangely limiting.

Even though he could walk out now, if he wanted to. Could organise a meeting in Sydney or Paris or Prague and be on a plane within hours.

Be in London within hours.

Max picked up the snow globe that now stood right next to his laptop dock: a penguin balanced on an iceberg encased in a glass bauble. He hadn't known what to expect when Ellie had given him the paper bag but it certainly hadn't been this. Delicate, intricate, mesmerising.

Like its giver.

He shook it, watching the tiny flakes fall on to the miniature black and white bird, turning the arctic scene into a fairytale. It *had* been a fairytale. For just a few days. But he was back in reality now.

Back in reality and ridiculously restless.

He wasn't sleeping well, straining to hear the waves crashing on a shore thousands of miles away; rolling over to put on arm around a body that wasn't there.

He'd always liked sleeping alone before. Liked the rumble of the city.

A knock on the door pulled him back to his surroundings, and he managed to return the snow globe to its place and refocus his attention on the document he was reading before his PA entered the room. His pulse quickened. Had Ellie been in touch? He'd asked Lydia to tell him if she heard from Ellie, but there had been nothing at all in over three weeks.

Was she well? Was she safe? She was probably busy with the shop, with her committees. Busy going to the pub with her friends…with that blond surfer who hadn't been able to keep his eyes off her. As long as it *was* just his eyes.

He made an effort to unclench his jaw. 'Yes?'

'You asked me to let you know when your father was back in his office. He arrived back ten minutes ago.'

'Thanks, Lydia.'

His father had been elusive ever since Max's return to Hartford. Once Max had verified that Great-Aunt Demelza's shares were valid he had done his best to track his father down so he could tell him of the change in ownership in person. It had proved impossible. In the end he had had to notify him by email.

His father hadn't replied.

Max leaned back in his chair and stared at the snow globe. *This was it*. Everything he wanted was within his grasp. He should feel elated, and yet the best word he could find to describe his feelings was hollow.

Empty.

He glanced over at the snow globe again. He swore the penguin was trying to tell him something.

It was a short walk to his father's office, which occupied the other top floor corner suite. Max's great-grandfather had settled in Hartford in the early nineteen-twenties to provide printing services to the city's insurance industry, but had soon branched out into book publishing and journalism. It was Max's grandfather who had taken the company into TV, film, and expanded out of the US.

But although they now had offices around the globe—publishing headquarters in New York, digital in Silicon Valley and Los Angeles—the heart of the operation remained in Connecticut. Where it had all begun.

The door to his father's office was closed but Max didn't knock, simply twisting the handle and walking in. To his surprise his father wasn't at his desk; he was standing at the window, looking out over the river beyond, his shoulders slumped. Would he concede defeat before the battle began?

Max hoped so. It might be necessary, but he had no stomach for this fight.

'Hi, Dad.'

'Max.' The shoulders straightened, and his expression as he turned around was one of familiar paternal affability. 'Good vacation? Where did you go? Cornwall?'

As if he didn't already know.

'I wasn't on holiday. I was in London and sorting out Great-Aunt Demelza's estate. Did you know she lived in the house your grandfather was born in? She left it to me. It's pretty special.'

'Are you going to sell it?'

That was his father. Not a trace of sentimentality.

Max closed his eyes briefly and saw the round white house perched high above the harbour, the golden wood of the polished floorboards, that spectacular view. 'No. I'm thinking of keeping it.'

Ellie's words floated through his head. *The village needs young families not more second home owners.* It might be a selfish decision but it was the right one. For now, at least.

'It wasn't all that she left me, Dad.'

His father's jaw tightened. 'Apparently not. The papers…they're legitimate?'

'Seems so. You realise what that means?'

'That we're equal partners. Well, you *are* my son, although it seems a bit premature for you to have so much control. You're still just a boy.'

Max breathed in, willing himself not to rise to the bait. 'We need to talk, Dad. Want to take a walk?'

Hartford, like many cities, had a gritty side, and many affluent families, like Max's own, preferred to live outside the city in large estates by the river, or in one of the quaint and historic small Connecticut towns.

But since he had moved into one of the many luxury apartment blocks catering for young professionals Max had grown fond of the old city, especially enjoying the riverside paths and parks which were vibrant public spaces, perfect for walking, running and cycling. He steered his father towards the river, glad to be outside—even if the temperature *was* hitting the high eighties.

He was even more glad that, unlike his father, he had taken advantage of the company's Dress-down Friday policy and was comfortable in dark khakis and a short-sleeved white shirt.

The park was full of people: families picnicking, personal trainers putting their clients through their moves, couples lying in the sun. Steven Loveday looked around at the buzzing space in obvious surprise. He probably never walked in the city, Max realised. He would be driven in to the office, to the theatre, to the high-end restaurants he frequented, but otherwise he spent his life on his estate or at his club.

'This is all rather nice.' He followed Max down the steep steps and onto the path. 'I had no idea this was here.'

'I guess you wouldn't have.' Max wanted this talk, had sought it out, but now it was time he was finding it hard to find the right words. 'I spoke to Mom.'

A smile spread across his father's face and he clapped Max on the shoulder. 'That's my boy. Has she seen sense?'

'I spoke to Mom and I told her exactly what I am about to tell you.' Max kept his voice level. 'It's not my place to arbitrate your divorce. That's between you guys. Personally, I think you need to go and talk to her face to face. She deserves that courtesy, at least.'

Steven Loveday stood still, incongruous in his handmade suit amongst the rollerbladers, joggers and families. 'Right...' he said slowly.

'She won't come after the company.' Max took a deep breath. *Here goes.* 'As long as I'm in charge.'

His father looked at him blankly. 'What?'

'Dad, our profits are down. We're losing some of our most valuable staff. Rumours are flying through the industry that we're on the brink of collapse. The publishers tell me that agents aren't entertaining our bids. We're losing ground.'

His father waved a hand, dismissing the litany of disasters. 'That was bound to happen after your grandfather died. We knew there would be some instability.'

'It's been over a year.'

'We have a strategy.'

'*No.* No, Dad, there isn't a strategy. I don't know what we're doing, the board doesn't know, and none of our senior directors have any direction. You're on a spending spree and I spend my whole time firefighting. It's not a strategy. It's a disaster.'

'Come on, Max, things are a little tight...'

'I own fifty per cent outright.' There was no point

rehashing the same old arguments. 'You own twenty-five per cent, with an interest in the other twenty-five. Your share is yours. You can do what you like with it. But I want you to sign the other share over to me now. Not when you retire. If you do then Mom will leave the company alone. The rest of the settlement is up to you two—but you owe her, and I think you know it.'

His father's eyes narrowed. 'And if I won't?'

'Then I'll go to the board and force a vote. I'm pretty confident that they'll back me.'

His father started walking slowly along the path. The colour had left his face and he looked every minute of his fifty-eight years. Guilt punched through Max but he ignored it. It was time Steven Loveday faced the consequences of his actions.

'Dad, you are about to have another baby. A chance to do it all over again.' Max didn't add *to do it right*, but the unsaid words hung uncomfortably in the air. 'You say you love Mandy. I hope you do. I hope for all our sakes that this time it's real. Spend time with her… with the baby.'

'Take early retirement? That would be convenient.' His father's words were laced with scorn.

'Or take an executive role. Dad, honestly, are you enjoying it? Running DL Media? Does it buzz through your brains? Is it the first thing you think of when you wake up, before you sleep?'

'Well…I…'

'Or do you miss the afternoons golfing, the long lunches? It's okay if you do, Dad. I'm just saying that running DL is all-consuming. And I don't think that's what you want.'

'And you do? You want to be like your grandfather? Work first and the rest of the world be damned?'

Max looked away, across the river. 'It's all I know. All I want.'

At least it had been. But it hadn't been work occupying his mind as he lay in bed fruitlessly chasing sleep over the last few weeks.

It had been a small terraced building on a steep road and the dark-eyed, toffee-haired girl who occupied it.

She hadn't been born and brought up in his world. She didn't know the rules.

She had no interest in timetables.

But when he imagined his future she was all that he could see.

'I don't see that I have much choice. You've won, Max. I hope it's all you want it to be.'

His father turned and walked away, leaving Max alone by the river.

He should be elated. The company was his. He had won.

But he had no one to tell, no one to celebrate with. He was all alone, and the only person he wanted to share his news with was on the other side of the Atlantic.

Maybe she should get a dog. Something to walk on the beach with, something to talk to. Uncritical adoration.

Ellie breathed in and turned slowly. The briny air filled her lungs and her eyes drank in the deep blue of a summer ocean. The roaring of the waves filled her ears. Trengarth on an idyllic summer's day.

It was perfect, and yet somehow it didn't fill her with the usual peace. Discomfort was gnawing away at her and she couldn't assuage it. Not with work—the shop seemed to run itself these days. Not with the festival— thanks to the brilliant volunteers making sure not a sin-

gle task remained to be done. And now not even a walk
on the beach helped.

Max was right. Watching wasn't enough. But she had
been on the sidelines for so long. How could she step out
onto the crest of a wave?

She stepped back onto the road, for once not turning
back to admire the view.

'Hi, Ellie, are you walking back? I'm going that way.'
Sam was breathing hard as he caught up with her.

'You are?' Ellie looked at Sam in surprise. 'Don't you
live in the old town?'

'Yeah, but I have some business on the hill.' He looked
vaguely uncomfortable.

She had seen a great deal of Sam recently. He'd been
walking on the beach at the same time as she had several evenings recently and always joined her. Twice he
had been at The Boat House when she'd popped in for
her regular Friday lunch and he'd asked her to sit with
him. He was on the organising committee, on her pub
quiz team. He had popped in to the shop several times,
to buy presents or ask for recommendations.

They'd laughed about how they must stop bumping
into each other all the time. And here they were. Again.

Ellie's stomach swooped and it was all she could do
to keep walking and talking normally. She'd suspected
that he liked her before. But now she was sure. He *liked*
her liked her.

Her hands felt too big, her legs too long, her laugh
too grating. She was hyper-aware of her every word and
gesture. They all seemed clumsy and fake. *Breathe,* she
told herself crossly. *Max* liked *you liked you and that
didn't worry you.*

And Sam was great. A catch. He had an interesting
job, he was funny, community-minded. He was hand-

some enough, if you liked fit, blue-eyed, blond-haired surfer guys.

Did she?

Or was she a little too fixated on dark-haired, caramel-eyed Americans?

Unobtainable dark-haired Americans.

She was supposed to be moving on.

'Sorry, what was that?' Sam had been speaking and she hadn't even heard him.

'The festival,' he repeated. 'It's going well.'

'It seems to be,' she agreed cautiously. 'Obviously it's early days yet, and we have a long way to go, but DL's London office have been really helpful. I think we're guaranteed some big names through them anyway, so that should put us on the map.'

Her phone beeped at this opportune moment and, thankful for the interruption, she smiled at Sam apologetically. 'I should get this. Go on without me. Honestly.'

He looked as if he might protest, but she turned away, pulling her phone out of her pocket as she did so. At some point she was going to have to let him know she wasn't interested.

Because she *wasn't* interested. Although how she wished she was. Darn Max Loveday. He was supposed to be the cure, not the poison.

The number on her phone was a London one, which wasn't unusual these days. She had never spent so much time on the phone, mainly to agents or publishers, trying to secure the names she wanted whilst considering the ones they were pushing at her. It was a real game of nerves, and to her surprise she got a buzz out of the negotiations.

'Hello?'

'Ellie? It's Andy Taylor here, Head of Retail Marketing at DL Media. We met at the industry awards the other week.'

'Hi, Andy. Is this about the festival? Because all my paperwork is back at the shop.' She dimly remembered him, but he wasn't one of her usual contacts.

'Festival? No, no. Actually, Ellie, I was calling you on the off-chance that you might be interested in a job. We have an opening here at DL Media and I think you might be the perfect candidate.'

Ellie stood in the street, time slowing down, until all she could hear was the slow thumping of her heart. Even the cry of the gulls, the chatter of children outside the ice cream shop faded away. That irritating, interfering man. Did Max have to try and sort out *everything*?

'Did Max put you up to this?'

'Max? You mean Max Loveday?' Andy Taylor laughed. 'Oh, no. He doesn't interfere at all with local staff, or any hiring below director level. No, it's your experience we're interested in.'

'My experience?'

Stop repeating things, Ellie or he'll change his mind.

'It's a retail marketing role. Obviously you run a really successful shop in a remote area, and I think that means you'd be able to bring a really valuable perspective to the role.'

He did? Ellie's heart and lungs seemed to expand, filling her chest with almost unbearable pressure. Her hard work had been noticed, appreciated.

'I know you live in Cornwall, and your shop is there, and this would be a really big change. But although this is a London-based post there would be some flexibility about working at home: maybe one or two days a week, depending on schedules. If that was what you wanted.

Would you be free to come in next week and have a chat about it?'

Ellie looked around at the dear, familiar village. The harbour curved in front of her. Just up the road was her own shop, her sanctuary. Her safety net. Could she leave it? Move on?

She swallowed, trying to get moisture back into her dry mouth, her stomach twisting.

But she had felt at home on the South Bank hadn't she? Had wondered what it would be like to be one of that confident sea of people at home in the city. Here was her opportunity to find out—and if it didn't work out she could always come back to the shop.

Besides, she might not even get the job. It was an interview...that was all.

'Next week is fine. The twenty-first? Yes, I'll see you then.'

See: she didn't need Max Loveday to move on. She didn't need him and one day soon she would stop wanting him too.

CHAPTER TWELVE

It made absolutely no sense to come all the way to London for just one day. Ellie had travelled up the night before her interview to make sure she was rested, on time and not too travel stained, although it was hard to look at her small, practical, budget hotel room and not yearn, just a little, for the opulence of the hotel suite she had occupied on her last London trip.

And as she had made the journey she might as well stay another day. Do some more sightseeing while she mulled over her next move. So here she was. With time on her hands. A tourist once again.

A tourist with a purpose. She was going to walk around central London and work out whether she could live here or not, even on a part-time basis.

The interview had gone well. *Really* well. More of an informal chat than a terrifying interrogation. She had found herself enjoying the experience and had to admit that the job, being a liaison between small independent shops and the publishers, sounded fascinating.

From the interviewers' enthusiasm and attention to detail Ellie was pretty sure they were going to offer her the role. She was also pretty sure that she would take it, with the proviso that she worked at least one day a week in Cornwall. Apparently plenty of people let out rooms on a weekday-only basis, and with two five-hour commutes in her week she would have plenty of time to catch up on paperwork.

Of course she would be insanely busy. She would have to appoint a shop manager, but she'd still do the accounts and work weekends, plus there was the festival. But she was young, healthy and oh, so single.

Ellie picked up her bag. That was it. She was on the verge of a new, exciting, dream-fulfilling experience and she would not mope around pathetically, thinking about holding hands on the South Bank. She was going to leave this perfectly adequate hotel room and she was going to have some fun whether she felt like it or not.

It was a warm, humid day, the sun hidden by low white cloud. Ellie hesitated outside the hotel's modest entrance, unsure which way to turn. Parks, palaces, museums, shops, exhibitions, theatres—the whole city was open to her.

It was almost paralysing, all this choice. She hadn't felt this way before, when she'd been here with Max. Then having no plan, no destination, had been exciting...an adventure. How was she going to travel and see all the places she had always dreamed of if she couldn't even walk down the street in her own capital city without panicking?

Ellie lifted her chin. Of course she could do it.

She set off almost blindly, walking through the bustling city streets. Four weeks since he had left. More than twice as long as she had actually known him. It made absolutely no sense that she missed him so badly. That it felt as if something fundamental was missing...some part of her like her liver or her lungs. Or her heart.

It made no sense that she instinctively looked for his ironic smile when committee meetings were particularly dull, that she missed his hand in hers on the beach. That she reached for him in her sleep.

He was the first person she wanted to tell when her mother called with updates on Bill's health. The person she wanted to share the amazing book she had just read with. The person she wanted to be sitting opposite her, coffee in hand, book open, reading in companionable silence.

It made no sense at all. But there it was.

Ellie had reached her destination. One huge shop, five storeys high, filled with books, books, nothing but books. It was a mecca for the bookworm, a source of inspiration for a fellow bookshop owner. She should be filled with anticipation, with the tingle in her fingers and the tightening of excitement in her stomach that exploring a new bookshop gave her.

Nothing. Not even a twinge.

Two hours later she emerged.

Five floors and she hadn't felt breathless once. Not a single display had moved her. She hadn't bought one book. Even the expensive piece of cake in the café had tasted of nothing.

It was no good. She was on the verge of an exciting new life and it was if she were dead inside. She needed to recapture some of that heady excitement from her last trip here. Maybe she should head back to the South Bank and see how much she enjoyed hanging out there in the daytime and on her own. See whether she really wanted to live half her life in the anonymity of the city.

Ellie couldn't walk at her usual rate. It was too hot and the tourists were out in force, stopping in front of her, ambling along and taking selfies at every landmark, no matter how insignificant. But it didn't take her long to reach Westminster Bridge. Last time she had walked over the bridge she had been holding Max's hand, with the promise of his kiss hanging over her like a velvet cloak; rich, decadent and all-encompassing.

In front of her the London Eye dominated the skyline. Ellie stopped in the middle of the bridge, her hands on the railings as she looked down at the wide swell of the Thames. So she missed him? That much was clear. The real question was, what was she going to do about it?

Slowly she retraced their steps, across the bridge and down the steps. The queue for the London Eye was already long and she scanned it eagerly. Hoping to see what? Their shadows? A faint wisp of Ellie and Max, still laughing in the queue?

No. No more mooning around looking for the ghosts of lovers past. She pulled her gaze away and marched on, only to be confronted by another queue. The queue for the London Aquarium. The missing piece from their last trip.

If she went in she would go alone. That had never been the deal. She should just walk on by, carry on with her plans. But her feet were heavy, her legs reluctant to move. Ellie stood still, tourists weaving around her, racked with indecision. Maybe she *should* go in. Her last and final act of being pathetic before she pulled herself together and thought about whether she wanted this job or not and where she wanted her life to go.

Just a few small decisions to make.

And then she saw it. A poster advertising tea with the penguins. *Today.* 'Diary it in,' he had said. Of course it had been a joke...a meaningless comment.

But still. It was a sign. She wasn't sure exactly what the sign meant, but no matter. A sign was a sign.

The queue to get in was ridiculous.

If Max had been there, there was no way he'd have

queued. He'd have paid top-dollar for a priority pass and probably been conveyed in on a chariot pulled by walruses. It must be nice to be rich.

Still, she was near the front at last. It was only a quarter to twelve, and she might as well enjoy the whole experience as she was there. Obviously there were several aquariums, zoos and animal sanctuaries a lot closer to home, but that wasn't the point. At all.

No, the point was that she was proving a point. She was taking a positive step. Taking control of her own destiny one very slow step at a time.

Finally she was at the front of the queue. Ellie's heart began to hammer.

'Oh, I'm sorry.' The girl behind the desk didn't look that sorry. She looked busy and tired and fraught. 'The tea with the penguins is all booked out. Do you want a normal ticket?'

Ellie stared. She had blown it. She couldn't even make a melodramatic gesture without messing it up.

'Miss?'

Ellie sighed and held out her bank card. She was here after all. 'Just one adult ticket, please.'

It didn't get easier once she was inside. The entrance was crowded with buggies, harassed families and small children slipping out of their parents' grasps to run amok. And everyone moved so *slowly*! You'd think they'd paid a fortune to look at each and every exhibit, to read all the noticeboards and interpretations, to watch the sharks feeding.

Actually, *that* was quite cool. But, no, she wasn't here to look at sharks.

Finally, *finally,* she managed to sidle past a large group, dodge a particularly active toddler and navigate her way through a group of texting teens. And there she was. At the entrance to the penguin room.

It was like entering an ice palace. White walls, white ceilings and low blue lighting. Windows on one side separated the black and white flightless birds from the spellbound watchers, giving them space to swim and play in peace. She felt a moment's pang for them, confined to this artificial room, unable to explore the wider seas, but at least they were safe from orcas and other predators.

For one long moment Ellie forgot why she was there, swept up in the icy atmosphere and the sheer wonder of the penguins, so graceful in the water, so comical on land. But she soon remembered her purpose and looked around. The room was busy, apart from a cordoned-off area by one of the viewing windows where several tables and chairs were set up. Cake stands and tea sets were neatly arranged on the tables.

Ellie inhaled, long and deep. There was no way he would have remembered that throw-away comment—and even if he had there was no reason for him to be here. But a quick look wouldn't hurt. Would it?

Of course he wasn't there.

Her chest tightened. Should she be disappointed? Heartbroken? Relieved?

Ellie watched a penguin dive into the water, its body hurtling at speed towards the pool floor before executing a neat turn and zooming back up to the surface. The truth was that she was none of the above.

She was determined.

She had queued for nearly an hour on a hot, humid day, and fought her way through the crowds. Not because she had expected to see Max; it wasn't even that she'd *hoped* to see him, amazing as it would have been if he was actually here. No, she had come here to work out what she wanted. It wasn't the most heroic quest of all times, sure. She hadn't fought a Minotaur or anything. But she had tested herself, tested her commitment, and now she knew.

Knew that there was no point leaving her happiness in the hands of fate, or hoping that coincidence would send Max back her way. If she wanted a life with Max Loveday she was going to have to go after it. Show him that she was no damsel in distress but an equal—and a far better match than some well-bred society girl who might know all the right people but would bore him to death within six months.

Really, she was going to be the one who saved him.

So that meant she needed to book her first flight abroad on her own. It wasn't going to be Paris or Rome. She was heading to the States.

Max leaned back in his chair and watched Ellie. His first incredulous happiness at seeing that she was actually here hadn't faded, but it was joined by amusement now as he watched her. Her jaw was set and she looked grimly determined.

He hoped that boded well for him. She might be planning his disembowelment.

'Excuse me.' He walked over to her, stopping behind her as if he were just another visitor, trying to find a spot to view the penguins. 'Are you meeting someone for afternoon tea? I have a table for two, right over here.'

'Max!' She whirled round, her hands against his chest, whether to ward him off or check he was real he didn't know. 'What are you doing here?'

'Afternoon tea, remember? Only they don't serve sushi. Apparently it would be a little insensitive in an aquarium. You can see their point...'

'Yes.' She bit her lip, her face an adorable mixture of confusion and joy. 'But it wasn't a real date. It was a joke.'

'Yet here you are.'

'I was in London anyway, so I thought...you know... while I was here I might as well come and...'

'See if I was here?'

'No.' Her cheeks were turning an interesting shade of red. 'I wanted to see the penguins.'

'And?'

'And what?'

He lowered his voice. 'Are they everything you hoped they would be?'

Her eyes were serious as they scanned his face. 'I'm not sure yet. I hope so. What about you? Are they living up to expectations?'

Max stared down at her, at the pointed chin, the delicate cheekbones, the candid brown eyes. 'Oh, yes...' Was that him? So hoarse? 'Everything I dreamed of.'

Her eyes fell, but not before he saw the spark of hope in them. 'You're sure?'

He took one of her hands in his. 'I've never been surer.'

At one level Max was aware that they were blocking a window, that people were moving past them, trying to look over their heads. That other conversations were taking place, children were crying, asking questions, pushing past him. But it was as if there was a bubble enclosing Ellie and him. They were in the room and yet apart from it. In an alternative universe of two.

He watched her inhale before she looked back up at him.

'What about your parents and DL?'

'Don't let it overwhelm you, but you are looking at the new CEO of DL Media. My father has decided to take an executive board position.'

She raised her elegantly arched brows. 'Decided?'

'That's the official line. As for the divorce: I'm out of it. My only request is that they behave themselves when they have to be in the same room.' He paused. 'At my wedding, for instance.'

Her lips parted. 'Your wedding?'

He held her hand just a little bit tighter. 'There's nothing worse than feuding exes at a wedding. Apart from midlife-crisis-suffering uncles hitting on the bridesmaids, that is. Don't you think?'

'I haven't really thought about it. Are you planning ahead, or have you brought your timetable forward?'

'I got rid of the whole damn timetable. Turns out you can plan for everything but love, Ellie.'

'Love?'

Was that a crack in her voice? He couldn't wait any longer. He'd spent the last eight hours practising elegant speeches but they had gone straight out of his head.

'I can be based in the London office most of the time. Obviously I'd need to go to Hartford regularly, travel a lot, but the UK would be my main home. I'd buy a place in London but spend weekends at The Round House, work from there whenever I could. Get that boat, walk on the beach, win the pub quiz. If you want to, that is?'

'Do I want to win the pub quiz?' Her voice was teasing but her eyes told a different story, shining with happiness. 'I already did. Twice.'

'But not on *my* team. And that's where I want you, Ellie. On my team—and I'll be on yours. For ever. I know it's fast, and I know I didn't make the best first impression, and I know you want time to work out who you are, and I respect that—'

He came to a halt as she put a cool finger to his lips. 'Max Loveday, stop babbling and tell me what you want.'

'I want to marry you, Ellie. Preferably right away. But I'll wait. We can take it as slow as you like.'

'That's a shame.' She stepped a little closer, one hand still in his, her other hand moving from his mouth to cup his cheek. 'Because I don't want to take it slow at all. I want to do it all, Max. Marriage, travel, babies, work. I want it all.'

'You do?'

She nodded solemnly. 'Although you might have to put up with me at more than just the weekends. I might be working in London during the week as well. Does that ruin your carefully thought out plans?'

'I'm learning to be adaptable. London? Really?' His mouth curved into a tender smile. 'Just when I thought you couldn't surprise me more.'

She narrowed her eyes. 'I was interviewed for a job at DL Media today. That didn't have anything to do with *you*, did it?'

'Not a thing. But I'll write you a reference. Although I'm not sure fiancés are acceptable referees, even if they *do* own the company.'

'Fiancé?'

She folded her arms. His cheek still tingled where she had touched it.

'I don't remember you asking. Not properly.'

He reached into his pocket. 'I don't have a ring,' he warned her. 'I want it to be perfect and exactly what you want.' He pulled out a box and dropped down on to one knee.

'Max! Get up!'

'What's that man doing, Mummy?'

Max was horrifyingly aware that the penguins were no longer the main attraction. The room was full of people and they were all looking, smiling and staring at him.

Oh, no—phones were out and pointed in their direction. She'd better say yes.

He took her hand, and as soon as he touched her he was back in the bubble. Let them watch and film.

'Ellie Scott, I love you and I want to give you the world. Will you marry me?'

He held up the box.

'I thought you said you didn't have a ring?' Her voice trembled as she took it from him.

'Open it.'

She slowly lifted the lid. 'It's a snow globe.'

'I had it made specially. Look inside, Ellie, what can you see?'

'Oh, the Eiffel Tower! And is that the Coliseum? And the Sydney Opera House? Does it snow in Sydney?'

'I'll take you to all those places and a hundred besides. We'll walk through the streets and eat in little neighbour-hood restaurants and get to the heart of everywhere we go. If we go together. Will you, Ellie?'

'Yes, Max. Of course I will. I'll go anywhere as long as you are with me.'

He got up and cupped her face in his hands. 'Are you sure, Ellie?'

'I'm completely sure. I love you, Max Loveday. All my life I've been too scared to reach out for what I want, but not any more. You've shown me that I can do anything I want to. And what I really want is to spend the rest of my life with you.'

* * * * *

BEWARE OF THE BOSS

LEAH ASHTON

For Isla.

Welcome to the world, honeybun!

CHAPTER ONE

WITH A GASP, Lanie Smith sat up abruptly, her floppy straw hat dislodging onto her lap and her towel a tangle amongst her hastily rearranged legs.

What on earth?

A shockingly cold nose pressing insistently against her knee answered that question. The large dog, its long red coat soaked in salt water and decorated generously with beach sand, nudged her leg, then flicked its liquid chocolate gaze hopefully in her direction.

'You lose something, buddy?'

Lanie leant forward, searching amongst the folds of her towel. The dog found its soggy-looking target first and snatched the ball up, backing a quick handful of steps away before going still and staring at her again.

'You want me to throw it?'

Knowing there was really only one answer to that question, Lanie pressed her hands into the sand and climbed to her feet. She shook her head a little, still fuzzy from her impromptu nap.

One minute she'd been reading her paperback…the next… She glanced up at the sky, looking for the sun, and breathed a silent sigh of relief when she realised it was still low and behind her. At least she hadn't slept for long.

Not that sleeping the day away would have been such a disaster. It wasn't as if she had a million other things to do.

The dog came closer and dropped the ball with a dull plop at her feet.

Hurry up.

Lanie couldn't help but smile.

'Okay, okay, buddy—here we go.'

With barely a grimace as her fingers wrapped around the slobbery ball—there was enough water here at North Cottesloe beach to wash her hands, after all—Lanie weighed up her throwing options. Back towards the water, from where the dog had obviously come? Or along the shore...?

'Luther!'

The deep voice stilled Lanie's movements. The dog momentarily glanced in the direction of the obviously familiar voice before refocussing his rapt attention on the ball.

A man loped across the blinding white sand towards her. He was shirtless, wearing only baggy, low-slung board shorts and a pair of jet-black sunglasses. The morning sun reflected off toned olive skin that glowed with exertion, and he ran a hand through slightly too long dark brown hair as he approached, leaving it standing in a haphazard arrangement.

Lanie found herself patting uselessly at her own brownish hair—which, in contrast, she was sure had *not* been rakishly enhanced by the combined effects of sand, wind and the fact that she'd done no more than loop it into half a ponytail before walking out of the house this morning.

'*Luther!*' the man said again.

The dog moved not a muscle, every line of his body focussed on Lanie's hand.

For the first time the man glanced in her direction.

And it *was* only a glance—as brief and uninterested as Luther's when he'd heard his owner call his name.

'Are you planning on keeping his ball?' the man asked, shifting his weight from foot to foot as he waited for her response.

Lanie blinked behind her own sunglasses. 'Pardon me?'

He sighed, twisting his wrist to look at his watch. 'Can you please give Luther his ball? Soonish would be great.'

The ball dropped from Lanie's fingers, but the big red dog pounced as excitedly as if she'd thrown it miles away. Now he crossed the short distance to his owner, and moments later the ball was whizzing through the air and into the shallow waves. The dog followed with huge, galumphing, splashing strides.

The man left too, without a backward glance, jogging the exact parallel distance from the lapping waves as he did every single morning.

'You're welcome,' Lanie said to his rapidly retreating broad shoulders.

What a jerk.

She knelt to stuff her towel and book into her canvas tote bag, and covered her windblown hair with her hat.

Well, at least now she knew.

In the past weeks she'd come to recognise most of the early-morning regulars at the beach—the dedicated open water swimmers who swam at seven a.m. every day, come rain, hail or shine. The walkers—both the walking-for-exercise and the walking-because-the-beach-is-gorgeous types. The joggers, the surfers, the sunbathers—and of course the dogs.

That man was also a regular. Unlike the others, who would greet Lanie with a familiar nod or smile each morning, this man appeared to be absorbed completely in his own world. He went for his run, his dog zipping about the shore in his wake—and then he left. That was it.

Dark and interesting, Lanie had thought whenever she'd seen him. *Private. Intense.*

Gorgeous. Obviously.

She wouldn't have been human not to wonder about a man like that. What did he do? What was his name? Was he married?

Not that she'd harboured any ridiculous daydreams. Lanie was, if nothing else, pragmatic.

But still—she'd wondered.

And now she had the only answer she needed. So, what was he like? *Rude*. Definitely.

Oh, well. No great loss—he could still add to her beautiful view each morning. A personality deficiency wouldn't impact on that.

With her shoes dangling from her fingers, Lanie followed a path through the green scrub-tufted dunes towards Marine Parade. Small white shells mixed amongst the sand dug into the soles of her feet. When she hit the footpath she dropped her shoes to the ground so she could step into them. The concrete was surprisingly warm, despite the lukewarm winter day.

It was Tuesday, so the Norfolk-pine-lined street was mostly empty, not crammed with cars fighting for every available space as was typical throughout summer weekends. Across the road, multi-million-dollar homes faced the cerulean ocean, with a single café nestled amongst their architecturally designed glory. The café's white-painted tables and chairs spilled outside, protected by brightly covered shade cloth sails and decorated with blue glass bottles filled with yellow daisies. Lanie's house was a two-minute walk up the hill—but a wave from the grey-haired man amongst the empty tables drew her attention.

'Lanie!' he called out, pausing his energetic sweeping to prop himself against a broom. 'Morning! Did you swim today?'

She smiled as she shook her head. 'Not today.'

'Tomorrow?'

They followed this script every day. 'Maybe.'

The man grumbled something non-distinct, but his opinion was still crystal-clear.

'Tell me what you *really* think, Bob,' she said dryly.

'Such a waste,' he said—just as he had yesterday—then patted one of the table tops. 'Coffee?'

Lanie nodded. Along with her early-morning beach visits, coffee at the eponymous Bob's Café had become part of her daily routine.

She slid onto the wooden chair, careful to avoid Bob's scruffy-looking apricot poodle who slept, oblivious, at her feet. Bob didn't wait to take her order, just shuffled inside to brew her 'usual': flat white, no sugar, extra shot of coffee.

On the table was today's newspaper, and automatically Lanie flipped it over as she waited.

A giant colour photograph almost filled the back page: a familiar, perfect, blinding white smile; slicked back, damp blond hair and eyes identical to those she saw in the mirror each day—except Sienna's were a sparkling azure blue, not brown.

'Hazel,' her mum always said. *'Not brown. If you only made more of them, Lanie, they'd be your best feature.'*

'Another gold medal,' Bob said, sliding a large mug and saucer onto the table.

Lanie shrugged. 'I know. She's doing really well. This is a great meet for her.'

Meet. Quite the understatement.

Bob raised his white-flecked eyebrows.

'I mean it,' Lanie said—and she did. 'I'm thrilled for her. Very proud of her.'

Her sister was in London, living Lanie's dream.

No, *Sienna's* dream. Lanie's dream had ended months ago, at the selection trials.

Lanie held her mug in her hands for a few moments, then raised an eyebrow at Bob, who still hovered.

'It's the relay tonight,' Bob said.

'Uh-huh.' Lanie took a too-quick sip and the hot liquid stung the roof of her mouth. She pressed her tongue against the slight pain, dismissing it.

Bob didn't push, but she felt the occasional weight of his gaze as he swept around her. He was a sports nut—pure and simple. Fanatical, actually—he had to be to have recognised her that first morning she'd emerged from her mother's house. *Lanie Smith* was far, far from a household name. *Sienna Smith*—well, that was another story. A story that could be read in the sports pages, in gushing women's magazines, or even in lads' mags accompanied by pictures of her in far more revealing bathers than her sister wore at swim-meets.

It didn't bother her. Her younger sister was suited to the limelight and she deserved it. Lanie was much happier in the shadows and perfectly satisfied with her accomplishments as a world-class relay swimmer. Besides, she certainly didn't crave the adulation that Sienna seemed to draw like a magnet.

Mostly satisfied. Lanie mentally corrected herself. *Mostly satisfied with her accomplishments.*

Absently she flicked through the sporting pages, full of photos of winners on podiums.

'Wish it was you?'

She hadn't realised Bob had approached her table again, and she glanced up in surprise. 'Of course not,' Lanie replied—snapped, really. Immediately she wished she could swallow the words. 'I'm retired,' she clarified, more calmly.

He nodded and drifted politely away again—but Lanie didn't miss the questions, and maybe concern, in his eyes.

She stood and left a handful of coins on the table, trying to ignore how her eyes had started to tingle and squint.

It was the sea breeze.

She slung her bag onto her shoulder and took big, brisk strides to exit the café and get home as quickly as possible.

She'd walked past three huge mansions, heading towards the street where her mother's small neat cottage was, when something caught her eye.

The glint of sun off a sweaty, perfectly muscled chest.

That man.

He jogged along the footpath on the opposite side of the road. His dog was now on a lead, intermittently gazing up at his owner in adoration.

Lanie felt herself tense, for no reason she could fathom.

She'd slowed her walk, but now she deliberately sped up—back to the pace she'd been before.

She didn't care about that guy. Didn't care if he was rude. Didn't care what he thought of her.

Didn't care what Bob thought.

Didn't care what her sister thought. Didn't care what anyone thought.

She held her head high and walked briskly past. With purpose.

But out of the corner of her eye she couldn't help but watch the man.

And notice that he paid her absolutely no attention at all.

It was as if she were invisible.

The knock on Lanie's front door later that night was not unexpected.

She headed down her narrow hallway, her slippers thudding against the hundred-year-old floorboards.

She flung the door open, and—as expected—behind the fly screen stood Teagan. Her long black hair was swept off her face and semi contained in a messy bun on the top of her head, and her eyes sparkled behind red-framed glasses.

Her oldest friend held up a plastic grocery bag. 'I have four types of cheese, olives, sundried tomatoes, and something I believe is called quince. The guy at the deli told me it was awesome, but I remain sceptical.'

Teagan bounded up the hall, as comfortable in this house as her own. As kids they'd split their time between their family's homes, although Teagan's family had long upgraded and moved on, while Lanie's mum had quite happily stayed put in the house she'd grown up in.

Lanie watched as Teagan pottered around the kitchen, locating a large wooden board and helping herself to cutlery.

She didn't bother asking why her friend was here as it was so obvious. Equally obvious was the fact that Teagan had ignored her when she'd politely declined her offer to hang out with her tonight.

'It's just another race, Teags,' she'd told her. *'I'll be fine.'*

Apparently she'd convinced Teagan about as well as she'd convinced herself.

Soon they'd settled on the rug in front of the TV, red wine in hand, cheese platter set out in front of them.

'You *do* know the final isn't until, like, two a.m.?' Lanie asked, her legs sprawled out in front of her.

'That's what coffee is for,' Teagan said between sips of wine. 'Besides, this current job I could do in my sleep. Hardly anyone calls Reception. In fact I'm starting to think they don't have any customers at all. You know…' Teagan paused, leaning forward conspiratorially. 'I reckon it's possible that it's all an elaborate front for something dodgy. I've always thought that my boss has shifty eyes…'

Lanie laughed out loud as Teagan outlined a typically outlandish theory. More than once Lanie had suspected that Teagan's preference for temping over a more permanent job was purely to get new material—whether they caught up for coffee, dinner or a drink, it was guaranteed that her friend would have a new story to tell.

As they ate—and polished off the bottle of wine—Lanie flicked from channel to channel of the sports coverage—heats of rowing, horses leaping over huge fences across country, cyclists whizzing around a velodrome.

'So, have you made a decision?' Teagan said a while later, her tone much more careful than before.

Lanie shifted uncomfortably. 'Has my mother been in touch?'

Teagan pulled a face. 'God, no. And it isn't like your mum's not capable of nagging you directly.'

Lanie's lips quirked unevenly.

Teagan drew her legs up so she sat cross-legged. '*I* was just wondering.' She paused. 'Worrying, maybe,' she added softly.

Lanie found herself biting the inside of her lip. When it happened twice in one day—first Bob, and now her best friend—that look really couldn't be misinterpreted.

They felt sorry for her.

Her whole focus had been aimed in one direction for so long. But now the pool wasn't calling her to training each morning. Her coach wasn't yelling at her. Her times weren't creeping down—or up. She didn't have another meet to aim for.

She had no goals.

Even though she wasn't the slightest bit hungry she reached for the cheese platter, busying herself with slicing bread and cheese and then taking her time to chew and swallow, not looking at Teagan

She mentally pulled herself into shape.

'I've decided not to go back to my old job,' she said, finally answering the question. 'It's time for a change. Managing the swim school is too much the same thing I've been doing for ever.' She attempted a carefree laugh. 'Although I can't imagine a job where my office doesn't smell of chlorine!'

Teagan, ever the good friend, smiled back, but she wasn't about to let her off the hook. 'So, the new plan is…?'

On the TV a rider toppled off his horse when the big grey animal slid to a stop before a hulking log fence. Lanie watched as he immediately jumped to his feet. She could see what he was telling everyone with his body language—*I'm fine!*—but the commentator was explaining in a clipped British accent that this meant he was disqualified. His dream was over.

The man patted his horse's neck, then leant forward until his silk-covered helmet rested against the horse's cheek.

Lanie knew *exactly* how he felt.

'I don't know—maybe I'll finish my business degree,' she said with a shrug. Three-quarters finished years ago, she'd abandoned it leading up to the national titles, intending to defer only for a semester or two. But then she'd made the Australian team, and everything had changed.

'Still living here?' Teagan's wrinkled nose conveyed exactly what she thought of that idea.

Lanie didn't know. She'd moved back in months earlier, after the selection trials. At the time it had seemed sensible—she'd taken extended leave from her job, needed a break from swimming entirely, and without an income she couldn't afford the rent on her little one-bedder in Scarborough without putting a huge dent into the savings she had earmarked for a house deposit. Her mum and sister had been focused on Sienna—not unusual in itself—so she'd reasoned that it wouldn't be too bad.

But they'd both be back soon.

'Maybe.'

Teagan raised an eyebrow. 'Hmm. You're always welcome to crash at mine. Or I can put a good word in for you at my temp agency?'

'And I can inadvertently work for an international drug cartel?' she asked with a smile.

Teagan stuck her tongue out at her.

So the conversation was over—for now.

Some time during one of the rowing finals Lanie noticed Teagan had fallen asleep sprawled against the front of her sofa. She padded over to extract the empty wine glass from her friend's hand, and then took her time washing up and tidying the kitchen.

She wasn't at all tired. Quite the opposite. In fact with every passing minute she felt more alert, more awake.

Before Teagan had arrived she'd considered not watching

the race at all. She'd told herself that it wasn't as if anyone would know—and she'd find out the result tomorrow, anyway.

But she hadn't really believed she could do that, and now she *knew* she couldn't. It wasn't quite the same, but she recognised how she was feeling: as if *she* was racing today.

The anticipation, the adrenalin, the nervous energy. Muted, but there.

From her kitchen bench Lanie watched the swimmers walk out for the men's hundred-metre breaststroke final. Watched them stretch and roll their shoulders, wiggle their legs about.

Then she watched the race—listened to the crowd, to the increasing hysteria of the commentators, and then watched the moment the winner won gold.

Automatically she smiled in reaction to the winner's smile, and then grinned to herself when she realised what she'd done.

See? She could do this. Tonight was just like any other night in front of the television. She'd watched her sister win two medals and been genuinely nervous and then over the moon for her. If she was going to have regrets, or be overwhelmed by jealousy or resentment or something equally unpleasant and inappropriate, she would have done it by now.

It really was just another race.

On the screen, groups of swimmers began to walk out to the pool. Sweden, in their uniform of vivid blue and gold. Japan, with all four women holding hands as they waved to the crowd. The Dutch in orange and grey.

And then the Australian team.

'Lanie?' Teagan poked her head over the top of the couch and blinked sleepy eyes in her direction.

'Perfect timing!' Lanie said, managing to sound remarkably normal. 'The race is just about to start.'

Her friend raised an eyebrow.

Okay. Maybe she didn't sound totally normal. But surely a little bit of tension was to be expected?

The swimmers had all discarded their tracksuits and onto

the blocks stepped the lead-out swimmer. Australia was in lane four, sandwiched between the United States and the Netherlands.

Teagan's eyes were glued to the television when Lanie sat beside her, but her friend still managed to reach out and grab her hand. She shot a short glance in Lanie's direction as she squeezed it—hard.

'You okay?'

Lanie nodded. 'Totally.'

'Take your marks.'

Pause.

Complete silence.

BEEP!

And they were off.

The first leg was good—strong. The United States touched first, but there was nothing in it. By the end of the second lap Australia had drawn level.

Then the third Aussie girl dived in, sluicing through the water like an arrow.

This was *her* leg. The girl was just like her—the fastest of the heat swimmers, awarded with the final relay berth amongst the more elite girls.

She was doing a brilliant job. Holding her own.

Would Lanie have?

She closed her eyes, squeezing them shut tight.

She imagined herself in the water. Remembered the way her focus became so narrow, so all-encompassing, that she didn't hear the crowd—didn't hear a thing. It was just her body and the water, and all she could control was her technique.

Stroke, stroke, *breathe*. Stroke, stroke…

The crowd—a world away—was suddenly much louder, and Lanie's eyes popped open. The anchor swimmer was in the water, and Great Britain had a chance for a medal. The crowd had gone wild.

Teagan squeezed her hand again, harder, and Lanie blinked, refocussing her attention.

Australia had pulled ahead. They were going to win.

And just like that—they had.

The girls had done it, and done it in style—in record time. They deserved every accolade the over-excited commentator was bestowing upon them.

They filled the television screen, swim caps stripped off, damp hair long around their shoulders, as they completed the standard pool-side interview.

'Lanie?' Teagan's voice was full of concern.

Despite her own mental reassurances that she was fine, and the many times she'd told herself she was a bigger person than to be jealous or resentful or whatever, she suddenly realised she wasn't.

A tear splashed onto her hands, and she looked down to where her fingers were knotted in the flannelette of her pyjamas.

She'd been wallowing. Treading water until this moment—waiting for tonight, for this race.

Why?

Because tonight was the end. The end of her swimming dream.

Teagan silently shoved a handful of tissues in front of her and Lanie dabbed at her cheeks. Blew her nose. And considered what to do next.

She needed to do something—anything. And she had to do it *now*. She couldn't wake up tomorrow and be the also-ran swimmer.

She turned to face Teagan on the couch. Her friend was so close to be as good as shoulder to shoulder with her, but she'd wisely not made a move to comfort her.

'I need a job,' Lanie said.

Teagan's eyes widened, but then she smiled. 'But no drug cartels?'

'Or anything involving swimming.'

Her friend's smile broadened. 'Consider it done.'

CHAPTER TWO

GRAYSON MANNING SHOVED his chair away from his desk, then covered the generous space between the desk and the door in quick, agitated strides.

Outside his office, his assistant's desk was empty.

He glanced at his watch, confused. It was well after nine a.m., and Rodney was always on time. Gray insisted upon it.

He frowned as he walked into the hallway. Thankfully a woman sat behind the glossy white reception desk. Behind her, 'Manning' was spelt out in ridiculously large chrome block capitals.

What was her name again? Cathy? Katie?

'Caroline,' she said, unprompted, as he approached—reminding him he'd guessed wrong last time he'd asked her a question, too.

'Caroline,' he repeated. He'd been told doing so was useful when remembering names—not that it had helped him so far. 'Where's Rodney?'

The woman blinked. Then bit her lip, glancing away for a moment. 'Um…Mr Manning, Rodney resigned…' A pause. 'Yesterday.'

Gray's jaw clenched. 'Our agreement with the agency specifies at least two weeks' notice must be provided.'

The woman nodded, her blond ponytail bouncing in agreement. 'I believe he asked your permission that his resignation be effective immediately.'

'I didn't agree to that.'

Caroline's lips twitched. 'I'm pretty sure you did. Rodney forwarded me your e-mail so he could organise cancellation of his building access and so on. It was there in writing.'

Gray pulled his phone from his jacket pocket and quickly scrolled through yesterday's sent messages. Yesterday had been stupidly busy—back-to-back meetings, a major issue with one of his contractors, and a lead on a new investment opportunity in South East Asia.

Even so, surely he would have noticed if… *Letter of Resignation.*

It wasn't even a vague subject line. He really needed to start paying more attention to his inbox. But then, that was one of the reasons why he had an assistant: to prioritise his mail, to nag him to respond to anything important, and to allow him to pay no attention to anything that wasn't.

The irony was not lost on him.

Without another word he headed up the hallway to the opposite end of the floor. To his father's office.

A mirror image of his own, Gordon Manning's office also had a smaller adjacent waiting area—although his was complete with an actual assistant.

'Marilyn—'

Unlike Caroline, the older lady didn't even attempt to hide her smile. She shook her head. 'Gray, Gray, Gray…'

'I need a new assistant.'

'So I hear.'

His lips thinned. 'Does everyone but me know that Rodney resigned?'

'A group of us had farewell drinks last night. Lovely guy.'

'I was unaware you were so close,' he replied dryly. 'He was only here a couple of weeks.'

'Two months,' Marilyn corrected smoothly.

Really? Since his father had announced his impending retirement six months ago, Gray could barely remember what day it was. He was working seven days a week, and easily twelve-hour days.

'Is my father in?'

'No, not today.'

His father hadn't been into the office in months. Initially his transition to retirement had been gradual—and Gray had been unsure if his father was capable of retiring at all. But soon Gordon's days in the office had been reduced to only a few hours, and then to nothing. And while Marilyn continued to manage his dad's life, now she did so exclusively via e-mail.

A month ago Gordon Manning had had his no-expense-spared retirement party and that had made it all official. But Gray wasn't silly enough to clear out his dad's office just yet—apart from the fact it contained about forty years' worth of god-knew-what paperwork, it would be a while before Gordon—or Gray, come to think of it—could imagine a Manning Developments office without a desk for its founder.

'So you can help me today? Fantastic. I need you to accompany me to a meeting in West Perth. And to sort out my flights for next week. And—'

But Marilyn was shaking her head. 'No need. Your new assistant should be here soon.'

Oh. The agency must already be on to it. Even so...

'I'd rather not have someone completely new to Manning with me today. This is a very important meeting. It's essential that—'

Marilyn's look froze him mid-sentence, exactly as it had frozen him many times before—although the vast majority of such glares had been twenty-five years ago. A kid learnt quickly *not* to mess with Marilyn.

'If you don't want a new assistant, be nice to the assistant you have.'

'I *am* nice.'

Her eyebrows rose right up beneath her dead straight fringe.

'Be nice to this one, Gray. Let's try for three months, this time, hey?'

* * *

Almost an hour later, Caroline ushered Gray's new assistant into his office.

'Mr Manning?'

He was just finishing an e-mail, so he barely glanced in the direction of the figure in his doorway and instead just waved an arm in the general vicinity of one of the soft leather chairs in front of his desk.

Absently, he heard the door thud quietly shut, and then the click of heels on the marble floor—but all his attention was on the e-mail he was composing:

I look forward to discussing the proposal further...

No. He hit the delete key half a dozen times, maybe a little harder than was necessary. He didn't want any discussion. He wanted a decision. The deal was already behind schedule. He needed a *yes* and he needed it last week.

I trust you'll agree...

That was even worse. He held down the delete key again, thinking.

But that was the problem. He was thinking too much. It was just an e-mail—an e-mail to an investment partner with whom he already had an excellent rapport. The proposal was little more than a formality.

Or at least it should be. But their last meeting had been... *off.* It had been subtle—more questions than he'd normally expect, more careful perusal of the numbers Gray had shown him. All perfectly normal things for a wise investor to do. The thing was that *this* particular investor had so much confidence in Manning that he was usually rather relaxed about conducting his own due diligence.

Quite simply—he'd trusted Manning.

But now...

Maybe it was a coincidence that this new-found caution coincided with Gray's father's retirement...

Gray didn't believe that for a second.

And it was damned infuriating.

Gray glanced up. His eyes landed on the woman's hands—long, elegant fingers, unpainted, neat, short tips. She was sluggishly rubbing each hand down her thighs, the movement slow but clearly triggered by nerves.

She wore trousers, not a skirt, he noticed.

'How do I finish this e-mail?' he asked. His tone was sharper than he'd intended, and Marilyn's words echoed momentarily.

His gaze shot to the woman's face.

As their eyes met her body gave a little jolt and she gasped—quite loudly.

Immediately one of those long-fingered hands was slapped to her mouth.

Her eyes widened as she looked at him.

And they were very lovely eyes, he acknowledged. Big and brown, framed by dark lashes—even though he was almost certain she wore no make-up. They watched him with unexpected intensity and an expression that was impossible to read.

He didn't understand. Surely his request wasn't so shocking? Abrupt, maybe, but hardly earth-shattering.

When the silence continued he shrugged, his temporary interest in her reaction rapidly morphing into frustration.

He didn't have time for this. The agency would just have to send someone else.

'I don't think this is going to work out,' he said, very evenly. 'Thanks for your time.'

He didn't bother to wait for her to leave, just gritted his teeth and got back to his e-mail.

Again he only half listened to the sound of her heels on the marble—although soon he realised she was coming closer, not going further away.

'Regards,' she said, from right behind his shoulder.

'What?'

He looked up at her. She was somehow bigger than he'd expected—taller, and wider through the shoulders. She leant forward slightly as she studied his computer, her long hair shining in the sunlight that flooded through the office's floor-to-ceiling windows.

'I'd delete all that stuff at the end, and just say *Regards*. Or *Sincerely*. Or however you normally sign off your e-mails.' She met his eyes, and this time she didn't look like a deer caught in the headlights. She watched him steadily, and there was a sharpness to her gaze that he appreciated.

Her eyes were definitely hazel, he realised. Not brown.

When he didn't say anything, she explained further. 'Judging by the e-mail trail beneath this one, you've been having this conversation for a while.'

Gray nodded.

'And you want a resolution? But you don't want to be seen as pushy?'

'Exactly,' he said, surprised.

'Well, then,' she said, as if it was the most obvious thing in the world. 'Sometimes saying less is more.'

She straightened up and took a step away from his chair.

Silently, he deleted his half-written sentence, ended the e-mail as she'd suggested, then hit *'Send.'*

Good. It was gone.

He stood, and with this action, the woman took another rapid step away. Then she rolled her shoulders back, and thrust out her hand.

'Elaine Smith,' she said, very crisply. 'Lanie.'

Automatically he grasped her hand. It was cool and delicate. And she *was* tall. But even in heels she was an inch shorter than him.

Her suit jacket was a dark grey and a little tight across the chest—and her soft pink shirt wasn't sitting quite right, with one side of her collar higher than the other. Combined with her loose, wavy hair and lack of discernible make-up, no one would call her perfectly presented.

He would call her pretty, though. Very pretty.

Gray rapidly dispatched that unexpected musing. The appearance of his employees was irrelevant. All he cared about was their ability to do their job.

And, despite her slightly odd initial reaction to him, there was an air of practicality to this woman that was appealing. Plus she'd been right about the e-mail.

Most importantly he needed an assistant, and she was here.

'I have a meeting in half an hour in West Perth.'

For a moment she looked at him blankly. 'So I have the job?'

He nodded impatiently. 'Yes, of course.'

A beat passed.

He sighed. 'Anything else?'

'Oh,' she said. 'No.'

He turned back to his computer and a moment later she walked away, her heels again clicking loudly.

He briefly wondered if she needed help figuring out how to log into her computer or anything—but then another e-mail popped in that he urgently needed to attend to, and that was that.

Surely it wasn't that difficult? She seemed smart. She'd figure it out.

Lanie almost collapsed into her new, plush leather office chair.

Her phone trilled its musical message notification from within the depths of her bag, but for now she ignored it.

Of course she'd forgotten to put it onto silent mode prior to her interview.

Thank goodness she hadn't received that message a few minutes earlier. She could just about imagine Grayson Manning's reaction to *that*.

But then would that have been such a bad thing?

If he'd stuck with his original conclusion—that she wasn't suitable—she'd have walked out of this office no worse than how she'd walked in: without a job.

With the added benefit of *not* working for Mr Grumpy Pants.

No. Not a bad thing at all.

And yet she'd had her chance to leave. She had her chance still to walk away. No one would force her to stay. Not even the employment agency she was working for.

Which reminded her…

Lanie fished out her phone. As expected, the waiting message was from Teagan. As she'd been whisked up to the twenty-fifth floor in a seriously shiny mirrored lift she'd tapped out an urgent message to her friend:

What did you do??!

Because this building was definitely not what Lanie had been expecting of her first assignment with the agency. Yes, she'd known the role was as a personal assistant, but after seven years managing the swim school she'd been unconvinced she really had the skills for such a role—but Teagan had been adamant. *'You'll be fine,'* she'd said. *'Piece of cake,'* she'd said.

Given her lack of relevant experience, Lanie had imagined she'd be working somewhere small. Somewhere that couldn't afford a true executive assistant. Somewhere she could kind of figure it all out as she went along.

Manning Developments was *not* that place.

Teagan's text message therefore did not surprise her at all.

I spruced up your CV. Just a little.

Right.

Lanie rolled her head backwards until it rested on the high back of her chair and stared up at the ceiling.

The sensible thing to do would be to leave. She didn't have the experience for a role like this, and if she stuffed it up then the agency, Teagan *and* herself would all look pretty bad.

It was sweet of Teagan—annoying, inappropriate, and dishonest—but sweet.

It should end here.

But she remained at her vast new desk. For the same reason she'd stayed in Grayson's office after she'd recognised him as the man from the beach.

For long seconds she'd searched for the cutting comments he deserved after his performance at the beach—but then, before she'd gathered her thoughts, she'd realised he'd just *dismissed* her.

Again. Just as he had at the beach, he'd carried on as if she was irrelevant to his world. Why on earth would she want to work for someone who would treat her like that?

But she couldn't let that man—*Grayson*—ignore her again.

So here she was. With a job she didn't really want, working for a man she didn't like.

Lanie wiggled the wireless mouse on the desk and the large flatscreen monitor blinked instantly to life, revealing a login screen.

Her gaze flicked to the still open door to Grayson's office, but then immediately away. That he would be of no help at all was obvious.

She stood and headed for the hallway—Caroline, the little plaque on the reception desk had proclaimed. She should be able to point her in the direction of IT Support or something.

She could do this. It couldn't be too difficult.

She'd figure out *why* she was doing it later.

CHAPTER THREE

THE LITTLE GREEN man started blinking, so with a coffee cup gripped firmly in each hand Lanie made her way across a very busy St Georges Terrace.

'Lanie!'

A fierce breeze whipped between the high-rise buildings, blowing her loose hair every which way and partially covering her eyes. Not that she needed a visual aid to identify that particular deep and demanding voice.

Calmly she stepped onto the footpath and Grayson met her halfway, jogging down his building's steps and deftly negotiating the sea of lunchtime pedestrian traffic.

'We're going to be late,' he said. 'Why didn't you say something?'

Lanie tossed her hair out of her face and met his gaze as she handed him his triple-shot latte.

'I did mention that there may not be time for a coffee.'

Grayson blinked. As always, he seemed genuinely surprised. 'Oh…' he said.

In the week she'd worked for him this routine had already become familiar. He was rather like a mad scientist—so utterly focussed on his work that the practicalities of life seemed beyond him.

It would have been endearing—except…

'Well, make sure it doesn't happen again.'

Lanie bit her lip.

Remember the money. Remember the money...

It was the money, Lanie had decided. The reason she hadn't already quit.

Thanks to Teagan's creativity with her CV, and her ability so far to fudge her way through the job, she was earning almost twice what she had at the swim school. And she needed the money so she could move out of her mother's place as soon as possible—before she and Sienna returned from Europe, preferably.

That was the only reason she was here. Nothing to do with that morning on the beach.

Lanie nodded tightly. 'I've got a car waiting for us.' She gestured with her spare hand in its direction, and to the driver idling illegally in the clearway. Grayson opened his mouth, but Lanie jumped in before he could get a word out. 'The laptop, projector and business specs are on the back seat.'

In response his eyebrows rose, just slightly. 'Good,' he said.

Again Lanie bit her lip. *How about a thank-you, huh?*

She pivoted on her heel and strode towards the car.

Remember the money. Remember the money. Remember the—

The toe of her shoe caught on something and Lanie stumbled. But before she had much time to register that the grey pavers of the footpath were rapidly becoming closer her descent was suddenly halted.

Grayson's arm was strong and solid and warm around her waist. In an effortless movement he pulled her upwards and towards him, so she was pressed against his impeccably suited body.

She tilted her chin to look up at him.

He caught her gaze—*really* caught it—and for a moment Lanie was completely speechless.

His eyes weren't just grey—they were flecked with blue. And with his face now arranged in concern, not hard with tension, he was somehow—impossibly—even more handsome.

Of course she already knew he was gorgeous. To pretend otherwise would be ridiculous. And, frustratingly, beautiful people didn't become less beautiful simply by their unlikeable behaviour.

Less *attractive*, though. They did become less attractive. He'd proved that, that day on the beach. And each day since then.

But right now Grayson did *not* seem unattractive. Right now, with the subtle scent of his aftershave and the warmth of his arm and body confusing her, he was anything but.

The side of her body he touched…no *everywhere* he touched, reacted to him. Electricity flooded through her.

'You okay?'

Because it was all she could manage, she simply nodded mutely.

He took a step away from her and amazingly she had the presence of mind not to follow him. She took a deep breath, rolled her shoulders back, and rebalanced on her own two feet.

She realised she was gripping her coffee cup hard enough to slightly crumple the cardboard, and made herself loosen her grip.

Then he smiled. It was a subtle expression—far from broad—but it was the first Grayson Manning smile she'd witnessed.

Once again her ability to form words evaporated.

He covered the short distance to the car and opened the door for her.

She slipped past him, not catching his gaze. With every moment she was increasingly aware that she *really* needed to pull herself together.

If she was going to keep working for Grayson she needed to erase completely from her subconscious even the smallest skerrick of romantic daydreams involving her boss.

Obviously the agency would not approve.

Secondly she—*Lanie*—did not approve. She might not

have extensive experience in the corporate world, but even she knew getting involved with your boss was…well, pretty dumb.

And thirdly, Grayson was not about to be overcome by lust when it came to Lanie Smith.

Lanie's lips quirked up at the idea of Grayson arriving at her front door to take her out to dinner. It was laughable.

She settled into the soft leather of the back seat as Grayson closed her door, and moments later he was sliding into the car from the opposite side.

Lanie took a good long gulp of her coffee, hoping that the addition of caffeine would help get her brain back to speed.

She fully expected Grayson to flip open his laptop as the car pulled way, or to make another one of his seemingly endless phone calls. But instead he turned towards her.

He cleared his throat, the sound unexpected and awkward in the quiet vehicle.

'Thank you for the coffee,' he said gruffly.

Lanie shot a look in his direction, not immediately sure she'd heard him correctly.

But his expression was genuine. Not quite contrite—that wouldn't be Grayson Manning—but still…

'Not a problem, Grayson.'

He nodded, then glanced away through his darkly tinted window at the passing traffic.

Without looking at her, he spoke again.

'You can call me Gray.'

The beach was near deserted the following morning. Gray's bare feet smacked rhythmically against the wet sand, his progress only occasionally punctuated with a splash when the waves stretched across his path.

Luther was well ahead of Gray, having abandoned his ball to begin enthusiastically digging a hole to China. Beyond Luther rocky fingers of coastline stretched into the ocean, and distant cranes for hoisting shipping containers formed blurry silhouettes against the sky.

It was cool—it was only July after all—and all but the most dedicated swimmers had abandoned the beach on such a dull and overcast day.

But today Gray needed to run.

Maybe he'd hoped the bite of the frigid air in his lungs would help. Or, more likely, it was that heavy ache in his legs that he craved.

Because out here he was in control. He could run as far as he wanted—further even than his body wanted to go.

And Gray liked being in control. He was used to it. Expected it.

He was in control of everything he did in both his business and his private life. He knew what he was doing and could plan with absolute confidence how things were going to work out.

By Gray's reckoning, his father's retirement should be no more than a blip on Manning's radar—after all, it had been many years since Gordon Manning had spearheaded a project. For the past five years Gray *had* been Manning's CEO in all but name. So Gordon's retirement was nothing more than a formality. Nothing would change except he'd eventually have to repurpose his dad's offices.

That was how it was supposed to be happening.

It was still how Gray thought it *should* have happened.

But it hadn't.

Things *had* changed.

That irritating e-mail from the suddenly cautious investor was just one example. Not of many—far from it—but enough to frustrate the hell out of Gray.

An extra question here or there shouldn't bother him. Or decisions taking longer than he felt they should. Or even that subtle, almost but not quite imperceptible shift in the atmosphere at meetings…

Even Gray had to smile at that. Since when had he been so sensitive to a change in *feel*?

Well, whatever it was that had changed—it *had*. And it did bother him. Because it wasn't just an irritation...all these questions and atmosphere-shifts ...it had the potential to impact his bottom line.

In fact it already was.

And Gray was *not* going to tolerate that.

In his peripheral vision, Gray noticed a lone figure walking near the dunes. As he glanced in her direction the woman waved, while her other hand firmly held an oversized floppy hat to her head.

Automatically Gray waved back, then refocussed. Deliberately he crossed from the wet sand to the dry, wanting the extra demand on his muscles the deep, soft sand forced from his body.

It turned out that, despite the many years since his dad had actually led a Manning project, for some of his clients Gordon Manning had been a very real and very important presence—somewhere behind the scenes.

The reality that it had truly been Gray they'd been working with—not Gray as Gordon's mouthpiece—didn't matter, and that exasperated Gray.

He deserved the trust he thought he'd already earned. He deserved his stature in Australia's business community.

A larger wave pushed far up the beach and Gray's bare feet splashed through foamy puddles as the water slid back into the ocean.

It also annoyed him that he hadn't realised this reality. That he hadn't fully understood what it meant to be Gordon Manning's son, regardless of his own track record and years of success.

So it was frustrating and exasperating and irritating...

But it was also...

Gray's time.

Now was his time to prove himself.

And nothing could be allowed to stand in his way.

Lanie dropped her arm as Gray disappeared into the distance. He'd waved each morning since she'd started at Manning, although he'd shown no sign of realising she was the woman he'd been so rude to on the beach that morning of the relay final. Now, knowing Gray, she doubted he ever would.

She'd considered telling him—but what would that achieve?

Lanie knew the answer to that: a blank stare, followed directly by a look that said *Why are you wasting my time with this?*

That was a look she was quickly becoming familiar with. At least now she didn't take it personally. Pretty much everything not immediately related to Manning and preferably relevant *right at that moment* elicited exactly that look.

'Which hotel would you like me to book for you in Adelaide?'

When he'd discovered he was not, in fact, booked into his favourite hotel, he'd booked himself in, then sent Lanie a helpful e-mail with the name of the 'correct' hotel for next time.

'For that presentation tomorrow, would you like me to include the numbers from the Jameson project?'

Turned out she'd guessed right with that one…

So a returned wave each morning was both unexpected and welcome. Although ignoring the woman he worked with every single day would have been quite a stretch—even for Gray.

With Gray and Luther little more than specks in the distance, Lanie started walking again and allowed her thoughts to circle back to where they'd been before the flash of Luther's red coat against the sand had distracted her.

It would be odd, she'd just decided, if she wasn't jealous of her sister.

Wouldn't it?

She didn't know. It was what had got her out of the house so ridiculously early on a work day. She needed the beach. The space, the salt and the sound of the waves… It was all as familiar to her as breathing.

Water had always helped her. Whether chlorinated or not, it was where she gravitated at times of stress. When her dad had left it had seemed natural. He was, after all, the reason she loved water. With an offshore mining job he'd rarely been home—but when he had he'd spent all his time at the beach.

As an adult, she looked back and wondered whether he'd simply tolerated the fact she'd clung to him like a limpet when he was home—rather than her more romanticised version in which she'd told herself she'd been his swimming buddy.

Because surely if he'd really wanted her there he would have bothered to stay in touch after he'd left. Or not left at all.

But if nothing else he'd given Lanie her love of water and the genes that helped her swim very quickly through it.

It had been a mistake to skip the beach earlier in the week. She needed to rectify it. Even today, with the wind whipping off the waves and gluing her long cargo trousers and thin woollen jumper to her skin, it was the right place for her to attempt to organise her thoughts and her reactions.

Sienna had e-mailed her overnight, full of post-championships euphoria. From the magnificence of the closing ceremony to how much fun she was having, through to how she was dealing with the rabid tabloid press after being seen out on a date with a British rower.

Lanie had seen the photos—and the headlines—as they'd made it to Australia too. *'Golden couple'. 'Winners in love'.*

Jealousy? Whatever it was she was feeling, she hadn't defined it.

Until Sienna's e-mail.

It hadn't been until right at the end, amongst all the glitz and excitement, that her sister had acknowledged how Lanie might be feeling. Her sister wasn't stupid, or heartless. A bit oblivious at times—but then, that was Sienna.

Somehow, though, Sienna's awkward attempts at making the contrast in their situations seem somehow okay had hit home harder than anything else.

How are you doing? It wasn't the same without you. You should be so proud of your personal best, though. Any other year you definitely would've made the team.

And so here she was, at the beach.

Walking today, not swimming—but the scale and scope of the ocean helped, just as she'd known it would.

She envied Sienna. She *was* jealous.

Today she allowed herself to be.

CHAPTER FOUR

THE UNEXPECTED SENSATION of warmth against his chest snatched Gray's attention from the report he'd been reading. He glanced downwards, to discover a trail of pale brown liquid trickling in multiple rivulets down his front.

A brief perusal of the obvious culprit—the takeaway coffee cup in his hand—revealed a leak beneath the lid.

He swore. Loudly. He had a meeting right in this office in less than twenty minutes.

Tossing the defective lid into the bin beneath his desk, Gray downed the rest of his coffee as he tapped a short message into Manning's internal instant messaging system.

Moments later his office door swung open, although Lanie paused before walking in. 'You said you had a problem?' she asked.

He stood, his gaze moving downwards as he surveyed the damage to his shirt and pulled the damp fabric away from his skin. With the other hand he gestured for Lanie to come closer.

Moments later her long, efficient stride had her by his side. 'Nice one,' she said, a hint of a smile in her tone. 'I don't suppose you have a spare shirt?'

'If I did,' he said, for the first time transferring his attention from the shirt to Lanie, 'would I—?'

His eyes met hers and he momentarily had absolutely no idea what he'd been about to say.

She stood closer than he'd expected. Or maybe it was just her height. When she was in her heels they were very nearly eye to eye, and he still wasn't quite used to that sensation.

Plus today she looked...*different.*

Her hair, he realised. It was tied back. It highlighted the striking structure of her face—the defined cheekbones, the firm chin—and her skin's perfect golden glow.

He'd thought her pretty when he'd first met her, but right now she looked...

As he watched she raised an eyebrow.

Gray blinked. 'If I had a spare shirt...' he tried again '...would I need you?'

He looked down at his ruined clothing again, yanking his mind back on track. So what if he'd noticed Lanie looked nice today?

Lanie crossed her arms in front of herself. 'What size are you?' she asked.

Not for the first time she'd pre-empted his next question.

'I have no idea.'

She didn't bother to hide her sigh. 'How can you not know that?'

Gray shrugged. 'I shop in bulk. Those couple of times a year I shop, I figure out what size I am then.'

He reached for his shirt, automatically sliding button after button undone. He'd tugged it off his shoulders and gathered the fabric in his hands before he noticed Lanie had backed off a few steps and was currently staring out the window.

'This is how I normally work out my size,' he explained, finding the tag beneath the collar. 'There you go. Turns out I wear a forty-two-inch shirt.'

'And you'd like me to go buy you a replacement?'

'Exactly.'

Not meeting his eyes, Lanie turned away from the window and took a step back towards the door. 'You know, I could've just checked the tag for you. No need to...' a pause '...undress.'

For the first time Gray noticed the tinge of pink to her cheekbones. He suspected the right thing to do would be to apologise. But with the words right on the tip of his tongue he paused.

'My shirt was covered in hot coffee,' he said, instead. 'And this way you can take the shirt with you. To check the size or whatever. Here.'

He thrust the shirt out in front of him.

Now she met his gaze, and hers wasn't bashful any more. It was razor-sharp and most definitely unimpressed.

He just shrugged. He'd done too much second-guessing recently. The equation was simple—he needed a new shirt and quickly. That was it. Anyone walking down the beach most mornings in summer saw a heck of a lot more skin than he'd just revealed to his assistant.

He steadfastly ignored the subtlest echo of Marilyn's words in his head. *Be nice to this one.*

Lanie reached out and their fingers brushed as she snatched the shirt away. Gray watched as her blush spread like quick fire across her cheeks, but her gaze never wavered from his.

'Thank you,' he said.

She raised the subtlest eyebrow, but remained silent.

See? He was nice. He checked his watch. 'You've got about ten minutes.'

Gray thought he might have heard Lanie muttering something as she strode out of the room.

Something about remembering money?

'He took off his *shirt*?'

Teagan's voice was incredulous as she raised the pizza slice to her lips.

'Uh-huh,' Lanie said, rounding her kitchen bench to join

Teagan at the dining table. 'I guess it's not that big a deal.
I've seen it all before at the beach.'

Teagan chewed thoughtfully for a few moments. 'You don't
think he was...like...coming onto you or something?'

Lanie just about choked on her own mouthful of pizza.
'*No!* I told you. This guy looks like he just walked off a
catwalk.' She shook her head in a decisive movement. 'It's
more likely he happily whipped of his shirt because he forgot I was female.'

Her friend narrowed her eyes. 'That's a pile of crap and
you know it. You're gorgeous.'

Said with the certainty only a best friend could manage.

'I'm not gorgeous,' Lanie said, and waved her hand dismissively when Teagan went to speak again. 'Not in the way
people like Grayson Manning are. Or my sister. My mum,
even. I'm just not one of the beautiful people. And, honestly,
if it means I'd carry on like Gray does, I really don't mind
my ungorgeousness.'

Teagan shook her head in disagreement, but thankfully
kept silent.

It had been a great disappointment to Sandra Smith that
her eldest daughter had inherited not only the height and ath-
leticism of her ex-husband, but unfortunately also the strong
features that were arresting in a man but not exactly beautiful in women. Thankfully two years later Sienna had come
along, and was every bit as beauty-pageant-pretty as Sandra.

'So what are his latest efforts?' Teagan asked, picking up
the unspoken cue to change the subject. 'Other than the emergency shirt-shopping expedition?'

Lanie shrugged. 'Same old, same old. Letting me know
he needs me to write up a report five minutes before five—
so I'm there until seven. Or asking me to book the best restaurant in Perth that is fully booked, for a very important
lunch meeting—so I have to go down there and sweet-talk a

table out of them. And then cancelling said meeting. Plus, of course, just the general expectation that I can read his mind.'

Teagan shook her head. 'You shouldn't put up with this, you know. I'm starting to feel bad. This guy isn't normal—trust me.'

An unwanted flashback to that more-than-a-glimpse of incredible bare chest she'd seen in Gray's office very much underlined that comment. No, Gray was *not* normal. She didn't understand why, but somehow in his office his chest had been just so much more *naked* than at the beach. It had felt personal.

Intimate.

She put her half-eaten pizza slice back down on her plate, suddenly no longer hungry.

'You *can* quit, you know. I'm sure the agency would find you something else—no problem.'

'I know that,' Lanie said. 'But it's not so bad. It pays almost double my salary at the swim centre, and I wouldn't get that anywhere else—anyone but Gray would see straight through my total lack of experience.'

Teagan's eyes narrowed. 'There you go again. Underselling yourself.'

Lanie snorted with her wine glass in mid-air. 'No. You were the one that *oversold* me, remember?'

Teagan rolled her eyes dramatically. 'A small detail. The fact is this guy has an awesome PA and he should know it. He's taking you for granted. Most people would've quit by now.'

Based on what she'd learnt in the Manning lunch room, most had. Lanie had a sneaky suspicion that one of the guys in Legal was running a book on how long she'd last.

'Teags, I could deliver his twice a day triple-shot latte nude and he wouldn't notice.'

Disturbingly, her friend's eyes widened. 'That's *it!*'

'I'm not flashing Gray Manning, Teagan,' she said dryly.

'No, no. Not that—at least not exactly.'

'Partial nudity, then?' Lanie said. 'You know, I reckon if I borrowed one of Sienna's skirts it would be so short and so small that—'

'You're not taking this seriously.'

Lanie raised her eyebrows. 'I didn't realise *you* were.'

Teagan's wine glass made a solid thunk as she placed it firmly on the table. She leant forward, meeting her eyes across the half-finished pizza.

'*Make* him notice you. *Make* him appreciate you.'

'And what would be the point?'

'Because you deserve it.'

It was lovely, really, what Teagan was doing. Lovely, and kind, and all the things that Teagan's friendship always was. Plus also one of the things it occasionally was.

Misguided.

'I'm fine, Teags,' she said. 'Really.'

She didn't need Teagan—or Gray as her proxy—to be her cheerleader.

She knew Teagan was worried about her—worried about how she was handling the continuing publicity around Sienna and her success.

But she was fine. She had a new job that paid well. A fresh start.

Not that working for a grumpy property magnate had ever been a particular dream of hers.

She looked across at Teagan. 'So you can put the pink hair dye or whatever you were planning on hold for now.'

'I was thinking more along the lines of a gorilla suit, but...'

And then they both laughed, and Gray and his shirtlessness was—mostly—forgotten amongst talk of Teagan's latest disaster date, the cooking-related reality TV show they were both hooked on, and anything and everything else.

Except, of course, swimming. Or Sienna.

* * *

Lanie's phone rang far too early the next morning.

She rolled over in the narrow single bed she'd grown up in, reaching out blindly with one hand towards her bedside table. Typically, she managed to knock the phone to the floor rather than grab it, so it took another twenty seconds of obnoxious ringing and fumbling around on her hands and knees in the inky darkness before said phone was located.

'Hello?' she said.

She'd been too disorientated to read the name on the screen, and besides it was most likely Sienna. Her sister hadn't quite managed to figure out the whole time difference thing.

'I need you to come over.'

The voice was deep and male. Definitely not her sister.

Lanie blinked in the semi-darkness. Dawn light was attempting to push its way under the edge of the bedroom's blinds with little effect.

'*Gray?*' she asked, although it was a rhetorical question. Of course it was. 'Do you know what time it is?'

'I have a flight to Singapore that's boarding in a few hours' time—so, yes, I do.'

There was a long moment of silence as Lanie considered hanging up on him.

'Oh,' he said eventually. 'I'm sorry. I woke you.'

Lucky.

'Can you come over?' he repeated. 'Now?'

'I'd rather not,' she said honestly. 'What's the emergency?'

Now it was Gray's turn to go silent. 'Oh…' he said again, and his surprise that she hadn't just dropped everything to come to his aid was apparent even in that single syllable.

At work Lanie could roll her eyes at his unreasonable requests—probably not as subtly as she should—or she could tell herself it was her job or whatever. But just before five in the morning…

No. There was a line, and Gray had definitely just stepped over it.

'It's my dog,' he said.

Instantly Lanie felt terrible. 'Is he okay?'

'Yes,' Gray said. 'But I forgot to organise someone to walk and feed him. Rodney used to sort it out for me, but I guess I didn't mention it to you.'

Lanie supposed he got points for not making *that* somehow her fault.

'And you couldn't e-mail me about it?'

'No,' he said. 'I need you to come over now so I can explain what he eats and where to walk him, and—'

'Okay, okay,' she interrupted on a sigh. There was no point asking him to write it down. Gray just didn't work—or think—like that. In his head it would be far more efficient for her to come over and for him to tell her. 'I'm coming over.'

Ten minutes later she knocked on Gray's front door. He lived only a few kilometres away from her, but unsurprisingly his house was right on the beach. It was gorgeous in an angular, modern, mansion-like way. At this hour of the morning the street was silent, save for the muffled crash of waves.

The door swung open, but before she could even say hello his back was to her as he walked away, already shooting out instructions. Luther, at least, bothered to greet her. He sat obediently for his welcome pats, then pressed his head against her thigh as she followed Gray down the hall. Lanie had thrown on an old tracksuit, and her sandals thwacked loudly against the pale, glossy porcelain tiles.

'So, Luther is a red setter,' Gray was explaining. 'And he's on this special prescribed diet as he has a few allergies. It's *essential* he only eats this food…' Gray opened up one of the many, many drawers in a huge granite and glass kitchen to point at neatly labelled tubs of dog biscuits. 'Otherwise he gets sick and—well, you don't want to know what sort of mess that makes.'

Lanie raised an eyebrow as she considered the size of Luther and the fact that every bit of the house she could see was decorated in shades of white and cream. 'I can imagine.'

Gray met her eyes for a second and one side of his mouth quirked upwards. 'I'd advise you not to.'

Automatically, she grinned back.

When he smiled, his face was transformed. She wouldn't say his expression softened—there was something far too angular and intense about Gray—but there was certainly a lightness, a freshness. And a cheeky, intriguing sparkle to his gaze.

Lanie took a step backwards and promptly walked into a tall stainless steel bin. Some sensor contraption obediently flipped the lid open, and the unexpected movement made Lanie jump and bump her hip—hard—against the benchtop.

'You okay?' Gray asked.

'Other than it being far too early in the morning for me to be co-ordinated?' she replied, raising a pointed eyebrow.

Nicely covered, she thought, giving herself a mental shake. The last thing she needed was another confusing beside-the-taxi or shirt-off moment.

'Sorry about that,' he said, not sounding sorry at all. He'd already walked off again, continuing his monologue.

Lanie rubbed the small, rapidly forming bruise on her hip as Gray described how this section of the house was secured separately from the rest and about some nifty automatic heating and lighting system he'd had installed so that Luther would be comfortable. Plus there was a Luther-sized door to the landscaped pool and garden that Lanie could now just see in the very early rays of sun.

At the end of his explanation, in front of a neat row of hooks hung with multi-coloured leads, Gray finished with a flourish, 'So Luther is *totally* fine whenever I go away.'

But Gray wasn't looking at her, he was looking at Luther, who had stretched himself out, oblivious, at their feet.

'You don't sound all that convinced.'

This whipped Gray's attention back to her. 'Of course I'm—' he started. Then, suddenly he crouched down and rubbed the big dog's head right behind his ears. He looked up to meet Lanie's gaze. 'No, you're right. I hate leaving him behind. Leaving him here is better than boarding him, but not much.' Another pause. 'I'll give you a list of walkers I've used before, and a couple to avoid—'

'I'll look after him,' Lanie said. She'd assumed she would be, anyway. Another invisible line on her job description: *Responsible for the care and walking of Mr Manning's red setter as required.*

'Are you sure?'

Lanie nodded. 'No problem. Although I'd rather take him home to my place, if that's okay? Easier than coming here twice a day.'

Gray smiled, again—a big, genuine smile—and Lanie found herself smiling back almost as hugely. It was impossible to do anything else in the presence of such high-wattage charm.

But then his brow furrowed. 'Do you have any experience with dogs?'

His obvious worry for his pet was beyond endearing. Luther rolled onto his back, baring his pale golden tummy in a silent plea: *scratches, please.*

'I grew up with a collection of my mother's small, fluffy lapdog terrors—honestly, anything Luther throws at me will be child's play. Besides,' she said, dropping to her knees to administer the demanded tummy-rubs and directing her next comment to the dog, 'Luther and I have an understanding—don't we, mate? I am the thrower of the ball—but he owns it.'

She grinned as she darted a glance at Gray.

'That's about right,' he said. 'He'll also love you for ever if you walk him down at North Cottesloe beach. It's his favourite.'

'I know,' Lanie said, slowing her hand's movement down to a glacial pace.

Gray's brow had refurrowed and he looked at her quizzically, as if she'd just said something very odd. 'How do you know?'

Lanie blinked. Her hand had gone completely still, and Luther writhed about on the floor a bit, apparently hoping to somehow wring another pat from her listless touch.

'Because I walk down at North Cottesloe beach. *All the time.*'

'Really?' Gray said. He was so close to her, kneeling by Luther's head.

He bumped his shoulder slightly with hers as he stood, and reached out to steady her. Instantly her skin went all tingly and warm.

'Yes,' she said, quite firmly. 'I walk most mornings. I see you and Luther a lot. You wave.'

At some point Lanie had stood too, and Gray dropped his hand from her upper arm.

'Oh…' Gray said, no longer in concerned-and-rather-adorable-dog-owner mode, but in vague-when-it-comes-to-everything-but-Manning mode. 'To be honest the beach is kind of my time out. I don't really pay attention to much at all.'

No. Definitely no points for that total lack of an apology. She'd convinced herself it was okay that he'd never connected her to that original morning they'd met because he'd noticed her now. He made the effort to wave. It had felt friendly—like a form of camaraderie or something. As if they were a team.

It was that guy on the beach with his dog that she reminded herself of when Gray was being particularly unreasonable, or autocratic, or pushy—or whatever other negative phrase she wanted to use to describe her boss.

But it wasn't even real.

Lanie was silent as Gray handed her a dog lead. He was

saying something about how he'd go and grab Luther's bed, and bowls and food to put in her car.

She watched his retreating back. He was in casual clothing for his flight—a faded old T-shirt, jeans that rode low on his hips. His shoulders were broad, and he had the type of strong, muscled legs that could never wear the currently fashionable, hipster skinny-guy jeans.

He was gorgeous and perfect—the type of guy that you didn't forget.

But the girl he worked with eight hours a day was evidently not worth noticing even when he looked directly at her and waved.

Gray had made her feel invisible that first day at the beach *and* ever since.

And Lanie Smith was *not* going to let that happen again.

CHAPTER FIVE

A MAKEOVER WAS not particularly original, Lanie knew. And Teagan had insisted it wasn't necessary—but she was just being kind.

Lanie did know—in an absent, better-get-round-to-it-at-some-point way—that she needed a haircut. And that the few suits she owned were nearly five years out of fashion and better suited to her at her race weight—not with the extra five odd kilos she was carrying now. *And* that it probably wouldn't hurt to slap on some make-up each morning. There was no chlorine fog to make her eyes water and her mascara run at Manning, after all.

So—a makeover it was.

Lanie twisted to slide the skirt's zip closed, then fussed for a few moments, tucking and plucking at the cream silk blouse.

She smoothed her hands down the fine wool fabric of the skirt, enjoying how it felt against her palms. The price tag dangled just above her hip, and she traced the sharp edges of the thick card with her fingers.

It was silly to delay the inevitable, but she wanted to enjoy how the clothes felt for as long as possible. Right now, before she turned to face the mirror, she could pretend she looked as good in this outfit as the mannequin also wearing it on the shop floor.

She wouldn't say she hated to shop—not exactly. She appreciated beautiful clothing, and was regularly tempted to try on the clothes displayed in shop windows—although she rarely did.

Like Gray, she had a tendency to shop in bulk—but unlike Gray she didn't do it in the name of efficiency. It was more that clothes and Lanie just didn't get along.

The way she imagined she'd look when she first saw the dress, or top or jacket on the rack and the way she *actually* looked never quite matched.

But this part she liked. Before she turned to face the mirror. The possibility that *this* outfit might look as amazing as she'd hoped.

'Come *on*, Lanie!' Teagan knocked on the change-room door impatiently. 'How does it look?'

Lanie shook her head as if to clear her thoughts. She was being ridiculous. Melodramatic. 'Just a sec.'

She spun around.

She looked…not bad.

Intellectually, she knew that.

The slim cut skirt helped emphasise what waist she had, and the delicate embroidery around the V neckline helped draw attention away from her broad shoulders. She stood up on her tiptoes to mimic heels and noted that her legs looked good—long and athletic.

Which, of course, was the thing. No matter the clothes or the shoes she was still tall, still strong and still slightly awkward. That was how people described her: *athletic*. Not elegant, or beautiful. And definitely not willowy—a descriptor regularly associated with Sienna.

But I'm lucky to be so tall, to have such strong shoulders. It's why I swim so fast…

She flung the door open, striking a pose. 'What do you think?'

Teagan clapped her hands together. 'Fabulous!'

It took a huge effort not to raise a sceptical eyebrow, but she managed. Teagan would only argue with her, anyway.

Her friend had a small mountain of clothes in her arms and she shoved them in Lanie's direction. 'Here—try these.'

'You know,' Teagan said through the door when Lanie was back in the change-room, 'it seems a shame to waste all these outfits just on Grayson Manning.'

'They're not really *for* Gray,' Lanie said carefully. She absently assessed the charcoal-coloured shift dress she wore—not good: it made what shape she had disappear entirely—before meeting her own gaze in the mirror. This and her upcoming visit to a hairdresser and beautician wasn't about looking good for Gray. It was about her not feeling invisible any more.

Teagan made a dismissive noise. 'Whatever. You look hot. You should come out with me one night.'

'I don't know—'

'And you can't use the early-morning training excuse any more.'

'It wasn't an *excuse*,' Lanie corrected gently. 'It was a fact. I was training to make the Australian team—not the local swimming carnival.'

'But you're not training now,' Teagan said—not unkindly, but with some emphasis. 'And you definitely need to start dating men who aren't *swimmers*.'

Lanie grinned at Teagan's tone as she tugged the dress off over her head. 'You make it sound like they have gills or something.'

'It's all that waxing they do,' Teagan said, and Lanie could just imagine her friend's look of distaste. 'It's not natural.'

Lanie laughed out loud. 'Fair point.'

She grabbed the next piece of clothing from the hook—another dress, this one in shades of chocolate, with a peplum detail at the waist.

'Although,' Teagan continued, 'I reckon I'd be happy if you dated *anyone*. It's been far too long. It can't be good for you.'

Lanie laughed again, but it was a touch more forced.

'What? A date a month keeps the doctor away or something?'

She stepped into the dress and tugged it upwards a little roughly.

Teagan snorted. 'Honey—a *month?* That would be awesome. But I reckon we're talking a year since that guy...what was his name?'

'Dominic. And it's not been a year.'

Although as she contorted herself inelegantly in front of the mirror to do up the back zip, Lanie did the calculations. Teagan was right—it *had* been a year. Fourteen months, actually.

And it had hardly been some amazing love affair. A guy she'd met at the swim centre. A good handful of dates over a month or so. He'd stayed over a night or two—but then she'd ended it.

She'd wanted to focus on her swimming—in fact she'd *needed* to. She'd known how hard she'd have to work to make the team and she hadn't been able to afford any distractions. Especially the distraction of a relationship in which she felt they were simply going through the motions.

Swimming had come first. *Always.*

Dress finally on, she pushed open the door to show Teagan.

'Oh, this is *definitely* my favourite!' her friend gushed.

Lanie turned this way and that in front of the mirrors that lined the wall across from the change room. She still looked like a tall, slightly gawky Amazon—but the dress worked her curves for all they were worth. 'It's nice...'

Teagan rolled her eyes. 'You're a lost cause, Lanie-girl,' she said. Stepping forward, she reached out to grab her hand. 'But I meant it before—you need to get out more. You've worked so hard for so long, you deserve to have some fun.'

'Mmm-hmm,' she said, and ignored Teagan's raised eyebrow. 'But for now I'm focussing on exorcising Ms Invisible, okay?'

* * *

Gray kept staring at their hands.

One was young, pale and perfect. Tipped with subtle pink polish, the fingers were laced through her husband's much larger, much *older* fingers. His nails were cut short and straight across in a neat contrast to the skin of his hands, which looked slightly oversized and baggy, scattered with the occasional sunspot—gained golfing, Gray could only presume, as his father hadn't exactly spent his working days outside.

Their hands lay linked on the crisp white tablecloth, between the fine china and sparkling cutlery of the table settings.

Tasha laughed musically at something Gordon had said, staring up at him with adoration. Gordon smiled back—a familiar smile. Loving and equally adoring.

Gray had seen it all before.

He looked back at their hands. Somehow it was *their hands* that surprised him.

He shouldn't be surprised. Tasha was wife number seven.

Yes, *seven*.

He'd been here before—to dinners just like this one, organised by the eager new wife, keen to establish a relationship between herself and her new 'son'. Not that any in the past twenty years had been stupid enough to refer to him in that way.

He knew this dinner—knew the infatuated smiles, knew he'd drive home tonight and wonder where exactly his father would buy this latest wife's new home when they inevitably divorced. He might even wonder whether his dad ever worried that his ex-wives would bump into each other at the local, ritzy, over-priced organic grocery store.

Gray knew the answer to that: *no.* His father had perfected the art of the amicable divorce. A multi-million-dollar home as a parting gift possibly expedited that goal.

Yet tonight he was surprised.

Because tonight his dad looked old.

Not just older-than-his-new-wife old—he'd been that for the past three wives, quite spectacularly—but just plain old, *old*.

He looked like a man with a thirty-five-year-old son who'd had said son when pushing forty himself. He looked retired. He looked like a smartly dressed, smartly groomed *old* guy.

Gray's eyes were drawn back to their hands again. Tasha was rubbing her thumb back and forth along his dad's knuckles.

It should have looked loving and sweet. Maybe it did.

To Gray, it looked obscene.

With a glance and a nod in Tasha's direction he excused himself from the table. He wouldn't leave—he'd done that once before, years ago, and the wife of that moment had been devastated. It had *not* been worth the subsequent months of that wife trying far too hard—and his father being angry with him.

He couldn't even remember why he'd walked out that time. This time he just needed space, some fresh air. His dad's place was a penthouse at the opposite end of the terrace to the Manning offices. The balcony was huge, but mostly empty, with moonlight reflecting off the panes of the bifold doors and something sparkly mixed into the pavers.

Gray walked to the railing, wrapping his fingers around the smooth, cool metal, and stared out, unseeing, to the spectacular Swan River. On the other side of the water streetlights edged the South Perth foreshore, and to his right headlights glowed as they crossed the Narrows Bridge in a steady stream.

'What was that about?'

His father's voice was gruff, but not angry, behind him.

Gray turned slowly and shrugged. 'I'm tired.'

He'd flown in from Singapore only hours before. His meetings hadn't gone as well as he'd expected. He'd hoped he'd be flying home with a signed contract. He wasn't.

Was he different without the reassurance of his father in the background? He didn't really believe that. He'd never needed his dad to hold his hand.

Next week he'd fly out again, this time to Vietnam: a new resort on China Beach and a tour for potential investors of the villas already built. He was determined to be on his game. To be the Grayson Manning he'd been the rest of his career.

'What do you think?' his dad asked.

It took Gray a moment or two to work out what his dad meant.

Oh, Tasha. He shrugged again. 'She seems nice.'

He'd never met her before. His dad didn't have elaborate weddings any more—he did Las Vegas, or Bali or—as this time—Fiji. He didn't even bother telling his son about it.

Not that Gray telling his dad what he *really* thought would have made any difference.

Why are you doing it, Dad? What's the point?

He knew the answer to that question, too: *Why not? I love her.*

Right.

And that theory had worked so well the previous six times.

For a brilliant businessman, renowned for his hard bargaining and measured decisions, Gordon Manning's approach to his love-life made absolutely no sense.

It went against everything Gray had been taught. He modelled his business manner on his father's—the way he never let emotion cloud his decisions. The way he always took the time to fully understand or analyse everything. His steely, unflappable nature in the boardroom. And yet Gordon had retired and walked out of that boardroom and—it would seem—straight into the arms of sales assistant Tasha. Three months later they were married.

Gray shouldn't be surprised.

But he was disappointed.

This obsession with the idea of love—and not just any love, but insta-love—and his bizarrely unwavering faith in the idea of marriage despite all evidence to the contrary, was his dad's quirk.

Quirk? Weakness would be more accurate.

'Tell me about Singapore,' his dad said.

Gray propped his weight against the balcony railing. Even in the limited light out here it was clear that his father was in default mode. The sharp, shrewd, intelligent mode that Gray was familiar with. The one that he understood, admired and respected.

Not sooky, moony, head-in-the-clouds mode, while his much younger wife caressed his weathered skin.

That version of his father embarrassed him.

'Singapore was fine,' Gray said.

He wasn't going to elaborate. He didn't even consider it. He'd had almost twenty years of grooming from his dad and he'd just been confirming Gray's instincts for much of the past decade. Whatever his clients and investors might think, he *didn't* need his father's advice.

Gordon raised an eyebrow. For the first time Gray noticed that it was made up of more grey than raven-black.

'You're retired, Dad. You've got more important things to worry about,' he said. He even nodded meaningfully towards the kitchen, where he could see the slim figure of Tasha as she fussed about busily.

It wasn't sincere and Gordon knew it.

But still his father didn't push. Instead he reached out and gripped Gray's upper arm. Gray was wearing a T-shirt and jeans—straight off the plane—and his dad's touch was surprisingly firm and warm where it overlapped cotton and skin.

He met Gray's eyes. They were a near mirror image of his own, the colour an exact reflection. His expression was intense and knowing.

But he wouldn't push. He never had. He'd once said Gray did enough pushing on his own.

'You're right there, son,' he said with false heartiness. 'But I've got to tell you, Gray, you're missing out. About time you settled down.'

Gray pasted on a false smile, managing a laugh, even. 'Maybe one day, Dad.'

But Gordon knew that was false and insincere too.

Because Gray had worked too hard to risk all that he'd achieved on something as fleeting, as distracting and as superfluous as *love*.

His father's relationships—and his own—were yet to convince him of anything different. At least he had the good sense to end his affairs after a few weeks or months, rather than taking his father's rather extreme option and getting married.

Together, Gray and Gordon walked back inside, their joint re-entrance eliciting a mega-watt grin from Tasha. This was familiar too—the new wife's concern that she had somehow formed a wedge between father and son.

Gray should tell her she had nothing to worry about.

Gordon and Gray's relationship never changed. And so it would remain—long after Tasha, in a shower of expensive parting gifts, was gone.

'Now, don't you look lovely!'

Bob grinned down at her, order notebook in hand. Lanie leant back in her chair to smile back up at him. Beside her Luther sat obediently, his liquid brown eyes beautifully pleading in Bob's direction.

'Thanks.' She reached up to tuck a strand of newly highlighted hair behind her ear. 'Just the usual,' she said. Bob didn't take the hint.

'Guess you didn't swim today if your hair's still looking fancy?'

Lanie forced her smile to remain in place. 'Nope,' she said firmly. 'Haven't swum in months. And you know what? I don't miss it at all.'

Bob's mouth formed into a perfectly horizontal line. He took a deep breath, as if he was going to speak again—but then didn't. Instead he slowly—he wasn't young, after all—dropped down to a squat in front of Gray's dog. As he'd done on each of the four days that Gray had been away, Bob miraculously produced a small bone treat—which Luther took, very politely.

The speed which he ate it was less so.

Bob headed back to his shiny chrome coffee machine without another word, and Lanie shifted in her seat so she could stare back out across the street to the ocean.

She could make a good guess at what Bob had been about to say. That he believed she should still be swimming was obvious. It was bizarre. Everybody else—the selectors, her coach, her team mates…heck, *herself*…had known it was the right time for her to retire. She wasn't going to be making some great comeback. She was done.

Everyone knew that—except for the kind old man who worked at her local café.

It was sweet, she supposed. Well intended. She was sure he didn't mean to make her feel uncomfortable whenever he asked his daily question.

And, to be honest, she didn't have a clue why she *did* feel uncomfortable. If anyone asked her if she'd made the right decision she'd answer immediately and honestly: *Yes, I have.*

So, yeah—it was a bit weird…that he asked her and that she reacted as she did.

It was getting warmer now—not summer-warm, but warm enough that in the sun like this, summer didn't feel quite so far away.

More people were at the beach each morning, too. Not Gray. He'd flown back from Singapore yesterday and then gone straight to a dinner. He'd wanted to come and collect Luther afterwards, but Lanie had been clear that it really was no trouble having him another night.

Besides, she hadn't really wanted Gray turning up at her house late at night. Her flannelette pyjamas did *not* feed into her plan.

Flannelette pyjamas were Ms Invisible.

Next time she saw Gray she was determined he'd be paying attention.

Also—she really didn't want to give Luther up just yet. Lanie reached out to rub him behind his ears and the big dog leant immediately—blissfully—against her.

She'd loved looking after Luther. Loved having a silent companion on her daily beach walks and the way he lay on her kitchen floor as she cooked.

She'd never considered a pet before—between her rigorous training schedule, her full-time job, regular travel for swim meets and the tiny apartment she lived in, it just hadn't been possible.

Lanie's lips quirked upwards. Except for the size of her place, they were exactly the same reasons she'd remained mostly single her entire adult life.

But she guessed things were different now.

Everything was.

Gray was already in his office—door closed—when Lanie arrived at work an hour and a half later.

She felt good. So far Caroline at Reception had complimented her on her new suit, while Marilyn had said lots of nice things about her hair—wanting to know the name of her salon, no less.

Not that she'd gone crazy with her efforts today. Some women looked like different people when they were made up—but Lanie wasn't one of them. She'd been genetically blessed with a few good things—long, thickish eyelashes, for one, and clear, smooth skin, for another. A bit wasted on her average-coloured eyes and too strong features, she felt—but hey, she wasn't complaining.

But even though she was wearing mascara and foundation today—and even a bit of eyeliner—Lanie didn't feel she looked all that stunningly different.

The clothes she'd bought with Teagan were probably the bigger statement. Well-fitting, and a size larger, her new pencil skirt and pretty salmon-coloured blouse flattered her shape rather than pulling against it. And combined with her hair—now cut in layers and with generous splashes of blond—it *was* quite an improvement.

So, while she hadn't exactly turned up as a different person—she didn't aspire too, anyway—she *did* look good.

Lanie was putting the finishing touches on a report—some impressive statistics related to the success of Manning's Singapore residential developments over the past five years—when the little instant messenger bar at the bottom of her desktop screen started to flash impatiently.

She clicked on it and a window popped up.

IMON

This was Gray's very own acronym: *In My Office Now.*

No *please*, of course. As usual, her jaw clenched and she silently seethed.

She'd come up with a series of her own acronyms, and her fingers itched to type them as they hovered just about the keyboard: *WPF—When Pigs Fly.* Or... *SYASNN—Since You Asked So Nicely, No.*

But instead she stood, straightened her shoulders, and brushed her hands down the fabric of her blouse and skirt. For now, this job was serving a purpose. So she held her tongue/fingers.

She grabbed a notepad and walked in her shiny, trendy new heels into Gray's office.

As usual, he didn't look up when she walked in. He was focussed entirely on his computer screen and instead simply waved vaguely in the direction of one of the chairs across from his desk.

This was part of the routine. The alternative was that he'd just start talking—or rather, barking directions. The fact he'd waved at the chair simply meant this was going to be longer than a ten-second conversation.

Lanie smiled. *Conversation.* Right.

Her tummy felt unexpectedly light and butterflyish as she walked to the chair.

Nerves.

She did her best to ignore them.

She settled into the chair, notebook at the ready. 'How can I help?'

Now Gray looked up. A quick glance—lightning-quick. He barely met her gaze before his attention returned to his computer.

'Have you booked my flights to Hoi An for next week?'

'Last week,' she said. 'You're flying direct to Ho Chi Minh, then a second flight to Da Nang. A car will meet you at the airport.'

She waited impatiently for him to look up. To notice the changes—to, for once, properly look at her.

He nodded, still staring at the screen. 'Do you have a passport?'

Lanie blinked. 'Yes.'

She'd renewed it leading up to the championships, so it was perfect and stamp-free.

'Right. I want you to come with me. Can you sort that out?'

'You want me to come to Vietnam?'

Finally he glanced up, as if surprised by her question. 'Isn't that what I just said?'

This time he did pause for a second, to catch her gaze.

Then his attention flicked over her—her hair, her face, maybe her clothes. Very brief.

Had he noticed?

Anything?

He typed something on his keyboard, the subtle click of each key seeming particularly loud today.

She knew what this was: she'd been dismissed.

She was supposed to go away and book her flights and that was that. Gray's brain had already ticked over to his next task.

He probably wasn't even entirely aware that she hadn't left the room.

'Why?' she asked.

Gray's head jerked up. As expected, his expression was very much: *Why are you still here?*

'Because I want you there.'

Again back to his screen and his oh-so-important e-mail.

'What if I have plans?' Lanie asked. 'The trip is over a weekend. I could have somewhere terribly important to be.'

Gray pushed back his chair a little and leant back. His gaze shifted a little. Focussed.

'Do you?'

Lanie shrugged. 'That isn't the point. If you can explain to me the reason why I need to jet off across the world at a moment's notice, I can then weigh up whether or not I'm able to do it.'

'Vietnam is hardly across the—'

'That isn't the point either,' she said.

Did his lips quirk up just momentarily? Lanie couldn't be sure.

'I thought everyone wanted to go to Vietnam. It's very beautiful.'

Lanie shrugged. 'I'd love to go to Vietnam—' she started, and immediately saw Gray's eyes unfocus. He thought it was sorted. The issue filed away. 'On a holiday. *Not* with my boss.'

The glint returned to his gaze. Another blink-and-you'd-miss it sense of a smile flicked across his lips.

'Right,' he said. He crossed his arms, but his attention remained on her. He cleared his throat. 'I'd like you to accompany me as this project is particularly important to Manning. We require further investors for a new luxury beachfront hotel. Interest hasn't been as I'd hoped, so the purpose of this trip is quite simply to convince a group of wavering investors that there is nothing better they could do with their money than hand it over to us for this project. I'll be there for three days—wining, dining, etcetera, etcetera.' His lack of enthusiasm for this task was obvious. 'I need you to keep me organised, to deal with the details I tend to forget. You did a great job while I was in Singapore, but our being in different countries is not ideal. It would be much more efficient to have you there with me.'

That was about the most Gray had ever said to her at once. He tended to talk in soundbites, and very much on a need-to-know basis.

Something else occurred to her. 'I assume I'll be paid overtime?'

He nodded. 'Of course.'

Lanie narrowed her eyes as she looked at Gray, as if she was carefully considering his request.

He held her gaze the entire time.

'Okay,' she said, after what she figured was enough time for him to stew about it. 'I'll come.'

Gray nodded sharply, then stood—and surprised her by holding out his hand.

She stared at it for a moment, before making herself step forward and reaching out her own hand to grip his.

His touch was firm and warm. Lanie felt a blush start to build somewhere around her chest and begin to creep upwards. No slower than the day when he'd stripped off his shirt and definitely no less heated.

And a blush just wouldn't do. Not now. She made sure her gaze remained firmly trained on his. Clear and direct, not flustered.

'Thank you,' Gray said.

Lanie dropped her hand from his as soon as she could. Immediately it was easier to think, and for the cogs to start moving again in her brain.

'Not a problem,' she said, although her voice cracked a little and she needed to clear her throat. 'I'll get back to work, then. I'll need to sort out my visa immediately.'

But now she was speaking to the top of his head. He'd sat back down.

'Mmm-hmm,' he said, reverting to the Gray she was familiar with.

Although that was okay. Because today she certainly hadn't been invisible—and it had *nothing* to do with her new hair or new clothes.

But what had she hoped to achieve, really? Did she want Gray to think she was attractive?

No. He was her boss.

Liar.

It was like that first morning at the beach. She wouldn't be human if she hadn't noticed Gray Manning running along the shore with the sun glistening off his sweat-sheened biceps. And wondered...

She wouldn't be human if she didn't want to impress a man like Gray.

And today he had noticed her—when for the first time in a very long time she'd said exactly what she was thinking. She hadn't censored herself—not for Gray, and not for herself.

Not the way she did when she told people she was okay after missing out on team selection. *'I swam a personal best. I did everything I could. I'm proud of getting this far. Of course I'm okay.'*

Not like telling Sienna how happy she was for her, telling her not to waste any time worrying about her. *'This is your moment, Sienna! I'm so proud of you, and that's all that matters.'*

And not like telling Teagan that she was fine working in a job that was so far removed from her dreams and aspirations that it was laughable—and that she was frankly terrified that she had nothing new on the horizon. Nothing new to strive for. *'It's actually really great, Teags, to have this time to re-calibrate. To think. I feel really relaxed, really calm—don't worry about me!'*

Today she'd spoken her mind—over something trivial, but still—and it had felt *great*. Better than the way she'd felt when Caroline had admired her suit or Marilyn had been sweet about her hair.

It was a tiny thing. A baby step.

But she knew she was going to do it again.

CHAPTER SIX

THE HUMIDITY, THICK and cloying, enveloped Lanie as she stepped from the plane onto the mobile staircase that led to the Tarmac. She'd worn jeans for the flight—perfect for Perth in August, but not ideal for Vietnam at the very beginning of the wet season. She could feel the heavy fabric clinging to her with every step as she headed for the bus that would whisk them the short distance to the terminal.

'Don't worry, we're about two minutes away from air-conditioning,' Gray said beside her, rolling up the sleeves of his shirt as he walked.

Lanie nodded, glancing in his direction. She'd half expected him to be completely unaffected by the weather—one of those perfect people who were always effortlessly cool and stylish, as if in their own separate temperature-controlled micro-climate.

Although she supposed she was already quite aware that he did, in fact, sweat. A disturbingly photographic memory of Gray running shirtless along the white sand of North Cottesloe beach flashed unhelpfully across Lanie's brain. She gave her head a little shake and cleared her throat.

Focus.

The small bus was almost full of tourists. Backpacker-types with nut-brown tans, families from toddlers up to grandparents, and a few couples that Lanie would put good money on being honeymooners, with their arms intertwined and bodies touching, despite the oppressive heat.

It was a different crowd from the arrivals in Ho Chi Minh a few hours earlier. There the plane had also had its fair share of travellers in business attire—quite fitting for Vietnam's bustling, rapidly developing economic centre and its population of more than twenty million. All Lanie had seen was the airport while in transit, but even so the sense of sheer activity had been apparent, and she wished she'd had the opportunity to venture outside and witness the uniquely crazy street traffic for which Vietnam was famous.

But Da Nang airport served a tourist centre and here life already felt slower. Although when she walked into the terminal Lanie quickly realised that *slower* was relative.

She'd expected something smaller. She'd been told by friends of a single baggage carousel and walls plastered with posters for local hotels and the tailors that Hoi An was famous for. Instead she was greeted by what seemed like acres of shiny tiles and high raked ceilings. Very modern, very international—not at all the regional Vietnam she'd expected.

'The new terminal opened about a year ago,' Gray explained as they waited to collect their bags. 'You could say that this area has well and truly been discovered by tourists. It's no longer a closely guarded secret.'

'That's why we're here,' Lanie said.

'Exactly.'

And although it was silly—after all, she didn't know any different—she felt a little disappointed that she hadn't been here earlier—before tourism and investors just like Manning had swooped.

Once they had their bags they headed outside into another wall of heat, and a crowd of neatly dressed men touting their taxi services. Many came right up close, offering to take their bags, wanting to know where they were staying, and insisting they could offer *'a very good price.'*

Everyone was smiling, and no one touched her—and yet it wasn't what Lanie had expected. She found herself shifting nearer to Gray as they walked—close enough to bump into him.

'Oh!' she said, stepping away. 'Sorry.'

But a moment later she bumped into him again, just as Gray told yet another extremely keen driver that they already had a car organized. This time as she went to apologise she felt Gray's hand on the small of her back.

Not wrapped around her. Not pushing her or directing her. Just *there*.

In the heat his touch was—of course—warm. Very warm. It went right through her thin T-shirt to her skin, and his hand felt strong and reassuring.

She let out a breath she'd had no idea she was holding,

His hand didn't move until they arrived at their car—which was low and white and expensive-looking.

A man in a crisp shirt—who *did* look completely unbothered by the weather—opened the rear door for her just as Gray's hand fell away.

'Thank you,' she murmured.

He just smiled and shrugged in response. *Not a problem.*

Gray walked around to the opposite side of the car as Lanie slid onto the creamy leather back seat.

When Gray joined her, the driver—who introduced himself as Quan—presented them both with small, chilled white towels and bottles of icy cold water. The car slid away from the airport almost silently as Lanie and Gray took advantage of both.

'So, what do you think so far?' Gray asked.

Lanie twisted the cap onto her water bottle and placed it back in its little tray between the front seats.

'Overwhelming,' she said, then grinned. 'Although it is kind of silly to be, I guess. I'm taller than *all* the drivers.'

This had only occurred to Lanie as she'd stood directly beside Quan—who was clearly inches shorter than her.

Gray tilted his head as he looked at her. 'Why would that make any difference?' he said. 'It's overwhelming for everyone the first time they come here—me included. I'm a lot taller than you and, trust me, I almost turned around and went back into the terminal the first time I visited.'

The image was so unexpected—tall, strong Grayson Manning hightailing it back into the glossy new terminal—that Lanie laughed out loud. 'Right. Besides, you aren't *that* much taller than me.'

Gray shifted in his seat to face her. 'What are you? Five-eleven?'

She nodded, surprised he'd noticed. 'Exactly.'

'So I've got three inches on you. I win.'

There was a mischievous hint to his tone that was new, and Lanie couldn't help but laugh again. Normally her height triggered comments like *Wow, that's really tall!*—and not in a good way. During her swimming career her body had been her tool, and the breadth of her shoulders and lankiness of her limbs a positive. She'd made herself look at her body objectively and monitored her weight, her skin folds and her lung capacity as if she were a racing car engine.

Yes, she had moments where she envied her more petite sister—when she went clothes-shopping, for instance. Sienna was more reasonably tall, at five foot eight, but with long, narrow feet like flippers and a freakishly good technique. Sienna had an elegance and a *normality* to her—no one ever made jokes about the air being thinner up there, or guessed that she must play basketball or something.

But overall she'd always seen her height as a good thing, and had told herself—firmly—that her moments of self-consciousness were a total waste of time.

More recently she was finding that more difficult. Now she was tall, quite frankly *not* a small person, and she wasn't even an athlete any more. Her size didn't make her special, and it didn't make her a potential champion. It just made her different.

And Gray didn't seem to think it was all that unusual. At all.

Lanie, for the first time since she'd arrived, felt the tension ease from her body. She settled back into her seat, and watched Da Nang city fly past her.

Growing up in Perth, she'd travelled to nearby Bali before, and to Singapore—and her swimming had taken her to Rome a few years ago, and to China. But as the car whisked them through the city the architecture was like nothing she'd ever seen before.

In pretty pastel shades the buildings were sandwiched together—the fronts tall and narrow but their structure stretching out long behind. Above them, power lines criss-crossed each intersection, looking rather alarmingly messily arranged and remarkably copious—as if every home's appliance had its own personal power supply.

Around them, the traffic mingled indiscriminately—luxury cars amongst rusted old overloaded vans—and everywhere, motorbikes. No one, including their own driver, appeared to pay too much attention to the road's lanes, or to progressing in single file. At each stop sign multiple scooters would surround their car and then shoot off ahead, two or three abreast.

And then, just occasionally, Lanie spotted a glimpse of the Vietnam she hadn't even realised she'd been searching for: a man walking along the footpath balancing two baskets from a pole across his shoulders, a woman on a pushbike in simple clothes of beige and brown, her face shaded by a traditional conical hat.

'Oh, did you see her?' she said enthusiastically, when she first saw the woman on her bike, and Gray leant across to see where she was looking. Soon she was asking him questions as Gray pointed out some of the French influences scattered throughout Da Nang—from the red-roofed architecture to the baguettes for sale at cafés alongside traditional Vietnamese *pho* soup.

Soon they'd left Da Nang and joined a busy road towards Hoi An. To their left was the ocean—China Beach—and to the right the marble mountains. More like hills than mountains, they thrust out abruptly from a flat landscape, covered in greenery and dotted with colourful pagodas visible even as the car zoomed past.

The traffic had thinned—not that that stopped the driver of every car or motorbike that came anywhere near them from leaning heavily on his horn. It seemed in Vietnam the horn was more about *Here I am!* rather than *Watch out!*

But soon their car was escaping the noise and the glare of the sun as it turned from the main road down a grand cobblestoned driveway, lushly shaded with towering palms.

Moments later the car came to a stop before a sprawling double-storey building—and here the French influences that Gray had mentioned were immediately apparent. Painted in shades of cream, the red-roofed building boasted elaborately moulded columns and a balcony that stretched across the entire second floor.

The hotel reception area was open-sided, with oversized wicker fans spinning languidly overhead. They were greeted by two women in traditional attire and handed seriously exotic-looking juice concoctions, and watched as their bags were unloaded and silently whisked away.

Gray's phone rang almost immediately. He answered it, making vague hand gestures as he disappeared outside that Lanie could only guess meant he'd be a while. She already knew she had the rest of the afternoon free, so she checked in and then followed another crisply shirted hotel employee to her villa.

It was one thing for Lanie to be familiar with this develop-

ment through her work with Gray back in Perth—on paper,
multi-million-dollar pricetags for a luxury beachside villa
weren't all that meaningful—but here, surrounded by this
opulent reality, it was something else altogether.

From Reception they passed the main pool area—a series
of infinity pools built on different levels, each with uninter-
rupted views to the private beach. No one swam today, or
lay in the canopied daybeds. The hotel was not yet open for
business, and none of the private residences had been sold.

Beyond the pools was the beachfront, and here Lanie was
deposited at one of the smallest villas—after all, she had no
need for multiple bedrooms. Entry was through a private
courtyard, lush with thick grass and edged with palms. Inside, the open-plan space was dominated by a raised central
section topped with an extravagant four-poster bed. Bifold
doors opened out from a small, exquisitely decorated living
area to a private deck and then to perfect white sand and the
ocean beyond.

It was absolutely beautiful.

Although it had only been a short walk from Reception to
her villa, the car's air-conditioning felt like a forgotten memory. Lanie's skin felt over-warm again, despite the cool sanctuary of the villa. There was an obvious solution to that, so
she unzipped her suitcase and pulled out a bikini.

With the two pieces of fabric in her hands, she paused.

The swimsuit was new, purchased with Teagan on their
shopping trip. The violet-coloured fabric was gorgeous, and
it flattered her now slightly less than super-fit shape. It was
the perfect bikini to wear at a place like this, but when Lanie
thought of the perfect, untouched, unused pools she'd just
walked by it didn't feel right at all.

Not the bikini's fault—but she didn't want to laze by a
pool, she realised. She didn't even want to simply splash
around in the shallows or order a cocktail while she relaxed
in crystal-clear water.

She wanted to *swim*. For the first time in ages. And a bikini simply wasn't going to cut it.

Minutes later she'd changed into the plain black one-piece suit she'd packed almost automatically. It was one of her training suits—built for efficiency, not glamour. But it wasn't about to worry her with the possibility of parting from her body at an unfortunate moment, so it was definitely the right suit for today.

She grabbed a fluffy white towel and hit the beach. To her right she could see activity in the distance, but here, on the resort's own beach, there was not another soul. Even the lifeguard's tall white chair was empty. She dumped the towel but resisted the temptation to hit the water immediately—instead she stretched, as she had every morning prior to training for as long as she could remember.

But then—finally—she was in the water. It was warmer than she'd expected, and shallower, so she ducked beneath the water and put further distance between herself and the shore with strong, easy underwater breaststrokes.

Breaking the surface, she treaded water momentarily, looking back towards the shore and the perfect white sand to her beautiful villa.

Lanie grinned. This was surreal—this was *not* where she was supposed to be right now. She and Sienna had had plans to travel together through Europe after the championships— but now it was just Sienna doing the travelling.

And here she was—in Vietnam for *work*, no less.

She was not supposed to be here, but she was unexpectedly glad she was.

Then, with one last look, she turned in the water and with a sure stroke and a powerful kick began to swim.

Gray swiped the phone to end the call, then placed it not entirely gently on the small writing desk in his villa.

Then he swore.

An investor who'd been booked in for the weekend had cancelled.

It should be okay—after all, the personalised tour of the residential properties that Gray had planned for this weekend involved a group of investors. Losing one was no disaster. He knew that, and yet it still bothered him.

Not that the guy had cancelled—it didn't even matter why—but because it had rattled Gray.

On the flight over he'd busied himself on his laptop while running through in his mind exactly how this weekend was going to proceed. In itself, that was not unusual. What *had* been unusual was his demeanour—he'd been tense and fidgety. Fidgety enough to be irrationally annoyed at how Lanie had so obliviously read a paperback for the entire flight, as if she had no idea how much was riding on this trip...

Which, of course, she didn't. And she'd offered numerous times to help during the flight. He'd assured her that she couldn't.

The fact was he'd had nothing to do on the flight either. Everything was sorted. Everything was planned to the nth degree. It *would* go off without a hitch.

There was absolutely no reason why it wouldn't.

He realised he was pacing the floor of his villa from one side of the room to the other, his gaze directed blankly to the limestone tiles.

This was a waste of time.

He needed to go for a run.

Gray's chest heaved as he slowed to a walk. He leant forward, his hands just above his knees, as he took in great, big gulping lungfuls of air.

His body was coated in sweat thanks to the still intense humidity even now, as the sun was just beginning to consider setting. The solution to that problem was obvious, and he'd turned to step towards the welcome waves…when he noticed her.

A long way out a woman was swimming. Her arms moved in confident, practised freestyle movements, her feet kicking up a neat stream of bubbles.

It must be Lanie, he realised—it could be no one else.

He watched her for a few long moments, surprised. Maybe he shouldn't be. She had such a tall and athletic frame it really shouldn't be unexpected that she swam—and swam well.

Not for the first time since that morning after he'd arrived back from Singapore he wondered about her. What did he know about Lanie? She'd shocked him that day with her forthrightness. No one had ever questioned him at work before—at least, not so blatantly. He realised it didn't reflect well upon him—and Marilyn's damn words again came to mind—but, honestly, people didn't say *no* to him. Ever.

But Lanie had. And that intrigued him.

She'd worked for him for weeks. And she'd always been obliging.

Although maybe she hadn't always been. He had a sudden flash of memory of just slightly narrowed eyes, a glint to her gaze. Subtle, but there.

Yes, she'd been obliging. But maybe she hadn't always been happy about it. Or with him.

Actually, that was disingenuous. He *knew* she'd been unimpressed with him at times—the days when he was particularly busy or distracted—and he *knew*—normally some time later—that he'd been less than polite.

But he hadn't really cared.

He'd figured she was being paid to do a job and that was that.

But now…now he was wondering what she really thought.

And as he watched her swim he wondered who she really was.

She'd told him that morning in his house that they'd shared

the beach many a time. He hadn't realised. Even now, considering it, he couldn't remember seeing her. But then, even if pressed, he probably couldn't describe *anyone* he saw at the beach each day. When he ran, he used the time to think. And the times when he couldn't face thinking he'd focus on his breathing. Or the thud of his feet on the sand.

It was just him and Luther and his thoughts—or lack thereof.

It wasn't personal that he'd not noticed her, which is why when he'd seen her reaction that morning—her shock and, hurt—he'd dismissed it.

Gray straightened and ran a hand through his damp hair. Lanie was pretty quick, he'd give her that—she cut through the water effortlessly.

As he watched her he wondered *how* he couldn't have noticed her.

Yes, he'd been focussed on the business. *Entirely* focussed on the business—it was all he did and all he thought about. Except for running.

He prided himself on his focus. Honed it, in fact.

But Lanie somehow—at least momentarily—had him questioning it.

He was intrigued.

In a single movement he pulled off his soaked T-shirt, dumping it on the sand, and—given he ran barefoot—he was instantly ready to swim. He didn't mess around with wading into the water. He simply dived into the shallows, the cool water a welcome relief to his heated skin.

Then he surfaced, spotted Lanie, and began swimming in her direction.

CHAPTER SEVEN

HER STROKES WERE easy. Relaxed.

She wasn't training today. She certainly wasn't racing.

She was just swimming.

Stroke, stroke, stroke, *breathe*. Stroke, stroke, stroke, *breathe*.

Slow. Easy. Effortless.

She wasn't wearing goggles so she kept her eyes shut in the water—besides, there was no blue line for her to watch at the bottom of the ocean.

Every now and again she'd remember to look up between strokes, to check where she was going. But really—aside from the risk of accidentally swimming too far—she was safe. She wasn't about to swim into a stray surfer or a boat.

It was just Lanie and this perfect, gorgeous slice of the South China Sea.

She let her mind wander to anything and everything.

Some of it was silly. She found herself wishing that Bob's little café would miraculously appear on the beach, just so when he asked *'Did you swim today?'* she could declare *Yes!*

But at other times her thoughts turned more serious corners.

Within the reassuring, regular rhythm of her breathing she let herself consider stuff that was far from controlled. Stuff she hadn't let herself consider in weeks. Mainly, *What was she going to do?*

Because—nice and unexpected as this trip to Vietnam was—a career as a personal assistant was not her dream.

She'd spent her life for as long as she could remember striving for her swimming goals. She'd put everything into it and shaped her world around it. She'd been driven and dedicated and *obsessed*, quite frankly. She'd had to be to get up at four-thirty each morning and head for the pool. To stare at that line on the bottom of the pool for lap after lap. To maintain the strict training regime and the diet and the lifestyle.

She'd known she wasn't as naturally talented as other swimmers, but she'd had the raw elements—the height, the shoulders, the legs—to propel her bloody fast through the water. But without quite the same intrinsic talent as her competitors she'd had to work harder. She'd rarely let her hair down. Rarely taken a day off.

Her life had revolved around swimming and her goal.

And now she needed something else to fill it.

Stroke, stroke, stroke, *breathe.* Stroke, stroke, stroke…

She looked up just prior to taking her next breath—and just about sank to the bottom of the ocean.

Ahead of her—within a handful of metres, basically in the middle of the South China Sea—was Grayson Manning.

Her lips must have dropped open because salty water filled her mouth, making her cough and splutter.

'Hey!' Gray said, swimming closer. 'Are you all right?'

He reached out towards her but Lanie shooed him away, treading water. 'Of course I'm fine,' she said.

She'd stopped her swim so abruptly that her hair half covered her eyes. Automatically she dipped beneath the water and then ran her hands through her hair as she resurfaced, so her hair was slicked back from her face.

The action had moved her closer to Gray—really close, actually. Close enough that she could see the water droplets on his eyelashes.

She'd meant to say something—something inane to fill

the slightly odd silence. But as she looked at him—treading water before her, with the remnants of the sun, making him squint in an unfairly attractive manner—she found herself swallowing her words instead.

And saying nothing at all.

Gray hadn't really thought too much about what he'd do once he swam out to Lanie. Just that it seemed the logical thing to do.

Lanie was swimming, he was surprised and curious about that fact, plus it was hot and he wanted to swim—so he'd swum out to her.

But now he was here he wasn't sure what to do next.

Right now his body seemed quite content just to stay here, simply *looking* at her.

When she'd done that thing—that neat little dive and elegant reappearance with her hair slicked away from her face in shades of dark blond and brown—it had been as if he was seeing his assistant for the first time.

There'd been moments, of course, when he'd noted Lanie's attractiveness. Her eyes he'd noticed immediately—right back at her interview. And then the first day she'd worn her hair tied back in a ponytail, rather than spilling forward and covering her face. He thought she'd changed her hair again the other week too—her hair framed her face rather than shrouding it. And she did have a nice face—a strong jaw, defined cheekbones and a long, fine nose.

But that was the thing—he'd noted these things and had thought them nice. That was it, no further consideration. But right now she looked a heck of a lot better than *nice*.

Her deep brown eyes seemed huge, set off perfectly by her lovely, lightly tanned skin and the hint of freckles across her nose. Without her hair as a distraction her face was revealed for what it was—striking, defined and different. She wasn't model-beautiful, but she was…*distinct*. Much more than pretty. Much, *much* more.

'I'm sorry I don't remember seeing you at the beach,' he said.

He hadn't planned to say that, and Lanie blinked at him for a moment.

'You swam out here to tell me that?' she asked, raising an eyebrow.

'Yes,' he said. Then, realising that wasn't true at all, added, 'No. Of course not.'

Lanie tilted her head, studying him as if he was a very, very strange sea creature.

He didn't even bother to explain.

'I didn't know you swam,' he said instead.

Her eyes widened dramatically. 'You didn't know I *swim?*'

He would have shrugged if it had been easier to do while treading water. 'How would I? We've already covered the fact that I've been oblivious to your presence at North Cottesloe beach for weeks, so I wouldn't expect me not knowing your extracurricular activities to be a surprise.'

Lanie's lips quirked up in a bemused-looking smile. 'Okay.'

They really were very close to each other. Lanie wore what he was pretty sure was a simple one-piece swimsuit, its practical looking shoulder straps visible above the waves.

'So you swim,' he said. 'What else do you do?'

'Is this *Get to Know your Employees Day* or something?'

Gray laughed. 'Not officially. Let's just say I meant it before. I'm sorry I didn't recognise you at the beach. It's not personal. I've been particularly…distracted these past few months.'

That last bit he hadn't meant to say at all.

But Lanie nodded. 'You spoke to me once, too. Before I started working for you. You weren't happy when I took too long to throw Luther's ball.' Her expression was unreadable as she waited for his response.

Gray grimaced. He didn't remember the incident specifically, but it sounded about right. 'I'm sorry about that, too.'

She nodded again, this time with a subtle smile. 'Thank you.' A pause. 'You were very grumpy that day.'

'I've been told I can be,' he said.

Lanie's smile broadened. 'Your sources are onto something.'

He couldn't help but grin back.

But then that slightly tense silence descended again. Water lapped against them both, making them bob up and down amongst waves that would not fully form until much closer to shore.

Gray caught Lanie's gaze, meaning to repeat his earlier question: *What else do you do?*

But she was still smiling, her eyes sparkling. She looked like—Gray didn't know what mermaids were supposed to look like, or water nymphs, or whatever, but he'd guess they looked like Lanie. Glistening with tiny droplets of water, she looked entirely natural in the ocean.

Much, much more than pretty.

His attention now was far from abstract. More so than even five minutes earlier.

He was looking at her not as his assistant but as a woman. Out here, both of them without the accoutrements of their roles—no suits, or laptops, or smart phones—it was impossible to think of her and of himself as anything but a man and a woman. It was all they could be out here.

Just a man and a woman. Alone.

Lanie's smile had fallen away and the sparkle in her eyes had shifted to something far more intense. Far more compelling.

One of them—her or him?—had moved a little closer.

He could see flecks of emerald in her eyes.

Something else he'd never noticed before.

As he watched she licked her lips, a bead of salt water disappearing with that little movement of her tongue.

Then, in a sudden splash of water, Lanie was not so close any more.

'Race you?' she said. Her voice was high-pitched.

'What?' He was trying to gather his thoughts, far from certain he had any idea *what* he'd just been thinking.

'Back to the beach.' Her voice was steadier now. She gestured parallel to the shore with one arm. 'Swim straight this way till we're in line with the lifeguard's chair, then first one out of the water wins.'

'And the winner gets…?' he prompted.

'I'll decide what I want later,' she said with a cocky grin.

Gray made a show of sizing her up. 'You sound extremely sure of yourself.'

Remarkably so. Sure, she could clearly swim, but he was taller and stronger.

'I am,' she said.

He considered offering her a head start but from the steely look in her gaze decided that would be a very bad idea. He guessed Lanie was the type of person who wasn't interested in winning any way but fair and square.

He could understand that.

'And if *I* win, I want—' he began.

'Doesn't matter!' Lanie said. 'You ready? Let's go!'

And just like that they were off.

He did better than she'd expected. Lanie had to give him that.

For the first half of the hundred-metre-odd swim he was her shadow.

But gradually—completely as she'd expected—she pulled away.

In fact by the time he emerged from the water in all his bare-chested glory she was already on her feet, hands on hips, waiting for him.

The sun was rapidly setting behind her and long shadows were thrown by the backdrop of towering palms. Gray walked in and out of these shadows as he moved towards her, water sluicing down his long, lean body.

Unlike that day in his office, this time Lanie properly looked. She looked at the heavily muscled width of his shoulders. At the defined—but not overly so—shape of his pectorals. The lightest sprinkling of dark chest hair. The ridges of his belly. The way his shorts clung very low on his hips.

He was gorgeous. She already knew that. She always had.

Her gaze travelled upwards again to meet his own.

He was looking at her as he had when they'd been treading water in the ocean. How to describe it? Maybe as the opposite of the way he usually looked at her—or rather the way he usually *didn't* look at her.

This look wasn't dismissive, or uninterested, or brief.

It was intense. Interested.

In what?

The same question had triggered their impromptu race. The race that had been supposed to clear her thoughts, to give her time to realise that she'd imagined whatever it was she'd seen in his gaze.

Standing here staring at him like this was not conducive to that goal.

She gave herself a mental shake before taking two steps towards Gray and holding out her right hand, as if they were meeting for the very first time.

'Elaine Smith,' she said, then added proudly, 'Retired Member of the Australian Swimming Team.'

'This is not what I expected,' Lanie said.

Gray paused in the narrow laneway. 'You said you wanted me to take you to my favourite place in Hoi An.'

Her prize for winning their race. Although he *had* pointed out that he felt he'd agreed to the race under false pretences.

She'd countered by mentioning that, had he bothered to read her CV when she applied for her job, he would have known exactly who he was swimming against.

Which was a good point.

Lanie smiled up at him. She wore a long, summery dress with thin straps that revealed sunkissed shoulders. 'I was imagining a temple. Or a view from a mountain. Or maybe a fancy pants restaurant.'

'So you're not the only one surprising people today?'

'I guess not.'

They *were* at a restaurant—although the word could only be used loosely.

At the end of a long lane—which itself stretched down from the main street of Hoi An town, about ten minutes' drive from the resort—was a collection of mismatched plastic chairs and metal tables. The lighting was provided by naked bulbs strung across the back of a pale yellow two-storey building with dark green shutters and a red-tiled roof that was about five hundred years old.

The contrast between the ancient and the new was stark, and should have been ugly. But somehow this place—completely packed with locals—wasn't ugly at all.

It was vibrant and authentic.

And, besides, the food was amazing.

Gray led Lanie to a spare table—no one greeted customers at a place like this—and then left her for a minute to pay. You also didn't get to order here, either.

As he walked back with a couple of cans of soft drink sold from a bucket full of ice, he watched Lanie, observing this place.

She looked relaxed, leaning back comfortably in her chair. Her gaze was flitting everywhere, as if she was trying to see and absorb everything: the details of the ancient houses that surrounded them, the raucous laughter from a table of Vietnamese women all dressed in modern Western clothes, the older woman who was yelling directions at the restaurant's staff as they ferried oversized tin or plastic plates to table after table.

He'd decided to come here without much thought, and really it wasn't the most logical choice. He'd meant for them both to eat dinner at the resort tonight, alone in their respective rooms, as he'd had plans to work late into the evening.

If he'd properly considered taking her out to dinner it wouldn't have been to this place. He would have taken her down to the banks of the Thu Bon river, where the streets on either side where lined with cafés and restaurants, all serving incredible food at tables located perfectly for hours spent watching the world go by.

Lanie smiled as he approached. 'This place is awesome,' she said. 'Like nothing at home.'

And instantly Gray was reassured. He'd been right to bring her here. She got it.

'Tourists don't come to this place,' he said. 'Quan, our driver, brought me here one night last year. It isn't the sort of place that appears in guidebooks, or in a glossy pamphlet at a hotel reception.'

'That's probably a good thing,' Lanie said as she poured her iced tea into a glass. 'If this morphed into a tourist trap it wouldn't be the same.' She took a sip of her drink and met his gaze over the rim of the glass. 'This way I feel like I'm in on a secret.'

Their food arrived—banh xeo: crispy deep-fried pancakes with a pork and mushroom filling baked into the batter. Gray showed Lanie how to add lettuce and roll the pancake before dipping it in a lime and chilli sauce.

He waited for her verdict as she took her first bite.

'Delicious!' she declared, and Gray felt as stupidly pleased as if he'd cooked the meal himself.

'I looked you up on the internet,' Gray said, after polishing off his first pancake. 'Elaine Smith, member of the Australian swimming team.'

Lanie met his gaze. 'And what did you learn?'

'That you were aiming for this year's championships.'

She nodded. 'That's correct.'

'And your sister is Sienna Smith.'

'So's that.'

Now she did break eye contact, her attention suddenly focussed on a stray beansprout she was twirling between her fingers.

'It must have been hard, watching her win after you missed out on the team.'

Lanie looked up and raised an eyebrow. 'You don't beat around, do you?'

He didn't bother to answer that question.

'That's not very sensitive of you, you know,' Lanie pointed out. 'Most people would assume that's a delicate subject for me.'

'Is it?'

Lanie shook her head, but said, 'Yes.' Then blinked, as if surprised by what she'd said.

But she didn't correct herself.

'Of course,' she continued, 'I'm absolutely thrilled for Sienna. It's amazing to see someone you love achieve their dream.'

'That sounds scripted.'

Lanie's eyes narrowed. 'I meant every word. What sort of person would I be if I didn't?'

'I didn't say you didn't. I'm just not sure why you mentioned it. We were talking about you, not your sister. I don't really care about what she did or didn't win.'

He reached for his can of drink, enjoying the play of emotions and reactions across Lanie's face. Shock, affront—and then careful consideration.

How had he not noticed how transparently expressive she was?

Well, the same way he'd not noticed that he'd hired a world class athlete. It was apparent such an oversight was not difficult for him.

'So you're saying it wouldn't bother you if I was insanely jealous, overwhelmingly frustrated and more than a little bitter that my baby sister—who only began swimming to copy me—has just gone ahead and done something I've spent my whole life dreaming about?'

'No,' he said.

Lanie gave a little huff of protest. 'Right. I—'

'I'd call you honest.'

Her mouth snapped shut.

She reached for her own glass and downed the remainder of the sparkling liquid in a single gulp. 'For the record,' she said eventually, 'I don't feel that way.' A long, telling, pause. 'Most of the time.'

Gray nodded. He believed her. 'Do you want to go for a walk?' he asked.

'Definitely,' Lanie said, already on her feet, as if keen to escape from the conversation as quickly as possible.

Minutes later they were heading down Le Loi Street, which stretched all the way down to the river. Red paper lanterns were strung across the street, and with motorbikes parked along the footpath the narrow street itself was full with foot traffic—only the occasional swift-moving bicycle or a motorbike heralding its arrival with a toot of its horn wove amongst the crowd.

It wasn't late, and many of the shops remained open. Each flung light across the street, and the walls of colourful fabrics inside drew tourists towards them like moths.

Lanie's walk had slowed almost to a standstill. 'Can I have a look?' she asked.

Gray nodded. Even he with his bulk-purchasing approach

to clothing had been attracted to the famous Hoi An cloth shops. Le Loi Street was almost entirely full of them—and this was far from the only street in Hoi An like this. From suits to shirts to evening gowns, tourists could have almost anything made to measure—generally overnight.

If he'd had more time on his fleeting business visits he might even have had a suit or two made. But he hadn't, and he definitely wouldn't have time this trip, either.

For the first time in hours—since he'd dived into the ocean, actually—the real reason for this trip rushed back to fill his brain.

Temporarily he'd felt as if he was on holiday. A tourist, not a businessman.

He'd followed Lanie into a shop, but now he turned and walked out the way he'd come.

Lanie ran her hand down the wall of neatly folded silks and satins. Here they were organised in shades from the palest pink to a blood-orange-red, and the textures beneath her fingertips varied from silkiest smooth to roughly textured to delicately, prettily embroidered.

The fabric covered all three internal walls of the small shop. Suiting fabrics—pinstripes, wool and houndstooth— were just across from her, but it was this pretty wall that interested her. It was funny, really, she'd never been a girly-girl, yet it was this rainbow wall of pastels that had drawn her from the street.

A young woman had approached her as soon as she'd stepped inside, her black hair shining beneath the bright shop lights. Now she followed Lanie with a thick file full of pages carefully torn from top-end fashion magazines. She kept flipping to a new page, pointing at some amazing dress and ensuring Lanie they could make it for her, saying how beautiful she would look in it.

Lanie tried to explain that she was just looking to little effect. She knew Gray's schedule for the weekend inside out, and there was *no* time for this—no matter how remarkably fast the tailors in Hoi An were.

Lanie smiled to herself. Her sister would think this hysterical—that *Lanie Smith* was disappointed she wouldn't have a chance to shop. Combined with her makeover expedition, she was practically a shopaholic!

But here—with this wall of fabrics and the stack of fashion books and files on the battered-looking wooden desk in the middle of the shop—there was a possibility that maybe she could get something made just for her. Something perfect and custom-made that would...

What?

That would make her beautiful?

Lanie's hand stilled on a roll of fabric and she realised she was digging her fingers into it—hard. Enough to tug it a little out of its shelf. The shop girl watched her warily, as if she was about to fling the defenceless fabric onto the floor.

'Sorry,' Lanie murmured.

She turned, searching for Gray. He'd been standing amongst the mannequins at the front of the shop, but now he was nowhere to be seen.

She strode outside, negotiating the parked motorcycles to stand in the middle of the street. Gray should be easy to spot—and he was, way down the street.

Now she didn't bother looking into each shop. Instead she walked far faster than the groups of turtle-slow tourists, her flat sandals slapping on the bitumen.

Gray stood outside a café, his entire attention on his phone. Behind him a blackboard sign proclaimed free wi-fi with any purchase and an untouched frosty colourful drink in his spare hand made it pretty easy to put two and two together.

'Gray?' she said.

He glanced up. Not a glance like earlier today, but the

type she was far more used to. The type that seemed to look straight through her.

It was so unexpected she took a step back.

'I need to get back to the resort,' he said, eyes still on his phone. 'I need to deal with this.'

They were supposed to be continuing their walk down to the river. He'd told her of oversized, giant *papier-mâché*-like sculptures that floated along its surface in the shapes of dragons and fish. And a market across the bridge entirely lit by thousands upon thousands of paper lanterns.

But she didn't bother mentioning it to him.

It was a timely reminder, really. A necessary one.

Gray was her boss and nothing more.

Whatever she'd thought had happened down at the beach clearly hadn't.

It was as silly and misguided as the idea that somehow just the right outfit could make Lanie Smith beautiful.

That was never, ever going to happen.

Just as Grayson Manning would never look at her as anything more than his personal assistant—who had used to be a swimmer, once.

CHAPTER EIGHT

GRAY WAS TENSE. Very tense.

Lanie sat at the end of a long table, her laptop set in front of her as she took notes.

There were no conference facilities at the resort, so one of the function rooms had been converted into a meeting room of sorts. Although—wisely, she thought—Gray had decided to leave the floor-to-ceiling windows uncovered. Subsequently there was no mistaking where they were, with a sweeping view over the pools all the way down to the gently swaying palm trees and the pristine private beach.

For the investors gathered around this table today there would be no forgetting that they were sitting amidst paradise.

The goal was that all of them would find it impossible not to buy a slice of it for their own—either as a private retreat and long-term investment or to visit a handful of times a year and rent out to the fabulously wealthy for the remainder.

It was what Gray did—invest in construction and development and then sell the completed properties. The Vietnam-based corporation with which he'd built this resort—necessary due to Vietnamese law—would retain ownership and management of the main hotel-style half of the complex, while it was the private villas Gray needed buyers for.

Lanie had kept an eye on the five groups of investors throughout the meeting—on the sharply suited couple who made absolutely no concession to the heat, through to the maxi-dressed, tattooed woman with crazy, curly red hair whom Lanie knew had made her fortune shrewdly on the stock market. She watched their gazes drawn back time and time again to the view—to the promise and the possibilities that Gray was spinning for them.

She reckoned two of the five groups were already ready to sign on the dotted line—no question. The others—particularly the suits and Raquel of the maxi-dress—needed more work.

That Gray could convince them she had no doubt. She'd seen him in action before—he was good. Very good.

But today...

He was tense. Definitely.

Gray abhorred the type of presentation in which someone talked at words on a wall or screen. Sure, he'd show short movies, or photos, or the occasional chart or whatever—but generally his skill was talking. That he genuinely believed in the property he sold—his 'product', so to speak—came over loud and clear to anyone who met him.

He was passionate about what he did. Lanie was sure that that alone sold many of Manning's properties.

So, as usual, he wasn't standing at the head of the room and presenting. He was sitting at the table, having a conversation with the investors and answering questions while cleverly weaving his sales pitch into everything he said. Occasionally he'd stand and walk over to the windows to draw further attention to the view, or he'd ask Lanie to hand out yet another glossy photograph, or the impressive projected rental return figures, or research on the estimated growth in tourism in Hoi An over the next five years.

He was as smooth and as polished as he always was.

But he was tense. It was subtle—very much so. When he stood and walked around the room Lanie could see the stiffness in his shoulders beneath his cream business shirt. When he answered pointed and at times abrupt questions he would pause just that little bit longer before responding. And today, rather than *I know* or *This will* he was saying *I believe* or *Expectations are*.

She hadn't really believed him when he'd told her last week that this trip was particularly important, and that was why she needed to accompany him. She'd figured they were basically throw-away words, because she knew at Manning *every* project was important—particularly from Gray's point of view.

But now she'd revised her opinion.

She didn't really understand. Based on her knowledge of Manning's financial state—admittedly gained more from osmosis than anything concrete—everything was going incredibly well. Manning had ridden the Western Australian mining boom over the past decade to remarkably profitable effect. The company had developed and sold the flashy head offices required by the mining conglomerates in the Perth CBD, and had also diversified to invest and build in the mining centres dotted across the state. With the boom, by all reports, now gradually dying down, this new push into tourism and South East Asia was somewhat of a risk, Lanie assumed, but as far as she was aware it was a calculated one.

Nothing Gray had said or done in the time she'd been working with him had ever indicated that the company was in trouble.

But today, for the first time, she wondered.

The meeting ended and Gray left with the group briefly—the resort chef was conducting a special Vietnamese cooking class for their guests. When he returned he closed the door behind him and Lanie watched as he let out a long breath—as if he'd been holding it for some time.

'What's wrong, Gray?'

She asked it automatically, without thinking.

Gray's gaze snapped up to meet hers. For a moment he

looked as if he was actually going to tell her—although maybe that was just wishful thinking.

Then his eyes went cold and flat.

'I have no idea what you're talking about,' he said.

Then, as if the exchange had never happened, he walked over silently, pulling one of the chairs away from the table to sit beside her.

He began talking, his attention on her laptop screen—certainly not on her—without any expression at all.

But every inch of his body radiated tension.

Not that Lanie had any intention of asking him about it again.

Gray knew he'd stuffed up with Lanie.

He walked along the path to her villa, rehearsing what to say. He wasn't getting very far.

She'd thrown him before. Her question—asked so matter-of-factly—had felt as if it had come from nowhere.

He'd told himself that this first day had gone well.

That he had nothing to worry about.

But then Lanie had asked her question…

No. That was unfair.

He'd known he'd been off since he'd left Perth. He'd just been refusing to acknowledge it.

It didn't mean it had come as any less of a shock that Lanie had noticed.

Had the table of investors noticed too? The possibility had floored him. Made him re-evaluate every moment of the day so far.

So, yes, he'd been rude to Lanie. He knew it.

But how to explain?

As if he could just come out with it: *You see, it turns out the reputation I've built over the past fifteen years isn't as rock-solid as I thought.*

It bothered him enough that *he* was bothered by all this.

That he clearly hadn't been able to shake off his frustration as completely as he'd intended.

Who cared that some of Manning's clients would apparently much rather his dad was still around?

It turned out *he* did.

He shouldn't be dealing with it at all.

So, no. He wasn't going to tell Lanie the truth.

But a simple apology wouldn't cut it either. It had become clear that his assistant was not about to nod and agree to everything any more.

And he needed her help tonight.

Gray jogged up the steps to the front door of Lanie's villa, but just as he raised his hand to knock it swung open.

Lanie stood before him in her one-piece bathers, towel in hand—and nothing else.

'Oh!' she said, taking a step back.

His gaze travelled down her body—he was male and breathing, after all—and confirmed that she looked equally amazing in her swimsuit today as she had yesterday.

Tall and athletic, with never-ending legs, she looked like the world class swimmer he now knew she was. One with subtle curves in all the right places and—his gaze made it back to her face—blush-red cheeks and a furious expression.

'What do you want?' she asked. Her tone was pure frost. 'I believe I've finished work for the day.'

The combination of a near naked Lanie and his lack of preparing anything reasonable to say meant he blurted his words out.

'How did you know something was wrong today?'

Instantly her eyes softened, but she crossed her arms across her chest, her towel hanging forgotten from one hand.

She raised an eyebrow, and what she was thinking was obvious: *Seriously?*

Gray ran a hand through his hair. 'If I was rude to you before, I'm sorry.'

Silence.

He tried again. 'I apologise for my behaviour earlier. You've been a huge help to me this trip, and it was unfair of me to lash out at you about something which is not your fault.'

Lanie raised her chin slightly. 'Better.'

Her arms had uncrossed, and now she was fiddling with the towel in her fingers. 'Do you want to go for a walk?' she asked.

Not particularly. But he wasn't about to quit while he was ahead. 'Sure.'

Lanie had hoped the addition of a summery dress over her bathers and swift exit from the too-cosy confines of her villa would help. She'd felt far too exposed—both literally and figuratively—in her swimsuit, and had figured the beach would give her the space—mental and physical—she needed.

It was only somewhat successful. Having a business conversation while half-naked and in what was effectively her bedroom was clearly not an optimum scenario. But likewise walking along China Beach with six feet two inches of Grayson Manning with his suit trousers rolled up and his dress shoes in his hand didn't feel anything like a meeting in his office back in Perth, either.

But still, it would have to do.

As usual, the beach was deserted. The lapping waves nearly brushed their bare feet and a gentle breeze ruffled the dense line of palm trees. The sting of the sun had lessened, but it was still warm against Lanie's skin.

Gray cleared his throat. 'Why did you ask if something was wrong today?'

It was obviously difficult for him to ask, and no less the second time around.

Part of her wanted to push—to make him tell her what was wrong first. She shot a glance at him as they walked side by side and noted the hard edge to his jaw, and the way his gaze was remaining steadfastly ahead.

No, he wasn't going to tell her.

'Well,' she said after a while, 'it wasn't any one obvious thing.'

Instantly she sensed Gray relax, and that reaction surprised her. What had he expected?

'I doubt anyone else noticed,' she continued, and now Gray's attention moved from something in the distance back to her. 'I've just watched you in so many meetings that the subtleties stood out for me.'

He nodded. 'Like what?'

So she explained.

At some point they both came to an unspoken agreement to stop walking, and sat in the shade beneath a palm tree, their legs stretched out in front of them.

Gray didn't interrupt as she spoke, and it didn't take all that long, really.

'Thanks,' Gray said when she'd finished.

They were both staring out at the ocean as the sun set behind them.

Lanie was making a move to stand up when Gray spoke again.

'It's about my father,' he said.

Lanie sat down again, looking directly at Gray. He'd gone tense once more, almost as if he was angry.

'Okay…' she said.

'You wanted to know,' he said, with an edge to his tone, as if she'd somehow forced it out of him.

She went to stand again. 'Don't do me any favours, Gray. You can tell me if you want. Or not. Up to you.'

He stood too, and in silence they headed back to the villas. Gray was walking much faster than before—big, generous strides. Certainly not leisurely.

Halfway back, he spoke again. 'My dad retired a few

months ago,' he said. 'For years he's been little more than a figurehead. He's been my mentor, I guess, but not active in negotiations or anything like that. So, logically, his official retirement shouldn't have made a difference to anything.'

'Has it?'

Gray came to a stop. He shoved both his hands into his pockets as he faced her. 'That's the stupid thing. It *hasn't*. At least I don't think so. Everything's fine. Manning's fine.' He seemed to realise something. 'Is that what you're worried about? Job security? There's nothing to worry about on that front.'

She should have been worried about her job, but no. She'd been worried about Gray.

Ha! How stupid. As if Gray would worry about *her*.

A memory of Gray's hand at the small of her back at the airport, and his concern that day when she'd tripped on the street, momentarily confused her. It was easier to think of Gray as her grumpy, unreasonable, thoughtless boss. Not the man who'd raced her to the beach, or who hadn't judged her when she'd revealed more than she'd meant to at dinner last night.

Certainly not the man who was talking to her so openly now.

It was disconcerting.

'It's good that Manning is okay,' she said. She blinked, trying to get her thoughts back in order.

Gray studied her for a long moment. 'It doesn't make any sense. If the business is okay, if I know what I'm doing, and if this particular project is no more of a risk than any other significant new venture for Manning, then *why on earth* am I second-guessing myself?'

Lanie met his gaze. 'Because you're human,' she said, echoing his words of the night before.

His attention flicked over her shoulder, maybe to the waves beyond.

She spoke carefully, not even sure herself what she was trying to say. 'It's difficult to be so directly compared to someone else. When your father retired it was natural that people would search for change. That they would judge you and weigh up your achievements against what had come before. You'll be benchmarked against him for a very long time.'

'Is that what people *really* do?' Gray said, a derisive edge to his tone.

Lanie shrugged and her gaze dropped to her feet.

'It doesn't matter if they do it or not. Maybe they don't. Probably they don't—not all of them, anyway.' She curled her toes in the sand. 'All that matters is that you *think* they do.'

The touch of Gray's fingers beneath her chin shocked her.

Slowly, he tilted her face up again, so she was looking straight at him. Into his eyes.

'Who are we talking about here?' he asked gently. Too gently.

She took a step back, annoyed. 'You. Me. Does it make any difference?'

His hand fell away. The sea breeze was cool against the skin he'd touched.

He started to walk again. Whatever had happened then— if it had been *a moment* or whatever—had clearly passed.

Lanie took a second to follow him, but he paused a few metres away to wait for her.

Together, they walked again, the quickening breeze whipping long strands of Lanie's hair out of its ponytail.

'So what do we do about it?' Gray asked at the base of the steps to Lanie's villa.

Lanie laughed out loud. 'I wish I knew.'

A moment later Gray followed suit, and they stood there laughing together about nothing really funny at all.

When they'd both gone silent again Lanie gestured towards her front door. 'I'd better get inside. Sort out some room service or something.'

In response, Gray looked at his watch. 'Damn, I lost track of time.' He looked up at Lanie. 'Can you be ready for dinner in fifteen minutes? We're having dinner in Hoi An town with the investors.'

Lanie grinned. *This* Gray she was comfortable with. 'So what you're saying is that you'd like me to accompany you to a business dinner tonight, *please?*'

He nodded, completely oblivious. 'Yes. I realised today that it would be good to have you there. I should've included you from the beginning.'

'Okay,' she said.

But Gray had already turned down her steps, never even considering she might decline.

'Don't be late!' he called out, not bothering to look over his shoulder.

And that was just so quintessentially Grayson Manning that Lanie was laughing again as she closed the door.

CHAPTER NINE

THAT NIGHT WAS the full moon festival in Hoi An town.

Gray explained the celebration as the group had dinner in a café overlooking the Thu Bon river. On the fourteenth day of the lunar month the streets of the ancient town were closed to motorised vehicles and the street and shop lights switched off. The result was a world lit only by lanterns and candle-light—and, of course, the light of the moon.

It was a night during which the locals celebrated their heritage, and Lanie and the investors all got to experience this first-hand, with a dragon dance on the street outside the open windows of the café: three young boys—one beneath the elaborate dragon's head, another as its body, and the third providing the beat with a makeshift drum.

Amongst the celebrations, and at this simple café where each meal cost only a few dollars, they were a million miles away from the luxurious resort where the investors had spent the day.

It was a beautiful spot. Across the river the ancient build-ings also housed restaurants, all with packed chairs and tables spilling out onto the street, dark except for the smattering of lanterns. The temperature was balmy but far from unpleas-ant, and the locals and tourists were out in earnest. A gentle buzz of happy chatter spread from the street to the shops and restaurants and back again.

Lanie thought Gray had chosen well. *This* was what Hoi

An was about for tourists—amazing, authentic Vietnamese food served in the ancient town without any airs or graces. As lovely as the beach and the five- and six-star hotels that were popping up along it were, it was Hoi An itself that had originally drawn people, and it was this town that would continue to do so. She'd been here two days, and that *this* was what it was all about was already clear to her.

Hopefully the group of investors would see that too.

After dinner a line of cyclos arrived to whisk them out of the ancient town to where three cars waited to drive them back to the hotel. Lanie had enjoyed her ride down to the river in the three-wheeled bicycle taxi, seated ahead of her driver between the front two wheels on a canopied bench seat padded in shiny red vinyl. One by one each investor climbed into their own cyclo and were driven away two abreast, so they could continue their conversations as they sped across the cobblestones.

Lanie and Gray had sat at opposite ends of the long table at dinner, Lanie's role simply being to keep the conversation going—especially with Raquel and another investor who was travelling alone. Unsurprisingly the evening hadn't been about business at all—a few cocktails and their guests had seemed to forget about work entirely.

Raquel grabbed Lanie's hand as she stepped into her cyclo. 'Thanks for a fun night,' she said, squeezing her hand. 'I've never had dinner with someone famous.'

Lanie laughed. 'Not quite famous.'

'Pfft!' the older woman said with a dismissive gesture. 'Famous enough for me!'

And then with a wave Raquel was on her way.

Lanie was still smiling as she turned back to the road, but it fell away when she realised how close she was standing to Gray. It was the closest they'd been all night—almost as close as they'd been that afternoon down at the beach.

Her skin goose-pimpled, even though it wasn't even close to cold.

Gray studied her steadily. His face was shadowed, but the full moon overhead and the lanterns that edged the street provided more than enough light for Lanie to see he was truly meeting her gaze.

'Famous?'

'Uh-huh,' Lanie said with a grin. 'Haven't you heard? Raquel thinks she might remember watching the women's relay final four years ago, and she might also have seen me on television. Therefore—apparently—I'm a star.'

'She's right,' Gray said, very matter-of-fact. 'You are.'

Then he immediately turned away to speak to the driver of the waiting cyclo.

Lanie blinked at his back for a moment or two, not quite sure what to say.

Tonight had been the first night in ages—months, even—that she'd really, truly enjoyed herself. Just as Raquel had said, it *had* been a fun night.

Of course amongst the plentiful food and drink her swimming career had come up in conversation. Lanie had forgotten how normal people reacted to it. To her family and friends—even in her old job—her achievements had long ago become part of the wallpaper. But Raquel had been impressed—seriously impressed. As had the others seated near them.

For a little while she had felt a like a star.

So she couldn't really tell Gray he was wrong.

'Lanie?'

Belatedly Lanie realised that only a single cyclo remained outside the restaurant.

'Are you walking back to the hotel?' she asked with a grin.

Gray smiled back—the first time she'd seen him do so all evening.

'No,' he said. 'That market I mentioned last night... We...'

a pause '…we ran out of time yesterday. But I think you'd like it.'

Lanie smiled again. 'Sure.'

He gestured at the cyclo for her to climb in.

'So you *are* walking, then?' Lanie asked, confused. 'I can walk with you. I don't—'

Gray shook his head. 'There's heaps of room,' he said. 'We can share a cyclo.'

Lanie took another look at the bicycle-like vehicle. It was admittedly slightly wider than the one she'd been driven in on. But still…

'Maybe for two *normal*-sized people.'

'Don't be stupid,' Gray said. 'Trust me—we'll fit.'

He neatly ended Lanie's protest by grabbing her hand and tugging her into the cyclo behind him. The driver started pedalling the instant they were seated, and for a few moments they were both silent as they turned off from the relatively busy road along the river to an empty back street.

Silent and…squished.

From shoulder to hip to toe they were pressed tight against each other. The skin of Gray's arm was hot against hers, and their knees bumped awkwardly with every jolt in the road.

And then Gray started laughing. Laughing so hard his whole body vibrated—and consequently so did Lanie's.

'So it turns out,' he managed eventually, 'we *don't* fit.'

It was impossible not to laugh with him.

Their detour took them past a street corner crowded with tourists. Amongst the throng a small band played traditional Vietnamese songs and women in beautiful sashed dresses danced with oversized fans that flicked and flickered in time with the music. As they headed back to the river Lanie began to relax just a little—or as much as was possible given their proximity.

After their laughter faded away they didn't talk for the remainder of their trip—although it wasn't an awkward silence.

Lanie had expected Gray to ask what she thought about the dinner. She'd definitely noticed a subtle difference—not so much in the stuff he couldn't control, as she'd still seen the hints of tension in his posture, but he'd shifted his language, reverting to the more confident phrasing that she was more familiar with.

But she was glad he didn't ask. It was nice to play tourist for just a little while.

She risked a glance in his direction.

His gaze was directed outside the cyclo at the many shop fronts and the boats moored along the river. In profile, Gray was every bit as handsome as he was from other angles. Although this close she noticed he wasn't quite as perfect as she'd suspected. His nose *wasn't* quite straight, and had the smallest bump near the bridge. His just-too-long hair had a couple of flecks of grey, and he'd even managed to miss a section while shaving. The tiny patch of stubble was unexpectedly endearing.

He must have sensed her attention because he turned to meet her gaze with a smile. Of course she smiled back.

It turned out that even now—when Gray's smiles were *almost* a regular occurrence—they had just as much impact on her. It was near Pavlovian—one smile from Gray and her insides went all gooey, with a dopey smile to match.

Of course she knew this wasn't a good thing. She'd told herself that many times—particularly in the past twenty-four hours and *especially* since he'd dragged her onto this cyclo. But what she needed to remember was that it was natural for the two of them to feel some sort of temporary closeness, given how much time they were spending together.

That was what this was. Nothing more.

The cyclo came to a stop at the base of a wide pedestrian bridge. On either side floated giant lantern-like sculptures— far taller than even herself—bobbing amidst the boats on the river. A tiger, a serpent, a fish and more—all glowing in shades of gold, red and green.

'Come on,' Gray said. 'We'll walk this last bit.'

He stepped out and then reached out a hand to help Lanie. Once she was standing, and while he asked the driver to wait for them, he kept right on holding her hand.

Lanie looked stupidly down at their joined hands, but let him tug her behind him as they crossed the bridge. His touch did such strange and crazy things to her. This was different from how she'd felt in the cyclo because—like down on the beach—she couldn't interpret it as anything but deliberate. Sensations fluttered in her belly that she really had no business feeling.

He was her boss, after all.

And he wasn't interested in her.

Are you sure?

More than once now she'd thought she'd seen something when he'd looked at her. As they'd swum together in the ocean. When he'd surprised her at her villa door in her bathers. That moment he'd raised her chin with a tender touch… And maybe now…

No. No, no, no, no, *no.*

She was being fanciful. Imagining things.

She should pull her hand away from his immediately.

But she didn't.

She wanted to kick herself for her weakness. What was she going to do next? Swoon at his feet?

They emerged from the crowd on the bridge to a wide expanse of road on the other side. As the crowd parted their destination was immediately obvious: the Night Market.

It was so beautiful that Lanie came to a sudden halt right in the middle of the street. Gray's hand dropped from hers, and with the removal of his touch he returned her capacity for speech.

'Wow!' she said. Which pretty much said it all.

'I thought you'd like it,' Gray said, looking pleased. 'Do you want to go explore?'

As if that question actually required an answer.

The market was small—only a single row of stalls, plus a line of freestanding carts and stands selling jewellery and souvenirs. But what it did have was an abundance, or even an overabundance, of light. Each and every stall sold lanterns— lanterns in silks and chiffon and lace and cotton and in every colour under the sun. And all were lit—rows and rows of them. Pendant shapes and diamonds, columns and spheres. Some with golden tassels, others without. Some delicately painted, others tiny and strung together on delicate strings.

All beautiful, all bright, all magical.

There was no other light in the market but that thrown by the lanterns—but it was enough. Lanie approached one stall and a woman immediately offered to make her a lantern on the spot, in any design she wanted. Any colour, any size, any painted decoration.

Lanie turned to Gray. 'I don't actually *need* a lantern...' she began.

Gray laughed. 'Neither do I. But I have two from here at home, in a cupboard somewhere.'

Once again he'd surprised her, and she found herself laughing back at him. 'Grayson Manning the impulse shopper?'

He slanted her a look. 'Do you honestly believe you're leaving here without a lantern?'

'Good point,' she said, and then embraced the inevitable by weighing up her many, many lantern options.

In the end she kept it simple—a sphere-shaped silk lantern in a blue that reminded her of the South China Sea, with today's date painted in delicate script at its base. What she'd do with it when she got home she had no idea—it wouldn't exactly blend in with her mother's décor. But of course that wasn't the point.

Directed to return in half an hour to collect her new lantern, Lanie took her time browsing the other stalls, exploring even more lanterns, plus jewellery, trinkets and silk fans. Tonight Gray didn't disappear. He didn't hover over her shoulder, either, but browsed the stalls with her, occasionally drawing her attention to the weird and the wonderful—like the unexpected discovery that one stall was selling, of all things, cheese graters.

Eventually they reached the edge of the Night Market. They stood together in a puddle of light thrown by the final stall's lanterns, both of them looking back the way they came.

'I read your CV,' Gray said out of the blue. 'I figured I should check for any other hidden talents I was unaware of.'

Lanie shifted her weight a little uncomfortably. 'Um…' she began. How to explain?

'For an elite athlete,' Gray went on, 'you've managed to squeeze a heck of a lot into your business career.'

Maybe she'd imagined his questioning tone, but regardless she needed to tell him. 'My CV—excluding the swimming part—is a little…uh…*creative.* A friend of mine made some adjustments without my knowledge.'

'So you lied to get your job?' he said. But his tone wasn't accusing.

'In a way…yes.'

A long pause. 'I should probably be pretty angry about that,' Gray said.

Lanie met his gaze, and even in the lantern light a sparkle was unmistakable. 'Probably,' she said. 'But you're not.'

He studied her. 'No.' A shrug. 'You're doing a great job. And you haven't quit. So that's in your favour.'

'I've heard you have an issue with people doing that.'

Gray sighed. 'Marilyn says I need to be nicer to my staff.'

'Marilyn is a very wise woman,' Lanie said. 'Although you *are* improving. You've been almost nice at least once this weekend.'

Actually, many more times than that.

'Have I—' Gray began, but then a couple with a huge, fancy-looking camera began talking to them in a language she didn't understand—although their hand gestures soon made their intentions clear. They wanted to take a photo down the length of the market and she and Gray were in the way.

So they stepped aside—around the side of the last stall and into almost darkness, with only a few lonely-looking lanterns hanging above their heads. The move had brought Gray closer to her—close enough that she needed to tip her head up to look at him.

'What was I saying?'

'Something about being nice,' she said.

'No, not that,' he said. 'Your CV. If all that experience isn't accurate, then what *have* you been doing for work? Or were you paid to swim?'

Lanie gave a brief laugh. 'No! Surprisingly, an unknown relay swimmer is *not* a target for lucrative sponsorship deals.' She briefly explained her old job at the swim-school, which she'd taken to support the limited government funding her swimming had received.

He looked at her curiously. 'Why are you working for me?'

'Because you're such a nice guy?' she said, trying another laugh. But this one was even less successful.

'No, I'm serious,' he said. 'Is this what you want? A career in business?'

Lanie wrapped her arms around her waist. Her stomach was feeling strangely empty, despite their recent meal. 'Why not?' she said.

Gray shook his head, and the small action made Lanie's jaw go tense.

'You're not young for a swimmer,' he said, oblivious to Lanie's narrowing eyes. 'So I'm guessing swimming has been your life for—what?—ten years?'

'Longer,' she said.

'So after all those years focusing on and striving for one

thing—being completely driven by your own goals and aspirations—you walk away to be my assistant?'

Lanie felt her nails digging into her waist. 'It was the right time for me to retire,' she said very tightly. 'And there's nothing wrong with being a personal assistant.'

'Of course not,' he said. 'If that's what you want.'

She couldn't listen to this. 'I don't have the luxury of *doing what I want*, Gray. Not many people do.'

Lanie didn't want to stand still any longer. She stepped away, needing to walk somewhere. Away from Gray.

But his hand, light on her upper arm, slowed her. Then his voice, quiet but firm, stilled her. 'What *do* you want, Lanie?'

She shrugged his touch away, not needing the distraction. Gray was standing directly below the small cluster of lanterns. Their light was inconsistent, putting his face into flickering shadow. She couldn't quite make out what she was seeing in his gaze—but she could guess.

Concern.

Pity.

'I wanted a gold medal, Gray,' she said. She spat the words out, as if it was a dirty secret. 'But you know what? I soon learnt not to be fussy. Then I just wanted a medal. Later it was enough to be on the team, to swim in a final. Then just being a heat swimmer was okay.' She paused, taking a step closer to Gray. 'I've got pretty good at downgrading my dreams. And how is it any of *your* business what my new dream is? Maybe I've just figured out that it's better to choose a dream I've got some hope of actually achieving.'

She dropped her gaze, staring at nothing over his shoulder. Somewhere at the back of mind she didn't understand her reaction. Wasn't this question exactly the one she'd pondered as she'd swum yesterday?

But then, maybe that was the problem. Yesterday she'd had no answers.

Today she still didn't.

She wasn't going to admit that to Gray.

She didn't even want to admit that to herself.

Gray shifted closer, and now the lantern light revealed his expression to her more clearly.

'Lanie...' he began, then paused.

If his gaze had held the pity she expected she would have walked away. If it had been compassion, or worry—everything she saw in Teagan's eyes and heard in Sienna's voice—she would have been gone. Out of there.

But it wasn't there. None of it was. He looked at her with... *something*. A mix of understanding and maybe respect?

Could you even *see* that in someone's eyes?

He reached for her again—this time for her hand. His fingers were warm and firm as they wrapped around hers.

'Don't do that,' she said, although she didn't pull away.

'Touch you?' he asked.

She nodded. 'You keep doing it. At the airport, the beach, just before...'

Lanie realised it sounded as if she'd burned every instance of his touch into her brain, and she felt a blush steal up her cheeks. He probably had no idea. It had probably all been subconscious actions—nothing to do with her.

'Why is that a problem?' His voice had become very, very low.

She was looking down again. At their joined hands. She had pretty big hands—they were in proportion with the rest of her—and long fingers. But Gray's made hers look normal.

Almost, but not quite, small.

'I can't concentrate when you do,' she said. And then immediately wanted to whisk those words away. She tried to make a joke. 'See? I don't know what I'm saying.'

But the atmosphere didn't lighten. If anything, the shadows in which they stood felt even more intimate.

Here at the end of the stalls there was no one. No tourists, no shopkeepers—nothing.

They were alone.

'Really?' he said. His grip shifted, moving a little way up her arm so his fingers brushed the sensitive skin of her inner wrist.

The tiny, delicate movement made her breath catch.

'You don't have to hold my hand, you know,' she said, her voice not sounding at all like her own. 'I'm not going to walk away. Not because you don't deserve it, but because I don't know how to get back to the hotel.'

Gray's lips quirked upwards.

'Maybe I'm not touching you for purely practical reasons,' he said.

Lanie didn't know what to say to that.

Her instinct was to argue. To say, *Don't be stupid.*

But as she looked up into his eyes, as she felt the gentle touch of his fingers and realised it was most definitely a caress, words failed her.

Electricity was shooting up her arm and her whole body felt warm. Different. Certainly not entirely her own as she felt herself sway towards him.

He was looking at her as he had in the ocean. With an intensity and a certainty that she didn't know how to handle.

She was familiar with a Gray who barely registered her existence. This Gray, who was making her feel as if she was all he was capable of looking at…whose gaze she felt travel from her eyes slowly, slowly to her lips…this Gray was completely overwhelming.

But, unlike that afternoon at the beach, she just couldn't make herself look away.

It was crazy. It was stupid. She wasn't even sure if they liked each other.

He'd moved closer. Close enough that she could feel his breath against her lips. Close enough for her to register that his breathing had quickened.

Had she done that?

His other hand reached out, but it wasn't gentle like the brush of his fingers against her wrist. No, his hand at her waist was firm and sure as it tugged her closer. A whisper away from their bodies touching.

It was as if he was impatient—as if he couldn't wait around for her to make up her mind about what was going to happen.

And it was *that*—that little glimmer of familiar Gray, exasperated, focused, impatient, *imperfect*—that shoved all the other thoughts and doubts from her mind.

Right here, right now, all that mattered was that she wanted to kiss him. Needed to.

And incredibly, remarkably—and unquestionably—he wanted the same thing.

She looked straight into his eyes and he must have seen what she was thinking. Instantly there was no longer any gap between them at all.

The touch of lips against hers was firm. There was no caution in his kiss. But then, would she expect anything less from Gray?

His hand slid from her waist to the small of her back, although Lanie hardly needed any encouragement to move even closer. Both her hands snaked up and around his neck, and her fingers into his too long hair.

She wasn't sure who deepened the kiss but it didn't really matter. All she knew was the brush of his tongue against her lips and then the amazing sensation of their tongues touching and tangling.

She leant into him, enjoying how broad and solid and *tall* he felt, needing to get closer to all that strength and warmth. His hands traced random patterns at her waist and then moved upwards to the bare skin at her upper back. There, his touch made her shiver—and wish that she had more of his own skin to explore than just the nape of his neck.

Lanie didn't know how long they kissed or how many times they broke apart to kiss at some other wonderfully perfect angle. It was a confident, passionate kiss, giving them both the time to explore each other's lips and tongue—and to experiment with kisses both soft and hard. And everything in between.

It was like no other kiss Lanie had ever experienced.

She'd never felt quite so involved in a kiss, never felt so focussed on the touch of mouth and hands. It was as if her whole world had narrowed down to this kiss, to this moment, and absolutely nothing else mattered.

Gray had pulled his lips from hers and was kissing his way along her jaw. The luscious sensation made her tremble and hold on tight as otherwise she had serious concerns her legs were incapable of holding her upright.

'Lanie?' Gray murmured against her skin.

'Mmm-hmm?'

'We should probably head back to the resort. I'm not one hundred percent on Vietnamese law, but I'm pretty sure if we stay here we'll be arrested.'

The words were light and casual, but they were enough to snap Lanie's eyes open.

She froze. Immediately in her line of vision was that poor, forgotten cluster of lanterns—at first a blurry mass of colour but, as reality rapidly descended, soon refocussed into sharp relief. For a moment she watched as they swayed in the evening air and the rest of her surroundings also rushed back into her awareness. The buzz of the market. Music playing, somewhere in the distance. And the almost silent swish of a bicycle along the street.

Oh, God.

Her fingers were still tangled in Gray's hair, and she was still pressed chest-to-chest to his body. She felt a hot blush accelerate up her chest as she yanked her hands away, but before she could step back Gray's grip hardened at her waist.

'Lanie?'

Keeping her eyes on those lanterns, she aimed for a tone

that was hopefully breezy and matter-of-fact. 'Now, we can't go getting arrested, can we? Wouldn't be good PR for the resort.'

More brittle than breezy. But it would have to do.

'No,' Gray said. For an instant his grip tightened again—but then he let her go entirely. Taking his own step away.

She should be relieved. It frustrated her that she wasn't.

She risked looking straight at him and he caught her gaze.

He watched her with questions in his eyes—questions she definitely had no intention of answering.

So she filled the silence before he could. 'We'd better head back to the resort. Busy day tomorrow.'

Gray nodded—a slightly awkward movement. Then he fished his phone out of his shorts pocket and led the way from the relative seclusion of the dark to the multi-coloured brightness of the market.

Lanie kept her gaze straight ahead as she followed him, just putting one foot in front of the other, trying not to think about *anything*.

But her body—her hormones or something—was determined to keep reminding her how she *felt*, and it took an effort to push all that away. She didn't want to remember how she'd felt in his arms. How she'd enjoyed the romantic flutter of his fingers against the skin of her shoulder almost as much as the more earthy, more blatant way he'd claimed her lips.

She wasn't doing too well on that front.

As they stepped back onto the bridge a woman ran up beside her, a sea-blue lantern in her hand. Automatically Lanie took it and thanked her, but she didn't really want the lantern any more.

Which should be unsurprising, given that Gray had so adeptly brought to her attention tonight that she had no idea what she wanted.

Except for a short while, in the darkness just beyond a wall of hundreds of rainbow-coloured lanterns, she'd definitely wanted Grayson Manning.

CHAPTER TEN

HE SHOULD HAVE SAID something in Vietnam.

Gray knew it. And he kept on knowing it with each painfully awkward conversation with Lanie back in Perth.

After their kiss beside the Night Market they'd travelled back to the resort in total silence. He'd studied her as she'd stared out of the window, trying to figure out what to do or say.

At the time the issue had been that what he'd wanted to do and what he'd known he should say were very different things.

Even in the back seat of that car, with Quan only metres away, the temptation to reach out and touch Lanie had been almost impossible to resist.

When they'd arrived back at the resort there'd been a moment when they'd both stepped out of the car and Gray had been sure Lanie had swayed towards him. He'd been sure that whatever barriers she'd built since their kiss were just going to fall away.

And even though he'd known exactly how wrong it was for him to want that to happen he *had* wanted it.

But then she'd given a little shake of her head—like a reminder to herself, maybe—and walked away.

Thankfully, somehow he'd had the presence of mind not to follow her.

But even so his behaviour had shocked him.

He was her boss.

Even his dad and his too-quick-to-love heart had never had an affair at *work*.

And to think he'd been so smug about his relationship history when compared to his father's: dotted with mutually convenient temporary relationships, but never, ever anything hinting towards permanency.

He'd decided long ago that marriage was not for him. His career was his life's focus—he didn't need or want anything else. No distractions, no loss of control, and certainly no risk of losing what he'd spent his whole life working towards.

Besides, he had no doubt that he'd inherited his dad's propensity for divorce. All he had to do was look at his track record with his staff—it was clear he did not do long-term well.

But apparently he did think it was okay to kiss his personal assistant. In public, no less.

Gray realised he'd read the same e-mail three times and was still yet to comprehend any of it—so he pushed his chair away from his desk, spinning it around so he faced his window, and the view down to the magnificent Swan River.

He should have said something in Vietnam. Or on the plane home. Or when they'd arrived in Perth.

So many opportunities and yet here they were—almost forty-eight hours after their kiss and he'd done nothing.

Except maybe subconsciously hope that the whole issue would just go away.

Kind of the way his memories of their kiss had so successfully gone away?

Hardly.

The opposite had happened, in fact.

Lanie Smith.

She was not like anyone he'd ever met...

She intrigued him.

And she'd understood that stuff about his dad—stuff he hadn't told another soul.

When he'd kissed her it had felt as if they'd been building up towards it. As if he'd been waiting for that moment. Wanting that moment.

And then, when they *had* kissed…

He hadn't cared about where they were, who he was or who she was. He hadn't cared about Manning, or the investors, or his dad, or his dad's new wife—or anything.

He'd just cared about kissing Lanie. And then, later, he'd just cared about getting her back to the resort and to his villa as quickly as possible.

But that hadn't gone so well.

He needed to talk to her.

As if on cue, an instant message from Lanie popped up on his computer screen.

Raquel would like to organise a meeting later today.

This was good—one of the potential investors for the Hoi An resort.

Great. Can you come into my office to organise a time?

Of course that didn't really make any sense—this was definitely a task more efficiently sorted by instant messages. But, well…no time like the present and all that…

His office door swung open and Lanie stepped inside.

She wore a simple outfit—a knee-length slim-fitting charcoal skirt and a pale blue shirt. She looked tall and elegant, with the shirt skimming her curves and her legs appearing to go on for ever. Having seen her in her swimsuit, he now knew they did. She also looked neat and professional, and the gaze she had trained in his direction—as if she was making herself look him dead in the eyes—was equally so.

It also revealed nothing.

She had a tablet in her hand, and she turned its screen to face him as she walked to his desk.

'You've got a few meetings already in your calendar today, but I think you can safely move this one.' She zoomed in on the appointment. 'Or otherwise—'

'Lanie,' he interrupted.

She watched him calmly. 'Yes? Do you have another suggestion?'

'I don't want to talk about the meeting,' he said.

'What would you like to talk about?' she said.

Again, very calmly. Although as he watched she shifted her weight awkwardly from foot to foot.

'I'll give you one guess,' he said.

Her eyes narrowed. 'I have no idea what you're referring to.'

'Don't play dumb. We both know what I mean.'

'And we've *both* been playing dumb very successfully, I thought,' she replied. Her attention flipped back to the tablet screen. 'So—'

This time Gray stood up, and Lanie went silent as he stepped around to her side of the desk.

'We need to talk about this.' He followed her lead and met her gaze—as if it really wasn't all that hard to be having this conversation. And as if his brain wasn't unhelpfully supplying unlimited memories of exactly how good Lanie had looked with her hair slicked back in the middle of the ocean.

Ha.

'Look, I'm not going to launch some sexual harassment suit, or anything, if that's what you're worried about. It was a mutual thing.'

The idea hadn't even occurred to him—although of course it should have.

What was wrong with him?

'No, that's not it. I just wanted to—' He searched for the right words. 'Clear the air.'

Well, that was lame.

'There's no need,' Lanie said. 'Don't stress. I haven't picked out a wedding dress or anything—I know it was a one-off, random thing. Two people travelling together, an

exotic location...' She shrugged. 'It was a mistake. I get it.
I know you'd never be interested in me in that way...*blah,
blah, blah*...and there's the whole you being my boss issue...'

Her gaze had shifted now, to a spot just over his shoulder.

His instinct was to correct her. What did she mean she
knew he'd never be interested *'in her that way'*?

She said it with such certainty—as if she truly believed
that he would have kissed any random work colleague he'd
been with that night.

The opposite was true.

'Lanie—' he began, then made himself stop.

What was he going to say? That in fact, *yes*, of *course* he
was interested in her in *that* way?

Was he really? She was nothing like the women he usually dated. She didn't look like them, and she certainly didn't
act like them.

And besides—what would be the point? He couldn't afford a distraction right now.

He remembered how she'd looked in the market, when
he'd questioned her about why she was working for him and
what she really wanted.

Her pain and frustration had been crystal-clear—and he
hadn't believed her for a second when she'd spoken of downgrading her dreams. As if she'd accepted that fate.

She hadn't. She was still processing the death of her dream.

She didn't need a guy like him to come along and hurt
her some more.

So, after far too long, he didn't say anything at all.

'Good!' Lanie said, all *faux*-cheerfully. 'Glad that's sorted.
Now—can we work out this meeting?'

'So!' Teagan said over the top of her hot chocolate. 'How
was Vietnam?'

'Beautiful,' Lanie said with a smile. 'Fantastic beaches,
and Hoi An town is amazing. I'd love to go back one day.'

There. Well-rehearsed and executed, Lanie thought.

A waiter placed an oversized slice of carrot cake between them. They'd met at a café near Teagan's place in Claremont, just beside one of the area's trendy shopping districts. Outside, people flowed past in a steady stream, expensive-looking shopping bags swinging from their fingertips.

'And how was your prickly boss? I can't imagine he'd be much fun to travel with.'

'Actually,' Lanie said, 'he wasn't so bad.'

That wasn't quite to script. She'd intended to say he'd been as difficult as usual—and as he had, in fact, provided a few decent grumpy-Gray anecdotes she even had sufficient material to back that up.

She'd figured it couldn't hurt—Teagan didn't know Gray. What harm would it do to perpetuate the idea that he was the boss from hell?

'Really?' Teagan said, looking disappointed. 'Damn. I was imagining you wearing one of those pointy hats, cycling around Vietnam searching for the perfect triple shot latte or something else equally unreasonable.'

'That's very specific,' Lanie said, and Teagan grinned. 'But, no. Honestly, he's not so bad.'

Teagan's eyes widened instantly. 'Pardon me? Is this the same guy?'

Lanie knew she should stop the conversation, but just couldn't do it. 'I don't know. He was almost *nice* while we were away. Seemed to want to get to know me better.'

He'd been more than nice, actually.

'You mean like a real-life *normal* person?' Teagan said with a grin. 'Wow. Amazing.'

And then the conversation turned to the famous Hoi An tailors, and Gray—at least from Teagan's point of view—was forgotten.

Unfortunately for Lanie it wasn't so easy to move on.

Part of her—a *huge* part of her, actually—wanted to blurt

it all out. She wanted to walk Teagan through her weekend blow-by-blow, so that together they could analyse what on earth had actually happened.

It was what she and Teagan normally did. In fact they'd just deconstructed her friend's latest date.

It didn't feel right not to tell her—but she just couldn't do it. It was hard to tell with Teagan. She'd respond one of two ways: either she'd be really concerned—both about Lanie and Lanie's job—or she'd go right to the other end of the spectrum and tell her to go for it.

And, given her conversation with Gray today, neither scenario was relevant.

It was—as she'd said—sorted. Over. There was nothing to analyse: quite simply it had been a one-off that was never to be repeated.

A mistake.

'Sienna was in *Lipstick* magazine this week—did you see?' Teagan asked.

Lanie nodded. 'With that rower in Paris, wasn't she? She looked really happy.'

She'd looked beautiful, in fact, with her new boyfriend in posed photographs taken all over the French countryside. Blissfully happy in a vintage convertible. Effortlessly gorgeous on a picnic blanket beside a picture-book lake.

'When does she come home?'

Lanie did the maths in her head. 'In a few weeks. She's meeting Mum in Dubai and they're flying home together.'

Teagan pulled a face. 'So you get them both at once? Lucky you.'

She had to laugh. 'It won't be so bad.'

'Is that what you're telling yourself?'

'It helps,' she said, grinning. 'And I can't move out, so I don't exactly have a choice.'

'Why not?'

Lanie swirled the remnants of her cappuccino in the base

of her coffee cup. 'I'm pretty sure I'm going to go back to uni. Finish that degree.'

'Really?' Teagan all but clapped her hands with enthusiasm. 'That's wonderful!'

She raised an eyebrow. 'Am I really in that much of a rut?'

'Yes,' Teagan said seriously, then clapped her hand over her mouth. 'Well, you know what I mean. This current job is okay, but it doesn't really *fit* you, you know?'

'But it's a similar job to yours.'

Teagan waved her hands dismissively. 'My temping jobs are about raising cash for my Grand Adventure.'

Teagan always referenced her planned year-long trip around the world as if it were capitalised.

'They're just a means to an end.'

'But why can't *I* have that?' Lanie asked. 'Why does everyone—' She stopped, correcting herself. Now was not the time to think about Gray again. 'Why are *you* so sure I should be doing something else?'

'Because you're the most driven, most focussed, most determined person I know. Do you think an average person would've kept on swimming, kept on believing, when their baby sister came through and did it all so easily? That takes guts, Lanie.'

'Or stupidity.'

Teagan glared at her.

But, honestly, sometimes Lanie did wonder.

The next morning Lanie went for a swim.

It was still colder than it had been in Vietnam, so she wore her wetsuit. The truly dedicated ocean swimmers simply wore their bathers, but while Lanie admired their dedication she wasn't about to give it a go.

Stroke, stroke, stroke, *breathe*. Stroke, stroke, stroke, *breathe*.

Just as she had in the South China Sea, she let her mind drift.

Should she go back to uni? Or continue to work full-time? Maybe even finally make use of the deposit she'd been so carefully accumulating and get her own place?

Was *any* of that what she wanted?

Gray's question had echoed within her skull all week. *'What do you want, Lanie?'*

Now she let herself acknowledge her answer to that question: she didn't know.

And that was terrifying.

Today, certainly, she didn't have an answer. So instead she just did what she knew: she swam.

Stroke, stroke, stroke, *breathe*. Stroke, stroke, stroke, *breathe*.

She lost track of the number of laps she'd done along the beach—she just swam until her shoulders ached and her legs were no longer capable of kicking.

Knee-deep in the shallows as she headed for the shore, a familiar splash of red came barrelling towards her.

'Luther!'

The dog leapt about excitedly in the water, running up close to Lanie and then running away back to the shore, as if to show her the way to go.

Unfortunately it was Gray who stood on the sand and who Luther kept returning to.

So her original plan to ignore Gray should she see him down here—after all, it wasn't as if he'd notice her—was not exactly going to work.

'Hi,' she said, coming to a stop in front of him. She tugged her goggles off over her swim-cap and swung them absently against her wet-suited thigh.

'Hey,' he said.

He was looking straight at her—right into her eyes.

A part of her—a big part—was horribly aware that she wore no make-up, that she definitely had the imprint of her goggles still encircling her eyes and that *no one* looked good in a swim-cap. Meanwhile Gray, with his hair ruffled all over the place by a swift breeze, and in running shorts and a T-shirt soaked with sweat, still managed to look gorgeous.

It was incredibly annoying, and maybe that was the reason for the sharpness in her tone. 'So you've bothered to notice me today?'

Oh, no.

It was supposed to be a teasing joke, but it so, *so* wasn't. She'd sounded hurt. Upset. Not at all like a woman who'd completely moved on.

'I don't know how I ever didn't notice you before,' he said. His words were low and...intimate.

The way they immediately made her feel—the way they made her body react—didn't help her mood. 'Yes,' she agreed. 'I am a bit of a giant woman, aren't I? Difficult to miss.'

She pivoted on her heel, spotting her towel a few metres to the left of Gray.

'That isn't what I meant at all,' he said, following her. 'And you know it.'

She snatched up her towel and then realised this was generally the point when she'd unzip the top half of her wetsuit. Briefly she considered not doing so—but then, what did she care what Gray thought?

As casually as she could she unzipped her top, peeling it down to her waist. She'd worn her new violet bikini today, and strongly wished she hadn't.

She didn't bother responding to his last comment. She didn't fully understand her frustration—in fact she had no idea why she was standing here so wound up with tension.

Why was she angry at Gray?

She glanced at Gray, meaning to say something—something about not being at her best this early in the morning, maybe—when the way he was looking at her stole the words from her throat.

He was most definitely checking her out. And she was almost one hundred percent certain that he liked what he saw. The intensity of his attention—of his *appreciation*—was like a physical touch against her skin, warm and tingling. It skimmed across her from her hips, where the wetsuit hung low, to the indent of her waist and upwards, over the small-ish curves of her breasts.

And finally to her face.

His gaze locked with hers, and she saw that he knew that *she* knew what he'd been doing.

He shrugged without even the hint of an apology. 'I have no idea how I ever didn't notice you, Lanie Smith.'

Then he turned and with Luther trotting obediently beside him walked away.

'See you at work,' he called out, and the words were whipped away by the breeze.

CHAPTER ELEVEN

THE NEXT MORNING, when Gray ran with Luther along North Cottesloe beach, Lanie was there again.

As he ran he'd occasionally search for her in the water—looking for the rhythmic splash of her kicks and the elegant way her arms sliced through the water.

When she emerged from the ocean Luther spotted her immediately and sprinted across the sand and through the water to get to her as quickly as possible. Gray couldn't have stopped him, anyway—but he didn't even try. Instead he followed in Luther's footsteps, meeting Lanie just as she stepped across the line where the sand switched abruptly from soaked and grey to almost blindingly pristine dry and white.

'Hey,' he said.

Gray wasn't sure what to expect. Yesterday at work she'd done her ultra-professional thing and it had been as if they were seeing each other for the first time that day.

Definitely not as if he'd all but imprinted the image of Lanie in that amazing bikini onto his brain.

'Hi,' Lanie said eventually—quite softly, as if she wasn't really sure talking to him was that good an idea.

He knew how she felt.

'I received an e-mail late last night from Raquel,' he said. 'She wants one of the three-bedroom villas.'

He'd planned to tell her at work, not here, but the words had burst out.

Lanie's face broke into a wide, genuine smile. 'That's fantastic!'

'Yeah,' he said as they walked to her towel. 'A big relief, too.'

He hadn't understood how much until right this moment. And Lanie got that too. She knew how important this deal was to him, and pleasure in his success was reflected in her expression.

After Lanie had stripped out of her wetsuit—she wore her one-piece bathers today, Gray noted with some disappointment—she towelled off and pulled on a tracksuit. Together they walked up the beach to the street. Gray had Luther sit while he reattached his lead to the dog's collar and he saw Lanie wave to someone. He followed her gaze to the tired-looking beach café—empty this early in the morning—and the man with the shock of white hair who was waving back to Lanie as he wiped down a table.

'Bob's my biggest fan,' Lanie said, then grinned. 'Quite possibly my only fan, actually.'

And then, together, they walked up the road, talking about the new deal—until Lanie turned up her street and Gray and Luther kept on walking along the parade.

'See you at work,' Lanie said.

But at work the beach was never mentioned.

'My dad's new wife dropped by last night,' Gray said as they walked along the beach the next day.

Lanie hadn't been surprised to see Gray waiting for her on the shore when she'd emerged from the ocean. She didn't understand why he was, but she did know seeing him watching her walk through the waves made her smile. And for now that would have to do, because she'd discovered that thinking about Gray—about any of this—was far too confusing. She didn't understand it, and certainly didn't understand Gray.

Today their conversation had been about not much—a bit

about work, but mostly nothing too important or serious—and they'd both gradually relaxed. But Gray's tone had shifted at the mention of his father.

'New wife?'

Gray nodded. 'Number seven.'

'Seven! Do you have any brothers or sisters?'

He shook his head. 'No, I'm the only one—the result of marriage number two. It was the longest my father remained married—almost three years, actually.'

'Are you close to your mum?' Lanie asked.

'We're in touch occasionally, but we're not close. My dad was really my primary carer as I grew up. He was great—very hands-on—and he'd often drag me with him to work rather than hiring a nanny or sending me to childcare. Mum went back to Sydney, where she's from, after they split, although I saw her on school holidays.'

'When you were—what? Three?' Lanie asked, incredulous.

'Two,' Gray confirmed. 'As I said, we're not close.'

Lanie nodded, but was unable to imagine a mother walking away from a child that young. For all her own mother's flaws, Lanie knew her mum loved her.

But then she guessed her father had done exactly the same thing just a few years later.

'My dad worked away,' Lanie said. 'And then left for good when I was eleven. He didn't even bother to stay in touch.'

Gray slowed down his pace just a little as he turned to her. 'So you don't see him at all?'

'Not once since he left.'

The words were matter-of-fact, but it irritated Lanie that she still felt a faint kick in the guts as she spoke. Her dad wasn't worth worrying about, and certainly not worthy of any remnants of hurt and regret.

'That sucks.'

Lanie shrugged. 'Hey, at least he gave me these shoulders,'

she said, with a grin that she only had to force a little. 'So, the new wife came over...?'

'Yeah.' Gray rubbed his forehead. 'I don't get it. It happens every time. These women inexplicably feel the need to *connect* with me. To *know* me. When I know it's a total waste of time. This one will be gone in a year—guaranteed.'

Lanie snorted with laughter. 'Wow. I can't see at *all* why this poor woman is feeling insecure around you.'

Gray looked so surprised at her comment Lanie laughed some more. 'Oh, come on. I can just imagine how you'd be around her. Probably like you were with me at first.'

And how he still was, at times. Not down here at the beach but at work, where he got so caught up in what he was doing that her presence seemed to cease to register altogether.

He opened his mouth as if he was going to protest, but then stopped. 'Possibly,' he finally conceded.

Ahead of them Luther had found a friend—a small black poodle—and together they took turns chasing each other into the water.

'But what if this one—wife number seven—is, in fact, *the one*?' Lanie asked. 'Isn't it worth getting to know her just in case?'

Now Gray laughed. 'She's barely ten years older than me. It's not going to last. My dad's one flaw is his inability to be sensible around women. For such a successful, accomplished, intelligent guy, his stubborn faith in love is bizarre. In that way I'm nothing like him.'

Lanie smiled. 'I never would've guessed.'

The Manning office gossip had confirmed what Lanie had already guessed: Gray's previous relationships had been both short-lived and superficial. Since his father had retired the consensus was that he'd been seeing no one at all, so complete was his focus on work.

'I'm not sure I agree that being a success and believing in love are mutually exclusive things,' Lanie pointed out.

'Maybe they aren't for some people,' he said. 'But my dad has lost millions with each of his marriages. And yet he keeps going back for more.'

Lanie had never heard Gray criticise his father, but his scorn for his dad's romantic history was obvious.

'And has that caused him financial difficulty?'

'With his early marriages, yes—although he argues now that it was what spurred him on to diversify the business, to take risks. Because he needed the money.'

'So he's a risk-taker in life *and* in love?' Lanie said.

'Yeah.' Gray didn't sound so happy about it.

'I think that's nice.'

They'd almost reached Luther, who was busily digging a hole now his poodle friend had left with his owner.

'Really?' Gray said. 'You don't strike me as such a romantic.'

Lanie wasn't sure if she should be offended by that. 'I like the idea of love. Of marriage and a happy-ever-after.' She paused, trying to think how to phrase this. 'But I guess more in an abstract way. Something for other people to do, not me.'

'And why not you?'

Lanie laughed. 'My longest ever relationship was two months,' she said. 'I'm not much good at them.'

She said it lightly, although Gray's gaze still sharpened as he looked at her.

'I don't know, Lanie, I—'

Gray's words were cut off by a loud yelp.

Luther.

The dog was holding his paw in the air.

Instantly, they both broke into a run.

Gray dropped to his knees in the sand, reaching out gently to inspect Luther's paw. Immediately blood splashed onto Gray's arm—blood that hadn't been obvious against Luther's dark coat.

Lanie spotted the culprit—the dog had managed to dig up

a small pile of broken bottles that some thoughtless person had long ago buried.

'He's got shards stuck all over him,' Gray said, worry heavy in his voice.

'Take him to a vet,' Lanie said. 'I'll clean this up so other dogs don't do the same thing. And I'll cancel your meetings for today.'

Gray just nodded as he hoisted Luther up into his arms, his attention entirely on his dog.

Lanie watched as he ran up to the street, faster than she'd ever seen him run before despite the heavy weight he was carrying.

Then she laid out her towel and started piling it up with glass, piece by piece.

By the time Lanie drove up to Gray's front door she knew she'd made a mistake.

She'd questioned her decision to drop by on her way home from work more than once. Firstly when she'd gone shopping in her lunch break for a large rawhide bone for Luther.

At the time she'd figured it could wait—she would simply give the treat to Gray at work tomorrow. But then she wouldn't know how Luther was.

In which case calling him should have seemed the obvious option. Except she could just imagine how that phone call would go. Odds were she'd call at a particularly inconvenient time, Gray would be all distracted, and she'd be lucky to get a handful of words out of him.

So she'd told herself dropping by on the way home from work—especially as it was kind of on her way—seemed reasonable.

Until she'd actually been in her car on the way here.

Was she breaking the rules? Did they even *have* rules around their daily beach meetings?

She had no idea.

She glanced at the bone on her passenger seat, complete with a big red bow, and pulled herself together.

She was worried about Luther and had brought him a present. That was it. No more, no less. If Gray thought that was horribly inappropriate and it meant the end of whatever it was they were doing at the beach then so be it.

Maybe the beach thing was over now, anyway.

It was never going to last, their semi-friendship. Kind of like that one-off kiss. She should have known it was temporary right from the start.

Right. So. Yes. She was going to go to Gray's house and give Luther his bone.

She'd laughed at the analysis that had required her to get to that point at the time.

Now—at Gray's front door—her hesitation didn't seem so ridiculous after all.

This was a mistake. She shouldn't be here. Gray wouldn't want her here.

She knelt down in her slim-fitting trousers to leave the bone at the front door.

Maybe she'd send Gray a text to let him know she'd left it. Or ring the doorbell and then run away like some eleven-year-old playing a prank.

That idea—and the image of her running down Marine Parade in her heels—made her giggle. She was still giggling when the door swung open.

'Lanie?'

She looked up from where she was crouching on his door-step—up long legs clad in faded jeans to his soft, ancient-looking T-shirt—to his bemused expression.

She shot to her feet. 'Oh!' she said. Then thrust out the bone she still held in his direction. 'I bought Luther a bone.'

'Thanks,' Gray said, and his lips kept quirking upwards, as if he was trying not to smile. 'Nice bow.'

'I thought so,' she said. 'Anyway, I didn't want to disturb you, so I'll just get going...'

'Do you want to see Luther?'

Lanie knew it was far from wise to stay any longer, and yet she found herself nodding enthusiastically. 'Yes, please. How is he?'

Gray held the door open for her, then followed her inside. 'He's okay. He needed some stitches, so he's a bit dopey from the anaesthetic, but he'll be as good as new in a few weeks' time.'

'That's excellent.'

Luther was curled up on a big cushion on the floor in Gray's lounge room. The huge windows showcased the rapidly setting sun and also provided an unobstructed view of the front porch. With the window's dark tinting on the outside she'd had no idea she was being watched. No wonder he'd been hiding a laugh—how long had she been dithering out there?

'Why didn't you knock?' he asked.

'I didn't want to bother you.'

'What if I don't mind being bothered?'

Lanie laughed. 'You hate being bothered.'

He shrugged. 'For you I'll make an exception.'

Suddenly uncomfortable, Lanie knelt down in front of Luther and scratched behind his long, floppy ears. He wore a large plastic cone to stop him licking his wounds, and looked most unhappy about the situation. 'Hey, buddy,' she said, low and soothing. 'You doing okay?'

Luther looked up at her with his gorgeous chocolate eyes and out of nowhere, Lanie felt her throat tighten.

What was she upset about? Luther, thank goodness, was going to be okay.

She stood up, walking briskly over to the kitchen to put some space between herself and Gray. 'Do you mind if I grab some water?' she asked.

Gray followed her—which wasn't part of the plan. So she moved to the opposite side of the bench as he found her a glass, needing that large slab of granite between them.

'I should've called you,' Gray said as he pushed her water across the counter top. 'Told you how he was.' He nodded in Luther's direction.

'No,' Lanie said, 'of course you shouldn't. You had Luther to worry about.'

He shook his head. 'I should've called you,' he repeated. 'I'm sorry.'

Lanie wrapped her fingers around the frosty glass. 'Okay,' she said. 'I'm glad you didn't come into work, though. I'm sure Luther appreciated it.'

Gray tilted his head back a little, as if he was suddenly intensely fascinated by his ceiling. He gave a short bark of laughter.

'That wasn't entirely why I didn't come in.' His gaze dropped to meet hers and he leant forward, gripping the edge of the granite with both hands. 'I didn't come in because I received *two* phone calls this morning while I was at the vet. Two more of the Hoi An potentials.' A pause. 'They're out.' He managed a humourless grin. 'Great timing, too.'

'Oh, Gray,' Lanie said, resisting the urge to go to him and…and *what,* exactly? She stayed put. 'I'm really surprised.'

'Me too,' he said. 'After Raquel signed up I thought I had it in the bag. That all that stuff we talked about in Vietnam really didn't matter—that nothing actually had changed since my dad retired.' He laughed again. 'That it was all in my head. Guess not.'

'It probably has nothing to do with you,' Lanie said. 'The investment just wasn't right for them.'

'What I do, Lanie, is target the right investors with the right projects at the right time. Those investors all had money to spend, and I'd hand-selected them. If the product was wrong for them that's *my* fault. If the weekend sales pitch was wrong for them, that's my fault too.' He walked to the fridge and grabbed a long-necked bottle of beer. Lanie watched as he twisted off the top and then just left the beer on the counter, as if he'd already changed his mind. 'So I stayed home this afternoon to mope with Luther.' He did that ugly grin again. 'Real professional of me.'

'I think you're being too tough on yourself,' Lanie said. 'I'm sure no one has a one hundred percent strike rate with this type of thing—not even your dad. You did your best. That's all you can do.'

His gaze jerked up to tangle with hers. Instantly she knew where this was going and took a step backwards before she'd even realised what she was doing.

'*Really, Lanie*? You think that doing your best is all that matters? I find that hard to believe.'

There was no point pretending she didn't understand what he meant.

Very deliberately, Lanie stepped forward again. 'I *did* do the best I could. I trained the hardest I could. I swam the best I could—my best time *ever* in the selection trials. I'm proud of what I achieved. That *is* all that matters.'

'You're right,' Gray said. 'Of course you're right. You should be incredibly proud of what you achieved—you *are* a champion. But I don't think you really believe that, do you?'

Lanie stared at her untouched water glass. 'I don't really think this is any of your business.'

'Why not?'

Her head jerked up. 'Because you're my boss and I'm your employee. This is all a bit personal, don't you think?'

All Lanie's sensible plans to remain on her side of the counter were ruined as Gray strode over to her. She crossed her arms, not about to back down.

'Is that all we are, Lanie?'

She nodded, very stiffly. 'Haven't we already covered this?'

'What are we doing at the beach each morning?'

Lanie shrugged. 'I swim. You run. We happen to do it at the same time.'

'Come on. That's crap and you know it. Why are you being so stubborn about this?'

Her eyes narrowed. 'I should get going.' She went to step around Gray. 'Bye, Luther,' she said.

But Gray grabbed her hand as she brushed past. 'Wait.'

She was right next to him and she twisted around to meet his gaze. 'Please don't touch me.'

He didn't loosen his grip one iota. But then she knew if she really wanted to pull away, she could. But she didn't.

She couldn't.

'Why can't I touch you?' Gray said, a dangerous glint to his slate-grey eyes. 'Because you can't concentrate? Why *is* that?'

Lanie glared at him. 'You know perfectly well what it is. You probably have women collapsing at your feet all the time. Don't act like you don't know the effect you have on women. You know *exactly* what you're doing.'

He took a step closer to her. Too close. But she felt frozen in place, incapable of doing anything but *looking* at him.

'Yes, I know what I'm doing,' Gray said, all soft and low. 'I can't speak for other women, but I have a pretty good idea what I do to *you*.'

Her body already felt hot, confused. Now an all-over mortified blush was added to the mix. Why did she have to be so transparent?

Finally her ability to use her limbs returned and she tugged her hand from his grip, taking a handful of steps away before turning to face him. 'What are you trying to prove? Just exactly how smug and arrogant you are?'

He walked towards her. Slow, deliberate steps.

'Has it ever occurred to you, Lanie Smith, that you have the same effect on me?'

All she could do was stare at him.

He took another step. Close enough to touch.

'I—' she began—but she really had no idea what to say. Her instinct was to deny—to shake her head and tell him that he was wrong, that this was unfair, that he didn't really mean that.

But would she actually believe what she was saying?

Did she really believe that incredible kiss at the Night Market had really been so one-sided? That their daily meetings at the beach were solely between work colleagues—or at a stretch, friends?

Or was it more that she hadn't wanted to acknowledge what was going on? That she didn't want to allow herself to consider—or hope—it was something more?

Because she knew she couldn't deal with another *no* right now. Another rejection. Another failure.

'What are we doing?' she managed eventually. 'What *is* this?'

Gray's lips quirked upwards. 'I have absolutely no idea. But right now I'd really like to kiss you.'

Well, when he put it like that...

What to do seemed obvious—the only thing possible. She reached for him blindly, her hand landing on his chest. Instantly his arms wrapped around her, pulling her close while he turned her, lifted her, and the next thing she knew she was sitting on the counter-top, Gray standing between her legs, her face cradled between his hands.

She'd never felt so delicate, so light—so sexy.

Then his mouth touched hers.

And just like at the Night Market suddenly it was as if this kiss was her whole world.

But this time there was no prelude, no preliminaries—it was immediately and completely desperate. He tasted delicious, fresh and clean, and he kissed her as if he'd been thinking about doing nothing else for weeks.

It was overwhelming—but also unbelievably good. With each and every kiss she felt her doubts flutter away.

That Gray was kissing *her*, that he wanted *her*, was obvious in every touch, every breath. His hands slid from her face to her waist, doing electric, shivery things to her insides as his hands moved upwards.

She had to get closer to him, had to feel his skin, and she tugged him closer, pushing his T-shirt up in messy handfuls of cotton.

His skin was hot beneath her palms—hot and firm and lean. He was kissing his way up her jaw to her throat and she heard his sharp intake of breath when she ran her fingernails along his spine. She gave a little laugh of surprise and felt his lips form a smile against her skin.

'Told you,' he said.

And she laughed again, before his hands, his mouth, just *him* swiftly converted it to a sigh. Then he was kissing her mouth again. And from then on that kiss—this night—was all that mattered.

CHAPTER TWELVE

'TELL ME ABOUT your swimming.'

Lanie turned on her side to face Gray in bed. He'd propped his head on his hand and his gaze traced over her shape beneath the bedsheet. Said sheet had dipped quite low on his side of the bed, and Lanie found herself distracted by how lovely all that naked skin looked in the soft light of Gray's bedside lamp.

She cleared her throat. 'Um…*that's* what you want to talk about right now?'

He grinned. 'It's not every night I have a swimming champion in my bed.'

'Former swimmer.'

'Oh, yeah,' he said, looking thoughtful. 'Good point. Come to think of it, I've had *many* former world-class athletes. It's easy to lose track with all those women collapsing at my feet.'

She shoved him in the chest, but ruined the effect by giggling.

'Hey—*your* words,' he said, then reached out to tug her on top of him as he rolled onto his back, so Lanie lay half on top of him.

She almost said something about her being far too heavy—but she stopped herself. Gray wouldn't listen. And besides, for once in her life she actually didn't feel all that big. In fact, she didn't think she'd ever felt more feminine. More pretty.

'So?' he prompted.

'What do you want to know?'

'How about you tell me what it's like to represent Australia.'

Lanie closed her eyes for a moment, thinking. It took a mental shift to refocus on her past successes. They seemed a lifetime ago.

'It's such a cliché,' she said. 'But, honestly, just being there was incredible. I wasn't expected to make the team—even six weeks before the trials I never thought I had a chance. I'd been unwell earlier in the year—a bad case of the flu—so even to make the team as a relay swimmer was a huge achievement. Then when I got there…'

She spoke for longer than she'd intended. Told him about her sense of anticipation before the relay heats, how the noise of the crowd had somehow drifted away as she'd stood on the blocks, waiting for the split second the previous swimmer touched the wall. How the whole meet had seemed surreal—even the weeks and months after.

Even now it felt as if that experience had happened to somebody else.

'It's an amazing thing you achieved—you do know that, right?'

Lanie caught Gray's gaze as he studied her face. 'Yeah,' she said honestly. 'I do know. No matter what else happens in my life, I'll always have that.'

'But you really wanted more.'

She blinked, surprised. 'Of course. At one point I had a chance of swimming in the women's hundred metres as well as the relay. I had a really good year. But then a couple of the younger girls caught up with me.' Lanie managed a casual laugh. 'As you mentioned once, I'm not all that young for a swimmer.'

'You're not old, either. Twenty-six, right?'

'Good internet searching,' she teased.

'Plenty of time for a new dream, then.'

Instantly Lanie went tense and rolled away from Gray to sit on the edge of the bed, her back to him. Her eyes scanned the room, trying to locate her clothing.

'Why do you do that?' he asked. 'Why can't you answer that question?'

'Why do you keep on asking it?'

Her shirt was just within arm's reach and she snatched it up, pulling it on over her shoulders in an awkward movement.

'Because the drive that got you so far doesn't just go away. No one trains that hard for so long without being a little bit obsessed.'

He paused. He wasn't telling her anything she didn't already know.

'I love my career,' Gray continued, 'and I love Manning even now, even when it isn't going as well as I'd like. I *need* it. I need that focus. It's different, but still I guess it's an obsession. I can't imagine not having it.'

It was on the tip of her tongue to argue. To tell him he was wrong, that it *was* completely different.

But maybe it wasn't. It seemed ridiculous that she and Gray could be similar in any way at all, but was it possible?

Lanie wasn't entirely convinced. Besides, he wasn't the first person to ask what she was going to do now. To want to know how she'd fill this new void in her life.

But he was the first person to persist when she didn't answer. The first person who seemed to *need* to know—as if it was incomprehensible to him that she could exist without a goal. Without a dream.

Because he knew that *he* couldn't.

So maybe they weren't so different after all.

With a sigh, she stilled her hands, her shirt still half unbuttoned. She twisted around to face Gray and pulled her knees back onto the mattress.

'I told a friend the other day that I was going to go back to uni. Finish a degree I started a few years ago.'

Gray nodded.

Lanie chewed on her bottom lip, knowing she could just leave it at that. She'd answered the question and now watching Gray watching her, she knew this time he wasn't going to push.

But he knew in a way Teagan hadn't that she wasn't all that sure going back to uni was the answer. It was clear in the way he looked at her. In the still lingering questions in his eyes.

'The thing is,' she said eventually, 'I don't know if that degree is what I really want. If it will lead me anywhere near where I want to go. Wherever that is.' There was a long, long pause. 'I don't know what I want at all.'

Her throat felt tight and she blinked away the prickling in her eyes as she crawled across the bed to Gray. He met her halfway and drew her into his arms.

Then she kissed him—because she desperately wanted to, and also because she didn't want him to see her cry.

The next day was Saturday, so they had breakfast at Bob's Café.

They didn't swim, or run, as Luther wasn't really up to either. Instead he curled up at Gray's feet, banging his cone-shaped collar on their chair-legs whenever he moved. It was warm, and they weren't alone in pretending it was already summer: the café was packed, as was the beach below them.

Bob came over with a menu, handing it to Lanie.

'Taking the weekend off?' he asked her.

She nodded, but Gray could see her smile was a little forced.

'I'll be back in the water on Monday,' she said.

'Good, good…' the old man muttered, then wandered away to take an order from another table.

Lanie leant back in her chair and propped the menu against the edge of the table. Her sunglasses-covered eyes were looking at Gray, and not at what they were going to have for breakfast.

'He doesn't give up,' she said. 'I don't get it.'

'Bob?' he prompted.

She nodded vigorously. 'First he was on about me swimming, and now that I am he's checking up on me. It's bizarre—like he's convinced I'm going to make some amazing swimming comeback or something.'

'Is that why he's asking?'

Lanie shrugged. 'Why else would he?'

Gray didn't know, but the man's persistence bothered him. Lanie wasn't going to swim competitively again. She'd made that clear. She certainly didn't need someone making her feel guilty about that, however well meaning.

'Do you mind if I ask?'

'Knock yourself out.'

A few minutes later Bob returned to take their orders.

'Lanie's retired,' Gray said, which wasn't exactly what he'd meant to say. There was an edge to his tone he also hadn't intended—but then, he'd never been known for his tactfulness.

The older man appeared unmoved. 'Yes, I'm aware of that.'

Lanie leant forward. 'And I'm not planning on competing again. When I swim now I'm not training. I'm just swimming.'

Bob turned to her. 'I know that too. So, what can I get you today?'

Lanie gave a little huff of frustration. 'Then why do you keep asking me about my swimming?'

For the first time Bob seemed to realise that Lanie was unhappy. There was a spare chair at their small table, and he pulled it out to sit down.

'It's simple, really, Lanie—you're a swimmer. A beautiful swimmer. You should swim. You're unhappy when you don't. I've seen you swim on TV before—I've seen the fire in your eyes and the joy you take to the pool. When you quit you were miserable.'

'I was miserable because I didn't make the team,' she clarified.

Bob shrugged. 'Possibly. But you're happier now you're swimming again.' He stood up again. 'Now, what can I get you?'

They ordered, and Gray studied Lanie as she sipped her coffee.

'That was kind of weird,' she said. 'But kind of nice.'

'Anyone who's seen you swim can see where he's coming from. You're something else in the water.'

A natural. His ocean nymph.

Gray smiled at such an uncharacteristically romantic idea. *Look what Lanie did to him.*

'Do you feel like a swim?'

Lanie raised an eyebrow. 'What? Now? It must be almost midnight. And,' she added, 'it's not exactly warm.'

The weather's premature attempt at summer had disappeared along with the setting sun. After breakfast they'd walked leisurely along the beach with Luther, enjoying the warmth and the salty breeze. Later they'd gone out to pick up Thai food for dinner, and by then it had been cool enough for Gray to wrap an arm over Lanie's shoulders as they'd returned to his car.

The action had surprised her—yet it had also felt somehow natural and almost normal.

Kind of like the entire weekend.

Now they sat together on one of Gray's soft leather sofas. Lanie had her feet curled up beneath her and a half-finished glass of wine in her hand. Gray was sprawled out beside her, his feet propped up on an ottoman. Beneath the bridge of his legs lay Luther, happily asleep and snoring softly.

'Why not? My pool's heated.'

Lanie grinned. '*Ooh, fancy.*'

'Only the best for Luther.'

She looked down at the slumbering dog. 'I don't think he's up for a swim.'

'No,' Gray agreed. 'And I can't say *he's* my preferred swimming companion tonight.'

His gaze caught hers and held—and its heat made Lanie's skin go hot, and somewhere low in her belly became liquid.

Lanie wondered if at some point she would get used to this. To her instant, visceral reaction to Gray.

Then he smiled at her.

A slow, sexy, smile.

No, she decided. She wouldn't—she couldn't.

Everything about Gray—the way he looked at her, the way he touched her, the sound of his voice—was almost too much. She'd never get used to it.

At the back of her mind a little voice niggled, attempting to remind her that she wouldn't get the chance to *get used* to Gray, anyway.

Lanie didn't know what this weekend was, but she did know that right now she couldn't think beyond it. And Gray certainly wasn't. They had tonight and tomorrow. That was it.

'I didn't bring my bathers,' Lanie said.

Another smile. 'I don't think that'll be a problem.'

The pool was deliciously warm.

Lanie swam its length under water, heading towards Gray's board-shorts-clad legs in the shallow end.

She surfaced beside him, standing. Her upper body cleared the water and her skin goosepimpled where it was exposed to the cool night air.

It was dark in Gray's garden, the only light coming from tiny uplights that glowed amongst the decking that surrounded the pool.

'You do realise you are very nearly naked in that get-up?' Gray asked. His gaze roamed over her—slowly enough to make her skin tingle.

Lanie glanced down at her underwear. She'd stopped at home earlier that day, so she was wearing her absolutely best lingerie—pale pink satin edged with white lace. Unfortunately at the time it hadn't occurred to her to grab her bathers, and underwear wasn't that great a substitute. As she'd expected, her bra clung to her like a second skin—and she didn't want to even *think* what the chlorine was doing to it.

'But I'm not naked,' Lanie said primly. 'I really do feel modesty is *quite* underrated these days.'

Gray's mouth curved upwards. 'Or,' he said, 'you're just chicken.'

Lanie sniffed deliberately. 'Well, I think I deserve a little more respect for showing some decorum—'

Her words ended on a shriek as Gray launched himself at her and they both ended up underwater. By the time they resurfaced Lanie was *sans* bra, and Gray held it aloft triumphantly.

Lanie couldn't help but grin back—especially as she realised it didn't bother her at all to be topless in front of Gray. How strange… Only minutes ago she'd almost lost her nerve while undressing beside the pool, but now—unexpectedly— it was okay.

Quite possibly Gray's *very* admiring gaze had something to do with it.

'You are gorgeous, Lanie Smith,' he said, soft and low.

Suddenly uncomfortable again, she automatically moved her arms to cover herself.

Gray's eyes narrowed. 'Don't,' he said.

'Gray, I'm not gorgeous—'

'Want to race?' he interrupted.

'What?'

'To the other end and back? Ready?' He didn't wait for her to reply. 'Go!'

He was off in a huge splash of water before she'd had a chance to register what was going on.

And because it was so ingrained in her she found herself swimming after him as fast as she could.

But even with a championship-quality tumble turn he still beat her back to the wall.

'I knew it!' he crowed, tongue firmly in cheek. 'That was just a lucky race in Vietnam.'

'How about we go again?' Lanie asked. 'This time both starting at the same time.'

Gray shrugged. 'I'd love to, but...'

'But?'

He grinned. 'This way we finish with me winning.'

Lanie laughed out loud.

But her laughter faded away to nothing when Gray stepped closer. He reached out to tuck a stray strand of soaked hair behind her ear.

'I like your hair like this,' he said.

'Wet, messy and knotty?' Lanie asked in disbelief. She reached up, patting at her hair ineffectually.

Gray's hand moved to still hers. 'Slicked back like this, so I can see your face properly.' He moved his hand from hers to trail a fingertip along her cheekbone, then down along her jaw. 'You have a lovely face.'

She shook her head unthinkingly and Gray's fingers slipped beneath her chin to still the movement. He tipped her chin upwards, so she was forced to meet his steely gaze.

'Let me say nice things to you, Lanie.'

She looked away, looked everywhere but at Gray—at the plants around the pool, the water surrounding them, then up at the moon.

But Gray still held her gently in place, and now he leant forward, his breath warm against the damp skin beneath her ear.

'I'm not making this stuff up, Lanie. I mean it.'

His words and his proximity made her shiver.

But not quite believe him.

And he knew. He sighed loudly in frustration. 'I'm not in the habit of lying.'

Lanie took a step backwards. 'You barely knew I existed until recently. Can you see how that might leave me a little unconvinced of your compliments now? From invisible to *lovely* or *gorgeous* is quite a jump.'

She could just process the idea that he was attracted to her, but the concept that she was anything approaching beautiful was a step too far.

'Lanie, I—'

She ignored him. 'You didn't even notice—'

She stopped, not liking the vulnerability in her tone.

'Notice what?'

She attempted a smile. 'My make-over. You know—new outfits, new hair, new make-up?'

Gray's forehead furrowed as he considered her words.

Suddenly Lanie wished she'd done as her mother had always taught her and simply thanked Gray for his compliment. She didn't even know what she was trying to achieve—did she actually want Gray to *agree* that, in fact, she wasn't even close to beautiful?

Really, there were far worse things to deal with than a man like Gray insisting on pretending she was something she wasn't.

'The day I asked you to come with me to Vietnam,' Gray said.

'Pardon me?'

His look was typical frustrated Grayson Manning. 'That was the first day you came to work after your make-over, or whatever. It was, wasn't it?'

Lanie nodded mutely.

'I thought so. Your hair was different. It reminded me of the day you tied it back for the first time. I remember I liked it.'

Another silent, incredulous nod.

He stepped forward, closing the gap between them again. He reached out, sliding a hand onto her hip beneath the water. Somehow she'd managed to forget her near naked state, but Gray's touch was an instant reminder. And now she didn't feel awkward or shy. Instead the soft breeze against her skin felt...amazing.

So did she.

'Why did you do it?' he asked softly. 'The make-over?'

'I was sick of being invisible,' Lanie said. 'And not just to you,' she added, only for the first time acknowledging that. 'But also in general. I've spent my whole life in my little sister's shadow.'

'You're not invisible, Lanie. I didn't pay as much attention as I should have, but I did notice you. Everything's been about Manning for me these past few months. It's all I think about it. It's all I do.' He paused, as if he'd just realised something surprising. 'Until now,' he said. 'Actually, ever since you argued with me about Vietnam.'

'Not agreeing with you instantly is *not* arguing,' she pointed out.

He shrugged his shoulders dismissively, but smiled. 'Since then, I can assure you, you've been far, far from invisible.'

His hand at her hip pulled her closer, then closer still, so she was pressed up against him, skin to skin.

She tilted her head upwards so their lips were only centimetres apart—but Gray didn't close that small gap.

'You're gorgeous, Lanie.'

He waited, her gaze caught in his.

'Thank you,' she said.

Then—finally—he kissed her.

* * *

They needed to talk about what was going to happen tomorrow at work.

Lanie knew that.

But she couldn't quite do it.

Of course neither of them had spoken about what was going on. Or about what was going to happen next.

All they had was this remarkable electric connection between them—but then, that was just physical attraction. Chemicals.

It didn't mean Gray wanted anything more from her than this weekend.

It didn't mean that *she* wanted anything more.

Did she?

They sat together on the balcony adjacent to Gray's bedroom. Dinner—a platter of cheeses and antipasto they'd thrown together—was on a small table, but they'd both stopped eating a while ago.

The sun was well on its way to dipping beneath the Indian Ocean's horizon. It was deep and red as it sank lower amongst the clouds it streaked in purples, oranges and gold.

Once the sun disappeared, *then* she'd talk to Gray.

But say what, exactly?

She had no idea.

Beneath them a cream-coloured, clearly extremely expensive sedan, turned into Gray's driveway.

Gray swore, and she raised an eyebrow in his direction.

'My dad,' he said in explanation, pulling himself to his feet.

And then, without another word, he walked back into his room. Moments later she could hear the thud of his feet on the stairs.

Lanie watched as a tall man—she would have instantly identified him as Gray's father anyway—opened the passenger side door for a delicate woman. She wore a polka-dot sundress, stacked platform heels and huge, oversized Hollywood sunglasses.

She looked exactly like the type of woman she'd expect *Gray* to date. Perfect, straight from the pages of a magazine—kind of the way Sienna was dressed in that Paris photoshoot, in fact.

Lanie looked down at herself. She'd only gone home briefly to grab some clothes, but her wardrobe didn't have anything like that woman's dress inside it regardless. She wore faded jeans, leather sandals and a loose camisole top. Very casual, very relaxed.

She'd felt good in what she was wearing. Thanks to Gray she'd felt good about everything she'd been wearing—or not—all weekend. Until about two minutes ago.

The front garden was now empty, and Lanie could hear the murmur of voices in the kitchen, followed by footsteps ascending the stairs.

'Lanie?'

Gray was standing at the doorway to his room and Lanie stood, stepping through the billowy curtains onto the thick carpet.

'My dad and his wife have surprised me with a home-made dinner.'

Gray sounded several notches below thrilled.

'Okay…'

And?

Lanie wished fervently that she'd got her act together earlier, or even that the sun had set faster. Then she would know what was going on—she'd know if Gray expected her to stay or if he wanted her to disappear into the distance.

As it was, she just felt terribly awkward. As if it was somehow her fault for being here.

She explored Gray's expression for some hint of what he was thinking.

But it was difficult. He wasn't even looking at her. Instead, he was looking past her—at the setting sun, maybe, or quite possibly at nothing at all.

Definitely not at *her*.

Lanie stiffened her shoulders. It had been so long since Gray had looked at her like this—or rather *not* looked at her, she'd forgotten how much it hurt. Or at least she'd thought she'd forgotten.

But just like that—just one dismissive glance—and she remembered. She remembered that first morning at the beach, when she'd felt invisible.

Last night he'd told her she was far from invisible.

Beautiful words she'd so pathetically wanted to hear.

But his glance now told her that was all they were—beautiful, *meaningless* words.

'Do you want to stay for dinner?' he asked.

She should have been pleased, but she wasn't. There was no question now about what Gray wanted her to do. And it *wasn't* to sit down for a cosy dinner with his family.

The simplest thing, probably the smartest, would have been to come up with some excuse for why she needed to go. Easier for her—she could pretend to be a breezy, fancy-free woman who had incredible weekend flings without a care in the world—and much, much easier for him. But she just couldn't.

'Do you want me to stay?'

She needed to hear him say it. She needed the answer to the question she should have asked hours ago: *What's going to happen tomorrow?*

Gray's gaze flicked to hers and held, and for once she wished he'd kept on looking out of the window. Because seeing him looking at her—truly looking at her when he spoke—meant she already knew the answer. And, stupidly, when she'd asked it she'd still held the smallest smidgen of useless hope.

'It's probably better if you go,' he said.

Lanie nodded.

There—she had her answer.

Tomorrow, nothing was going to happen. Because whatever they'd had, it was over.

She followed Gray out of the house, past the curious glances of Gray's father and his beautiful, perfect wife and out through the front door.

He didn't walk her to her car. He barely looked at her.

She was—once again—utterly and completely invisible.

He muttered something about work, but Lanie could barely hear a thing past the furious mix of anger and humiliation that powered through her veins.

Lanie considered skipping her morning swim the next day.

In fact lying in bed for as long as possible had very significant appeal.

But a mixture of things—Bob's words, partly, but mostly her own need to feel the drag of the ocean against her skin—hauled her from her bed. Earlier than normal, though. With luck, she'd be long gone before Gray made his way down to the beach. If he came down at all.

She didn't wear a wetsuit. The perfect almost-summery weather had persisted, although it was still far from warm this early in the morning. She thought maybe the full brunt of the cool water would help knock some sense into her.

Or something, anyway.

Stroke, stroke, *breathe*. Stroke, stroke, *breathe*.

It was her racing breathing pattern, and her stroke rate was well up. This wasn't a leisurely swim while she let her mind drift. She was powering through the water, slicing through it as fast as she could.

Every muscle in her body ached. She hadn't warmed up properly. She hadn't intended to swim like this—to swim this fast.

But she couldn't help herself. She needed to do this.

Needed to remind herself of the speed she was capable of. Of her power.

This she could control. She couldn't control the outcome of the team selection trials. She couldn't control the contrast between her sister's success and her own. She couldn't control whether Gray wanted more from her than a weekend. And it seemed she certainly couldn't control how she felt about that.

But she *could* control her body. She could harness the height and the strength she'd been born with, the years of training and perfecting her technique. She could swim, and swim brilliantly.

Her arms tangled in something and she came to an abrupt halt. She gasped, treading water, as she took a moment to register exactly what she'd swum into.

Seaweed—browny-green and curling. She pulled it from her arm, then rotated on the spot to look back towards North Cottesloe beach.

She was breathing heavily. She was far from race-fit and her body wasn't used to such punishment.

But, strangely she quite liked the ache in her lungs, the way her chest was heaving and the way her legs felt heavy as they moved in the water.

She felt alive. Wide awake. Not in that fog of hurt and anger she'd been existing in since she'd driven away from Gray's house last night.

She'd been so, *so* stupid.

As if Gray had *ever* suggested he wanted anything more from her than an opportunity for them both to explore the unexpected electricity between them.

He hadn't promised her anything. He hadn't even implied.

And yet she'd relaxed into his world with him over the weekend—she'd relaxed around *him*. She'd let down the walls that she'd so carefully built—walls intended to keep her from hurt just like this.

She was angry with him for the way he'd treated her last

night. But mostly she was angry at herself. She should never have allowed herself to be in that situation. It should never have happened.

She swam back to the shore much more slowly, taking her time and keeping her head above water as she swam leisurely breaststrokes. It seemed Bob was onto something, although today she couldn't say that swimming was making her happy.

But it helped.

CHAPTER THIRTEEN

JUST BEFORE NINE A.M., Lanie strode into his office.

He'd been there for hours, arriving even before sunrise. His theory had been that the familiarity of work would be a good distraction.

The fact he even needed a distraction bothered him. His time with Lanie was never going to be anything long-term, let alone permanent. He'd always known that, and he assumed Lanie had too.

He hadn't really planned on it being *quite* so short, but really it was for the best.

His father's raised eyebrows and blunt questions after Lanie had left only underlined that.

'Who is she?'

'A work colleague?'

'Not a girlfriend?'

'No.'

'You're sure?'

'Absolutely.'

At the time he'd answered his father's questions honestly.

She wasn't his girlfriend. But later he'd felt uncomfortable, as if he'd lied.

Which was just stupid.

Now he just needed to apologise to Lanie for the awkwardness of last night and for causing her rushed exit—and that would be that.

But he didn't really believe that. He had a pretty good idea what was going to happen. The odd thing was, he wasn't happy about it.

Lanie came right up to his desk. Onto it she dropped a brilliant white envelope, his name neatly typed on its front.

'My letter of resignation,' she said.

Yes, exactly as he'd expected.

'You don't have to do that.'

She laughed. 'Ah, I think I do, Gray. You made that pretty clear last night.'

He pushed his chair back and came around to her side of the desk. He could see her considering and then resisting an impulse to back away. She stood her ground, of course—it was what she did.

He could count on one hand the other people who stood up to him, but he liked it that she did. Really, *really* liked it.

She'd forced him to see her properly, to really notice her—and to want to understand her.

Over the weekend he'd begun to think that maybe he did.

Which was fanciful. A weekend plus a handful of walks along the beach was nothing. It was as silly a romantic notion as his imagining of Lanie as an ocean nymph.

That should have been the red flag—the flashing stop sign he'd needed. At the time he'd ignored the warnings. It had been his dad arriving with his head still in the sparkling, naïve clouds about Wife Number Seven that had finally galvanised him.

He wasn't about to get caught up in the moment the way his father was so apt to do. To extrapolate a simple weekend of fun into something much, much more. No way.

Especially now. Manning couldn't afford the risk.

'I mean it. Although of course I understand if you want to move on. But you're welcome to stay. I'm sure we can retain our professional relationship.'

Lanie snorted with laughter.

'Professional like how we kissed in Vietnam? Or, even better, how we spent most of the weekend naked in your bed? Yeah, that was *super*-professional.'

She was trying to brazen it out, but he didn't miss the pink hint to her cheeks.

He didn't know why he was trying to argue with her. She was right. Their working together was not a smart idea. Standing this close to her only made that reality more clear.

Despite how inappropriate it was to be thinking it right this second, all he wanted to do was reach out and touch her. To drag her into his arms and carry on as if yesterday evening had never happened. To take them back to those moments as she'd watched the sun set over the Indian Ocean and all he'd been watching was her.

'I believe my contract requires two weeks' notice,' she said, when he remained silent. 'I'll honour that, of course. I'm sure the agency will be able to find a suitable replacement in that time.'

Gray just nodded.

He tried to hold her gaze, tried to interpret what she was thinking. Usually it was easy—she had such a direct way of looking at him. Direct and open, as if all her thoughts and feelings were on display.

But this morning it was different. She wasn't looking straight at him. She was looking at a spot on his shirt, or over his shoulder. Not at him.

She turned on her heel to walk away, but he reached out, touched her arm.

Just enough to stop her rapid exit—then his hand fell away.

'I apologise for last night,' he said. 'I was very rude. I—'

'Don't worry about it,' she said with a dismissive wave of her hand. 'It's fine.' She laughed. 'I don't think our weekend was really an appropriate prelude to dinner with the in-laws, do you?'

She made their weekend sound...like what?

He couldn't argue with her. She made it sound exactly as it was—a bit of fun. A fling. A weekend. Nothing more.

'You've got nothing to apologise for, Gray. We both knew what we were getting into, and it was fun while it lasted. But I think we can both agree it's for the best that it's over. You're not interested in anything long-term. And I…' There was a long, long pause. She swallowed. 'We both know that my life is messy right now. I need to sort myself out, figure out where my life is taking me now I don't have a medal to reach for. You've actually helped me realise that. And you're right— this job is *not* where I should be. Especially now.'

He didn't want to believe her. She'd been upset last night. Angry.

As if he'd hurt her. But she spoke today as if she'd wanted nothing more than he had.

As if she agreed that it was for the best it was over almost before it started.

Did she mean it?

He gave himself a mental shake. Of course she did. And if she didn't what was he going to do? Would anything about the situation change?

Of course not. He knew he'd done the right thing. He should be glad that she agreed—that in fact he hadn't hurt her feelings the way he'd feared.

What sort of person would he be if he wasn't?

'You don't have to give notice,' Gray said. 'Actually, if you'd prefer, you can finish immediately.'

Lanie blinked and her mouth dropped open. 'But you have meetings all day, and I'm only halfway through that report—'

'I'll manage,' he said, cutting her off. 'Really. And I'll pay out your notice period, too, to give you a chance to find another job.'

She bristled. 'If I'm not working for you, you're not paying me.'

He shrugged. 'Then it's up to you.'

She chewed on her bottom lip.

'Okay. I'll finish up what I'm working on. It should only take a few hours.'

Then she nodded sharply, as if to confirm her decision, before finally walking out of his office.

After lunch Gray had a meeting across the city that ran well over time. By the time he returned Lanie was gone, her desk completely spotless.

It was for the best.

Teagan had arrived with a very large box of chocolates.

She thrust them at Lanie as she opened the door. 'I have no idea what this is about, but I thought calories and soft centres might help.'

'I'm sorry to worry you,' Lanie said. 'Honestly, it's not that big a deal…'

Her friend held up her phone to Lanie as they walked into the lounge room, her text message clearly displayed.

'Ahem…' she said, '"*Call me, please. I need to talk to you.*" And no smiley face. So I knew it was serious.'

'I sent it at a low point of my day,' Lanie said. Just after she'd resigned. 'It was possibly over-dramatic.'

Teagan studied her sceptically. 'Right. Because you're *so* inclined towards hysterics.'

Lanie located a bottle-opener and went to work uncorking the Cabernet Sauvignon she'd picked up on the way home. When Teagan had called she'd asked her to come over after work instead. At the time she'd thought it would be easier than explaining the past few weeks over the phone. But now she had a sneaky suspicion she'd just been delaying talking about Gray.

But she did need to talk. She figured she'd just get it all out and then it would really be done. Over.

Although that was what she'd thought resigning would achieve.

Right in the middle of pouring the wine, Lanie found she couldn't wait any longer.

'I slept with Grayson Manning,' she said.

Teagan dropped the box of chocolates on the floor.

Most of the bottle of wine later, Lanie lay stretched out on her mother's overstuffed sofa, swirling the last of the wine in her glass. Across from her Teagan was sprawled in an armchair, her long legs overhanging the arm and swinging rhythmically to the sounds of late-night radio and the hits of a decade ago.

'You know,' Teagan said, 'I think this is a good thing.'

'How, exactly?'

Her friend turned her head on the chair's arm to look at her. 'I thought you needed to go out and have some fun. And I like that you finally did something even vaguely less than sensible.'

Lanie rolled her eyes. 'I slept with my boss, then quit my job without any other source of income.'

'See?' Teagan said. 'That's so unlike you. I like it.'

Lanie had to laugh.

'It's addictive, you know,' Teagan said. 'Doing impulsive things. Living your life in the moment.' She studied Lanie as if pondering something. 'It's a real pity you didn't get more than a weekend with this guy. Stretch the fun out a bit longer, you know?'

Lanie had told Teagan everything—almost.

She'd described the Night Market, their walks along the beach, that kiss on top of his kitchen bench...

But what she hadn't spoken about was the details. Their conversations. The sense she'd gotten sometimes that she was seeing a part of Grayson Manning that others didn't get to see—when he talked to her about his doubts, his father, or even his unusual view of relationships. And along with that came the knowledge that she had shared more with Gray then she'd shared with anyone—even Teagan.

He knew how to slide beneath her defences. He seemed to understand her. To *get* her. To push her buttons.

And she was different around him. It was ironic—the man who'd once made her feel invisible had triggered a…a quiet confidence, maybe. Definitely an edge. Gray's behaviour had pushed her to stand up for herself, to say what she was thinking.

To do what she wanted.

And where had that got her?

To her mum's lounge room, with a demolished box of chocolates and too much wine for a week night.

Gray sank back into his office chair. He didn't relax into it because he certainly wasn't relaxed. He more collapsed, actually.

Because that phone call had just made it official. He'd sold one villa—to Raquel—and that was it. The other investors were out.

Logically, he knew this wasn't a big deal. He'd had projects before that had been more of a slow burn. Others had sold in weeks, snapped up immediately. But then, this was something different for Manning. A new venture. He should expect progress to be slow. A delay was not a disaster. Yes, he had more capital than he'd like tied up in the resort. But they *would* sell. He did truly believe that. He needed to trust his instincts, to believe this development had been a savvy business decision. He'd entered a growing market at the right time. He would make money on this.

He did believe that.

But looking at the situation logically didn't make it any less frustrating. It didn't stop him from really, really needing some caffeine.

He leant forward again, lifting his hands above the keyboard to type out an instant message—but then paused. His new assistant was good. Über-efficient.

But really he was perfectly capable of getting his own coffee.

Besides, maybe a walk would do him good.

Was it the new venture? Or him?

Or, even better, a run.

It was mid-afternoon, so he hadn't really expected to see Lanie at the beach.

Still, he found himself scanning the waves for her, for that familiar way her body cut through the water.

She wasn't there, of course.

He ran hard, his feet leaving deep imprints in the wet sand as he propelled himself through the shallows.

He wanted to tell Lanie about what had happened today.

As he'd driven home he'd considered calling his dad instead.

But what was the point?

Gray already knew exactly what he'd tell him—and it would be no different to what he was already telling himself.

He just needed to carry on as he always had. To ride this wave and not let his frustration impact on the way he did business. Maybe it had in Vietnam, and the fact he'd allowed that possibility was infuriating. It couldn't and wouldn't happen again.

He hadn't changed. Manning hadn't changed. Eventually everyone would realise that.

He just wished they'd hurry up.

So, while his dad would understand, would be reassuring and say all the right things, going to him would feel as if he was doing exactly what many people seemed to think he'd always done: running to his dad for help. He hadn't done that and he wasn't going to start now. Gray *was* Manning now. On his decisions, his ideas, the company's success or failure rested.

So, no, he wasn't about to go running to his father. But he *did* want Lanie.

Not for business advice, or to tell him it was going to be okay—or anything meaningless like that. He wanted her because she understood this. She understood what it felt like to want something so badly and to be ultimately the only one in charge of your fate. When it came down to it, it had been just Lanie alone in that swim-lane. And it was Gray alone at Manning.

Gray's run slowed right down to a jog, then to a walk as he took big, heaving, breaths.

He looked out onto the ocean—out to the distance from shore where Lanie usually swam.

This beach was a world away from any aquadic stadium.

The kind of stadium she'd never return to.

For the first time the reality of that hit Gray.

All along he'd compared Lanie to himself. He'd sensed her passion, her drive to achieve. And he'd pushed her, unable to comprehend that a woman like her could be satisfied working for him. Could be satisfied without a new dream to chase.

But that was the thing. It was not possible to compare their dreams.

Here he was, furious with himself for a less than successful business transaction.

But he had another chance. Tomorrow. Next year. Next decade.

If he was stupid enough to lose everything, even to lose Manning, he could always start again.

There was no deadline on his dreams as long as he believed in them.

But Lanie…she didn't get another chance. She didn't get to go back and try again. To take a different tack, to review her training routine, to wring some non-existent bit of extra speed out of a body he was sure she'd honed to perfection.

She'd done everything right—her absolute best—and it hadn't been good enough.

She had to live with that. She had no other option.

And he'd been ignorant enough to push her. To question her. To think he was somehow helping by pointing out that she needed something new to strive for.

As if he had a Plan B for *his* dream. Manning was it. It was everything.

All he had.

His breathing had slowed to normal.

He should go home, have a shower. Maybe go back to work, or at least log into his e-mails from home.

He had lots of work to do. New projects to focus on. New investors to target.

But for once none of that excited him.

All he could think of was Lanie, swimming alone.

Lanie's mouth dropped open when she opened her front door.

'What are you doing here?'

A few weeks ago Gray had watched Lanie fidget outside his house as she over-thought how to leave her present for Luther.

Tonight Gray had done exactly the same thing. He still didn't know if this was a good idea—but it was too late now.

'I'm sorry,' he said.

Lanie raised her eyebrows. 'I know. You said so in your office. And, just like I said then, you have nothing to apologise for. I knew—'

'Of course I do,' he said. 'And you know it. I'm sorry for being such a bastard that night—because I was—but that isn't why I'm here.'

She crossed her arms and just looked at him, waiting.

'Can I come in?'

She shook her head. 'No.'

He took a deep breath, trying to organise his thoughts.

'I didn't get it,' he said. 'Actually, I *can't* get it. It's impossible for me to get it. And I'm sorry that I assumed I did.'

Lanie looked at him blankly. 'Pardon me?'

'Your swimming,' he said. Instantly Lanie tensed before his eyes. 'How you're feeling. What you should be doing now. I don't have a clue, and it wasn't my place to push you. To question you. I had no right, and I'm sorry.'

Her gaze had dropped to the wooden porch they were standing upon, but slowly she lifted her eyes until she met his.

'You weren't so wrong,' she said. 'You didn't ask me anything I wasn't asking myself.'

'That doesn't make it okay,' he said. 'You're strong enough to find your own new path.'

'I am,' she said with a slight smile. 'But you probably did speed things up a little. That's not a bad thing.'

There was a long pause. This was probably the point when he should leave, but he didn't.

'I miss the beach,' he said.

He didn't need to elaborate. She knew what he meant. Not the beach itself, but the two of them together there. Walking, talking. Laughing.

He could see her wavering, ready to deny him. Her eyes had narrowed and she'd taken a step forward, as if she was going to push him away physically as well as verbally.

But then, it was as if she deflated before his eyes.

'Me too,' she said. Then her gaze sharpened and she pasted on a plastic smile. 'But, hey, it was kind of fun while it lasted, right?'

'Does it have to end?' he said.

Her lips firmed into a thin line.

'You seriously want someone to walk with at the beach each morning?'

She was deliberately taking him literally, not making this easy for him at all.

But, really, could he blame her?

'I don't know what I want,' he said. 'I just know that I've wanted to tell you things—serious things, stupid things—I don't know how many times in the past weeks.'

Something softened in her gaze, but it was subtle, barely perceptible.

'And I know that I've wanted to touch you. To hold you. To kiss you. A hundred times more often.'

He was doing it again—tapping into this previously undiscovered romantic streak. It bothered him, made him uncomfortable—but not enough for him to wish back the words.

'What are you saying?' she asked. 'That you want more than a weekend together?'

'Yeah,' he said. 'More than a weekend.'

'And…'

'That's it,' he said honestly. 'That's as far as I've got.'

He knew it wasn't much, but it was all he had right now.

Her arms had dropped to her sides and she took a step forward. Then she seemed to think better of it.

'So you're saying we should live in the moment? Keep on doing this together for as long as it lasts?'

He nodded.

'That's pretty vague, you know.'

He did.

But then she took another step forward and reached out, touching his hand. He watched as she traced her fingers upwards, along his arm, up his bicep to his shoulder, then, finally curled them behind his neck.

She was close to him now. So close he could barely think.

She stood on tiptoes, her breath warm against his cheek.

'Okay,' she said, incredibly softly.

And he knew instinctively that even Lanie hadn't been sure what she was going to say right up until that moment.

That was how fleeting this was—whatever it was they had.

It wasn't a good idea. They both knew that.

But kissing her now, beneath the light of her front porch,

was the best idea he'd had in weeks. As was picking her up in her arms, despite her immediate half-hearted protest that she was far too heavy, and carrying her inside.

CHAPTER FOURTEEN

SOFT CONVERSATION DRIFTED into Lanie's subconscious.

Voices—women's voices.

She rolled over in her narrow bed and in her half-asleep state found that odd.

A few hours ago she'd definitely not been able to roll over so easily. Instead she'd been rather pleasantly squished up beside Gray.

But clearly he was no longer in her bed.

Lanie's eyes blinked open.

It was still dark in the room—not even a pre-dawn darkness, but proper, middle-of-the-night black.

She reached out blindly with one hand to turn on her bedside lamp, then flopped back against her pillow. In the corner of the ceiling hung the ocean-blue lantern she'd had made in Hoi An and she stared at it sleepily, thinking.

So Gray hadn't stayed the night.

Maybe that was how this new 'living in the moment' thing was going to work.

Lanie didn't know how she felt about that. She didn't know how she felt about the whole thing, actually.

But—no. Wait.

That was Gray's voice she heard. In the kitchen.

Lanie sat up, suddenly wide awake.

That *was* Gray's voice in the kitchen. Talking to her mum. And her sister.

Oh, no...

She leapt to her feet, fumbling about for a shirt to pull on. Moments later she was all but running down the hallway.

And there, in the kitchen, was Gray—in boxer shorts only, a hip propped against the benchtop. Across from him, perched on barstools, were Sienna and Lanie's mother. A small mountain of luggage sat waiting in the lounge room beyond.

'I didn't realise you were back today,' Lanie managed. She'd been sure it was tomorrow—although, to be honest, she hadn't paid too much attention. With an early-morning arrival, she'd just assumed she'd wake up one day this week with Sienna and her mum home again.

And of course that day was today—the night Gray was here.

She should have been more careful—but then, last night had hardly been planned.

'We guessed that,' Sienna was saying, with a very pointed look in Gray's direction.

'I thought someone was breaking in,' Gray explained, 'and then realised that was unlikely with their own key.'

Sienna laughed prettily, tossing her blond hair over her shoulders. For a woman who had just been on a plane for twenty-four hours or more, she looked remarkably well rested. And as beautiful as always.

Grey smiled back—men always did around Sienna—but then excused himself to get dressed.

The instant he'd left the room the questions started.

'Lanie, surely you aren't...?'

'Is he your *boyfriend*?'

'Who *is* he?'

Their surprise, shock and disbelief were obvious. And seriously unflattering.

'He's a friend,' she said quickly as Gray returned to the room. Now fully dressed, in jeans and a T-shirt, he was no less attractive than the boxer-shorted Gray.

To keep herself busy Lanie started to fuss around the kitchen making tea, while Gray answered Sandra and Sienna's questions.

He was doing well, really, given he clearly didn't want to be there. Lanie didn't want him to be here, either—this reality of Gray, her mum and her sister together was not one Lanie had ever expected to experience.

Gray said little. He didn't need to. The two other women filled all the spare conversation space and more. Lanie remained off to the side, watching them as she sipped at tea she didn't really want. Sienna was in her usual fine, flirtatious form—that was just who she was. Lanie knew it wasn't anything more than that, but still it irritated her.

And then Sienna brought out her medals.

As they were fished out of her sister's handbag and placed carefully in their boxes on the counter, Gray took a step towards Lanie, but she shook her head subtly. *No.*

Before she removed the lids Sienna's hand stilled and she met Lanie's gaze.

Lanie saw concern there. Hesitation.

But she also saw a mixture of excitement and pride—as if her little sister couldn't wait to show them to her. As if she was desperate for the praise of her big sister.

Lanie had never considered flying to London to watch Sienna swim. At the time she just *couldn't.* And she hadn't regretted it—until now.

Now she wished she'd been there to see these medals the day Sienna had won them.

Lanie smiled—a small smile that became broader when Sienna let out a breath she must have been holding.

Immediately Sienna reached for the boxes, and soon the medals were shining brilliantly beneath the kitchen's downlights.

They were beautiful, and far bigger than Lanie expected. She couldn't help but walk over, reach out and lift one from its padded bed. She weighed it in her hands and ran her thumb over the embossed surface.

Sienna was watching her with a worried expression. So was her mother—and Gray.

But there was no need.

That these medals were Sienna's—the result of *her* work, and *her* dreams and *her* achievements—was clear.

These medals weren't about Lanie. Not about her disappointment, or about what would have, might have...could never have been.

With a medal still in her hand, she went to Sienna, wrapped her arms around her and held her tight.

'I'm so proud of you,' she whispered.

And it was as simple as that. It was all that mattered.

Lanie walked Gray to his car. It was about two in the morning, but the idea of Gray returning to her tiny bed now her mother and sister were home seemed ludicrous.

It was perfectly still—still enough that Lanie could just hear the sounds of the ocean at the end of the road. She'd pulled on a pair of jeans, but now wrapped her arms around her body against the cool edge in the salty air.

'You okay?' Gray asked.

Lanie smiled. 'Yeah,' she said. 'I am.'

Gray reached for her, but she made herself step away.

'Lanie?'

She shook her head. 'I don't think it's a good idea,' she said. 'This. Us. Whatever it is.'

She had to push the words past her lips.

'Why not?'

Her gaze flipped up to the streetlight a few metres away. Its brightness made her blink as she stared at it.

'I think I've spent enough time in the past few months focussing on the wrong things. On my failures, my disappointments.'

'You're no failure, Lanie,' Gray said, his tone definite. 'Don't say that.'

'I know,' she said with a smile. 'I'm getting that now.' And Gray had played a big part in that—more than he'd ever know. 'I *did* fall short of my goals, and that hurts. A lot. But I need to move on.'

He nodded, letting her explain.

'The thing is, Gray, I don't think I can handle another failure right now. At least I can't handle one that's guaranteed. I need to believe in myself again.' She swallowed. 'So I can't do this with you. It's not going to work. We both know that.'

'But what do you want from this?' he asked. 'How can you be so sure it's going to fail?'

She laughed, but sadly. 'Of course it's going to fail. You can't even articulate what you want—neither of us can. But I know what you *don't* want. You don't want love, and you don't want for ever.'

She gave him a second—a moment to contradict her—but he remained silent.

She bit her lip, angry that her throat felt tight.

'That's what you want, Lanie? Love?'

Stupidly, she hadn't really considered the word in relation to herself. She'd just known that Gray didn't want it and had focussed on that.

But of course it was what she wanted. She turned her gaze back to him, looking him straight in the eye.

She had an awful feeling that love was something she already felt.

Could he see that in her gaze? She thought so, because his eyes drifted away.

'I think I get it now,' she said. 'That dismissive thing you do. I thought you were rude, or arrogant, but it isn't that, is it? You want to keep your distance from people. If you don't engage they can't get too close. Then there's no risk of any type of distraction—from Manning, and from your goals.'

He looked at her now, his gaze hard. 'You don't know what you're talking about.'

'I think I do, actually,' she said. 'I think for years I've been doing the same thing. My life was all about swimming—training, competing, day after day. There was no space left for anything else, and I didn't want anything else. But,' she said, with a smile, 'the good thing is that *now* I do have space. I have space for new dreams, new goals, new experiences, new relationships—and, I guess, for love.'

She'd only realised this as she'd been speaking. For the first time in months it was as if a whole new world was opening up before her—full of opportunities far beyond her swimming career.

Adrenalin pumped through her veins. Excitement.

Sienna's medals had been the catalyst, but this had started long before. Maybe that day she'd first stood up to Gray. Or when she'd finally believed in the way his body responded to hers. New emotions. New reactions.

Gray was shaking his head. 'You're wrong, you know. My whole career is about building relationships.'

'*Working* relationships, Gray. Not real ones.'

He laughed. 'Like my dad's marriages? Right. Or my mum's relationship with me? Or yours with your father, even? If that's what real relationships are, I don't want a part of one.'

Which was it, exactly.

Her gaze lifted to that streetlight again. She was discovering that right at this moment she was more like Gray than she'd realised. She couldn't look at him. Not now.

'Goodbye, Gray. This was fun while it lasted.'

He opened his mouth as if he was going to say something. But then he didn't.

Instead he looked at her—*really* looked at her—in a way that made Lanie wish she could take back everything she'd said. That made her want to throw herself at him and hold him and kiss him, take whatever it was he *could* offer for as long or as little time as he could.

There was passion and connection and maybe even something else in Gray's gaze.

But it wasn't enough.

She needed more now. A lot more.

And Gray wasn't capable of giving her what she needed. Or at least he didn't believe he was—and that was exactly the same thing.

He'd not contradicted her. He'd not even said he was willing to give it a try.

He was letting her end this and he was going to walk away.

That told her everything she needed to know.

So she let him.

One month later

It was a Friday night in an inner city pub, and Gray had met his dad for a drink. It was a celebration of sorts—three months since Gordon's retirement.

Gray couldn't say that everything at Manning, or his relationships with his clients and investors, was one hundred percent back to normal. But it was a heck of a lot closer than a month ago.

Nearly everyone was relaxing into the change, and Gray could sense a gradual return to the trust in him he'd once taken for granted.

And he thought *he* had relaxed into the change too. For a long time he'd had no idea he'd even needed to —nor even acknowledged that Gordon's retirement was a major change for him. Not just the people he worked with.

It had been Lanie who'd made him figure that out. Lanie swimming alone in the ocean, working her way through the biggest change in her life with so much dignity—and also moments of weakness.

Those moments were okay, though. Necessary, even.

So he too was allowing himself to be less than perfect. To adjust. To—as Lanie had told him—accept that he could do no more than his best.

It was all he and she could ever do. And that was okay.

It appeared to be working, too. This week he'd sold one of the Hoi An villas.

'It's over. With Tasha,' Gordon said out of the blue.

'I'm sorry to hear that,' Gray said, taking a sip of his beer.

'But not surprised?'

Gray shrugged. 'No.'

Normally that was as far as his conversations with his father went in relation to his divorces.

'What happened?' he asked, surprising himself.

Gordon raised his eyebrows, but answered the question. 'It wasn't working,' he said. 'It didn't turn out as either of us had expected.'

'And what *did* you expect?'

His father smiled. 'The perfect marriage, maybe?'

'What's that?'

Now a laugh. 'Maybe that's the problem. I don't know. Not what I keep on getting, anyway.'

'So why keep on trying?'

Gordon put down his beer glass as he studied Gray. 'I don't know. Each time it seems like a good idea. The best idea, even.'

'It's a good thing you're better at learning from your mistakes in other areas of your life,' Gray pointed out.

'Ah,' Gordon said. 'That's the thing, Gray. I married seven very different women. Given I didn't marry any of them twice, you could say I *did* learn.'

Gray laughed.

Their conversation shifted to more familiar territory—business, mostly. But Gray found himself studying his father and trying to understand how he was feeling.

Because surely—given he'd just separated from a woman he'd supposedly loved—there should be some evidence of… he didn't know… Hurt? Anger? Sadness?

He'd never been able to relate before. When his father had announced his separations—the ones Gray could remember, anyway—he'd paid little attention. As his dad said, Gray had always expected the demise of each relationship. It had never been a surprise.

He'd felt a little smug, actually, that once again he'd been proved right.

But this time he felt ashamed of his previous behaviour. His father must be devastated to have lost such a connection with another person. To have lost that spark, that magic, a person to share your day with. To laugh with. To share *everything* with.

And yet as his father related some golfing anecdote Gray didn't see any of that. No sadness. No regret. Nothing.

'Did you love her?' he asked, interrupting his father.

The older man's eyes widened. 'I thought I did,' he said, after a long moment. 'But no. I didn't. If I had, I don't think I'd feel so relieved that it's over.'

Yes, that was it. *Relief.* That was his dad's overriding emotion. As it had been in every divorce that Gray could remember.

Relief. Wasn't that what he should be feeling when it came to Lanie?

She'd done the right thing by ending it. She'd been absolutely right. Their relationship hadn't been going anywhere.

And, more importantly, she *did* deserve more than that. A lot more than that.

She deserved everything she'd spoken about that night—to live her life beyond her swimming career and to fill it with experiences, and joy, and definitely with love.

In which case, why was he thinking about her now?

Now, weeks later—weeks since he'd seen her, given he'd

changed his daily running track. He'd figured it wouldn't be fair to Lanie to share her beach.

Or fair to him…

He went to take another long drink of his beer—only to realise his glass was empty.

He had no idea what his father was saying, but he nodded occasionally as he tried to pull his own thoughts together.

He did know one thing: he *wasn't* relieved that things had ended with Lanie.

Lanie sighed as she unknotted her apron and hung it on a hook in the café's small office.

Bob grinned as he looked up from counting the day's takings. 'You'll get used to it.'

She smiled back. 'Honestly, you'd think after all my years of swimming I'd be fit enough to run about all day.'

'Maybe that should be your plan when you reopen the place—an underwater café. Then you could swim the orders out to customers.'

Lanie tilted her head, as if giving the idea serious consideration. 'You know, you could be onto something.'

Five minutes later, with her bag swung over her shoulder, she headed for the beach. The little café shut each day at five p.m.—something she *did* plan to change when her purchase of the café was finalised—and at this time of year there were still hours of daylight remaining.

The sand was only sparsely dotted with people—a few sunbathers, a handful of dogs, and some kids splashing about in the shallows. The afternoon sea breeze had kicked in, and it urged small white-tipped waves from the ocean. One hopeful surfer bobbed just behind the waves, and far, far beyond him a lone container ship was silhouetted against the sky.

Lanie dumped her bag, quickly tugged her cotton dress off over her bathers, then pulled her swim-cap on over her hair. Lacing her fingers behind her back, she stretched her shoulders and chest slowly, then moved through the remainder of her stretching routine. She finished by sitting on her towel, her fingers wrapped around her feet as she pulled them gently towards herself to stretch the muscles of her hips and legs.

Now was normally the point when she leapt to her feet—ready and raring to go, to feel the shocking coolness of the ocean against her skin, and then minutes later the satisfying burn in her lungs.

But today she paused.

The sun was still high in the sky, and it made her squint as she stared out to the horizon.

She should be feeling good. Fantastic, even.

The moment Bob had told her he was retiring and selling his business she'd known taking over the café and his lease on the building was the right thing for her to do. It had taken every cent of her savings, plus a substantial loan, but she figured her own home could wait, and for now she was living in the two tiny rooms at the back of the café.

Lanie now knew she couldn't work for anyone but herself—and not just because of her experience working with Gray. She needed to feel in complete control of this next phase of her life—good or bad, *she* was in charge of what happened next. That meant a lot to her.

But this was going to be good. She truly believed it—especially when she was down here at the beach.

This place reassured her.

Here she was in her element. The ocean didn't think she was tall or awkward—in fact amongst the waves she felt alive, strong, powerful. Elegant in a way she'd never felt in a fifty-metre pool. There she'd compared herself to others—to the girls on the blocks either side of her, to her sister.

Someone was always faster, prettier, or more talented.

But here in the ocean she let go of all that. She stopped judging herself. Stopped judging others.

It was impossible not to—out there it was just her in the water. No stopwatches, no competitors, no finish line.

In the water sometimes she even felt beautiful.

She never had before—except, of course, with Gray.

She shook her legs as if to chase the memories of Gray away.

There was absolutely no point thinking of him, although knowing that didn't really stop it happening. Especially when she swam.

Lanie clambered to her feet and slid her goggles over her eyes.

Stroke, stroke, stroke, *breathe*.

The sun was about to start moving towards the horizon as Lanie swam towards the shore. She pulled her cap and goggles off and held them in one hand as she dived beneath the surface, finger-combing her tangled hair away from her face.

Moments later a splash a few metres to her left grabbed her attention. A tennis ball, bright yellow, bobbed beside her.

Its owner made himself apparent almost immediately, leaping through the water until his paws didn't reach the bottom, then thrashing about enthusiastically as he paddled to the ball.

Luther.

True to form, the dog ignored her entirely, his focus exclusively on his prized possession. He snatched the ball up into his mouth, then swiftly made his way back to the sand—only to drop the ball as soon as he got there, then look back at Lanie, his body tense with anticipation.

'I can't throw it from out here, mate.'

A male voice—Gray's voice—immediately to her right.

As if the dog understood he happily trotted a few metres up the beach, then dropped to his stomach, the ball between his paws. Waiting patiently.

Of course Gray was here, if Luther was. But still, having him so close was unexpected and disconcerting. Or at least that was the reason she gave for the way her tummy immediately lightened at the familiar sound of his voice.

She'd been swimming back, but now the water was shallow enough to stand, so she did as she turned to face Gray. He was standing in the water too, his hair slicked back and his bare chest gleaming in the sun.

'Hey,' he said.

'Hi.'

For long minutes they just stood there. Lanie didn't know what to do or to say.

'Bob told me you bought his café,' Gray said eventually.

She nodded. 'Yeah. He's spent the past month teaching me everything he knows, and then he's leaving me to it.'

'You'll do great.'

'That's the plan.'

The terribly awkward conversation segued into an even more awkward silence. Lanie realised she was still splashing her cap and goggles about in the water, so she made her hands go still.

'I'm glad you came back to the beach. Luther loves it here. I hope you weren't avoiding it because of me,' she said. Her gaze drifted to the shore and she wished herself back at her towel. Or at home. Anywhere but here.

Because it had been bad enough thinking about Gray over the past few weeks. Standing metres away from him was impossible.

'Of course I was avoiding it because of you.'

Her attention snapped back to Gray. 'Oh,' she said. 'You shouldn't.'

'Why not?'

She attempted a blasé laugh. 'I'd hate for one simple weekend to ruin North Cottesloe beach for you for ever. Seems a bit dramatic, don't you think?'

'But that was the problem, wasn't it, Lanie? It was more than just a weekend.'

Lanie's realised she was gripping her goggles so hard that they were digging into her palms.

'You didn't seem to think so,' she said, then immediately wished the words back.

She needed to end this conversation now. It was pointless. They'd covered all this before. And it hurt just as much the second time around.

'What if I was wrong?'

She made herself meet his gaze, trying to ignore the pathetic butterflies of hope that swirled around her stomach. 'Were you?'

He nodded. 'I used to think that love was a weakness. A possible chink in my armour. A risk—a complication that I didn't need and that could distract me and shift my focus from what was really important.'

'Which is Manning,' she said.

He shook his head. 'No. It's part of it—but now I know it's not everything. It's not even close to everything I need in my life. My dad knows that too. That's why he keeps searching for love. He definitely doesn't always make the right decisions, but I can no longer deride him for trying. We've been talking a lot, and I think once he was in love. He keeps searching for that feeling again.'

Gray had stepped closer—or maybe the waves had pushed them closer together.

His gaze was still locked with hers, and he was now near enough that she could see the intensity in his eyes. And she could certainly feel it. Right now she had no doubt she was all he was seeing.

Maybe right now she was all that mattered.

It was an overwhelming sensation. But it drew her towards him like a magnet.

Another step through the lapping waves. So that if she reached out she could touch him.

'I don't want to be like him,' Gray said. 'I don't want to spend the rest of my life searching for something I once had.'

'Or getting married seven times?'

He laughed out loud. 'I can't see that happening.'

No, but Lanie could too easily imagine Gray shutting himself off from the world, keeping his distance in the guise of arrogance.

Gray took that last final step. The step that made her tilt her chin up to look at him and made each deep breath she took bring their bodies dangerously close together.

'I love you, Lanie,' he said.

After everything, it seemed almost too simple. Too basic and straightforward when everything about their relationship had been complicated and confusing.

But it was far from simple.

Could she do this? Could she risk herself again? Could she risk the all too familiar pain of rejection and failure?

The possibility scared her. Terrified her, even.

But as she looked up into Gray's eyes she didn't see any doubts.

And when she searched inside herself she couldn't find any either.

She wouldn't take back a moment of her swimming career, even though it hadn't ended the way she'd dreamed.

Besides, this was love—not sport.

Sure, there were risks, and no guarantees.

But their love wasn't dependent on others. On injury, or illness, or team selection policy.

It was just her and Gray.

'I love you, too,' she said softly, just loud enough to be heard over the gentle splash of the ocean.

Then she was in his arms and kissing him, with the taste of salt water on her lips and the bite of the sun warm against their damp skin.

On the beach, Luther barked—loudly.

It took a while, but eventually they broke apart.

'I think he wants someone to throw his ball,' Lanie said, smiling.

And, hand in hand, they walked back to the shore, together.

* * * * *

RED VELVET KISSES

SHERELLE GREEN

To my cousin, Shenelle, for your advice and constant encouragement. When we get together, there's never a dull moment, and it's been that way ever since we were kids. Your comic impersonations, spirited personality and infectious smile bring joy to others. You're so easy to get along with, but there's more to you than meets the eye. In order for people to truly get to know you and see what's inside your heart, they must take the time to peel back the layers of your personality, to find the treasures that lie beneath. You have such passion for delicious dishes, and I love your unique and warm demeanor. When I was thinking about the qualities that I wanted Lex to have, you were definitely my muse. Thanks so much for all the inspiration!

Prologue

"To buy or not to buy," Lexus Turner said to herself as she admired the pleated lilac babydoll in her hand. She'd been in Bare Sophistication lingerie boutique for over thirty minutes and had yet to find something sexy to purchase. Earlier that morning, she had listened to an audiobook of a female motivational speaker who stressed the importance of feeling and looking good. Lexus didn't have a special someone in her life, but she was tired of the frumpy, yet comfortable, undies she often wore.

Would this even cover anything? she thought to herself as she observed the uncomfortable-looking tiny silk thong that accompanied the babydoll. She then pulled out the silk G-string placed next to the thong. *Now this I like.* She may have been contradicting herself by disliking the thong yet liking the G-string, but to her there was a big difference. The couple times she'd worn a G-string, she felt as if she was wearing nothing at all. The one and only day she wore a thong, she'd felt as if something was stuck between her butt cheeks all day. That feeling had caused her to not-so-discreetly adjust herself by shaking her leg as she walked.

She looked through the rack at the other lilac panty options. "Oh, now this is different," she said as she held up a panty with a slit in the middle for easy access to her feminine treasures. She could only imagine all the naughty things one could do in a silky lace boyshort with a slit in the center of the panty. It was attached by intertwining ribbons on each side adding to her visual imagination.

"Oh, yes, I love this," she said aloud as she paired the silky lace boyshort with the pleated lilac babydoll. "Perfect match."

"I think you settled on a great set," a deep voice said behind her. Startled, Lexus turned around quicker than anticipated, running right into the solid chest of the man with the low timbre voice. She jumped back from the intensity of the direct contact and misjudged her steps. The oversight of the large rack caused her to trip over her feet and sent her tumbling right into a pair of powerful bronzed arms.

"I'm sorry, I didn't mean to startle you," he said as he helped her regain her balance.

Lexus tried to speak, but she couldn't formulate any words. *Oh...my...goodness.* The man looked tastier than the tiramisu she'd sampled earlier at a local coffee shop. His eyes were chestnut brown with gray specs sprinkled in the coloring. And from what she could tell by the outline of his clothes, he had the body of a god. She was pretty sure she was drooling, which probably didn't look sexy at all.

She tried to stop her eyes from looking him up and down in admiration, but she couldn't help it. He was wearing jeans and a button-up with quarter-length sleeves. He looked slightly familiar and had the sexiest deep dimples she'd ever seen on a man. She couldn't have met him before because she was sure she would have remembered a man this fine.

"Do you need me to help you with that?" he asked.

Lexus squinted her eyes together in confusion until she followed his gaze and noticed that all of the belongings from her purse had fallen out and were scattered across the floor.

"Oh, crap," she whispered as she bent down and began picking everything up. The man bent down to help her, and although Lexus wanted to tell him not to, she still couldn't speak. She'd met attractive men before, but none had left her speechless.

"You sure do have a lot of lipstick," he said with a laugh as he handed her two of the six tubes that had fallen near his feet.

Come on girl! Say something, Lex chanted in her head. Still nothing. Not a single word. Instead, she gave him a big smile and tried to make a sexy *I love lipstick and look good in it* sort of laugh, but it came off as an *I have issues please don't ask me any more questions* type of laugh.

Big fail. *Why do I even try?*

"Would you like me to ring that up for you," he asked as he picked up the lilac babydoll and boyshort that had fallen on the floor, as well. Lexus timidly nodded her head in agreement.

Making her way to the counter, she admired his walk

and the way his butt moved in his jeans. She looked down at her outfit, wishing she'd chosen to wear cute skinny jeans, a flattering top and stylish shoes rather than leggings, a simple T-shirt and gym shoes that needed a good cleaning. She'd just left a nearby workout facility so she was sure the once smooth edges of her hair were now in little curly cues. Her fellow cofounders at Elite Events Incorporated always told her to dress in sexier workout gear, but she never listened. *I should have taken their advice. Or at least worn a headband.*

When they got to the register, he began ringing up her items. She noticed that his eyes lingered on the panties a little more than the babydoll. When he lifted his face back to her he seemed amused. She couldn't tell if he wanted to flirt with her or laugh at her since it seemed she had no business buying such raunchy underwear. The fact that she couldn't tell the difference from the expression on his face was even more unsettling.

"You don't talk much do you?" he asked her as he bagged her items.

"Hahaha, um, yeah. Oh, boy do I." *Huh! What did she just say?* The amused look on his face turned into a hearty laugh. Lexus only felt it fitting to awkwardly laugh along with him although she saw nothing funny about her current situation.

"You're adorable," he said as he handed her the receipt. *Adorable?* Lexus thought as she raised an eyebrow at the man. She definitely didn't want the hot guy thinking about her as *adorable, cute* or any other word best used to describe a bunny, *not* a woman he found attractive. She had to hightail it out of there before she embarrassed herself any further.

Grabbing her bag, she flashed him a small smile before turning to the door. She arrived at the front entrance of the boutique just as a woman was entering. "Thanks so much sweetie," the woman said as she hastily made her way to the man that had helped her and gave him a tight hug. "You're the best," she continued as she gave him a kiss on the cheek.

Oh, well...you win some, you lose some. And there was no doubt in her mind that she wasn't winning this man even before his girlfriend walked into the shop.

When Lexus stepped outside, the hot August air did nothing to calm the inferno the man inside the shop had ignited within her. She hastily walked to the edge of the block before rounding the corner. Briefly stopping to lean on a nearby wall, she took a couple minutes to think about the recent course of events. The motivational audiobook she had studied said that she should take charge of her life and be aggressive. Well, she definitely hadn't taken charge of that situation. And even though she didn't have an aggressive bone in her body, she'd wished she had at least tried to be the aggressor back in the lingerie shop.

"It doesn't matter. He has a girlfriend anyway," she reminded herself as she thought about the exchange between him and the woman who entered the store when she was leaving.

Getting up from the wall, Lexus put her headphones back in and began listening to the motivational audiobook she'd downloaded through iTunes. She only had a couple hours to get ready before her business partner and cousin Cydney Rayne's dinner party in the Chicago River North area. Cyd had just gotten back from a weeklong vacation in Anguilla with her boyfriend, Shawn Miles.

As she walked back to her condo the words coming through her headphones almost made her want to cut off her phone completely. "You are in control of your own destiny. You can be the aggressor. In order to love someone else, you have to love yourself. There is nothing wrong with a vocal woman. You can do it. Just give it a try."

Lexus blew out a frustrated breath as she continued to listen to the voice coming from her headphones. "Yeah, yeah…be the aggressor. I got it," she huffed aloud.

Lex hopped off the CTA Red Line train and glanced at her cell phone. She was rarely late, but the glass of red wine she'd had after returning home from the lingerie shop had caused her to fall asleep. When she woke up, she'd realized she only had thirty minutes before the dinner started.

"Hello, I'm here for the Cydney Rayne dinner party," she said to the hostess when she arrived at the restaurant.

"Right this way miss." Lex followed the woman to the private room. After apologizing for her tardiness, she gave hugs to everyone in attendance including her other two Elite Events business partners, Imani Rayne-Barker and Mya Winters. She took one of the two vacant seats at the end of the dinner table when Cyd's boyfriend, Shawn, tapped his fork on his wineglass.

"Now that almost everyone is here, we have an announcement to make," Shawn said.

"Shawn and I are engaged!" Cyd finished as she stuck out her hand to reveal a gorgeous three-carat diamond ring.

"Oh, my gosh, congratulations!" Lex exclaimed as she jumped from her seat and rushed over to hug Cyd, followed by others offering their congrats.

"I guess I missed something," said a familiar baritone

voice from the doorway of the room. *What the heck is he doing here?*

"Everyone," Shawn said gathering the attention from the group and making his way to the man. "This is one of my best friends and my business partner, Micah Madden. He just moved to Chicago last month and if he accepts, he will be my best man."

Lex watched with eyes wide open as the two men embraced while Micah shared his congrats. She barely heard Cyd's story of how Shawn proposed in Anguilla because she was too busy staring at Micah, hoping that he wasn't the same person she thought he was.

Unless he has a twin, that's definitely him. As if he knew she was analyzing him, his eyes landed on her and slowly looked her up and down before he began walking toward her. She had to get out of there.

"I'll be right back," she said to the group of women, although they were too busy listening to Cyd's story to hear her. She turned and walked around the table in the opposite direction Micah was walking.

Once she was in the hallway, she slipped into a nearby bathroom and took a deep breath. *He's just a man. A normal man.* She glanced at her reflection in the mirror. Who was she kidding? He wasn't a normal man. He was a fine man. A tempting man. A man with a nice round butt begging to be grabbed. Lex was a sucker for a man with a nice butt. *And why the heck am I just meeting him!* Shawn and Cyd had been dating for eight months. She didn't remember Micah at any of Shawn's previous get-togethers since he hadn't lived in Chicago. But she definitely knew his name. Both Cyd and Shawn had mentioned him on more than one occasion.

Last year, Cyd had planned a series of appreciation

events for the Peter Vallant Company and had gotten kidnapped at the winter formal. Shawn and Micah had been securing the series of events and Shawn had saved Cyd from a crazy woman who'd become obsessed with her. Micah had been at the formal, but Lex hadn't arrived until after he was assigned to watch Cyd so their paths had never crossed that night. If she hadn't had another event that day, she probably could have met him that night and saved herself some embarrassment. Usually, when Lex met an extremely attractive man for the first time, she performed a ritual to help settle her nerves. The ritual started with a quick pep talk in the mirror similar to the one she was giving herself now and it ended with a conversation with Mya who often gave her witty things to say so she could keep the guy on his toes. An unprepared Lex equaled embarrassment and she had already been embarrassed enough for one day.

"Okay girl," she said to herself. "You can't hide in here forever." Fluffing her curls and reapplying a coat of red lipstick, she exited the bathroom, running right into a solid chest. Caught off guard, she tripped over his feet and twirled around so suddenly that she sent them both tumbling to the ground.

"Ouch," she said, landing hard on the man. When she heard him let out a loud groan, she looked up at his face. *Oh, great.*

"I'm sorry," she said as she attempted to get off of him.

"We have got to stop meeting like this, lingerie girl," Micah said, not easing his grip on her. *Lingerie girl... that's kinda cute.* Unfortunately, the way her purple summer dress was gathered high on her thighs was not cute at all. She was sure a part of her panties were showing.

"Can you let me go now?" she asked as she struggled

out of his arms. He finally let her go. When she stood, she nervously glanced around to see how many people were around to witness their fall.

"You're so adorable," he said to her before taking a step forward.

Here we go with this word again. She took a step back. "I'm sure you say that to your girlfriend, too." *Real subtle Lex.*

"What girlfriend?"

"The one who kissed you on the cheek in the lingerie shop today."

"That woman was my cousin, Winter Dupree," Micah said with a laugh. "She owns Bare Sophistication lingerie boutique and she needed me to watch the store for a few hours. The store just opened and she doesn't have much staff right now."

Cousin? Just kill me know. "And on that embarrassing note, I think I'll go back to join the group," she said leaving him in the hallway.

"Don't turn around. Just keep walking," she said to herself. But even with the warning, she had to know if he was staring at her. When she reached the end of the hallway, she slightly turned her head. Micah was still standing there with his hands in his pockets and a sly smile on his face. He looked handsome. And downright dangerous. *Mercy.*

Chapter 1

Three months later...

Lexus Turner stared out of her window seat on the CTA bus as she admired the holiday shops and boutiques festively decorated along the Magnificent Mile. She loved living in downtown Chicago, but driving in traffic often made her nervous, so she opted to take public transportation instead. Doing so allowed her the opportunity to admire her beautiful city and embark on some of the best festivities Chicago had to offer.

Lexus completely ignored the loud hustle and bustle of Chicagoans getting on and off the bus as they made their way through downtown for an array of winter festivities. When she reached her stop, she stepped off the bus and breathed in the crisp November air. Soft flakes were beginning to fall and the loud salt trucks caused a few pedestrians to take cover under store awnings to avoid the swinging salt from the trucks' brushes. Some people disliked the busyness of the city, but Lexus loved the constant activity and noisy atmosphere.

As she made her way into the tall skyscraper and arrived on the floor where her company was located, she admired the new logo that was intricately painted on the main office glass door. When Lexus, Imani, Cyd and Mya had joined forces and founded Elite Events Incorporated, they could have never predicted their company would take off so fast. They each ran their respective divisions while alternating as lead planner on each event the company booked. Lexus considered herself lucky to be able to run a successful business with those closest to her.

"Good morning, Ellie," Lexus said to the office assistant as she began removing her snow-white scarf and jet-black peacoat.

"Good morning, Miss Turner."

Before she made it completely through the second glass door that separated the lounge from the main office, Cyd met her halfway.

"Lex! Great, you're finally here," Cyd said as she led her through the hall to the back of the floor where the conference rooms were located.

"Why the rush, Cyd?" she asked with a smile as her warm brown curls bounced around her shoulders.

"Well, we need to decide who will lead a 35th anniversary party that Micah Madden wants to have for his parents. He has a meeting down the street so he dropped by the office a few minutes ago. Mya told him we could all meet with him before he leaves for his own meeting," Cyd explained.

The smile fell from Lex's smooth caramel face the instant she heard that Micah was in the office.

"Judging by the look on your face, that's exactly how I thought you would feel," Cyd said with a giggle. "That's why I came out of the room to warn you."

Three months ago Shawn proposed to Cyd and she happily accepted. The two were getting married next summer and Lex and Micah were both in the wedding party. Unfortunately for Lex, that meant she would be seeing a lot more of Micah as the wedding grew closer.

"A meeting? How convenient. Seriously, Cyd, I don't even understand why he has to plan a 35th anniversary party for his parents anyway. Why not plan a 40th anniversary party like any other normal person."

"Actually, the percentage rate for people who have 35th anniversary parties is very high and increasing every year," Micah said, standing behind Lex and Cyd. "My parents have never had a grand anniversary party so I think it's long overdue."

Crap, what are the odds, Lex thought to herself as she dropped her head to the floor. *Of course he's standing right behind me.* The man always had a way of sneaking up on her.

"I wasn't trying to sneak up on you," Micah stated, sensing her thoughts. "I had to step into the hallway to take an important phone call."

Lex recovered from her embarrassment and lifted her head before turning around to face Micah.

"Hello, Lexus Turner," Micah said as he extended his hand to greet her. There he was…in the flesh. The one man she wished didn't occupy so many of her thoughts. Most people called her Lex instead of Lexus, but her full name rolled off his tongue as if he said her name every day. Better yet, by the deepness in his voice, you'd think he said her name every night.

"Hello, Micah Madden," Lex said, taking her cue from him and saying his full name, as well. "It's good to see you again."

Micah stood there observing her, his eyes burning a hole through her snug-fitting sweater dress. When his eyes left her dress and reached her lips, they lingered there for a while. On instinct, she licked her rosy colored lips trying to stop the pulsating feeling between her legs. Every time she was near him, she couldn't help but be consumed by his presence. The first quality she studied on him today were his muscular arms that were clearly visible through his white fitted dress shirt. The second quality she observed were his perfect white teeth and sexy dimpled smile. The third quality she liked was his unique sense of style. The man could wear a pair of sleek slacks and slim black tie like no other, and always looked as if he'd just walked off the runway.

"Likewise," Micah finally replied as he finished appraising her. "You look very nice today LG." She wished she knew why he thought it was okay to call her LG. He had started calling her LG two and a half months ago at Cyd and Shawn's official engagement party. It was short for lingerie girl. No one knew what it meant except for the two of them and when anyone asked, she never told them. He always called her LG after initially greeting her as Lexus. *What is with this guy?* If she ever got the nerve, she would question him about it. She wanted to question him now, but she couldn't. Secretly, she liked the way it made her feel. Even saying the nickname he'd given her, Lex thought he made it sound heavenly.

Cyd cleared her throat.

"Oh, and you look very nice as well, Cyd," Micah replied.

"Why, thanks," Cyd said as she flipped her jet-black hair over her shoulders. "It's so nice of you to finally notice that I'm standing here. I was about to tell you both to take it to the bedroom."

"Cyd!" Lex exclaimed loudly. "Really?"

"No, she's right," Micah interjected. "We should handle this." At Lex's raised eyebrow he continued. "I meant that we should get started with the meeting. I wasn't referring to the bedroom comment."

Lex breathed a sigh of relief.

"Unless there's something you want to tell me," Micah stated aloud, looking solely at Lex.

"Nope, nothing to tell," she responded a little too quickly.

"You two are hard to watch," Cyd said as she shook her head and glanced from Lex to Micah. "Let's just go into the conference room. Imani and Mya are waiting."

While Micah and Cyd were making themselves comfortable at the conference table, Lex decided to pour a much-needed cup of coffee. She took her seat next to Imani, but not before she cut Cyd a slicing look of irritation.

Cyd responded to the look by innocently lifting her hands and eyebrows in indication that she didn't understand what Lex was referring to.

"Ha! Yeah, right," Lex said aloud, although she hadn't intended to.

"Is everything okay?" Imani asked.

"Yup, everything is fine," Lex replied. *As long as I keep my hormones in check.*

"Great! Now let's get down to business. As you all

know, Micah would like to throw a 35th anniversary party for his parents in their Arkansas hometown. First things first, we need to decide who will lead this event."

"I think Lex should handle this event," Mya quickly replied.

"I agree," Cyd added.

"Sounds good to me," Imani continued after Cyd.

"Great. Then, it's settled," Micah said as he stood to shake each woman's hand before finally reaching Lex.

"I have to get to work. But let's set a date to meet and discuss my needs."

Lex was a little taken aback by his comment and the fact that her partners had decided she would be the event lead. Micah was still holding her hand when he voiced the last words. *Did he mean work needs or personal needs?*

"Both," Micah said as if reading her thoughts again.

"I'm sorry, what did you say?" Lex asked in confusion. Everything was happening too fast and she couldn't react that quickly. "Never mind, I will call you to set up a preliminary meeting for the anniversary party. Is there any day this week that doesn't work well for you?"

Micah finally let go of her hand and flashed another priceless smile.

"Any day this week works for me." He winked, clearly entertained by the fact that, once again, she was ignoring his advances. With that, he gave a quick nod to all the women and left the conference room.

"What just happened here?" Lex asked Mya in particular after Micah was out of earshot. "Last week, I thought we both agreed that we would figure out what Micah wanted for the anniversary party before deciding who would be the best planner since Imani and Cyd already have a few events lined up."

"I don't remember us saying that," Mya responded as she pretended to be occupied with straightening a stack of unruly papers. "I talked to Micah when he first got here so I already knew that it worked best with your schedule."

Imani and Cyd both laughed. While eyeing her friends and partners, Lex tried to figure out exactly what scheme they were trying to get away with.

"I'm pretty sure that's what we discussed," Lex said raising her voice a bit. "And what do you mean it worked best with my schedule. He didn't even say what date he was interested in so you couldn't possibly know what worked best."

"Yes, he did," Mya answered. "His parents never had a real wedding, but their actual wedding date is Valentine's Day. He said that he wanted to plan their anniversary sometime next month before New Years, or after if that's too soon. Like I said, I'd already talked to him."

"That soon?" Lex exclaimed. "Why did we agree to plan this party? It's already November!"

"We've planned plenty of parties with way less time," Imani responded. "Besides, you still have another two weeks left in this month."

"And let's not forget that last year, I planned the formal for the Peter Vallant Company with way less time than you have," Cyd added. "I had about two weeks to plan that entire event. If I can make that work, you can definitely make this work."

Lex crossed her arms over her chest in annoyance. Her body language was a clear indication that she was pouting, but she didn't care. She felt as if she was the focal point of the joke, and being the main focus of any joke was *not* a good feeling.

Mya's smartphone vibrated. "Lex, I'd love to continue this conversation but I have to meet with a client to discuss the grand opening event for their new clothing store."

"Of course you do," Lex said sarcastically. Imani and Cyd had their phones in their hands as well, and if Lex was a betting woman, she'd bet any dollar amount that one of them had texted Mya to give her an excuse to leave the conference room.

"I have to go, too," Imani stated. "I have to tweet about a couple upcoming events and I have to update our page on Facebook."

"I should probably call the florist for my wedding to confirm my appointment next week," Cyd interjected. "Besides, I'm sure you have to start working on a game plan for the anniversary party."

"Ugh," Lex responded in annoyance. "I know what you guys are doing and it won't work."

"Sweetie, that childlike pout doesn't look good on you," Cyd said with a laugh.

"Besides, we don't know what you're talking about," Mya added.

"Oh, really," Lex said sitting upright in her chair while uncrossing her arms and bracing both hands on the conference table.

"Look, I'm not blind. I know Micah has a thing for me. But y'all know I'm not going there with a man like him."

"Lex, listen to yourself," Cyd said. "Micah is educated, successful and sexy. Plus he's a bit of a bad boy. Trust me, women in Chicago have been drooling all over him ever since he moved here this past summer."

"But he's only interested in you," Imani added.

Rubbing her hands over her face, Lex tried to ignore what they were saying. She couldn't date a man like him.

He was too easy to fall for and after everything she'd been through, she wasn't willing to risk her heart again.

"You guys know what I went through with Evan."

Imani reached over and softly touched Lex's hand. "Lex, we all know that Evan's craziness made you swear off men. But you can't let him define your future. You need to move on from that situation."

"I know," Lex replied. "But it's not that easy. He controlled every part of me in high school and college. If I hadn't seen the light after Gamine's death, I would have never realized the type of man he was." When her grandmother, Faith Gamine Burrstone died a few years ago, a light switch had finally been turned on in Lex's head.

"Sweetie, Evan Gilmore was the ultimate a-hole!" Cyd exclaimed. "We all blame ourselves for not always speaking up when it came to our true thoughts about him. But Micah Madden is not Evan Gilmore."

"Not even close," Mya added. "You're twenty-eight. You need to date a real man."

"I have dated real men," Lex said, defending herself. "Remember Reginald Collins?"

"Right, how can we forget nerdy Reginald," Cyd cynically replied. "I still don't understand why you wasted your time on someone who didn't even like to kiss in public...or private I presume."

"That's not true," Lex responded. "He was just very selective on how and when he showed his feelings." She wouldn't dare tell them that even though they'd dated for over seven months, they hadn't had sex and had barely even kissed.

"A peck on the cheek is not a kiss," Imani stated. "And that's all we ever saw him give you...a light peck on the cheek. Even with that peck, he did it sloppily."

"He sure did," Mya agreed. "It made us gag just watching it. Like he wanted to open his mouth and French kiss your cheek, but decided against it. Awkward."

"Okay," Lex said drawling out the word. "Enough about my last boyfriend."

"If you can even call him that," Cyd mumbled beneath her breath.

"Anyway," Lex continued, "since I don't have a choice, I will plan the anniversary party. But I want to make it clear that I will continue to look at Micah in a completely professional manner."

"Hmm, and how is that working out for you so far?" Mya said, laughing. Imani and Cyd followed suit and joined in the laughter.

"Oh, you guys didn't see them in the hall earlier," Cyd said, ready to spill all the juicy details.

"Oh, do tell," Imani said, rubbing her hands together.

"My work can wait," Mya said, making no attempts to leave the room as she'd previously been prepared to do.

"Well I don't think I need to stay around for this," Lex said as she gathered her stuff and walked out of the conference room. Before the door fully closed, she heard the women giggle as Cyd explained how she'd made the situation even more awkward for her and Micah when she had suggested that they take it to the bedroom.

Chapter 2

When Lex got to her office, she quickly shut and locked the door. Slipping off her winter boots and replacing them with her ballerina flats, she took a seat in her cozy chair behind her large mahogany desk. She then twirled in the seat until she was facing her window with a partial view of Lake Michigan.

"I knew I should have called in sick today," Lex said to herself. It probably wouldn't have even mattered. Micah Madden had been a constant distraction to her stable psyche since she'd met him in the lingerie shop.

"Lord, give me strength," she said as she shook her head and softly closed her eyes. She needed to avoid his advances and treat him like any other client. Otherwise, she had no doubt that she'd lose herself in him.

A soft knock on her door interrupted her thoughts. "Coming," Lex said loudly for the person on the other side of the door to hear. As soon as she opened the door, she wished she'd first asked who was behind the closed door before crossing the room.

"Yes, Micah?" she asked with more disdain in her voice than she'd intended.

"Well, I'm happy to see you, too, Lex," he said, his filled with laughter.

She stood back to let him enter her office. "I thought you left," she said, making sure her behind swayed when she walked back to her desk.

"I was almost out the building when I remembered that I needed to give you a few notes I had about my parents. You know, their likes, dislikes…that sort of thing. That way, you can start planning now if you'd like." He reached out his hand to give her a typed sheet of paper.

As Lex took the paper, she made sure their hands didn't touch. The last thing she needed was any close contact. She glanced up at him again. Their chemistry was undeniable and it seemed the more she saw him the harder it was to ignore how badly her body wanted him. Her mind was saying, *Heck no, you better stay away.* But her body was screaming, *Girl, what in the world is wrong with you? Sleep with him already!*

Lex cleared her throat and briefly looked at the paper again. When she looked back up to Micah, he glanced from the paper she was holding to her eyes and flashed one of his infamous half smiles. He had to know she was daydreaming about him. He was a smart man and probably felt the heat emanating from their bodies just as strongly as she could.

"Well, I guess I'll be going then," Micah stated as he turned to leave her office. Lex followed, heading to the door so that she could lock it behind him. She didn't need any more interruptions until the afternoon. When he reached the door, he quickly turned to face her, completely catching Lex off guard and causing her to run directly into his chest.

"Why do you always do that," Lex squealed as she tried to back away from him. But she couldn't. Her feet wouldn't move the second she gazed into his piercing eyes. He began taking deep breaths, his eyes slowly dragging over her entire body. Lex couldn't breathe. She feared that he would make a move if she so much as batted an eyelash. She wasn't sure how long they stood there before he finally said something.

"You can't fight it for much longer."

Just watch me. "I don't know what you mean," Lex said, deciding to play stupid. Micah stepped a little closer to her, further invading her personal space.

"Sooner or later, I will have you positioned spread-eagle style on my bed."

"I should smack you for saying that," she quickly replied, surprised by his blunt comment.

"But you won't," he responded, getting even closer to her. "You wouldn't hurt me."

"You don't know what I'd do," Lex replied, trying to sound as sassy as she could under the circumstances.

"Yes, I do," Micah said. "But that's not all I want to do to you."

Lex squinted her eyes. She shouldn't ask him to go on, but she was way too curious to end the conversation there. "What else do you want to do to me?"

Micah glanced at her lips before looking back into her eyes. "You'll see soon enough."

Concluding that he wasn't saying anything more, she finally exhaled. Her eyes dropped to his lips before she could stop them. She positioned her foot so that she could take a step back from him, but he moved toward her again, stalling her in her place.

"Be careful LG," he said as he took one finger and dragged it over her lips. "I'm usually not a patient man so your time avoiding me is almost up." She gasped out of surprise, but didn't move away from his touch. Her gasp gave him the opportunity to slightly dip his finger into her mouth. He then took his lipstick-smeared finger into his mouth and gently sucked the tip.

"I can only imagine how good you really taste," he said before taking another long look at her lips.

"Ew, I don't know where your hands have been," she stated as she took a step back from him. She huffed aloud, irritated at herself for not initially smacking his hand away, and aggravated at her mouth for wanting to suck his finger longer.

"Maybe not," he said as he moved closer again, this time bringing his face close to her ear. "But I can tell you where my hands want to go."

Once again, she gasped. Lex tried to think of a comeback, but her mind was blank, replaced by a feeling that was becoming all too familiar when she was around Micah Madden.

"See you soon," he said as he walked out her door. Once he was gone, she leaned against her closed door and chastised herself for not being stronger.

"How in the world am I going to plan this anniversary party?" she asked herself. She had too much baggage and she needed a safe guy...a predictable guy. *Not* the type who represented every wet fantasy rolled into one hot male specimen.

Walking away from the closed door, she went back to her desk in hopes that Micah wouldn't invade her dreams later.

Micah twirled his keys around his finger as he made his way to his parked Mercedes-Benz. Micah and Shawn had finally decided to name their security firm M&M Security and headquarter the company in Chicago. After leaving the police force, Micah had wanted a new start so he didn't mind where the company was located. And after he had met Lex, he'd been even more satisfied with the location. He wanted Lex in the worst way possible and his needs went way beyond the bedroom.

Sliding into his leather seat, he pulled out of the circular parking garage and into Chicago's morning traffic. He hadn't lied about his meeting. He had to meet with a potential investor in the security firm in two hours. But first, he had to meet with Shawn to discuss a few details.

Although he'd only been in Chicago for six months, he had grown quite fond of the city. Leaving his job as a police officer in Arkansas had been the best decision he could have made. He enjoyed being in business for himself and he knew he had to leave the police force after realizing that it was way more corrupt than he could have ever imagined.

He turned off of Michigan Ave. onto a side street, minutes away from the M&M Security office. His thoughts instantly returned to Lex. When he'd arrived in Chicago over the summer, he was glad he could check on his cousin and see how her new lingerie boutique was doing. He had hoped that a woman would catch his eye, but he definitely wasn't prepared to meet Lexus Turner. He hated to sound shallow, but Lex was not the type of woman he was usually attracted to. Lex was the type of woman you wife and he was more accustomed to dating the type of woman you simply bed.

Her natural beauty had captured him from the moment he first saw her. And her clumsiness and failure to form a complete sentence around him had only intrigued him more. He couldn't explain why he was so fascinated by a woman who'd made it clear that she wanted nothing to do with him. Gone was the unsure, wide-eyed woman he'd met in the lingerie shop. She'd been replaced by a woman who avoided his advances every chance she got and she wasn't afraid to tell him no.

Micah turned up his radio and instantly, Jay-Z's latest hit filled the car's speakers. Pulling up to a stop sign, he delayed at the sign to let three women cross the street. They took their sweet time walking, too busy flirtatiously looking at him through the front glass of the car. The one with the tight jeans, boot heels and slim winter coat caught his eye. When she turned around, Micah noticed that she was the same woman who had approached him several times at a bar near his office. Micah flashed her a smile and she waved just before stopping at the corner of the sidewalk and crooking her finger to indicate that she wanted him to pull over. *Flirting with other women will definitely get my mind off Lex.*

He pulled over as directed and watched the woman seductively walk in his direction. *Lex would look better in those jeans,* he thought. Micah shook his head, annoyed that even a woman as attractive as the one walking toward his car could not take his mind off Lex.

"Where are you headed to?" the woman voiced as she leaned over his car window, licking her lips in a way he assumed was supposed to be attractive.

"I'm headed to work," he replied with a smile.

"I live right around the corner. Do you have some time to spare?"

The smile began to fade from Micah's face. *This is what you pulled over for...right?* "In fact, I'm already late so I should go," he continued, brushing her off. She took the hint and stood up from his car window.

"Why did you even pull over?" she huffed with an irritated frown.

"My mistake," he said as he gave her a slight wave and took off. *Crap.* It wasn't like him to be so into a woman who wouldn't even give him the time of day. He knew Lex was attracted to him, but he didn't understand why she spent so much time ignoring his advances when she could clearly feel the chemistry. On several occasions when they were out with their friends, Micah would catch Lex staring at him with wistful eyes full of lust. He wasn't extremely cocky, but he knew he was a damn good catch, and women—like the one he just left— had been throwing themselves at him since he'd arrived in Chicago. All except for the one woman who he craved more than he had ever desired any woman.

When he arrived at M&M Security he greeted the receptionist before making his way to Shawn's office and knocking on the door.

"Come in," Shawn announced. Micah walked in and sat down in a nearby chair.

"What's wrong?" Shawn asked, reading the tense look on his face.

"Man, I'm only gonna tell you this because I know you've been there," Micah said as he let out a frustrated huff of air. Shawn laughed as if he already knew where the conversation was headed.

"Does this have to do with Lex?"

"Of course it has to do with her," Micah exclaimed. "I had a meeting with all the ladies this morning and within minutes, Lex was informed that she would be the event planner for my parents' anniversary party."

"Isn't that a good thing?"

"It is, but it's what happened after I left the office that caught me off guard."

"What happened?"

Micah dragged his long fingers across his face. "Remember that woman from the bar the other night? The one who wore those blue stilettos and tight jeans? We danced a few times before you and I left."

"Yeah, I remember."

"Well, I ran into her on my way to the office and she invited me back to her place."

"In the middle of the day? Man, some women are bold nowadays," Shawn said shaking his head. "But from the annoyed look on your face, I'm assuming you declined her offer."

"Sure did," Micah said as he dropped his head to the floor.

"So I guess the self-imposed streak of celibacy continues," Shawn said with a laugh.

"You know when I turned thirty this year I promised myself that I would stop sleeping around."

"Sleeping around with so many women, yes. Not sleeping with any women period, no."

"I've been too busy trying to get settled in Chicago to think about having sex with random women. Besides—" Micah glanced out the side window in Shawn's office "—there's only one woman I have my eye on, and until

Lex accepts the inevitable, I don't think I'll be satisfied with any other woman. That sounds crazy, right?"

"Well, considering I know the type of man you used to be, hell, yeah. But I understand," Shawn responded leaning back in his desk chair. "I felt the same way about Cyd, but luckily, Cyd didn't make me wait that long. Plus, I heard that Lex was in a serious relationship for years, one that went terribly wrong. According to Cyd, she's sworn off dating real men."

"So that means what? She dates fake men?"

"I don't know. Cyd and I got distracted so we never finished the conversation."

Micah didn't even bother asking what had distracted Shawn and Cyd since he already knew. Nor did he bother to ask about Lex's old relationships because he'd asked Shawn before and he said he needed to ask Lex. So he would just have to find out from her. There was way more to Lex than met the eye, and he was determined to figure it out. He'd spent the past few months observing her and patiently waiting for her to stop fighting the desire she was trying to hide. Now he was done waiting. Micah never had to persistently pursue a woman, but Lex was making him work for it. But if he left it to her they would never get together, so it was time for him to stop letting Lex control the course of their nonexistent relationship.

"Then I guess I will just have to show Lex that I don't plan on going anywhere."

"And I assume your sudden desire to throw your parents an anniversary party plays a part in your plans?"

"That and the fact that they deserve a celebration," Micah said, rubbing his hands together. "Up until now, I've been giving Lex time to realize that she can't fight the attraction forever. But I think it's time to lay out all the stops the only way a Madden man knows how to."

"I'm afraid to ask," Shawn said with a laugh as he pulled out a folder that contained notes on the investor they were meeting with in an hour. "Well, Romeo, I can't wait to see how this plan of yours plays out. In the meantime, let's get ready for our meeting."

Micah was barely listening to Shawn as he went over the notes in the file. His mind was already racing with different seduction tactics. *Time for you to see things my way, Lex.*

Chapter 3

"Ya'll couldn't possibly expect me to agree to this," Lex shouted as she slammed a piece of paper on Imani's desk. It had only been three days since she'd seen Micah and he was already working her last nerve.

"Let's be reasonable, Lex," Imani said as she stood from her chair and walked around her desk. "If a client needs us to travel we almost always accommodate their needs."

"She's right," Mya said, entering Imani's office with Cyd by her side. "Our main goal at Elite Events Incorporated is to make every event we plan a memorable experience. We achieve this by putting our all into every event we plan."

"Please save the speech for someone who didn't help cofound this company or create part of the mission statement," Lex said as she turned slightly to Mya and raised a hand to cut her off.

"Someone's bitchy this morning," Cyd said as she plopped down in a nearby chair. Lex cut her eyes at Cyd before taking a step back so she could face all the women. She took a couple deep breaths before she continued her rant.

"Look," she stated firmly. "Micah's request that I accompany him to his Arkansas hometown to get to know his parents better should *not* be a requirement."

"How is this any different than when you and I attended several family outings to get to know the families of Kaydence Walters and Justin Phillips before we planned their wedding and prewedding festivities earlier this year?" Mya asked.

"Or when Cyd and I spent three days with the families of Brooklyn Hathaway and Wyatt Lexington for the exact same reason before we began planning their wedding?" Imani interjected.

"All of that didn't require us to leave Chicago. Did any of you actually read this piece of paper before agreeing to his contract?" Lex asked as she picked up the paper from Imani's desk and waved it in the air. "Well let me inform you of Mr. Madden's ridiculous requests."

She flipped some fallen hair out of her face before she gripped the paper with both hands. "Number one—the event planner must meet with me in person once a week to ensure we are on schedule with the plans. Number two—the event planner must agree to at least three dinner meetings as my daily schedule is too busy for morning or afternoon consultations. Number three—the event planner must attend the winter festival in my Arkansas hometown during the month of December."

She placed the piece of paper back on the desk before looking at her partners. The smirks on their faces were really starting to get under her skin. "I don't think anything is funny about this situation!"

"Well, if you were looking at the situation through our eyes, maybe you would," Mya said with a laugh and shrug of her shoulders.

"Oh, lord," Cyd said getting up from the chair. "Lex, we know you're pissed off, but honestly, we've done more for clients before. You're usually so accommodating and you rarely complain so we can only assume that you like Micah more than you have let on."

"Oh, please," Lex said, waving off the comment. "I just value my time and with Christmas right around the corner, it irritates me that Micah is trying to occupy so much of it."

"Or," Imani responded as she placed her pointer finger in the air. "Spending that much time with Micah irritates you because you can't avoid him like you have been lately."

She sighed deeply. Lex was tired of arguing about the same subject and was even more tired of convincing herself they were wrong when she knew, deep down, that they were right. She dropped her head down to the floor before lifting it back up.

"I give up," Lex said taking a seat in the chair Cyd had just vacated. "You guys are right, but I just don't get it. Why is he even into me when he can have his pick of women? I've constantly ignored his advances."

"Do you hear yourself?" Mya asked raising an eyebrow. "Why not you? He'd be lucky to have you."

Lex wasn't so sure. The ladies didn't know how embarrassing it was the first time she'd met him. And once she realized she would have to see him again, she'd decided that she could either be that pathetic woman he met in the lingerie boutique, or she could act indifferent to him, which somehow came off as dislike. That wasn't her intention, but anything was better than being submissive to his charm.

She covered her face with both hands. "I'm done talking about Micah. Like I said before, I have too much baggage to even consider dating a man like him. Besides," she said getting up from the chair and smoothing out her dress slacks. "I've avoided his advances for this long so I'm sure another month or so will be a piece of cake."

"Are you sure about that?"

Lex jumped at the sound of Micah's voice in the doorway. *Oh, no...how much did he hear?* From the sly smile on his smooth brown face she could only assume he'd heard way too much.

"I hate when you do that," she said placing her hands on her hips and glaring at him. The man made her tense, and Lex hated feeling on edge. And why was he just standing there not saying anything? *Fine! If he wants to stand there and stare at me, I can do the same thing.* The only problem with that plan was that Micah had mastered the act of seduction and the thoughts reflected in his eyes made her heart beat ten times faster than normal.

"Your office assistant, Ellie, told me I could go directly into your office. I went there first," Micah finally said.

"Hmm. Funny that she didn't make you wait in the lobby." Lex looked around at her partners knowing that one of them had probably given Ellie the okay to add Micah to the list of people who could stop by without appointments. Otherwise, there was no way he would have been allowed to see her without first calling and scheduling an appointment.

"Can we talk?" he asked, his stare still unwavering. Today he looked more casual in jeans, a black polo and black peacoat. He removed his winter hat and instantly, Lex wished she could run her fingers through his soft natural black curls.

I really wasn't prepared to see him today. "Sure," Lex answered as she walked around the chair and accidentally bumped into it. She slightly stumbled before Micah's strong arms caught her.

"This feels familiar," he voiced as he helped her to her feet without releasing his hold.

"Uh-huh…sure does," she replied breathlessly. *Don't look at his lips! Don't look at his lips!*

"Ready to go to your office?"

Crap! Man he has sexy lips! Soft and inviting… Why did he have to look at her like that? Like his main purpose was to always be her hero. *Say something!*

"Oh, um, yeah, okay, that works, um, let's." *What the heck did I just say! Great! Now I'm back to sounding like a blubbering idiot.* At the sound of a few giggles, Lex turned her head, having forgot that Imani, Cyd and Mya were still in the office and were witnessing the entire scene.

Way to go, Lex! How about you have a couple more embarrassing moments so that your friends will really have something to talk about.

As he followed Lex to her office, Micah couldn't hide the smile that crossed his face. Lex was frazzled, and he loved when she got nervous around him. She had the same affect on him, but he could hide it better than she could.

He'd heard enough of her conversation with her partners to know that Lex was having a hard time avoiding his advances. And he was sure that she disapproved of the extra paragraph in his contract that ensured they would be spending a lot of quality time together over the holiday season.

"How about we go to the café on the corner for brunch?" Micah asked when they arrived at her office. When she turned around to face him, she twisted her mouth and squinted her eyes.

"I thought your contract said you are really busy in the mornings and afternoons."

So she did read that part. "That's true, except today I had to run some errands so I'll be going into the office later this afternoon."

"How convenient," Lex said as she began tidying up her desk. Micah could only assume she was trying to look occupied while she contemplated her response. He didn't mind because it gave him the opportunity to observe her more than he had in Imani's office. She had no idea how attractive she was. On occasion, he'd overheard her say that she assumed he liked the model-type. Little did she know, he much preferred her five-four petite frame and nice round ass that he was sure would fit perfectly in the palm of his hands.

"Okay, let's do brunch," she replied, breaking his thoughts. She sat down to remove her ballerina shoes and put on her winter boots. She'd barely made eye contact with him since they arrived at her office. He smiled as he thought about the last time he was in her office.

When she stood, she went to grab her coffee mug, but accidentally spilled the remaining contents on a stack of papers.

"Oh, shoot," she shrieked, grabbing some tissue and

dabbing the papers. It took all of Micah's focus not to laugh. He didn't want to make her even more uncomfortable. *Her clumsiness is so cute.* Only then did she chance a glance in his direction. He couldn't read her expression at first, but he was glad when he heard her laugh. He laughed along with her.

"Being around you makes me *more* clumsy."

"Well, being around you makes me do a lot of things I don't normally do," he said. *Like be celibate for over three months.* If his brothers knew, there was no doubt in his mind that he would be the object of their jokes for days. He was Micah Madden after all… Bad boy turned good and lover of all things female. Unofficially voted in high school as the number one panty snatcher and the sexiest. *Celibate for over three months?* Definitely a new record for him.

"Let's go," she said as she grabbed her coat. They walked half a block to the café in a comfortable silence. Lex wore a slight smile, and he wondered what she was thinking.

"You have a nice smile," he said after they ordered a couple of sandwiches and drinks. He had her order first so he could pay for both meals. When she looked hesitant, he reminded her that he was the one who'd invited her to brunch. Luckily, she didn't argue with him and they retreated to an empty corner table in the café.

"Thanks," she said, meeting his eyes. "I like your smile, too."

A compliment? "Finally warming up to me, huh?"

"Don't push your luck," she said with a laugh. "I have to be nice now that I'm planning your parents' anniversary party."

Micah bit into his sandwich and observed her in between eating. "From what I hear, you're always nice. Cyd consistently calls you the nice one."

Lex nodded her head in agreement. "That's usually true...except..."

Micah searched her eyes. "Except when it comes to me, right?" he finished when she didn't continue. Lex gave him a soft smile and tilted her head to the side.

"How about we start over?" she asked.

"Meaning, you want me to forget about the incident at Bare Sophistication?"

Her cheeks flushed. "Yeah, that wasn't my most shining moment."

"I beg to differ," he said, trying to ignore the way she licked her lips after the last bite of her sandwich. "You were so adorable that day. At the lingerie shop and then the dinner party."

"Not really," she said as she went into her purse and put on an extra coat of lipstick.

"Maybelline and Covergirl must love you," he said, nodding to the tube in her hand. Her eyes grew big as she shoved the tube back in her purse.

"My mother is a lipstick fanatic and so was my grandmother. I guess you can say they passed their fascination with lipstick down to me."

"Well it looks great on you," he responded as his eyes dropped to her ruby lips. She had perfectly shaped lips... lips that craved to be devoured. She began fidgeting with the sheer pink scarf around her neck.

"So, what did you want to discuss today?" she asked.

"Well," Micah said, clasping his hands together, "I know you received the contract so I wanted to make sure you were okay with everything."

She tilted her head to the side before leaning slightly

forward. "To be honest, I wasn't too happy that your contract was already approved and signed off on."

She stopped talking, but it seemed she still had more
to say. "Is that all?" Micah asked.

"No," Lex said letting out a deep breath. "Since I'm
the lead planner for your parents' anniversary party, I
would like you to go through me for everything you need
in the future. No more going behind my back to my partners. Deal?"

"That's reasonable," Micah said. "But in my defense,
I only went to them because you always avoid me."

"I'll work on that," she said with a smile. "I did have
a question about the December winter festival in your
hometown. What day did you want me to arrive for the
festival?"

She is not gonna like my answer. "Um, here's the
thing. My family plays an important part in the festival and my parents are on the town council, so I will be
down there for eight days."

"Okay," she said before taking a sip of her water. "So
do you want me to arrive on the first of the eight days or
toward the end of the eight days?"

"I need you to be there for the *entire* stay."

"What!" Lex yelled as she braced both hands on the
table. Micah looked around at the curious glances from
people sitting nearby before he leaned in closer toward
her.

"I was originally thinking I could plan their anniversary here in Chicago, but that wasn't really logical.
It makes more sense for the party to take place in Arkansas."

"So exactly why would I need to be down there the
entire time you're there? We plan long-distance parties

all the time at Elite Events Incorporated. We have vendor contacts everywhere, including Arkansas. Venues, florists, DJs…you name it!"

"Cranberry Heights, Arkansas, is not your typical Arkansas town. In order to plan the type of anniversary party my parents will love, you have to get to know the town and the people who live there."

Lex scrunched her face in irritation. *So much for us getting along.*

"Where would I stay?" she asked.

"My parents' house is large so you can either stay there with them like I will, or at the town's B and B."

"What reason will you give your parents as to why I'm visiting."

I was hoping she'd ask that question. "I'll tell them we're dating and I wanted to show you the town."

"Absolutely not," Lex said raising her voice again. "You have got to be kidding me."

"Do you have a better idea?" Micah asked.

"Yes," she said, crossing her arms over her chest. "You could go to the winter festival by yourself and avoid having to lie to your parents altogether."

Micah glanced at her chest before meeting her eyes again. "No can do. And quite frankly, it's in the contract and you asked me not to go to your partners about this so I was assuming that meant you'd be accommodating."

"Is Arkansas country living or city living?" she asked.

"Both," he said with a laugh. "You have something against farm animals?"

Instead of responding, she stood up and began putting on her coat. *I guess we're leaving,* Micah thought, taking his cue from her and putting on his coat, as well.

"You don't have to walk me back to the office," Lex said when they reached the outside.

"Okay." They stood there in silence for a few moments before Micah spoke again. "So, will you come with me to Cranberry Heights for the entire stay?"

She dodged a couple of groups of people walking by. "I'll have to think about it." She continued looking at him straight on.

"I understand," Micah replied. "Let me know your decision at Imani and Daman's party this weekend," he continued before turning to walk in the direction opposite of her.

"Wait," Lex said, gently grabbing his arm. "You were invited to Imani and Daman's Friends-giving?"

"Is that what they are calling the party?"

"Yes. Since we all spend Thanksgiving with our families, Imani and Daman plan a Thanksgiving with their close friends."

"Well, yeah, that's the party. Daman invited me last week."

"Great," Lex huffed.

"Tell me how you really feel."

"Sorry," Lex responded quickly. "I'll let you know my answer then. See you later." With that, she put on her hat and began walking back to her office building.

"Have a good day," Micah yelled after her. She turned slightly and gave him a half smile.

She's gonna say yes. She really had no choice. Micah knew exactly what he was doing when he put that clause in his contract. He was sure visiting his hometown was the perfect way to take her out of her element and, hopefully, get her to see another side of him. She was used to these pretty boys, and Micah definitely wasn't that. He was rough around the edges and damn proud of it. He intrigued Lex. He could tell. But she wasn't all the way convinced yet.

"Watch out, Lex," he said aloud to himself. She was a challenge and if there was anything Micah loved as much as he loved women, it was a challenge.

Chapter 4

Micah stepped out of his car and jumped in place three
times before making his way to the parking meter. Although he had on two layers of pants, a turtleneck, a
hoodie and a scull cap, he was still cold. He loved running by the lake and refused to let the chilly Chicago
weather stop the workout regimen he'd developed over
the summer.

Apparently, he wasn't the only one refusing to let the
thirty-five degree weather halt their workout routine. The
parking lot was half full and even the threat of snow
didn't stop a few people from bringing out their bikes.

Micah put in his headphones and scrolled to his workout playlist and then stuffed his phone in his armband.
Stretching at a nearby bench, he glanced at the white
frozen lake and started his five-mile run.

When Micah and his five brothers were growing up in
Arkansas they used to watch reruns of *Good Times* and

imagine how it would be to live in Chicago. Early last year when he quit his job of seven years and announced he was starting a business with Shawn, his brothers and mom had been supportive, but his dad not so much.

Micah didn't know what he had to do to get his father's approval. At family events, he pretended as if it didn't matter that all of his brothers had a good relationship with their dad. But, deep down, it hurt to know that his dad viewed him as the black sheep of the family. Micah visited his parents more than any of his brothers, but no matter what, his relationship with his dad remained non-existent. He hoped that planning the anniversary party would finally change the way his dad viewed him.

Micah nodded to a few runners passing by and moved out of the way of a couple bikers. His adrenaline was finally pumping and warming up his body. He cupped his hands together and blew into them before taking out his gloves that he'd forgotten were stuffed in the pocket of his hoodie. The view of the skyline was beautiful even in frigid temperatures.

Even though he left the Arkansas P.D. with no intention of ever returning to the force, he was still grateful that he'd had an opportunity to be a police officer. The P.D. forced him to change his ways and focus more on helping people make better choices. He'd run into a number of lost young men with no male role models around to help show them the difference between right and wrong.

His phone rang, breaking his thoughts. "Hey, Shawn," he said as he stopped by a nearby tree and continued to jog in place.

"Hey, man, I was hoping I caught up to you. Cyd just got off the phone with Lex. She told her that she wouldn't be going to Imani and Daman's Friends-giving tonight."

Micah scrunched his face. "Did she say why?"

"She said she needed some time to herself, but Cyd told me she thought it had something to do with you being there tonight, as well."

Micah knew that was the case, especially since Lex had yet to let him know if she would be attending the winter festival. "Cyd's right," Micah replied. "I know what it is. I'll call Lex and tell her it's safe for her to come to the party."

"Okay, good luck, man."

"Thanks." Micah hung up the phone and promptly dialed Lex's number. It went straight to voice mail. He tried twice more just in case it was a bad connection, but both times the call went to her voice mail again.

Micah called Shawn back. "She's not answering," he said when Shawn picked up. "It's going straight to voice mail, so I assume she turned off her phone."

Shawn laughed before telling Cyd that Lex had turned off her phone, and then informed Micah that he was putting him on speaker.

"Micah, what number are you calling?" Cyd asked. He rattled off the number to her.

"That's her work cell number. I'll give you her personal number so you can save it in your phone." Micah entered Lex's personal cell number in the notes section of his phone before thanking Cyd. He dialed the new number, and she answered on the third ring.

"Hello," she asked.

"Hey, Lex, it's Micah." The other line was silent for a few seconds.

"Oh, what's up?"

He laughed into the phone. "I was just trying to figure out why you cancelled on Imani and Daman tonight. If it was because you promised me an answer about the winter festival, then I'd like to take the pressure off you."

"What do you mean?" she asked softly.

"You don't have to give me an answer tonight."

"Then when would I need to give you an answer?"

"How about next week?" She was quiet for a moment, and Micah wondered if she was finished with their conversation.

"You must think very highly of yourself to assume that you're the reason I cancelled my plans tonight," she finally said.

"Well, isn't it?" Micah questioned.

"No," she answered. "I realized I had double-booked tonight and I've been super busy lately. So instead of choosing which party to go to, I decided to take a free night to myself. And for your information, I already know my answer to your request."

Micah smiled, hoping her answer was the only answer he wanted to hear. "And that is?"

She sighed into the phone. "Wipe that smile off your face, I can feel it through the phone." She let out a slight laugh. "I'll stay in Cranberry Heights for the duration of the festival."

Micah did a celebratory fist pump before responding. "I knew you'd make the right decision."

"Yeah, well you didn't give me much of a choice."

"Then I'll see you tonight? Everyone wants you there."

There was another pause before she responded. "See you tonight, Micah."

After he hung up the phone, he sent Shawn a quick text telling him that Lex would be attending the party tonight after all. A gust of wind made him shiver and he decided to cut his run short and head back to his car. Lex said that he wasn't the reason she had cancelled on the party, but he didn't believe her. It didn't matter either way because not only was she going to the party now, but she was also accompanying him to his hometown. And he planned on taking advantage of every moment he spent with her.

Lex lightly shook her wrist and watched the red wine swirl around inside her glass. She couldn't stare at her wine all night, but she could definitely plan to stare at it long enough to avoid Micah, who had invaded her space in Imani and Daman's kitchen. Their large estate with a gorgeous view of Lake Michigan had an enormous basement that Daman deemed the man cave and the entire six bedroom, five bathroom home had more than enough space to host their bimonthly get-togethers and holiday gatherings. But somehow, Micah had managed to pop up in the same room she was in three times tonight.

She didn't care that Cyd, Imani and Mya were in the kitchen, as well. Not only was the wine helping her hide her discomfort to his presence, but they were too consumed with talking about their newest clients at Elite Events to notice her lack of interest. She could feel her body heating in desire as he bent over in the fridge to grab a beer bottle.

Lord have mercy, she thought as she stole a couple glances in his direction. His loose-fitting blue jeans did nothing to hide the imprint of his butt, and his black-and-gray button-up seemed to only accentuate his muscular arms. And Lord knew she was infatuated with muscular arms. She'd never had the pleasure of dating a man who was as fit as Micah. Guaranteed, her ex, Evan, was in shape, but he definitely didn't have a body that looked that good.

He turned from the fridge quicker than Lex had anticipated and caught her staring. He shot her a half smile before popping off his beer cap and taking a quick swig. She took a sip of her wine as a distraction and was glad when a few people entered the kitchen to say their goodbyes. She was relieved when Micah took that time to leave the kitchen, as well.

"I have a great idea," Cyd exclaimed, clasping her hands together. "Since most of the guests are leaving, how about we play a group game or something."

"Well the guys are downstairs playing cards," Imani said. "What type of group game did you have in mind?"

"A drinking game!" Cyd exclaimed.

"What are we, in college?" Mya chimed in.

Cyd cut her eyes at Mya. "What's wrong with a drinking game?"

"I agree with Mya," Lex added. "We're too old for drinking games."

"Well, I'm with Cyd," Imani said, getting up from the stool she'd been sitting on. "Let's play."

"Of course you both want to play a drinking game," Mya responded crossing her arms over chest. "With Daman and Shawn here, you can both get drunk and make love to them afterward. What are Lex and I suppose to do when we get all drunk and horny."

"Oh, come on," Cyd said as she shook Mya's arms loose. "Daman still has a couple single friends here and flirting never hurt anyone. Besides," she continued as she glanced over at Lex. "Don't you want to see Lex try to ignore her attraction to Micah?"

They cannot be serious. "Um, I'm not playing," Lex said.

"It won't be fun without you," Imani said as she leaned in to hug Lex.

"You mean, it won't be fun if you don't have me to laugh at."

"What if we promise not to laugh?" Cyd asked. *Oh, brother.* They weren't going to let her back out of the group game easily.

"I'm only playing the game if Mya agrees to play, too." All eyes turned expectedly on Mya.

"I'll play," she said with ease as she shrugged her shoulders. Lex squinted her eyes at Mya in frustration.

"Great! I'll go get the guys so we can gather in the grand living room!"

"I'll come with you," Cyd said as she followed Imani out of the kitchen.

Lex flared her hands once Imani and Cyd were gone. "Um, Mya? What happened to the two of us sticking together?"

"A girl can't change her mind?"

Lex blew out a frustrated breath. "Not when there's so much at stake!"

"Okay, maybe I missed something. What exactly is at stake by us playing this game?"

Lex thrust her head to the ceiling and closed her eyes. If she admitted that she didn't trust herself around Micah when alcohol was involved, that would mean she would have to admit that her self-control was low around him. She wasn't even ready to admit that to herself so she definitely wasn't going to admit that to Mya.

"Whatever," she said brushing it off. "Let's just go get this game over with."

As they rounded the corner and walked the hall that led to the grand living room, Lex's heart was beating so fast, she swore she could actually hear the sound of it echoing through the hall. She felt as if she were walking into the lion's den, with Micah being the lion and her, his prey. *You got this, girl. It's just a game and he's just a man.* But the minute she entered the room, she knew she was in trouble. His piercing brown eyes landed on her, breaking the little cool she had.

Cyd had already directed everyone in a circle and the cards on the large coffee table were spread sporadically in a circle, as well.

"What is this game?" Lex asked as Cyd, she and Mya took a seat next to one another in the circle, as Cyd had instructed to with her index finger. They'd played group games before, but this wasn't their usual Q&A game and it definitely involved more liquor than usual.

"It's called circle of death or ring of fire. Whatever name you like most. I personally like circle of death so that's what we're calling it tonight."

Say what? Circle of death? Who in their right mind would play a game called circle of death? Lex finally noticed the beer can in the middle of the table. Shot glasses and mixed drinks were also in front of everyone. She lifted up one of the red cups and inhaled. *Tequila? Oh, heck no. I'm not drinking this!*

"Um, Cyd?" Lex asked, holding up the red cup. "What's in this cup?"

Cyd gave her a sly smile before responding. "That's tequila my dear, but don't worry, I watered yours down with juice. And before you tell me you refuse to drink it, how about I explain the rules of the game? Because if you pick your cards right, you may not have to drink that much."

Lex flashed Cyd a fake smile before she put the cup down.

"You'll be fine," Mya whispered in Lex's ear before glancing across the room. "I got your back."

She followed the line of Mya's eyes and landed right on the same person she'd been trying to avoid the entire night.

"Yeah, right," Lex whispered back. Lex could handle her liquor and usually loved a good game. But having Micah in the room made her nervous, and her friends knew that tequila was her kryptonite. Therefore, she avoided the stuff like the plague.

"Lex you pick a card first," Cyd prompted. *Please be a good card. Please be a good card. Yes, a three! Wait, what's a three?*

"I have a three," Lex said to the group. "What does that mean?"

"A three stands for *me*," Cyd said. "Which means you have to take a drink."

Of course that's what it means. Lex reached for the red cup.

"Not that one," Cyd said. "Your first drink has to be a shot."

"Fine," Lex said through gritted teeth. She swung back the shot and placed the glass back on the table with more force than necessary.

"Mya, you're next."

Mya picked a four, which meant that all the women had to drink. "I hate this game already," Lex said in what she thought was a whisper. She glanced at Mya,

Cyd and Imani in time to see them all trying to stifle a laugh. When she glanced across the table at Micah, he seemed to be holding back a laugh, as well. Lex loved a good laugh just as much as the next person, but lately, it seemed that all jokes were on her.

Chapter 5

Since it was the group's first time playing this particular game, Cyd had stated they would only go a couple rounds. Micah thought it was nice to revert back to their college years when drinking games were a thing of the norm, but most people in attendance were in their upper twenties and thirties, so their tolerances weren't nearly as high now as they were back in college.

Micah could tell that Lex was trying her best to keep her composure because, apparently, liquor made her a lot bolder. She wasn't shy about batting her eyelashes in his direction, and on a couple occasions he saw Mya hold Lex's hands down to her sides. Each time, he wondered what Lex was about to do that caused Mya to grip her hands.

"It's you turn, bro," Shawn said breaking his thoughts. He'd surprisingly pulled a number that hadn't been pulled yet.

"Cyd, what's a five?" She glanced over at Shawn and gave him a slick smile before she answered Micah's question.

"Well, like I said, there are many different versions to this game. But for tonight, a five means that we have to play *never have I ever*. Let's just do a rotation around the circle and each person says something that they have never done before. For kicks, let's put up five fingers, too. If you have done it, we trust that you'll be honest and put down a finger if you have. If you run out of fingers, participate anyway for fun."

Seems simple enough. "Okay," Micah said as he tried to think of a good *never have I ever* confession. "Never have I ever been fired from a job," he said deciding to keep it general. He may have quit his fair share of jobs when he was younger, but never had he been fired from one. A couple of Daman's friends and one of Imani's friends put one finger down.

"Never have I ever hot wired a car," Daman said next, receiving a few groans from a couple men, Micah included.

Imani was next. "Never have I ever been arrested." Micah was hesitant to put down a finger with Lex watching him so closely, but he promised to be honest.

"Didn't you used to be a cop?" Lex blurted out. *Damn, I knew she was looking.*

"Yes" was all Micah said. If she wanted to know the story, she'd have to wait.

"My turn," Cyd said. "Never have I ever skinny dipped," she continued as she gave Shawn a hard stare.

"Baby, I told you I didn't like how that lake looked," Shawn said firmly. "Besides, you're forgetting about the whirlpool in Carbondale last year."

"Making love to me in a hotel whirlpool is not skinny dipping," Cyd said poking her finger at Shawn's chest.

"What about all those times in Anguilla?"

Cyd blushed and lowered her voice. "Oh, yeah, all those times in the ocean…swimming pool…natural spring pool."

"TMI guys," Mya said shaking her head with a laugh. "We can still hear you and that sounds like a conversation for the bedroom."

Shawn and Mya took turns next, and then it was finally time for Lex's turn. *She's beautiful,* he thought as he watched her contemplate what she wanted to say. She had gotten up from her chair and was now sitting on the floor with her legs crossed. The color of her skinny jeans and blouse made him think about the lilac lingerie set he'd seen her purchase a few months ago. Damn, what he'd give to see her in that. Her hair was pulled up in a high ponytail and once again, she was wearing lipstick, only today, it was a color he hadn't seen before. She caught his eyes before she spoke.

"Never have I ever done anything in my life that was spontaneous or against the rules." Micah took note of the sad look in her eyes as she glanced around the room and saw finger after finger drop from people who had done what she confessed she hadn't.

When the next person went, his eyes still remained on Lex. She was playing with the rim of her cup, but her mind looked as if it were miles away. Before he could think about what he was doing he interrupted the game.

"Sorry everyone, but I think I need some fresh air," he announced. "Lex, would you like to join me on the patio outside?"

She gave him an incredulous look. "It's like twenty degrees out there."

"I'll get our coats."

She still looked skeptical, but luckily, the women talked her into joining him. He hadn't been outside yet, but he'd heard Daman talking about the rectangular bonfire table and outdoor furniture they had on the patio.

"It's freezing," Lex said as soon as they stepped outside into the darkness.

"Let's sit over there." He pointed to the chairs stationed around the bonfire. He sat on the bench and she took a seat two chairs away from him. He observed her as she blew into her hands before rubbing them together to stimulate friction. Even with the wine and tequila, she still didn't look completely relaxed.

"Why don't you sit here by me so I can warm you up?" She turned up an eyebrow at him. "I just meant we would stay warmer if we were sitting closer together. More body heat," he continued. She didn't need any more convincing as she began to move to sit beside him.

"So," she said, slightly turning to face him, "what were you arrested for?"

Man, she wasted no time asking me that. "How about I tell you that story when you're a little more sober."

"I'm sober now."

"Not completely."

"Nothing's wrong with my listening skills."

He searched her face. "I think I'll wait."

She looked disappointed. "Can you at least give me a hint?"

Micah laughed as he shook his head. "You already know that I used to be a cop, so clearly I'm not a bad person."

"I never said you were a bad person, but you do seem like a bit of a troublemaker," she said, brushing away a few strands of hair that had escaped from her ponytail.

"How can you tell?" he asked. "You've barely given yourself a chance to get to know me."

"Oh, I can tell," she said with a laugh. "You get this sneaky look in your eyes right before you're about to do something or say something to rattle someone's nerves." *So she has been paying attention.*

"That's not enough to label me as a troublemaker."

"Hmm…okay. From what I've observed over the past few months, I can tell that you're arrogant, cocky and a womanizer."

"Whoa," he said as he placed his hands over his chest. "Arrogant and cocky…at times, yes. Why? Because I'm a confident person. But a womanizer? That's far from the truth."

She gave him a look of disbelief. "You're a class A flirt, Micah, and I'm sure you'd screw anything with a skirt and not even care about how she felt afterward."

Ouch. That hurt. Especially coming from Lex. "Okay, yeah, I like to flirt. And I love being surrounded by beautiful women. But what man doesn't?" Micah got closer to Lex to make sure that she was listening to every word. "But I'm selective in who I date and who I sleep with. A womanizer is a selfish, egotistical prick that manipulates women and cares too much about himself. Whereas, I like to cherish women. I value their opinion, and although I've chased a few skirts in my time, now I'd much more prefer to date just one woman."

Her eyes grew bigger, and he noticed a quickening in her breathing. She didn't say anything and slightly turned her head away from him, so he continued.

"You see, Lex, for months I've been trying to get to know you but, apparently, you have already convinced yourself that I'm no good for you. Now, I'll admit that every now and then I can cause a bit of trouble, but I promise," he said as he lightly touched her chin to bring her face back toward him, "my kind of trouble is pleasurable and satisfying."

He watched a range of emotions cross her face, the most prominent emotion being interest. He'd seen that look on her before, but tonight was different. Tonight he'd learned that Lex was the type of woman who followed the rules. She thought before she took action and if something was out of her comfort zone, she backed away from it. Micah knew he was definitely standing outside of her comfort zone blocked by a gigantic electric wall. But he wanted to blow her fuse and he was pretty sure now was his chance to push her a little further.

He leaned in closer to her and to his surprise she began leaning forward, as well. When they were mere centimeters apart, she hesitated and slightly parted her lips, releasing a small fog only visible in the frosty breeze. *Keep going, Lex.* He wished he could grab her and finally get the kiss he'd been waiting on for months. But he needed her to make the decision to move just a tad closer first. Her breaths grew quicker, letting out faster puffs into the cold air that matched his own and mingled into one white cloud between them.

"Remember what you said during the drinking game?" Micah asked, noticing a cute small brown freckle on her nose that he hadn't seen before.

"During never have I ever?" she asked breathlessly.

"Yes," he said. "Don't think, just do." She searched his eyes before dropping to his lips. She leaned in a couple more centimeters. *That's close enough,* Micah thought as he crashed his lips to hers. He expected her to be surprised, but instead, her hands went around his neck as she softly moaned into his mouth. She tasted just like he'd imagined she would...sweet and tangy with a hint of wine and tequila from the game they'd been playing.

He probed her mouth open even farther and slipped his tongue deeper inside when she parted her lips more. She moaned softly into his mouth and gripped his neck even tighter, lightly massaging the back of his head as she did. The seductive way she moved her hands just made him want to kiss her harder...longer...until they were both breathless and craving for oxygen. What was it about this woman that pushed him to the brink of insanity? He'd never been this intrigued by a woman before, nor had he enjoyed a kiss quite like this. When she moaned into his mouth again and slipped her tongue even deeper, he knew he had to stop before he lost complete control of himself.

He broke the kiss, heaving rapidly as his lungs filled with coldness. Her cheeks were pink and her lipstick smeared. Evidence of just how thoroughly he'd devoured her mouth. "That was some kiss," he voiced, saying the first thing that came to mind. In all honesty, he didn't know what to say because all he wanted to do was to continue kissing her.

Her eyes grew from seductive to big and cautious. *Oh, no...what is she thinking.* Before he could even ask her what was wrong, she hopped up from the seat, said she had to go and hightailed it back into the estate.

Micah wanted to go after her and knew whoever was still at the party would take one look at her flustered state and swollen lips and be able to tell she'd just gotten thoroughly kissed. But he couldn't move from his spot on the bench. He looked down at the bulge of his pants and tried to will it to go down. But it was useless. There was only one person who could make it go down and, unfortunately, she'd run from him once again.

"Way to go, Madden," he said to himself as he unbuttoned his coat and hoped that the harsh wind would help him calm down.

As soon as Lex stepped back inside Imani and Daman's estate, she went straight toward an empty bedroom that was a couple feet away from the door with a window that overlooked the patio. She kept the lights off when she entered and softly shut the door behind her. Taking a deep breath, she pushed back the curtain to see if Micah was still sitting by the bonfire.

He was right were she'd left him and by the look on his face, he was just as affected by the kiss as she was. She had never been kissed like that, and even with the cold temperature, her body felt like it was on fire. She brought her hand to her lips, a little surprised by their swollen state. He put every man she'd kissed in her past to shame, and if that kiss was any indication of how good he was in the bedroom, she was in trouble.

While she watched him stare at the bonfire, she wished she knew what he was thinking. There was something so rugged and mysterious about his demeanor, and even though she wished she wasn't curious about him…she was. She wondered what led him to become the man he was today. And what had he been arrested for? He ran one hand down his face and smiled. *To be inside his mind,* she thought, wondering what his smile was about. She hoped he was smiling because he was thinking about her. His response to her accusation about him being a womanizer had left her speechless. Not only had she offended him, but she'd also made assumptions based off little fact. He probably thought she'd kissed him because she was a little intoxicated, but she'd only pretended to drink the last couple times she was prompted to during the game, so she was alert. She'd kissed him because at that moment, she wanted to know exactly what his lips felt like…tasted like. For months, she'd convinced herself that kissing him wasn't what she wanted to do, but in that moment, she decided to do something she didn't do often. React before thinking about the consequences.

He pushed his coat off a little more and dropped his head back. He'd unbuttoned his coat despite the fact that the weather outside was slowly growing even colder. He placed both hands over his face and sat like that for a couple minutes. When he adjusted himself on the seat, she couldn't see his face, so she opened the curtain a little more, moving closer to the window to get a better angle.

He placed his elbows on his knees before standing. His face looked strained for a moment, until he shook out his arms and rolled his neck. When he stretched his arms in the air, his back was turned to Lex. She watched him completely remove his coat and throw it on the bench before shaking out his arms for a second time. *It's freezing! Why in the world is he removing his coat?*

Her question was answered the minute he turned around and she noticed the massive bulge in his pants. She gasped and brought her hand to her mouth, wondering how she'd missed it when she was outside with him. He looked down at his pants before looking up to the sky. Watching him standing outside, completely aroused just from sharing one passionate kiss with her was enough to wet her center to the core. She placed one leg in front of the other, clasping her thighs together as tightly as she could.

I wish I had the nerve to invite him back to my place. She quickly shook her head at the thought. "Where did that come from?" she asked herself quietly. He began pacing back and forth, the bulge in his pants slowly diminishing. She quietly giggled to herself when she finally realized that the only reason he was still outside was because he was trying to calm himself down before heading back into the estate.

He jumped in place a couple times before grabbing his coat and turning toward the window Lex was standing at. "Oh, crap," she said before dropping the curtain. The lights were off so there was no way he could see her. *But he looked right in my direction, so maybe he did see me standing here.*

She quietly made her way to the door just as she heard the back door leading to the patio slide open. When she saw the knob turn, she quickly jumped behind the bed.

"Lex, are you in here?" Micah whispered into the bedroom. When she didn't respond, he said her name again. *This is stupid,* she thought when she imagined how crazy it was for a grown woman to be hiding behind the bed. She slowly rose, and was happy to find him still in the doorway looking into the dark room, unaware that she had been hiding.

"I'm here," she said softly as she reached the door. He pushed the door slightly open, leaving it cracked so that the light from the hallway could seep in.

"So you were watching me outside," he said as more of a statement than a question.

"Only because I wanted to make sure you were okay since you didn't follow me back inside."

"Did you enjoy watching me when you thought I hadn't noticed?"

She knew what he was doing. He was trying to make her feel uncomfortable, but she didn't want to give him the satisfaction. *Just be honest.* "Yes, I did enjoy watching you," she said confidently. His face was half hidden by the darkness, but she didn't miss the grin that crossed his lips right before he bent down to kiss her again.

You should stop him, she thought as her arms took on a mind of their own and curled around his neck. *He's your client and if you don't stop him now, he'll think he can kiss you whenever he wants.* His hands went around her waist and pulled her closer to him. Once again, his mouth explored hers, lighter than before, but still just as demanding. She was just about to push him away when she heard him let out a deep groan as one hand sprawled across her back, while the other gently cupped her butt. She could feel him getting excited all over again, and the fact that he didn't care that she could feel the length of him excited her way more than she wanted it to. *Okay, maybe you can enjoy this last kiss before you tell him it could never happen again.*

And that's exactly what she did.

Chapter 6

Lex looked at her cell phone for the fourth time in the past thirty minutes. Usually, it only took her about ten minutes to get her eyebrows done, but the place she normally went to closed early on Fridays. She'd taken one look at herself in the mirror and knew she had to tame those bad boys before she met Micah for dinner.

She glanced around at the women in the waiting area to make sure no one was watching and slowly eased the back of her feet out of her heels. She was furious with herself for wearing heels to impress a man today of all days. It had been raining nonstop and not only were her feet wet and her shoes squishy, but her hair had decided to do a half straight, half curly look on its own. She'd spent all last night straightening her hair and this morning, she'd feathered it as well to add bounce and depth. Years ago, she'd grown out her relaxer and promised to never look back. Although she loved that her hair was healthier than it had ever been, Chicago was a hard city to maintain non-chemically-treated hair. Whether she straightened it or wore it natural, it sometimes decided to do exactly what she wished it wouldn't do.

"Mam, we're ready for you," the salon assistant said to Lex. *Thank goodness!* She hadn't seen Micah in a week and since they were leaving for Arkansas in a few days, she had to set some ground rules that she knew he wouldn't like. After the intoxicating kisses they'd shared a week ago, it would be hard to ignore his advances but she had to. She would be there to do a job…nothing more. And the quicker Micah realized that, the easier it would be to convince herself that he was no good for her.

"All done," the eyebrow specialist said to her after she was done threading her eyebrows. Lex settled the payment and tip and left the salon.

Goodness, she mouthed as she noticed several people on the corner trying to hail a taxi. The bus stop was a couple blocks away, and the new umbrella she'd just bought was clearly for fashion and not rain. She wouldn't have a weapon against the rainfall.

She decided to walk across the street from the other taxi hopefuls, and luckily she was able to get a taxi right away. When she arrived at the sushi restaurant that Micah had chosen for dinner, she was just on time for their reservation.

"Hello, Micah," she said, taking a seat at the table he was already at.

"Hi, Lex," he replied, watching her every move as she removed her coat. She had chosen to wear a black skirt that hugged her curves in all the right places and a blue blouse with a few ruffles in the center that offered a peak of her cleavage. She completed her outfit with modest silver jewelry and sleek black pumps. All her partners in the office earlier had mentioned how great she looked, but more importantly, she felt great.

"You look amazing," he said to her after she'd sat down. The appreciation in his eyes momentarily stole her breath and made her forget about her aching feet.

"Thanks…you look great, too," she responded, taking note of his sharp black suit and name-brand loafers. She hadn't seen him in a suit in a while and, apparently, seeing him all dressed up still had the same affect on her. She crossed her legs under the table and tried not to look too closely at his lips, which was a challenge as neither one of them said anything. In the comfortable silence, all they could do was observe one another. Instead of looking at his lips, she looked at his hair, noticing for the first time that it looked different than she remembered.

"Trying something new with your hair?" she asked. His curls were a little fuller at the top and the sides were cropped short in a fade that made his devastatingly sexy look even more masculine.

"Just changing it up a bit," he said, shrugging his shoulders and flashing her a smile.

"It looks nice." *So nice that I wish I could run my fingers through it.* Before her mind could wander any more, the waiter came to take their order. Lex had more than a few questions about the daily special and the top-rated dishes at the recently opened sushi restaurant. After a few minutes of back and forth discussion with the waiter, she finally placed her order and turned back to Micah as he placed his order, as well.

"So I take it you really love sushi?" Micah asked.

"I'm a huge fan of sushi, but I like all types of food."

"What's your favorite dessert?" he asked.

"That's easy! Anything red velvet!" *Who didn't love mouthwatering chocolate,* she thought. *I bet he's even tastier than chocolate.* She shook her head, reminding herself that comparing Micah to anything that was mouthwatering would surely make her drool in public.

"I actually love red velvet cake myself. What's your favorite type of food?"

She took a sip of her water and smiled before responding. "Honestly, I love food too much to pick just one type. Indian. Italian. Greek. Soul food…I could go on forever."

"I see," he said with a laugh. *Just great, Lex…way to sound like your favorite pastime is eating.* Which it was, but she didn't need him to know that.

"Based off the questions you asked the waiter, I can tell you have a great food palate."

Good, he seems more interested than turned off. "My dad is a huge foodie and a great cook so I guess you can say I got my love for food from him."

"Do you love to cook like your dad, as well?"

"Definitely," she answered just as the waiter placed their plates on the table. "When I was little, I would watch him in the kitchen all the time so naturally, as an adult, I mirrored a few of his techniques and turned them into my own."

"Hmm, techniques. So you're a whiz in the kitchen, huh?" he asked as he popped a piece of sushi into his mouth.

"I throw down every now and then," she said, nodding her head. She took out her phone and snapped a quick pic of the sushi before uploading it to her Instagram account and hash-tagging the restaurant.

"Sorry," she said when he was looking at her curiously. "I'm a bit of an Instagram fanatic and I love tagging things from new restaurants and events."

She slid her phone over so he could see a few of the images. "Most of these are foods I cooked myself."

"Nice pics," he said after he'd scrolled through several. "Any chance you'd ever let me taste some of your cooking?"

Everyone knew how much Lex loved cooking, but she hadn't cooked for a man in years. "We'll see," she said, taking her first bite of food and glancing at him as she chewed. He was charming and she hadn't really seen this particular side of him before, not that she'd given him much of a chance. He hadn't said anything about the kiss and if she hadn't known how much he enjoyed it at Imani and Daman's party, she would have questioned if the feelings were one-sided.

Conversation between them flowed easily as they talked about a few more things related to food, cooking and random shows on the Food Network.

"So you're a fan of *Top Chef?*" she asked, surprised.

"Sure am," he said, flashing his pearly whites. "Although I probably can't cook as good as you, I like to watch *Top Chef* and a few other shows on the Food Network to brush up on my skills."

My, oh, my. I love a man that can cook! If there was any weakness that Lex had besides a man with a nice butt and muscular arms, it was a man with good teeth and a love for cooking.

"I'll cook for you, if you cook for me," she blurted out without thinking.

"Just name the place and time sweetheart." His astute smile was unmistakable and his statement triggered something inside her. *Sweetheart?* He hadn't called her that before and the fact that she'd gone about eight years of her life being called sweetheart by a man she'd rather forget existed was unsettling. This wasn't how the conversation was supposed to be going. She liked how easy it was for her to talk to him, but she hadn't addressed any of the issues she had planned to discuss at tonight's dinner.

He steered you away from your plan, the voice inside her head taunted. Lex lived off plans. That was how she made sure her life ran in order, leaving little room for mistakes. But Micah was a mistake that she wished she could convince herself to make. Not only was he not in her life plan…he stood for everything she convinced herself she didn't need. This was exactly how her ex had trapped her. Charming her and calling her pet names. His favorite was sweetheart. As a matter of fact, the only name he called her was sweetheart. *Ugh!* Micah could have called her anything but that, and she'd still be captivated by him and the conversation.

"Micah, there's something we need to discuss," she said ignoring the confused look on his face.

"Are you okay Lex?"

"Yes," she said directly. "I forgot to tell you at the party that although I agreed to go with you to the winter festival, we will have to refrain from kissing and behave professionally."

"Um, okay," Micah said, looking at her with concerned eyes. "But my parents think they're meeting a woman I'm dating. Won't it be weird if we don't kiss."

"Everyone won't expect PDA."

"Knowing how I am…they will."

She wished his statement didn't warm her body. "Well, if we have to share a kiss or two for show, that's fine. But nothing more. And I will stay at your parents' home because if they are anything like my family, they won't allow me to stay at the inn when we are supposed to be dating. But we must have separate rooms."

"That can be arranged," he said, searching her face. "Did I say anything to offend you?"

She sighed as she contemplated the right words "No, you didn't say anything," she lied, finishing the remainder of her food. He seemed as if he wanted to ask her more, but her phone rang, halting their conversation.

"Sorry, I need to take this call," she said to Micah as she rose from her seat and went to the waiting area of the restaurant.

"Hi, Mom."

"Oh, Lex, so glad I got you! Is there any way you can stop by the house tonight?"

Lex glanced at her iPhone to check the time. "It's almost 8 p.m. If I take the train, I still won't get out to the suburbs until about 9:30. Can this wait until tomorrow?"

"Oh, okay. I understand," Linda Turner said into the phone in disappointment. "Your father and I are driving to Tennessee with your aunt and uncle, Hope and David, and we leave at 4 a.m. tomorrow. But it's okay, I guess it can wait until later. I just really wanted to see you before we left."

Lex recognized the tone in her mother's voice and knew it was definitely not okay. Her mom was more than just a mother. She was one of her greatest confidants and Lex hated to hear her disappointed.

"Okay, Mom, I'll stop by. But I won't be able to stay long."

"No, you're right, sweetie. I don't want you traveling home this late. I'll just see you when you get back from Arkansas."

She'd told her mom the entire story and the way Micah conned her into going to Arkansas with him. To her dismay, her mom thought the entire situation was hilarious.

"Excuse me, Lex," she heard Micah say behind her.

"Hold on, Mom," she said before placing her hand over the phone and turning her attention to Micah.

"Yes."

"The waiter brought the check so I went ahead and paid and grabbed your coat and purse since this place is getting pretty packed with the late dinner crowd. Would you like to go across the street for coffee so we can talk about the Arkansas trip?"

More time with you would be too tempting, she thought. And though they still had more to discuss, she now had other plans.

"Sorry," she said to him. "I have other plans tonight." She saw the hint of disappointment in his eyes and tried not to enjoy it too much. For the past ten minutes she'd been acting pretty firm toward him and although she knew he didn't understand her change in demeanor, she couldn't help it.

"Okay, do you have any time tomorrow?"

She tilted her head and looked into his eyes. She didn't have any plans tomorrow except a bit of winter cleaning, but he didn't have to know that. *I wonder if I should make him think I have a hot date?* She was normally honest with men, not caring one way or another if they knew the truth. But Micah rattled her nerves too much and she was slowly realizing she enjoyed toying with him when she could.

Don't do it Lex, her inner voice warned. "Sorry, but my plans tonight may be *exhausting,*" she said, ignoring the warning and emphasizing the word *exhausting.* "My companion may keep me up too late." As she watched the displeasure spread across his face, she secretly relished in the fact that he wasn't ready for their night to end.

He didn't say anything. Instead he just stood there watching her closely. When she felt her nerves roll into a ball at the pit of her stomach, she pushed the feeling away. She felt liberated…in control. Powerful. Feminine. Strong.

"We'll just catch up when our schedules match, Micah," she continued.

"Baby, you better stop lying to that man." Her mother's voice filled the front of the restaurant. The high-pitched voice caught her off guard and caused her to almost drop her phone. She glanced down and realized she'd accidentally hit the speakerphone key. *Stupid touch phone.* She tried to click the speakerphone off, but it wasn't working.

"That man just asked you a simple question and you are making up excuses not to spend time with him. If he's as sexy as you say he is, then you should take him up on his offer for coffee."

"Mom, you're on speaker," Lex yelled into the phone. "I'm trying to get you off, but I can't," she said nervously, tapping the phone.

"Am I still on speaker?" her mom asked.

"Yes," Lex answered, not daring to look up at Micah.

"Oh, good. Put the phone near Micah."

"He can still hear you mom."

"Micah?" her mom called out.

"Yes, Mrs. Turner?" Lex finally glanced at him, mortified to see him grinning from ear to ear.

"Is there any chance you can drive my daughter to my house right now? Her father and I have something important to give her."

You have got to be kidding me. "Mom, he can't do that."

"Of course I can, Mrs. Turner. We're leaving the restaurant now."

"Micah, this isn't necessary."

"Oh, yes it is," her mom responded. "Lex, let Micah bring you over here. And your father and I want to meet him."

"Mom, we'll be there," Lex said, accepting defeat. "See you soon," she continued, prompting her mom to disconnect the call.

As soon as her mom hung up, her phone conveniently unfroze. All she could do was shake her head and look down at the floor. Without looking into his face, she grabbed her coat and put it on before taking her purse. *So humiliating.* Stuff like this would only happen to her.

Chapter 7

Once they were outside, she looked up at him again, happy to see that he was no longer smiling. The sunlight was gone, but the streetlights and snow on the ground still illuminated the area. Micah pointed his hand to the left for her to walk in that direction.

"How far down did you park?" she asked.

"Three blocks," he answered, falling into step with her. When they had walked two blocks, she couldn't take the silence anymore.

"Don't you have anything to say?" she asked him.

"Nope, nothing," he stated frankly. *Oh, I get it. He's paying me back for lying to him about having a date.*

Why did men make things so complicated? Micah always threw her off, yet she says one little white lie and he gets all bent out of shape.

She looked at him again. His face hadn't changed.

"Okay, fine," she said tossing her hands in the air. "I'm sorry for lying to you."

"I can't believe you lied," he said as he turned to her with a solemn look on his face. "My ex used to lie to me all the time."

He placed his head down and grew silent again. *Just great, Lex. Lie to the guy who has a history of women lying to him.*

"Well I truly am sorry, Micah. I was just trying to get you back for all those times you made me feel uncomfortable."

"Because you think I'm such a bad person." His voice was desolate, and Lex felt even worse. She reached out to touch his hunched-over shoulders. When she did, he caught her wrist and brought her to him. She gasped out of surprise.

"What are you doing?" she asked Micah, attempting to push against his chest but instead, she rested her hands there. He flashed her a mischievous smile.

"You're not upset at all, are you?" she asked him, finally catching on.

He laughed before he responded. "What type of sensitive men have you dated in the past that would cause you to believe I was upset about something so small."

Evan would have been furious. "I thought I'd hurt you're feelings," she said, feeling gullible that she'd fallen for his antics once again.

"Hurt my feelings?" he said, looking into her eyes. "Words don't break me. Besides…you think I'm sexy."

"My mom said that, not me."

"I've never met your mom, so I can only assume that she was quoting what you've told her."

He was leaning in closer to her and she knew what he

was about to do, yet she wasn't trying to stop him. In fact, she wanted it just as much as he did. When he was close enough to almost touch her lips, an ambulance flew by, disrupting the moment. It was the chance Lex needed to push away from him.

"Are we near your car?" she asked, walking ahead of him.

"It's a couple cars down," he said, following behind her. When they reached his car, he opened the passenger door so that she could slide in.

When he was walking around to the driver's side, she let out the breath she'd been holding. Her night wasn't really going the way she'd planned.

"Just so you know," she said, turning to Micah when he got in the car, "I meant what I said earlier. No more kissing."

He shook his head and laughed as he started up the engine.

"I mean it," she said, trying to sound forceful.

"I heard you when you said it in the restaurant," he said, turning his attention to the road. When they stopped at a light, he looked over to her, determined and resolute. "But if you think I'm forgetting about those explosive kisses we shared, then think again. You'll see."

See? What would she see? She wasn't sure she could handle seeing anything more Micah had to offer, which she was sure was a helleva lot.

"What's the address?" he asked, breaking her thoughts. She rattled off the address so he could plug it into the GPS system in his car.

"Let's go meet moms and pops," he said with a slick smile. She didn't dare respond to his comment. Words had gotten her in enough trouble tonight. Instead, she turned to look out her window and prayed that news of her introducing Micah to her parents wouldn't spread in her family like wildfire. Having one set of parents believe they were a couple was enough drama for one holiday season.

After a thirty-minute drive, they arrived at her parents' house. She had no idea what her parents wanted to give her, but she knew it had to be important if they wanted her to come visit them this late. When they pulled into the driveway, her parents were already opening the front door.

"Hey, baby," her dad said, embracing her as she stepped inside the house. She hugged her mom and her dad before introducing them to Micah.

"Mom, dad, this is Micah Madden. Micah, these are my parents, Linda and Ethan Turner."

"Nice to meet you both," Micah said, hugging Mrs. Turner and shaking hands with Mr. Turner. Lex smiled as her dad sized up Micah. Since she was an only child, her dad was extremely protective, especially after her relationship with Evan.

"Why don't we go sit in the family room," her mom stated after they removed their coats and shoes. When they sat down, she observed each parent, wondering why they seemed so anxious.

"Would you like me to wait in another room?" Micah asked, clearly sensing their apprehension, as well.

"No, that's not necessary," Mrs. Turner stated.

"What's going on?" Lex asked.

'Well, sweetie," Linda said, slightly glancing from her to her dad, "your father and I were able to locate something and were so excited to give it to you that it couldn't wait until Christmas." Her mom pulled out a white box with a blue bow tied around it that had been sitting on the table near the large sofa.

"Open it," her mom said, handing her the box. She looked at her parents inquisitively before untying the ribbon and opening the box.

When she removed the tissue paper, her heart skipped a beat. She let out a soft gasp as she clenched her chest, overwhelmed by what she saw. *It can't be...* She picked up the delicate gold brooch and ran her hands across the gems and diamonds. She hadn't seen the brooch in years and thought she'd never see it again.

"How did you find it?" she asked her parents.

"Your father was with some friends in Michigan and he ran across the brooch in an upscale pawnshop."

"What," Lex exclaimed. "Michigan! He sold my brooches to a pawnshop in Michigan!"

"Sweetie, that doesn't matter," her mom responded. "What matters is that your father was able to find it or better yet, the brooch was able to find him."

Lex knew her father often checked pawnshops to see what hidden treasures were waiting to be found. It was truly a miracle that he had found this one. "This must have cost you a fortune," she said to her dad.

"Nothing's too expensive for my baby," her dad said as he gave her a wink. Lex walked over to where her parents were sitting and gave them each a huge hug as she thanked them while rubbing away a couple tears that had fallen.

"Did you find the others?" she asked, although she already knew the answer. If they had, they would have given them to her.

"No, I didn't," her dad responded, sounding crushed.

"Well then, I'll make sure I cherish this one." When

she returned to her seat, she met Micah's curious glance before dropping her eyes back to the brooch. She heard her mom tell her father to join her in the kitchen before they vacated the room.

Once she was alone with Micah, she figured now was a good time to mention a part of her past that she often tried to forget.

"This brooch is one of three," she said, turning her head to face him. "When I went off to college, my grandmother Faith Gamine Burrstone, my mom's mother, had given me one of three brooches that were given to her by a dear friend. She knew I always loved them, and when I was little I used to sneak into her room, put on her lipstick and fancy wigs and stick one of her brooches on my shirt as I pretended to be her. I couldn't get enough of playing dress up with Gamine's stuff," Lex said with a slight laugh.

"Every time she caught me, she just smiled, gave me a kiss on the cheek and told me that one day, she would give me a brooch when I was old enough to hear the story behind them. I was surprised and honored when at eighteen, she had decided to give me a brooch from her collection…but there hadn't been a story to go along with it. She said that there would be a story she'd tell me later when I was ready to hear it."

Lex momentarily glanced back at the brooch as emotion clogged her throat. "When she passed away six years ago, she left me the other two brooches in her will along with the story that I'd waited most of my life to hear. It changed me at the time of her death, and it was exactly what I needed to hear in my life at that moment."

She glanced back at Micah, a little surprised at herself for what she was about to share with him. It was a topic, she rarely spoke about…mainly because she had a hard time admitting to herself that the woman too cautious for her own good had been reckless in her past decisions.

"The day I received the story and the other brooches was the day I decided to divorce my ex-husband, Evan Gilmore." She stared into his eyes, waiting for the look of shock or surprise to cross his face, but it didn't.

"Did someone tell you I was divorced before?"

"Not at all," he said as he took her hands in his. "And I'm sure divorcing your ex wasn't easy."

"It wasn't," she responded, glancing at their intertwined hands before looking up to his face. "On top of being the worst husband in the world, he also robbed me of my youth, among other things. A week before I was moving out of our home, we were robbed and the thieves managed to take everything I cherished in life… including all three of my grandmother's brooches. I always suspected Evan was behind the robbery, and so did my family. My suspicions were confirmed a year after our divorce when one of Evan's old coworkers told me that he had overheard Evan at the gym the day before the robbery gloating to a couple other men that if I got half of what he had earned, then it was only fair that he take the things I loved, as well. So my dad finding this brooch is priceless…"

"I'm sorry to hear that," Micah said with concern written across his face. "What did he do that made him the worst husband?"

She opened her mouth to say more, but then closed it quickly. *How can I possibly explain the depth of the hurt he caused?*

"You can tell me when you're ready," he said, sensing her hesitation. "But I do have one thing to say."

I don't want your pity, she thought. He reached up to touch her cheek. "The hardships and pain that we must go through sometimes may feel unbearable. But it's those situations and circumstances that make us stronger and wiser. It may not feel like it sometimes, but your relationship with your ex made you stronger...not weaker."

His words melted her heart in a way that no one else had. So many of her friends and family knew about her relationship with her ex, yet Micah had managed to listen to part of her story without judgment or pity. The man looking at her with his rich brown eyes was not flirting or joking like he normally did. He was compassionate, and although she knew she shouldn't kiss him, that was all his words made her want to do.

She leaned closer to him, enjoying the glint in his eyes when he, too, realized that she was going to kiss him. She never took the initiative to kiss a man, especially a man like Micah. Her lips softly brushed his at the same time that her hands clasped the back of his neck. He quickly took over, dipping his tongue into her mouth. She sighed from the sweetness of his lips. The kiss wasn't too hard or too soft... It was perfect with just the right amount of pressure. She could go on kissing him forever, which was exactly why she needed to end it before they lost control.

When their lips broke apart, she didn't feel the same anxiety she felt around Micah the last time they'd kissed. This time, she felt comforted, calm, and...protected. Those were feelings she hadn't felt from a man in a very long time.

Chapter 8

Micah stood in the kitchen listening to Mr. Turner explain the best way to smoke a turkey. It was the fourth dish that he'd pulled out of the refrigerator since he and Lex had arrived. When Lex had told her father that Micah enjoyed cooking, it hadn't taken him long to have him taste a range of dishes he'd previously made.

"Now taste this macaroni and tell me if you can pinpoint my secret ingredient," Mr. Turner said, handing Micah a small plate. Micah tasted a bite of the macaroni and turned toward the kitchen entrance, wondering where Lex and her mom had run off to.

"So...what do you think?" Mr. Turner prompted. Micah turned his head back to Mr. Turner at the sound of his voice.

"Hmm...did you add a little cayenne pepper?" he asked.

"Exactly," Mr. Turner said, snapping his fingers. "Plus a special cheese that you can only import from Italy." *Lex wasn't lying about her father's love for cooking,* Micah thought as he laughed to himself. He'd learned more cooking secrets from Mr. Turner in the past hour than he had on several Food Network shows.

Mr. Turner's checkered glasses and animated expressions reminded Micah of his uncle Barry, who used to wear unique glasses and spoke with such emotion when he was passionate about something. They would have gotten along wonderfully and since they were both talkers, he couldn't imagine them running out of things to say. Too bad his uncle Barry was no longer here and his own uptight father wasn't blessed with the gift of gab.

His mind drifted back to Lex. He knew it had been hard for Lex to tell him she had been divorced, but little did she know, it explained a whole lot about her character. Now Micah understood why Lex seemed so dismissive of him at times. Her ex had put her through a terrible marriage followed by a hellish divorce, and then taken things from her that she held dearly.

"Micah, are you ready to go?" Lex asked as she entered the kitchen wearing a smile that he couldn't seem to get enough of. Her mom trailed closely behind her. It was obvious that Lex had gotten her natural beauty from her mother, although she favored both of her parents a great deal.

"I'm ready," he said before turning back to Mr. Turner. "It was nice to meet you, sir, and I enjoyed our conversation."

"It was nice to meet you, too," Mr. Turner said shaking his hand. "Make sure you take care of my daughter in Arkansas."

"I will." After bidding goodbye to Mrs. Turner, Micah escorted Lex to the car. They plugged her address into the GPS and began the drive to her home. Glancing over at Lex, he smiled when he noticed the content look on her face. He didn't know if it was the brooch or their conversation that made her seem more at ease. But he figured it was probably a combination of both. At every stoplight on their drive to the expressway, he couldn't help but glance over at her.

"Any reason you keep staring at me," she asked, turning from the window to look at him, trying to hide the smile on her face.

"No reason," he said, looking from the road to her. He thought she would question him some more but she didn't. She leaned her head against the seat and her eyes fluttered closed, another good sign that she was getting more comfortable around him.

Halfway through their drive, Lex's breathing was even and peaceful as she slept. She wore a slight smile on her face that made him wonder if she was dreaming about the kiss they'd shared. He hadn't planned on kissing her in her parents' home, but when she had leaned toward him, he couldn't help but capture her lips.

His personal cell phone rang and he briefly wondered if he should let the car pick up the call or answer on his Bluetooth. He chose his Bluetooth so he wouldn't disturb Lex.

"Talk to me."

"Hey, Micah. It's Shawn."

"What's up, man?"

"I just heard from the Wellington brothers. We got their investment, but there are still a few minor things we have to do before they sign the contract. I already asked our lawyer to go over the termination clause and other details."

"That's great news. I'm meeting with Grant and Parker Inc. in Little Rock, Arkansas, next week. I think we're pretty solid and can count on their investment, but of course I'll update you after the meeting."

"Sounds like a plan. Landing that account would be our biggest yet. Good luck in Arkansas."

"Thanks, man," Micah said before hanging up and glancing at Lex to make sure he hadn't disturbed her sleep. He had been looking forward to their trip to Arkansas ever since Lex had agreed, but after tonight, he was even more anxious to see what the coming weeks would bring.

"Excuse me, Driver. How much longer before we get to Cranberry Heights?" Lex asked after seeing nothing but open fields for the past half hour.

"The welcome sign for Cranberry Heights is right up the road, mam," the driver replied. "Then it's about ten minutes until we get to the Madden manor."

Just as the driver had stated, the welcome sign came into view. She stared out the window and admired a cluster of horses running in a meadow. She honestly couldn't remember the last time she'd seen so much outland. She had expected to be traveling with Micah to Arkansas, but last minute, she'd changed her flight and told him she would meet him a day after he arrived, claiming she had some last-minute work to finish. But in actuality, she had been overanalyzing what type of clothes to pack and gathering everything she would need for a two-week trip. Not to mention, most of her brain had been occupied with thoughts of Micah's sweet kisses, wondering what it would feel like to have his mouth in other places.

A large banging noise distracted her from her thoughts. "They must be setting up for the winter festival, right?" she asked the driver.

"Most of the festival is already set up, but they are preparing for the kick-off parade tomorrow morning. All of Cranberry Heights comes out for that festival as well as a few neighboring towns."

"Interesting," Lex stated as she observed the men and women decorating the parade floats. She cracked her window to let a little air into the heated vehicle. The fifty-five degree Arkansas weather was a big relief from the eighteen degrees she'd left in Chicago, but the Arkansas residents appeared to be as bundled as Chicagoans. The town seemed quaint and festive. Lex's family was big into the holidays, but she had a feeling she was in for a surprise here in Cranberry Heights. Already, she'd seen signs advertising a variety of winter activities.

As they passed through the part of town that she assumed was downtown, and turned on a long coiling road with houses in the distance, her mind became occupied with thoughts of Micah again. Her parents had enjoyed meeting Micah and although they'd promised not to mention their visit to other family members, she knew better. *If I weren't so attracted to him, I probably wouldn't even care...* But the fact that she was so attracted to him was exactly why she did care. Guaranteed she was a little clumsy by nature, but around Micah she oftentimes felt more awkward than usual, and instead of coming off as sexy, she came off as a klutz. *Maybe I should just head back to Chicago?* she thought when she remembered that

Micah's parents would be under the assumption that she was dating their son.

"Mam, we're here," the taxi driver said to Lex as they pulled up in front of Madden Manor. She rubbed her hands together, a sign that she was anxious, as she stared at the massive house, not yet ready to get out of the vehicle. The large white house was gorgeously decorated with an array of Christmas decorations. She could only imagine how amazing the house looked at night. Pine trees surrounded the right and left side of the home, and a rustic welcome sign was displayed on the front door. Lex was in awe of the entire decor and probably would have sat in the car gazing at the house even longer if the driver hadn't tapped the window.

"Sorry! I was admiring the decorations," she said as she finally got out of the vehicle. "How much do I owe you?"

"Mr. Madden already took care of it," the driver replied as he began wheeling her bags up the gravel sidewalk.

"At least let me give you a tip," she said after him, pushing the fifty-dollar bill back in her wallet and reaching for ten dollars instead.

"No need, mam," the driver said with a smile when they reached the front porch. "Mr. Madden already took care of that, too. Enjoy your stay."

After the driver left, she turned toward the front door and was just about to ring the doorbell when the door flew open.

"You must be Lexus," said an older woman with soft brown hair, creamy mocha skin and kind eyes. Her facial features were warm and inviting and, immediately, Lex felt comfortable.

"I'm Cynthia Madden, Micah's mother. My son has told us so much about you. Come in out that cold dear."

"Nice to meet you, Mrs. Madden," Lex said when she stepped inside the foyer.

"Now, do you prefer Lexus or Lex? Micah mentioned both names to us."

At least he had the decency not to mention LG or lingerie girl as one of my nicknames. "Lex is fine," she replied, unbuttoning her winter coat. "You're home is so beautiful."

"Thank you," Cynthia replied as she took and hung up Lex's coat. "My husband doesn't always appreciate my interior decorating skills, but I always tell him that it's important for our guests to feel as if they are in their home away from home."

"I agree," Lex replied, following Cynthia into the living room. "What smells so delicious?"

"That would be my apple crumb pie," Cynthia said with a smile as she led Lex to the living room. "How about I bring you a slice and a cup of coffee before I give you a tour?"

"That would be great," Lex replied, her mouth already watering.

"Then, I'll be right back. Please make yourself comfortable. Micah is getting firewood from the shed so he should be back shortly."

After Cynthia left, Lex took the time to admire the decorations inside the home. The large pine tree was decked out in silver-and-gold ornaments while green vines wrapped around the staircase. Antique Christmas angels were delicately placed throughout the few rooms in the house that she could see from where she stood in the living room, and white lights outlined the top of the ceiling in every room.

The soft Christmas music playing in the background reminded her of her grandmother's home during the holidays. Her grandfather still made sure the house was decorated for the holidays, but her grandmother Gamine had an extra special touch that the family had missed since she'd passed away.

Lex breathed in the earthy scent of pine and cedar as she walked over to the massive fireplace to admire the red velvet stockings hanging there and on the near wall. There had to be about twenty stockings in total. *Why on earth are there so many?* Her eyes grew bigger when she zoomed in on a stocking with the name Lexus written on it.

"That's so sweet," Lex said to herself.

"My mom is the sweetest person I know," Micah said behind her before he placed an armful of wood in the black wrought iron log rack. *Don't watch him bend over,* she reminded herself when she felt her eyes following his movements. She focused on a quilt placed over the side of the couch for distraction, admiring the unique patches and warm colors. *Thank goodness we have separate rooms.* Just being in the same vicinity as Micah now was hard enough. She couldn't imagine how it would be if they had to spend the night in the same room.

"I'm glad to see you have arrived safely," Micah said, coming to stand close to her. She turned to face him and immediately wished she'd focused on a spot behind him instead of on him directly. His striking stance demanded her undivided attention.

"You look good," Micah said as his eyes traveled the length of her. Before she'd left for the airport this morning, she'd chosen to wear a pair of skinny jeans, a white blouse and brown boots. She didn't want to seem as if she was trying hard to impress him, but in actuality, it had taken her almost an hour to pick out her outfit.

"You look good, too," she said observing his loose-fitting jeans and beige button-up. "We complement each other."

"I agree," he said, his eyes dancing with laughter. "We look good together."

Wait, I didn't mean it like that. "I meant our outfits complement each other."

"That, too," Micah replied as he glanced at her lips. He took a step toward her and she wondered what he was going to do.

"Don't worry," he said as he reached out his arms to pull her closer to him. "I was just going to hug you," he whispered in her ear. The mellow tone of his voice made her skin tingle with desire. She was slowly learning that everything Micah did was for a purpose. So the calculated way he pulled her into his embrace and the way his lips brushed against her ear were both things that he'd done on purpose...perhaps, just to rattle her.

"Yeah, I'm sure that was the only thing on your mind," Lex responded with a slight laugh after he released her. He flashed her a smile showing off his deep dimples. *Goodness he's sexy.* She really loved the curly Mohawk style he wore and he had a sort of rugged look about him today that added to his sex appeal.

"Well, I have to tell you, Lex," Cynthia said, returning with a piece of pie and coffee, "I don't think I've ever seen my son smile that way at a woman. You must be someone special."

Lex glanced at Micah to see how he would respond and was intrigued to see that he was still smiling.

"Mrs. Madden, I noticed the stocking with my name on it," Lex interjected, changing the subject. "Thanks so much for including me even though I won't be here for Christmas."

"Didn't Micah tell you?" Cynthia asked as she placed a cup of coffee and slice of pie on a nearby coffee table.

"Tell me what?" Lex asked, looking from Micah to his mother.

Cynthia gave Micah an incredulous look before explaining. "Next week, we are having an early Christmas celebration with our guests who are residing in the B and B this month."

"Oh, I didn't know that," Lex responded, picking up the pie to take a bite. *That would explain all the stockings.* "Sounds fun! I'm looking forward to that. And this pie is wonderful, Mrs. Madden."

"Thank you, dear," Mrs. Madden said with a smile.

"Is the B and B nearby?" Lex asked, taking a sip of the coffee.

Cynthia glanced at her son again. "Madden Manor is also a B and B. It's actually the only one in town. We currently have all of our rooms occupied except the room that you and Micah will be sharing together."

Chapter 9

Sharing together? Lex thought, almost choking on her coffee and spitting it all over the living room. Oh, heck no, she must have heard her wrong. "Micah and I are sharing a room?" Lex asked after she quickly placed the coffee back on the table and cleared her throat.

"Of course you two are. My husband and I weren't born yesterday. You're both adults and we're filled to capacity because of the festival."

"Well, um, right. Adults. That's us," Lex said with a nervous laugh. "We are adults. That we are. Two adults who are dating and sharing a room together. That's normal." She sounded confused even to her own ears. And she couldn't stop laughing or talking in between laughs.

"Yes, it is," Mrs. Madden said as she drew her eyes together in concern. "Are you okay, dear? You seem a little nervous about something."

"Me? Nervous? Not at all. Never nervous. Not me." *Pull yourself together Lex! And please stop this awkward laugh lingo!* Lex told herself as she cast her eyes to the ceiling. *You sound like a crazy lady.*

"I just can't wait to see how big this manor is," Lex exclaimed, waving her hands for implication and spinning around in a circle. When she stopped her 360-degree spin, she was finally able to keep her mouth closed. She knew her face looked flushed and her cheeks were puffed out in annoyance, but she couldn't help it. Micah had guaranteed her that they would have separate rooms, and she wasn't prepared for Mrs. Madden's news.

"Are you sure you're okay, cupcake," Micah said, stepping in front of Lex and rubbing his hands up and down her arms. "You do seem nervous, but you have nothing to be nervous about. I'll take great care of you while you're here." He then lowered his voice and glanced over to his mom and explained that she was nervous about country living. *Cupcake? Country living?* She could deal with the pet names and staying in Cranberry Heights, but playing house with Micah every night was *not* in her plans.

Lex put on her best award-winning smile and willed her hands to stay by her side, and not react on instinct and push Micah away. Micah's back was now to his mom so Cynthia couldn't see the spec of challenge in his eyes that dared Lex to declare their relationship as false. Well, she had news for him. Now that she had committed to this charade, she was going to put the couple of late-night theater classes she'd taken in college to good use.

"I know you'll take good care of me love muffin," Lex exclaimed pinching Micah's right cheek. When he smiled even harder, she pinched his cheek harder.

"Ouch," Micah finally said, pushing her hand away

and releasing his hold on her. "Save your spunkiness for later, baby," he said with a wink.

Oh, I can't stand him. "Mrs. Madden, how about that tour?"

Cynthia looked inquisitively from Lex to Micah before clasping her hands together. "Okay, then. Why don't you sit down and finish your pie and coffee. I'm going to wash a few dishes, then we can start the tour."

"I'll help you, Mom," Micah said, not giving Lex time to question him without his mother present.

Two things came to mind as Lex stole a glance at Micah and his mom when they walked out of the living room. One, she never had a choice where she was staying since her only options had been Micah's parents' place and the town's B and B, which turned out to be the same place. Two, she barely trusted herself around Micah when they weren't residing in the same living quarters. She had absolutely no idea how she could control her hormones with him sleeping right beside her in bed.

She's so nervous, she can barely concentrate on the tour, Micah thought as they made their way from the library to the east wing of the manor where several of the bedrooms were.

Madden Manor was one of the first homes built in Cranberry Heights so it had a lot of history. When his parents had moved there when he was in high school, he hadn't appreciated the home or the town. Now that he was older, he valued both a great deal.

"Here is the bedroom you both will be staying in," his mother stated as they arrived at the end of the hallway. Micah was glad that they'd gotten the most secluded guest bedroom in the house. It was also one of three bedrooms with a connecting bathroom.

"It's beautiful," Lex stated as she browsed around the room, her eyes briefly stopping on the massive wooden canopy bed before moving to the French antique furniture.

"It smells amazing in here," she stated as she glanced at his mother.

"That's my special ginger and cinnamon holiday blend in the oil burner on the nightstand. There is a burner in every bedroom. I started creating special oils when my husband and I decided to turn our home into a B and B. There used to be another B and B in town, but it burned down a few years ago and the owner decided not to rebuild it. The only option guests have is to reside here or a neighboring town."

"I love it. I remember you saying you are full to capacity. Where is everyone?" Lex asked.

"My father took the guests on a historical tour of Cranberry Heights," Micah answered. "Most of the guests arrived a couple days ago for the festival."

Just as Micah had responded to Lex's question, they heard the sound of chatter and commotion coming from downstairs.

"That must be them now," his mother said as she began making her way to the door. "Micah brought your bags up here when I was washing dishes. I'll let you both freshen up before dinner, then I'll introduce you to everyone."

"Okay, and thanks so much for your hospitality," Lex said. Micah's mother gave a soft smile before she exited the room. He cracked the door and took a seat on the burgundy chair in the corner of the room as he watched Lex walk to her belongings and open up her suitcase.

"Do you mind if I take the drawers on the left side of the bed?" she asked. Micah shook his head and laughed. *She's barely glanced my way since we stepped into this bedroom.*

"I don't mind. I took the drawers on the right already anyway."

"Okay, that works," she said as she began taking out jeans, tops and socks. He liked the way she curled her nose as she took out every outfit, and he wondered what she was thinking about. Suddenly she stopped unpacking and glanced over her shoulder at him. "Are you just going to sit there and stare at me while I unpack my clothes?"

"I was thinking about it," Micah said as he crossed his arms behind his head and leaned back in the chair. She turned to completely face him with disapproval written all over her face. *You've really pissed her off now, Madden.*

"You've got a lot of nerve, Micah," she said as she began walking toward him. "First, you add this obscene clause in your contract with Elite Events forcing me to accompany you on your hometown visit. Then, you ask me to agree to this imprudent plan of yours to allow your parents to assume we're dating. And as if things couldn't get any worse, we have to sleep in the same room when you promised me my own space."

When she stopped her rant, she looked at him as if she wanted him to explain why he'd done those things. But truthfully, he didn't have much to say. "Everything you said is true," Micah stated as he rose from the chair and went to stand in front of her. "I added that clause in the contract and I knew it was unorthodox. I came up with a plan that I knew my parents would eat up. And I promised you a separate living space while you're here, and now we will be breathing the same air every night."

Lex's eyes enlarged before she spoke again. "And…" she said, rotating her hands to imply that she was waiting for him to say more.

"And what?" he asked with a shrug of the shoulders.

"What about an apology?" she asked, placing her hands on her hips.

"LG, I'm not apologizing," Micah said with a laugh.

"Don't call me that," she said through gritted teeth.

"But you'll always be lingerie girl to me," he said, stepping closer to her. She may have worn an annoyed look on her face, but the air around them was charged with awareness. "Unless you'd rather I call you runaway girl."

She squinted her eyes together and tilted her head to the side. "Why would you call me runaway girl?"

Did she really have to ask? "Maybe because every time we get too close, you get scared and run away. It's what you do."

Her face displayed a mixture of interest and embarrassment. "You don't know me," Lex said, stepping closer to him. "Like now," she said, removing her hands from her hips and crossing her arms over her chest instead. "I'm not running now…am I?"

Micah wasn't one to stand off with a woman, but if he really thought about it, usually the women he dated ran after him…not away from him. She looked like she wanted to back down, but she stood there.

"Are you daring me to give you a reason to run to prove something to me?" Micah asked, dropping his eyes to her lips. "Or are you trying to prove to yourself that you can handle being around me without running."

She licked her lips and uncrossed her arms, returning her hands to her hips. "Want me to be honest?" she asked.

"Always," he answered.

"A little bit of both," Lex said quietly. "I'm cautious in my approach to a lot of things and when I'm uncomfortable, I run." The look in her eyes made Micah think back to the drinking game they'd played at Imani and Daman's estate. He didn't know if he was taking the moment out of context, but he felt as if Lex was giving him permission to push her to her limit. Whether that limit be with him or otherwise, he was ready to accept the challenge.

"I have a proposition for you," Micah said, ignoring her wary look.

"In addition to the propositions you've been giving me since we met?"

"This is different," he said, collecting his words. "While you're here in Arkansas, I want you to indulge in something with me."

She raised an eyebrow at his statement. "Meaning?"

"I want you to try and do or say something that's out of your comfort zone each day. And at least one has to be something you do without thinking about the consequences."

Her features softened and he could see the wheels in her head turning. He wanted to add that taking a chance on him would be something spontaneous and out of her character, but he didn't want to push her. She was thinking too hard already, but he didn't mind it at the moment. It gave him the opportunity to observe her more closely than he had earlier. She had no idea how sexy she was. It wasn't an over-the-top sexy or a blatant sexy. Lex had more of a natural sex appeal that surfaced when she wasn't even trying.

She sighed and shuffled from one foot to the other. *I wonder if she realizes that she's still staring at me.* Her mind seemed miles away so he figured she didn't notice. Otherwise, based on his past experience with her, she would have turned away so that her thoughts weren't so visible to him.

He had a remedy for all her thinking. Every part of him was drawn to her so he could only imagine how good it would be when they finally made love. She had to accept that fact in her mind first, but that was a big reason why he wanted her to come to Arkansas. He was hoping a change of scenery would put her in a different state of mind. Although many would call him a city boy now, he still had country roots. He only knew city-girl Lex, and now he was hoping to see another side of her.

"Okay, Micah," she said, breaking his thoughts. "I accept your proposition to live a little more spontaneously while I'm here in Arkansas."

A slow smile crept on his face the instant he heard her agree to his proposal. "You won't be sorry," he said, not caring if she picked up on his excitement.

Micah wasn't sure what Lex was about to say before there was a knock on the door.

"You can push it open," he said to the person on the other side of the door. When his father came into view, Micah's smiled slightly faltered.

"Hello, son," his dad said walking into the room. "And you must be Ms. Turner." His dad reached out to shake Lex's hand. "I'm Mason Madden, Micah's dad. It's nice to finally meet you."

"It's nice to meet you, too, Mr. Madden," Lex said, returning his handshake. "And please call me Lex."

"Very well," his dad responded before turning his attention to Micah. "Your mother wanted me to let you know dinner will be served in ten minutes."

Micah and his dad hadn't talked much since he'd arrived so he knew his father was making an effort since Lex had arrived. "Thanks, Dad," Micah stated. It didn't matter how old Micah got, he couldn't ignore the look of disapproval on his father's face. His father looked as if he was going to say more, but decided against it.

"Very well," his dad said as he left the room. Now it was Micah's turn to busy himself and avoid any questions.

"Did you and your dad get into an argument?" Lex asked. *Yeah,* Micah thought with a strained laugh. *About twelve years ago and he still has yet to forgive me.*

"Not recently," he answered instead. Lex's inquisitive eyes were evidence that she had a lot more questions to ask.

"Can I ask you something else?"

Not if it's about my dad. "Sure, what's up," he said as he stepped into the bathroom to wash his hands. She followed behind him and let out a sigh of amazement.

"It's gorgeous," she said running her fingers over the granite countertop before she made her way to the waterfall shower and separate whirlpool tub. "I can't believe this is the room your parents let us stay in."

"I can," he said, grabbing a paper towel to dry his hands. "I've never invited a girlfriend to stay with me at Madden Manor before so I knew my mom would go all out to make you feel at home."

Lex gave him a soft smile before examining him again. "About my other question," she said, standing closer to him. "Do you and your dad have a close relationship?"

"That's a loaded question," Micah said, leaving the

bathroom and making his way to the door. "The short answer is, it's complicated. But it's time for dinner so let's discuss this another time."

He didn't give her a chance to respond and walked out of the bedroom. He was aware he was being slightly rude, but talking about his relationship with his dad would have left a negative tone in the bedroom and that was definitely the last feeling he wanted to have lingering in the air.

Chapter 10

"We're here folks," Mason Madden said to the small bus of Cranberry Heights visitors. When Micah's parents had informed the guests that they would arrive two hours before the kick-off parade to secure their seats, Lex had felt right at home. Oftentimes in Chicago, one had to arrive early to all public events to secure a good spot. It seemed the same was true for the town of Cranberry.

The sidewalks and streets were already filled with residents and visitors excited for the parade to start. Holiday music was playing on speakers located on every street corner and happy families were dancing and singing along. Lex had been to plenty of parades in her lifetime, but there was something mesmerizing about the sight she was seeing today.

"Let's set up here," Cynthia Madden said to the group as she pointed to one of the few open spaces left. Lex

opened the lawn chair that the Maddens had given each
of the guests and continued to observe her surroundings.
There were four couples and two families residing in the
B and B, and Lex had enjoyed all of their company at
dinner. She sighed when she thought about Micah last
night. At dinner, he'd done his best to keep up appear-
ances and appear unaffected by whatever had happened
between him and his father in the bedroom, but Lex could
read between the lines.

While the other guests had eagerly dived into Mrs.
Madden's scrumptious apple crumb pie, Micah had informed her that he had to take care of a few things before the parade. She'd planned on staying up and waiting
for him to return to the room, but she'd fallen asleep
and hadn't awaken until the next morning only to find
his side of the bed empty. She should have been thrilled
that she'd avoided the first awkward night with him, but
instead, she felt as if something was missing since she
hadn't seen him since yesterday evening.

"Mind if I keep you company," Cynthia asked, breaking Lex's thoughts. "Micah is still helping a few of the
parade participants set up."

"I don't mind one bit," Lex replied as she helped Cynthia open her chair. She had only known Micah's mom for
a day, but she felt like she'd known her for years. When
Cynthia looked over her shoulder and gave her husband
a soft smile, it made Lex think about the upcoming anniversary party she was planning, and she figured now
was a great time to ask Mrs. Madden some personal
questions.

"You and Mr. Madden seem so close. Is it too personal
if I ask how you and your husband met?"

"Of course it's not too personal," Mrs. Madden said as

she draped a blanket across her and Lex. "I met Mason about thirty-six years ago when I was in New Jersey, the state I grew up in. I had gone into a restaurant with my boyfriend at the time and I'd noticed Mason instantly. Mason had been dining with some friends of his, but by the look of interest on his face, I could tell he noticed me, too. That day is memorable to me for a couple reasons. That was the day I was proposed to twice. And it was also the day I met the man of my dreams."

"How did you receive two proposals?" Lex asked, completely engrossed in the story. Cynthia smiled before continuing.

"My boyfriend at the time proposed to me at the restaurant. I knew he would propose soon, but what I didn't expect was the knot in the pit of my stomach coercing me to say no. I said yes, ignoring my body's warning and convinced myself I'd made the right decision. As soon as my date excused himself to go to the bathroom, Mason walked over to my table and told me congratulations before he leaned down to whisper in my ear..."

"What did he say?" Lex inquired when Mrs. Madden appeared to be lost in thought. Cynthia placed her hand gently over her heart and tilted her head to the side.

"He told me that I should not have accepted the marriage proposal. And when I politely asked him why, he said, with confidence and vigor, that he was the man I was supposed to marry and that if I left with him that day, he was positive we'd be married that time the next year."

"Oh, my goodness," Lex exclaimed as she propped one leg up in her chair and did a ninety degree turn to face Cynthia. "How did you respond?"

"I slapped him in the face," Cynthia said with a laugh. "I couldn't believe he had the audacity to even approach me after I'd just accepted a marriage proposal. But then, something strange happened that made me rethink my decision."

"What was that?"

"While I was berating him for being so rude, he bent down and captured my lips in the most seductive kiss I'd ever had. A kiss that was seen by all the patrons at the restaurant, including my fiancé of ten short minutes."

"I can't believe Mr. Madden did that."

"Neither could half the people in the restaurant." Cynthia continued to smile as she finished the story. "The restaurant manager actually escorted my fiancé back to the table and asked Mason to leave the restaurant. Of course, being the stubborn man he is, Mason refused to leave without me." The look of contentment that Cynthia had on her face whenever she stole glances at her husband melted Lex's heart.

"Mason was always a bit of a bad boy and he was never one for following rules. At least that's how he was when we were younger. Having children made him more responsible and forced us to both grow up."

"What did you do when they kicked Mason out of the restaurant?"

"I did what I thought was right and followed my heart," Cynthia said looking straight into Lex's eyes. "I told the manager and my fiancé that if Mason had to leave, then I was leaving with him, and I handed my fiancé back the ring. Surprisingly, although the manager, my ten-minute fiancé and I were shocked, the person who seemed the most surprised by my choice was Mason. As soon as we stepped outside the restaurant, he asked me why I'd chosen him when I didn't know anything about him. At first, I wasn't sure how to answer. But the more I looked into his handsome face, the more my heart melted. So I told him the only thing I could…the truth."

"What was the truth?" Lex asked, hanging on Cynthia's every word.

"The truth is something that still remains true today," Cynthia continued. "I told him that the kiss we shared made me feel more alive than anything I'd ever experienced, and I wasn't ready to let that feeling go. Right then and there, Mason kissed me again with more emotion than he had in the restaurant. The kiss was so amazing, it left us both breathless and at a loss for words."

Love at first site in the truest form. Lex had heard stories of people who fell in love instantly, but this story seemed like a scene plucked right out of a classic romance movie.

"Neither of us had realized that we had an audience, or that Mason's friends were witnessing the scene with wide eyes of disbelief. I remember the ring that Mason was wearing on his pinkie finger that day. In front of all those people, some strangers and some not, he asked for my hand and placed the ring on my finger. He didn't propose marriage, but he did propose a promise that if I moved to Little Rock, Arkansas, with him and allowed him to court me, he'd make sure our marriage was always filled with love and devotion."

"You've got to be kidding me," Lex exclaimed as her hands flew to her mouth. "Obviously, you eventually moved to Arkansas, but what did you say to his proposal?"

Cynthia looked at Lex and laughed. "I said yes and met him in Little Rock two weeks later. Six months later we were married and ten months after we were married we had Malik, my oldest son."

"From New Jersey to Arkansas! That's so brave of you," Lex said in disbelief. "I went through a really bitter divorce over six years ago. Knowing what I know now, I can't imagine changing my entire lifestyle for a man."

Cynthia reached over and gently squeezed her hand. Lex wasn't sure why she'd shared that information when she rarely acknowledged that she'd been married before, but she felt compelled to share it with Micah's mom. "I can tell two things by your statement," Cynthia said. "First, your ex-husband was not the man you were supposed to be with because God had other plans for you. And second, my son hasn't given you a proper kiss yet that will make you so weak in the knees that you can barely speak."

Lex wasn't certain how her face looked, but she was pretty sure a deer caught in headlights was accurate.

"When a man truly kisses the woman he knows he wants to spend the rest of his life with, that kiss will touch the depths of her soul and build a permanent home right on top of her heart. A lot of people thought my relationship with Mason was just lust or a case of bad-boy syndrome as my friend used to call it. But Mason and I knew differently. After the type of kiss that we shared, we owed it to ourselves to try and have a relationship. We celebrate our 35th anniversary soon, so as you can see, I have no complaints and six beautiful sons to show for it."

"Six sons!" Lex repeated loudly before she could stop herself. Cynthia gave her a puzzled look. *If you were dating one of her sons, of course you'd already know how many siblings he has.* She knew he had brothers, but not five of them. "I mean…I can't imagine not having a daughter. It must have been hard raising all boys."

"It sure was," Cynthia said with a laugh. "Boys and

girls are totally different breeds. I felt like I was pregnant for a few years straight. I'm sure Micah has told
you how tall all his brothers are. Imagine making the
newspaper every time you have a son with the headline
being, Local Resident Breaks New Record With Largest
Baby In Arkansas."

"I can't even imagine that," Lex said, making a note to
ask Micah about the names of his siblings while she was
in town. The only brother she knew about was Malik,
who had attended Imani and Daman's wedding. "When
did you and Mr. Madden move to Cranberry Heights?"

"Two of my favorite ladies," Micah exclaimed, not
giving Cynthia a chance to answer. He bent down to kiss
his mom on the cheek before turning toward Lex and
planting a soft kiss on her lips. Usually, she'd be caught
off guard by the kiss, but after talking to Micah's mom,
the kiss felt natural. He lingered above her mouth for a
while, both of them soaking in the sight of each other.
He smelled masculine and woodsy, a combination that
aroused every part of her body despite the cold air.

"Having a good time," he asked, his eyes remaining
locked to hers.

"I'm having a great time." *Even better now that you're
here.* She wished it weren't true, but it was. *I wonder if
I'll ever have a love story to share in the future?* Evan
definitely wasn't her fairy-tale story, but he took the cake
for worst nightmare ever.

"You'll have that moment soon," Cynthia said, glancing
between her son and Lex. *Huh? Did I ask that out loud?*

"What moment?" Micah asked, finally stepping back
from Lex. *Okay, good. It was in my head.* But, by the way
Mrs. Madden assessed her meant she'd probably keep an
eye on Lex to see how she reacted to Micah while she

was in Arkansas. Her best option was to fake her attraction to him when they were around his mom so that she couldn't read the truth in her eyes, but would still assume they were dating. *How can I fake attraction when I'm already attracted to him?*

"Micah, dear, how about you sit next to Lex and I'll go sit next to your father."

"Thanks, Mom," Micah said, grabbing his mom's hand to help her out the chair.

"I enjoyed our conversation," Cynthia said before turning to walk toward her husband.

"Me, too," Lex said with a smile. When she was alone with Micah, she rested her head on his shoulder, wishing that the conversation with his mother hadn't put her in such a sentimental mood. She loved hearing the love story, but she hated the affect the story was having on her. When she divorced Evan, she vowed to never get close to another man who could make her lose herself and become consumed by him. Everything about Micah was intoxicating in the most seductive way imaginable.

She lifted her head off his shoulder and pretended to observe her surroundings when in actuality, she wanted to steal glances at him. When he caught her eyes, they made her pause as if she hadn't seen his eyes before.

"I'm glad you're here," he said, his eyes remaining on hers and not on her lips where they usually ventured when he got her attention.

"I'm glad I'm here, too," she said, ignoring the chill that whipped in the air, twirling her scarf around her head. When she laid her head back on his shoulder, she was certain that Arkansas had a lot more in store for her. *Oh, well...there are way worse things to be consumed by than a man like Micah Madden.*

Chapter 11

Micah had no idea exactly what time it was, but if he had to guess, he would assume it was close to 3 a.m. The parade had been amazing and the time he'd spent with Lex had been even better.

After the parade, he'd introduced her to several towns-people who were close friends with his parents and informed them that he was planning a surprise anniversary party for them. As suspected, every person they spoke with was eager to attend and claimed it would be the biggest celebration in town history. When Lex's eyes landed on him questionably, he had to explain that not a lot happened in Cranberry Heights. Even marriages were few because a lot of couples found solace in Cranberry Heights after they married, while those raised here were eager to get out. It was a great town, but it had taken a hard hit after the economic downfall, leaving many future residents on a search to find something better. The winter festival was one of the few annual events that brought back old residents, new residents and tourists alike.

Although the day may have gone great, the night was an entirely different story. *This is ridiculous!* Micah thought as he discreetly glanced over at Lex. He knew she wasn't asleep, but she was adamant on pretending to be. When they got back to Madden Manor and retired to their room, Lex had gotten all antsy and jumpy. Last night, Micah had crept into the bedroom after Lex had fallen asleep and she had been sprawled on the bed snoring softly. She'd looked so cute and he didn't want to wake her, so he slept on the couch and was gone before she woke up.

Now, not only was she as quiet as a mouse and had been for the past two hours, she also hadn't moved a muscle. There was no way that wild sleeper from last night was the composed sleeper lying beside him in bed right now. They were separated by several oversize pillows and concealed under a soft velour cover, but he could still feel the heat between them lingering in the air, hiding under the sheets, and taunting his state of mind.

Damn! I feel like a horny-ass teenager. It was bad enough he was hard as hell with no signs of going down before sunrise. But even worse, he was lying still, not moving an inch, all because he knew she was doing the same damn thing. He'd been reduced to one of those lame men who shared beds with women they weren't sleeping with. *I can't do this every night...especially when she's within arms reach.*

Deciding to test his theory and see if she was really sleeping, he moved a couple inches toward the middle of the bed to see what she would do. Within seconds, she scooted a little more toward her edge of the bed. *Really? All this just to avoid being next to me?*

He moved another inch toward the middle of the bed, only this time he had to move halfway on the pillows that separated them. Just like the last time, Lex moved over closer to her edge of the bed. Micah mouthed an expletive and raised his hands in the air in disbelief before bringing them back down to his side. Tilting his head without raising his body, he glanced past the cover to see how much space she had left on the bed.

She's almost out of space, he concluded, deciding to cross over the pillow-drawn line in the center of the bed and enter Lex's sleeping territory.

Micah pushed on his forearms and lifted himself at the same time that Lex began sliding closer to the edge. His thigh brushed against her butt and in a frenzy, Lex scatted even farther to the brink of the bed until there was nowhere left to go but down.

"Shiitake mushrooms!" Lex yelped when her butt hit the floor…hard.

"Shi ti what?" Micah said as he bent over the bed to see if she was okay while trying to contain his laughter. Lex ignored his outreached hand and flew to her feet. The moonlight seeping through the curtain danced across her face, illuminating her features.

"Shiitake mushrooms," Lex repeated, readjusting her pajamas and denying Micah a free peep show. "I try not to swear so it's what I say in place of the *S* word."

Is she for real? Micah knew some women and men who preferred not to spit out curse words every second, but Lex was spurting out a word he'd never heard anyone use to replace a curse word.

"Good for you," Micah said still trying to contain his laughter.

"Shut up," Lex spouted as she pushed on his shoulders and thighs, trying to get him to move over to his side of the bed.

"What did I say?" he asked, playing the innocent role.

"You know darn well what I mean, Micah," she said still pushing him. "I can tell you want to laugh. I can hear it in your voice."

"So you say *shiitake mushrooms* in place of *shit* and you say *darn* instead of *damn?*" he asked, unable to resist taunting her.

"Shut up," she said again, pushing against his body even harder. "A lot of people say darn."

"I know. I'm just giving you a hard time. I like getting you all hot and bothered and this is the most your hands have been on me since we met."

Lex jumped back from the bed, and missed a step. "Fudgesicles," she shrieked, when she hit her foot on the bedpost. Her hand flew to her foot and she began hopping around in a half circle around the bedroom.

Micah threw himself back on the bed and released the hearty laugh he'd been trying to contain ever since Lex fell to the floor.

She shot him a dirty look before releasing her foot and wobbling back to the bed. He didn't miss the look of hurt on her face as she turned her back to him.

"I'm sorry," Micah said, reaching out for her arm. "I shouldn't laugh at your expense, but sometimes, you do the funniest things and I can't help but laugh."

"People laugh at me all the time," Lex said in a defeated voice. "Out of all of my close girlfriends, I get teased all the time because I'm a little clumsy."

I was supposed to be seducing her...not upsetting her.
"I'm sorry, Lex," Micah said as he pulled her into his arms, taking note of how great she felt pressed against him. "I didn't think about how you would feel. I apologize for hurting your feelings, but you're unique and unlike any woman I've ever met. That's one of the reasons I'm so infatuated with you."

Her body began shaking uncontrollably. *Damn, I really messed this night up.* Just when he was about to apologize again, he heard her let out a chuckle. When she looked up at him, she was giggling...not crying.

"What the..." he said as it hit him she was joking around.

"Remember when you made me feel bad when we were walking to your car the other night back in Chicago," she said, sitting up in the bed. "Payback sucks doesn't it?"

"Payback, huh," he said, sitting upright. "I think the joke is really on you."

Her eyes twitched in confusion. "How so?"

"Well," Micah said drawling out the word while moving closer to Lex, "your mini performance gave me the opportunity to be next to you unlike I have before."

She gave him a skeptical look. "What do you mean?"

So glad you asked. "When you gave me the sad puppy-dog eyes, I was able to pull you into my arms, giving me the opportunity to feel your soft curves."

Her eyes softened, so he continued. "As I held you, I felt you relax in my arms...a sign that I'm growing on you."

"So, exactly how is the joke on me?"

"You don't get it, do you?" he asked with a slight chuckle. She shook her head to imply that she didn't.

"During that brief moment when you were trying to prank me, I had further decided that I wasn't going another night without tasting you again."

Micah placed both hands on either side of her thighs and pulled her into the center of his legs. She slid across the Egyptian cotton sheets with ease and her eyes widened in surprise and anticipation. The soft gasp that escaped her lips was barely audible. Her once mellow breathing now increased its pace. With one target on his mind, Micah's eyes zoomed in on her lips before pressing his mouth to hers.

It's been too long, he thought as he parted her mouth with his tongue and pulled her to him even closer. She only tensed for a moment before her body relaxed beneath his tender grasp and her mouth explored his with the same hunger. Micah vaguely remembered telling Lex that he would wait until she made the next move. But that was before he'd arrived in Arkansas and learned they would be sharing a room. Even so, he also knew giving her control was the validation he needed to kiss her and not feel guilty about it. Being so near her without touching her was absolute torture, but somehow, he convinced himself to listen to the more logical part of his brain and forced himself to stop kissing her.

"Sorry," Micah said, removing his hands from her hair, not remembering when his hands had even ventured to her hair in the first place. Their legs were tangled in the sheets, evidence that he'd still gotten more carried away than he'd planned.

He threw his head to the ceiling and puffed out a long breath before rotating his head to crack his neck and shifting his focus to Lex once more. After hours of lying in bed, he'd adjusted to seeing in the dark, so although her back was to the moonlight, he could read the question in her eyes.

"What are you questioning?" he whispered. "The fact that I kissed you?"

She slightly tilted her head to the side. "Actually," she said, brushing her tongue across her own lips. "I was curious why in the world you stopped…"

Gathering up as much courage as she could, Lex wrapped one hand around the back of Micah's head and pulled his lips back to hers. She pushed his back to the bed and straddled him, her lips never leaving his.

For years, she'd told herself that kissing a man the way she was kissing Micah was the type of kiss she could live without. *What was I thinking?* As their tongues mingled in the sweetest conversation, her hands roamed over his muscular arms slightly squeezing his biceps. He groaned at her touch and the erotic sound prompted her hands to continue their journey. She ventured under his shirt, finally able to touch his mouthwatering six-pack that she couldn't wait to see in daylight. She guessed the movement was what Micah had been waiting for because his hands that had been residing on her back, eased to her butt, fully cupping both cheeks.

"I knew you would fit perfectly in my palms," he said in between kisses. His words flowed through her like a cascade of water and elevated her desire. Slowly and seductively, she began rotating her hips, enjoying the feeling of him growing beneath her. Faint moans echoed in the room as they kissed, bit and sucked on each other's lips, both attacking one another with a starvation that food couldn't even satisfy.

In a quick move that caught her off guard, Micah

wrapped an arm around her waist and switched their position. He left a trail of wet kisses along her neck before moving to her breasts and delicately cupping them. He pushed her pajama shirt aside, a nipple escaping the constraints of the cotton fabric.

"Oh, my," Lex responded when his tongue grazed over one nipple while squeezing the other through the material. It had been way too long since her nipples had gotten any action, and Micah was definitely giving them the attention they deserved.

He left her breasts and lifted her shirt completely off, softly kissing her stomach and stopping at the drawstring of her pajama shorts.

"Lex," Micah said trying to get her to focus on him.

"Yes," she said as she lifted her head off the bed.

"Do you mind if I take these off?"

She briefly thought about the implication behind his request and what would come next if he removed her bottoms. She didn't take long to decide.

"Yes," she said, making sure she sounded confident. "You can take them off."

He gave her a sly smile before he undid the drawstring and slid the shorts off her. His hot fingers ran down her thighs followed by his daring tongue, each lick and touch hotter than the last. *What is he doing to me?* Lex was so wrapped up in the moment, she didn't feel him nudge her legs open until his tongue was on her center, lapping up her sweet juices.

She bucked off the bed giving Micah the opportunity to slide his hands under her butt, bringing her closer to his mouth. He dipped his tongue in and out of her core with determined precision, hitting her sweet spot with every lick. The ends of her toes curled into the sheets and her back lifted completely off the bed.

On their own accord, her hands gripped his face, not knowing if she should push him away or bring him even closer. When he plunged two fingers into her and encircled his mouth around her clit, her dilemma was forgotten. She gripped his head and held on for dear life as his long fingers played with her instrument while his mouth sang a sweet song in a way no man had ever done before.

Lex rolled her head to the ceiling and wailed a soft cry as she released an orgasm so strong she lost all sense of reality. Falling back to the bed, she closed her eyes, not believing that she'd been denied the sexual satisfaction of a man with a lethal mouth who knew how to please a woman.

"Shame on all the men who are too selfish to satisfy a woman in that kind of way," she said aloud, needing to voice the words for her own benefit, since until tonight she was one of those women.

"Told you I was the sweetest kind of troublemaker," Micah said, inching his way to her. He lay on his back and rolled her on top of him. Lex ran her fingers down his body with every intention of easing him inside her, when suddenly, he pulled her up by her thighs, stationing her center right above his mouth, the position forcing her on her hands and knees.

"We aren't having sex tonight," he said in the sexiest voice she'd heard yet. "But I do want to make you come as many times as possible."

She looked down between her legs to get a better view of him. The sight she saw nearly stole her breath. "Do you want me to lie back down?" she asked.

"No…just lower yourself onto my mouth," he said, still beneath her. "As if you're going to sit on my face."

Face sitting… She'd heard it was amazing from other women, but she never thought she'd have a man this irrefutably sexy asking her to willingly sit on his face. *I wish I could keep him in this position forever.* The thought made her close her eyes in embarrassment and surprise that she would even think such a thing. But Micah was daring her to live in the moment and had been since they had met.

Oh, my goodness, she thought as she spread her thighs more and slowly eased down onto his mouth. *This is really happening.* With each low movement, she could feel his warm breath teasing her wet center, anxiously awaiting the connection.

"Are you ready?" he asked in a deep raspy voice. She opened her mouth to tell him that she was, but the only word to escape was a pleasurable whimper of absolute satisfaction as his tongue dipped in her core and twirled around inside her.

Chapter 12

Lex slowly opened her eyes and glanced at the empty spot on the bed beside her. She briefly recalled Micah whispering in her ear that he had to get up early to assist with some activities at the festival and wouldn't be finished until 2 p.m. He seemed so involved in the community, and Lex would have never guessed that about him before visiting his family in Arkansas.

She took a long stretch and yawned before pushing the sheets and cover off her body. She was still naked, a sight that brought a small smile to her lips. Last night had been amazing and Lex couldn't believe that she'd willingly participated in such naughty behavior. She always attracted men who were all too eager to tell her how they could please her in the bedroom, and even if Lex had given those jerks the time of day, she knew that not one of them could have delivered the performance that Micah had last night.

Imagine how great he is in bed. She no longer wished to convince herself to stay away from Micah and she actually didn't think she could even if she tried. He wasn't just a sexy man, or a passionate man. He was a man who cared about pleasing her and put her needs before his own. She didn't want to think about Evan after such an amazing night, but she had to because being married to a man like him was what made her appreciate how Micah had handled her last night.

"Eeekk," she squealed as she kicked her legs in excitement. "What have you done to me, Micah Madden?" Not only did she feel like a new woman physically, but mentally, she felt relaxed and refreshed. *I guess it's true what they say,* she thought. *Orgasms really do relieve built-up tension.* She'd always thought it was a myth, but clearly she'd been wrong.

Lex stood up and gave her body another much-needed stretch, enjoying the freedom of being naked. You'd think living on her own she would've walked around naked every now and then, but she didn't. Right now, walking around naked until she showered and dressed for the day felt right.

She smirked to herself as she began singing one of her favorite holiday songs. She took it one step further and made up a dance to go along with her vocals. Gliding across the floor, she moved to the sound of her own voice, feeling more liberated than she had in a long time. She proudly hit the last note of the song, reminding herself that every woman should indulge in a little *me* time.

After her song, she went into the side drawer and got

out the clothes she would be wearing for the day along with her cosmetic bag.

"I much prefer you without any clothes on."

Lex yelped aloud and dropped everything she had in her hands at the sound of Micah's voice. Her hand flew to her heart as she swiftly turned around to find him standing in the doorway of the bathroom.

"What on earth are you still doing here?" Lex asked, oblivious to the fact that she was still naked. "You said you'd be busy until 2 p.m."

Micah gave her an amused look. "When was the last time you checked the clock?"

She looked over her shoulder at the clock on the night-stand. "Oh, wow, is it really 2:30?"

"It sure is, sunshine," he said, leaning against the wall wearing a white T-shirt and worn jeans. There were a few paint stains splattered on his clothes so she assumed whatever he did today included painting.

"I helped paint the inside foyer of the town hall," Micah said, reading her thoughts. Clearly captivated by Lex, his eyes perused her entire body with keen interest.

"But I'd much rather talk about how sexy you look and the fact that last night, I didn't notice how many cute brown freckles you had on your body."

"Oh, crap," Lex shrieked as she yanked the white sheet off the bed and covered her body. "Why didn't you say anything?" she asked as she began picking up the belongings that she'd dropped.

"I didn't know I had to remind you that you were naked," he said as he let out a robust laugh. "Plus I enjoyed watching you sing and dance. Your voice is amazing."

Although her family and close friends knew she could

sing, she rarely sang in front of them. "My parents placed me in voice lessons when I was younger," she told him. "Up until I was ten, I did voice-overs for numerous Chicagoland companies for different toys or musical books."

"You just keep amazing me lingerie girl," he said, moving toward her. "Did you mean what you said before you got out of bed?"

Lex raised an eyebrow at him when he reached her. *Got out of bed?* "Um, how long were you watching me?"

"Long enough to hear you say 'What have you done to me, Micah,'" he repeated in a girlie voice as he slightly flared his arms in the air.

"I did *not* sound like that," she said punching him in the arm. His eyes ventured to her hair and she figured she must look a complete mess. She brushed one hand over her disheveled hair before covering her mouth with the same hand.

"What are you doing?" Micah asked inquisitively.

"My hair is a mess and I still have morning breath."

"Seeing your hair like this let's me know that I did something right last night," he said with a wink. "And I don't mind morning breath." He removed her hand from her mouth.

"But I do," she said raising her hand back to her mouth. "And I had no idea I slept that long."

"I guess I'm to blame for that. We were up until 6 a.m."

"Did you even get any sleep?"

"Barely, and I don't have time for a nap either," he said. "Would you mind accompanying me to Little Rock today? I have a business dinner there with a potential investor and they are bringing their wives."

Kinda like a date?

"I'll go. How far is Little Rock?"

"Um, with the way I drive, it's about two hours…not too far," he answered before removing her hand again and glancing at her lips.

"Hold that thought," she said when he started leaning in to kiss her. She went to the bathroom and brushed her teeth, trying to ignore the fact that he was watching her do so and was blocking the door so she couldn't close it.

"So after last night I guess privacy is out of the question?" she asked in between brushing.

"Pretty much," he said with a smile as he brushed his hands over his goatee and looked her up and down. That was another quality that she really liked about him. Despite the fact that she was sure she looked like a swamp creature with her hair all crazy and her lips swollen from kisses, he still looked at her as if she was the most beautiful woman he'd ever seen. Given that he was such a good-looking man, she knew he attracted beautiful women all the time and she was sure they were those type of women who would never let a man see them in this state.

"Why do you like me?" she asked, walking past him to the bedroom.

"Why wouldn't I like you?"

"What exactly do you like?"

"What is there not to like?"

She twisted her mouth to the side. "Why am I really in Arkansas?"

"Why do you think you're in Arkansas?"

She placed one hand on her hip and turned to him. "Why do you keep answering my questions with a question?"

He took a step forward, stopping centimeters from her face. "Why are you asking me so many questions?"

"Because I really want to know," she said sincerely, her voice barely above a whisper.

Instead of responding, he closed the distance and gently placed his lips on hers. Her unanswered questions were forgotten, as she got lost in his intoxicating taste.

On the drive to Little Rock, Lex and Micah had given Cyd and Shawn a call to see how plans were going for the wedding. Micah was excited for his friend to finally marry a woman who understood him and loved him as fiercely as he loved her. When his brother Malik had first introduced him to Shawn, they'd hit it off instantly. Although they'd matured into respectable men and dedicated their lives to the safety of others, both had gone through a bad-boy streak that some may argue was still part of their personality.

Now Micah and Lex were sitting in his parents' Highlander in comfortable silence.

"I want to make a pit stop before we get downtown," he said to her, never taking his eyes off the road. There was so much more about him that he wanted her to know and understand.

"Okay," she responded. "Are you going to tell me where?"

"I want it to be a surprise," he said, preferring to see her reaction to the location when they arrived.

Twenty minutes later, they entered a part of the city east of downtown, where Micah had spent most of his childhood. As they drove through the low-income neighborhood, he noticed Lex tense. She was always full of questions so he figured she had questions now, but for some reason, she didn't say anything.

They passed several corners that were filled with young

men either hanging out with nothing to do, or discreetly selling drugs. Although Micah hadn't been around the old neighborhood in years, he still felt comfortable in his original hometown.

When they arrived on his old block, Micah shook his head thinking about how much his family's lifestyle had changed after they moved to Cranberry Heights.

"Here we are," Micah said as he pulled over in front of a small boarded-up home.

Lex glanced at the house before setting her eyes on him. "What did you want to show me?"

"This is it," he said pointing to the house. "This is the home I grew up in."

Her eyes widened as she turned back to the house. "How long did you and your family live here?"

"Until I was sixteen," Micah said. "My mom and dad had moved here back when the neighborhood wasn't as bad as it is today. My dad grew up in the area and was the director of a community center six blocks away. My mom taught at the elementary school that was right next door so they both chose to live close to their jobs."

"That makes sense," she replied.

"It did," Micah said. "My mom took off work for a while when she began having children, but she remained a substitute teacher."

"Are you the second oldest after Malik? Your mom mentioned that she had six sons. I knew you had brothers, but I had no idea there were six of you."

"You guessed right. Malik and I are less than two years apart," he said. "My brother Malakai was born after me, followed by fraternal triplets, Crayson, Caden and Carter."

"Oh, my goodness! Your mom didn't mention triplets.

That's nuts! I like the *M* and *C* name combo, though," she said with a laugh. "Was that done purposely?"

"You catch on quick, Turner," he said, joining in her laughter. "Before we were all born, my parents had decided if they had boys, their names would begin with *M* like my dad's. If they had girls, their names would begin with *C* like my mom's. Years after having three sons, my mom wanted to try for a girl and convinced my dad to have one more child. To both of their surprise, they were informed they were having triplets. Neither one of them was prepared for the news since natural reproduction of triplets was so rare. But my dad is a twin, so he was less surprised than my mom. Giving up her hope of having a girl, she gave the triplets names that begin with the letter *C*."

"Your mom is a warrior," she said with a smile.

"She is and I love her for it," he agreed, turning his head at the sound of a garbage can falling over due to a stray cat.

"What about your dad? Raising six sons could not have been easy."

"It wasn't," he said. "Especially when you have a son like me who was constantly getting in trouble."

"How so?"

Micah turned in the driver's seat to face her. "Growing up in this neighborhood can be hard for a young man trying to come into his own. Malik was known as the intelligent brother. Malakai was the creative one. And the triplets are years younger than Malakai so they were just developing their individual personalities. Me on the other hand…I had the street smarts."

Micah glanced at the front window, the white fog slowly overtaking the entire glass. "Since my mom was a teacher, she made sure we all studied as much as possible. I guess you can say I was born smart because I rarely studied, but I always got good grades. In my adolescence, my boredom resulted in me pranking teachers, spray painting the sides of buildings, and pickpocketing tourists downtown."

"Please tell me you did not steal from people," Lex exclaimed.

"I never stole anything big, but the friends I had growing up convinced me that stealing from people who had money, wasn't stealing."

"You mean like Robin Hood."

"Something like that," he said with a laugh. "Any money I took I usually spent on food for people in the neighborhood who didn't have enough to eat. I wasn't thinking about the consequences back then because all I knew was that I wanted to give back to the community in some type of way. School bored me, girls bored me and, quite frankly, life in general bored me."

"What else did you get into?" she inquired.

"What didn't I get into…" Micah turned back to face her. "When I became a teenager, I learned that I could survey a situation and come up with a solution instantly. I didn't just have sales skills. I knew how to strategize and create different tactics that delivered results. I didn't want to do anything reckless like sell drugs or get into gambling, so instead I decided to put my skills to use in another way."

"Like what?" she asked with interest as she shifted in her seat.

"I began discreetly following around some of the drug dealers in the area who all worked for the same leader. I observed the way they interacted with others in their group and enemies from neighboring areas. After about a month of following around some of the biggest dealers in my neighborhood, I approached one of them who I knew from school and asked him to set up a meeting with his boss and I."

"You've got to be kidding me," she said, resting her head on the headrest. "Why would you set up a meeting with the head drug dealer?"

"To tell him what his organization was lacking. I told him that although he was running a good system, he could be running it much smoother. I gave him a strategy plan on how to increase his sales and reduce the number of killings in the area. The plan also included a way to have a less violent relationship with enemies."

If Micah could think of one word to describe Lex's face, *astounded* was the first word that came to mind. He expected her to be surprised, but he needed her to know that being who he was in the past molded him in a positive way, although what he had done back in the day weren't his most shining moments. Her mouth opened, and he held his breath to see what she would say. "So... you helped drug dealers sell more drugs?" she asked.

Chapter 13

Helped drug dealers sell more drugs? "In a way, I guess I did," he said. "But my main goal when I constructed my plan was trying to reduce the number of killings in Little Rock. So in my mind, I figured I would go to the source and create a plan to do that. I never thought about the consequences, I only thought about my main goal."

She searched his eyes, and Micah tried his best not to fidget under her scrutinizing observation. He turned down the heat in the SUV, growing hotter under her gaze. He really didn't share his past with too many people, but he'd decided a while ago that he wanted a future with Lex, so he needed to be honest with her.

"I've never told this story to another woman," he said, unable to take the silence any longer. "In order to understand the man I became, I wanted to tell you about the man I used to be, no matter how stupid the decisions were I made in my past."

She was quiet for a moment longer before she squinted her eyes together. "You say that like you believe I think you're a bad person after hearing the story," she finally stated.

"Not a bad person," he said. "But I do recognize that I didn't always make the best decisions and I have to live with that."

"How long did you help that drug dealer?"

"For a few years, only when they needed a new strategy," Micah said, letting out a deep breath. "The killings in the neighborhood did reduce 20 percent from previous years, but I think my parents knew I was doing something I shouldn't have. Like I said earlier, I maintained good grades, so my relationship with them was fine until a terrible fire destroyed the community center and the school. Both my parents lost their jobs."

"Oh, no," she said as her hands rushed to her chest. "What did your parents do?"

"My mom started substitute teaching at another school and my dad began working odd jobs. Malik and I were both working at a local grocery store, so we handed over our checks to our parents to help with the mortgage and our brothers. Although Malakai wasn't old enough to work a real job, he began selling his artwork to shops downtown."

"That was really responsible of the three of you," she said, lowering her hands to her lap. "If they didn't know exactly what you were doing, what strained your relationship?"

His jaw twitched at the memory and he turned to stare out the foggy front window again. "My dad got into an altercation with the dealer I was helping when he saw him unnecessarily rough up another man pretty bad. I happened to be with my dad and told him to stay out of it, but my dad wanted to make sure the guy was okay. When the dealer confronted him, I was able to clear up the confusion and get him to step off my dad. But my dad wasn't stupid. He asked me about my relationship with the guy, so I fessed up, tired of hiding the truth."

Lex reached between them and lightly placed her hand on his. The gesture made him return his focus on her. "My mom and my brothers were disappointed in me, but when I told them I was changing my ways, they began to forgive me. My dad, on the other hand, was a different story. My uncle Barry, who lived in Cranberry Heights, found out the town was in need of a community director and contacted my dad. He interviewed right away and got the job. We all uprooted to Cranberry Heights, and the town was so impressed with my dad that within years, the townspeople suggested that he run for mayor."

"I had no idea your dad was mayor," she said with surprise.

"He was until a few years ago," Micah stated. "He fell into the position years ago after my uncle, who was mayor at the time, was killed in a car accident. My dad was chosen as the interim mayor and the position became permanent. When my parents decided to open up a B and B in town, they devoted all their focus on that, and my dad decided not to run for mayor anymore."

"I'm so sorry to hear about your uncle."

"Thanks," he said. "It was hard at the time, but that was a long time ago."

She searched his eyes with curiosity before asking the question he knew was coming. "So, why is your relationship with your dad still strained?"

Micah shook his head at the thought. "When we moved,

I still maintained contact with a few friends that I've had over the years. They weren't all dealers, but some of them weren't good people either. My closest friend at the time was the worst, and my dad warned me to stay away from him. He had thought that moving from Little Rock and me getting accepted into Fisk University in Tennessee would finally allow me to shake off those bad relationships. But instead, I convinced myself that my dad had forgotten where he came from, and I wasn't going to be that person."

He briefly paused as he continued to reminisce about his past. "While that friend was visiting me in college, something serious happened that caused me to eventually transfer out of the school. I later found out that him and his boys were reckless everywhere they went. That's when I realized that it wasn't enough to just be a good person. You had to surround yourself by good people and I had been hanging around all the wrong people."

Her eyes crooked in inquiry. "Is that when you were arrested?"

"The one and only time," he replied, still irritated with himself. "The case was dropped based on false accusations, but the damage to my relationship with my dad was done. Our relationship has been tense ever since."

"What happened to get you arrested?"

Micah stretched in his seat. "Let's save that for another conversation," he said, brushing his hand against her chin. "Just know that I'm a different man than I once was." *And I desperately need you to believe me.* She glanced out the window before glancing at him. The expression on her face was unreadable.

Lex watched a range of emotions cross Micah's face while he talked about his past. From the short time she'd spent with his family, she really enjoyed being around them. And in a way, hearing Micah recap his past only made her respect his family more.

"Can I ask one last question and then we can change the subject?" she asked.

"Shoot," he said confidently, although she read the hesitation in his eyes.

"How did you become a police officer?"

"After I transferred schools, I finally understood my purpose. I'd grown out of the thuggish days and decided to pursue a career helping others...mainly young men. I wanted a fresh start and I figured going to school in the Midwest would be a nice change. I double majored in Criminal Justice and Computer Science and graduated from Michigan State University in three years by taking classes every summer. The week before graduation, I was encouraging students to go to college at my old high school and was approached by the Little Rock chief of police about enlisting in the police academy. I thought it was a great way to make a difference in my old neighborhood, so I took a shot at it."

"That's so great," she said.

"It was," he agreed. "I was one of the best cops at my station and things were going great, until I realized there were more dirty cops than good cops in my unit so I put in a request to transfer. Malik and Shawn both knew each other from their FBI days, so when Shawn heard about my dilemma, he told me about his dream to open his own security company. I knew it was the break I'd been waiting for so I quit my job and teamed up with Shawn."

As she sat there, completely indulged in Micah's story, she realized that it wasn't just his story that intrigued her. It was him as a man. The way he thought. The goals he had. The way he made her feel. If she wasn't careful, she would fall head over heels in love with him. She no longer knew if falling for him was a bad or a good thing, but what she did know was that being vulnerable to a man made her nervous.

Worry lines were visible on his forehead and she realized that he was waiting to hear her response to his story. Usually, his eyes would roam over her lips and her body, but this evening, he was different. His eyes remained on hers, waiting for acceptance and understanding.

"You certainly have many layers, Micah Madden," she said softly as she turned in her seat so that her back was now pressed against the door. "You're a great man. Your story is part of what made you who you are, and just as you told me, your experiences have made you stronger not weaker. I admire your determination to help young men figure out that they have options."

"The world is theirs to conquer," he added, giving her a smile of relief for the first time since they'd arrived in his old neighborhood.

He's so cute. Looking at her with gleeful eyes, he looked every bit of sixteen sitting across from her, rather than the thirty-year-old man that he was. He glanced at the clock before turning the heat back up.

"Are you ready for dinner?"

"Let's go," she stated, turning back around and buckling her seat belt. "Thanks for bringing me here and sharing your story," she said once they'd started driving.

He flashed her a million-dollar grin. "Thank you for listening to my story with an open mind."

The conversation with the wives of the investors had been entertaining. Halfway through dinner, Micah had winked at her, a sign they had agreed he would give if the dinner meeting was going well. By the time they all said their goodbyes, there was talk about finalizing a contract, and a promise that Micah would bring Lex along for the next dinner. Grant and Parker were a huge account and she was so proud of Micah for representing his company so well. They made a good team, and tonight they'd put on a performance better than most seasoned couples.

"This was so much fun," she said to Micah as she removed her peacoat, keeping her eyes straight ahead on the road as they headed back to Cranberry Heights. He'd removed his coat thirty minutes ago and ever since he did, all she could think about was running her hands up and down his hazelnut abs. She squeezed her legs closer together. *Lex Turner! You know better! You can control your emotions.* Her encouraging thoughts weren't helping. Her panties were drenched...a situation she had *never* been in before.

"I'm glad you had a good time," he said, his eyes leaving the road to glimpse at her. She told herself not to glance back at him, but she couldn't help it. She turned her head to look at him and quickly turned back to the road before she reached his eyes. There was no doubt in her mind that she'd be even more uncomfortable during the car ride if she looked at his face. *His sexy face... masculine jawline...neatly groomed goatee...sop them up with biscuit lips.* She shook her head to clear her mind. *Look at the road, Lex. Straight ahead. Into the dark. Not Micah's creamy hazelnut complexion.* Her head slowly turned toward Micah again. *No, wrong way. Look outside,* she reminded herself, causing her to whip her head back forward.

"I got you," she said aloud, frustrated that her mind and body weren't listening to each other.

"Are you okay," he asked glancing from her to the road.

"Yup," she answered quickly, remaining in her same position.

"Are you sure?"

"Sure am."

"Absolutely positive?" he asked.

"Indeed."

They passed a large sign stating they were close to Cranberry Heights, followed by a highway sign with restaurants and gas stations on it. "Mind if I make a stop?" he questioned.

"Go right ahead."

"Do you want some dessert?"

"Sure. Why not." *Now who's asking all the questions!*

"What are you in a mood for?"

"You," she said breathlessly as she dropped her head to her hands, tired of answering all his questions. "Just you." She finally looked over at him, not caring that her desire was on display. He searched her eyes, remaining silent for a moment.

"I thought so," he finally said with a smirk, turning back to the road. *Of course he knew.* It seemed lately, he knew how she felt before she even knew how she felt.

"Well, now you know," she voiced in irritation, leaning her head on the seat. She was more aggravated by her lack of self-control than his accurate assessment of her yearnings.

"Then I guess we better fix that," he stated, yanking the car over a lane and hopping off at the next exit.

"That sign said there were a least a couple more stops until we got to our exit."

"I know," he said, driving like a bat out of hell. He turned off the main road onto a narrow gravel road with meadows on either side that rose taller than the car.

"If this is the time when you confess that you're really a serial killer, I only ask that you kill me quickly." Because of the bumpy road, she had a tight grip on one of the door rests while her other hand gripped her seat.

"I'm not a serial killer, but I should tell you now that I can't be held responsible for my actions," he responded, looking in her direction for the first time since he jumped off the expressway. "Because the wicked things I want to do to you are definitely illegal."

Good. God. Almighty. His stimulating words kissed every part of her sensual body. She threw back her head, thinking the best thing to do in this situation was pray to the goddess of love. Closing her eyes and clasping her hands together, she prayed.

"Dear lover goddess, please endorse the sins I am about to partake in. I know not what is right, for all I want to do is wrong," she reached her hands in the air before bringing them back together. "For tonight, I ask that you give me the stamina to sustain all that I can, the courage to let all my inhibitions go, and the ability to twist my body in ways inhumanly possible. For tonight, I allow myself to go to a place I've never gone before," she peeked one eye open to find that the car had stopped in front of an old house. "Amen."

"Amen," Micah said in a raspy voice. "I don't know whether I should be on high alert because you just said a prayer before we make love or if I should say a prayer, too, because listening to you made me feel dirty."

In one swift move, he lifted her off the seat and onto his lap. "Truthfully, the only thing your love request made me want to do is get you naked as soon as possible and have my way with you."

In that moment, she realized she'd been waiting her entire life for a man to make her feel this way...for a man to truly get her. She felt special. Desired. Appreciated. "Then what are you waiting for."

Chapter 14

Micah couldn't move fast enough. He opened the door and stepped out with Lex in his arms. He didn't place her on her feet until he got to the porch to open the front door. He knew he had to act fast and turn on the lights before she got spooked. After all, they were in the middle of nowhere.

He found the light switch and flipped on the living room light. He rushed over to two heaters and put them on, then turned on a lamp so he could cut the main lights back off. He wanted the lighting to be as intimate as possible.

"Does anyone live here?" she asked as he pulled down the Murphy bed and pulled covers and sheets from the closet.

"Not yet," he said as he tried his best to place the covers on the bed. "The owners moved out nine months ago and I bought the place."

Her eyes grew bigger. "You plan on moving back to Arkansas?"

"No," he said, laughing at her expression. "I plan on fixing it up and renting her out. I own a property in Little Rock, too, that I would have showed you if we had time."

"You're full of surprises, aren't you," she said coming from behind him and wrapping her arms around his back while he made the bed. It was finally warming up in the room. Either that, or he was getting heated from her touch.

Her arms wrapped around him felt so right. She felt right. Even in this unfurnished house, *they* felt right. Micah turned around to face her. He never would have thought the woman looking at him now was the same woman who'd walked into the lingerie shop several months ago. The woman he'd met that day had been innocent, cute, endearing and a little bit clumsy. And even then, he'd been intrigued by her. But the woman staring back at him tonight was an entirely different one. Tonight, she was confident, captivating and downright sexy.

She bit her bottom lip before slipping her tongue in and out of her mouth. When her tongue slid back out of her mouth, he crushed his lips to hers. Her sweet moans filled the air around them and encouraged him to take the kiss deeper, exploring her mouth from one side to the other.

She stopped kissing him to remove her boots. He imitated her actions and removed his, too. Deciding to waste no more time, he pulled her sweater over her head, eagerly tugging down her leggings, as well. Her hands flew to his button-up, gently undoing the first couple buttons before standing on her tiptoes to yank the shirt over his head. When her hands moved to his pants, he stopped her and removed them himself.

"If your hands go anywhere near that area, this will be over before it starts," he huffed in a rushed breath. His voice sounded strained even to his own ears. A clear sign that he had to have her tonight. Right now.

He took a moment to stand back and observe her lacy bra and panty set. Although he'd seen her naked last night and this morning, this was the first time she allowed him the benefit to look as he pleased. He briefly studied her face to make sure his blatant appraisal of her wasn't making her nervous. He was satisfied that her eyes mirrored the lust reflected in his own. "You're absolutely breathtaking," he told her, vocalizing the words floating around in his mind.

From day one, he'd known he wanted her even if she hadn't wanted to acknowledge the fact. Now, her look solidified her acceptance of the intimate step they were taking in their relationship.

With two snaps of his fingers, her bra fell to the floor, followed by her panties. He lifted her from the floor and gently placed her in the middle of the bed, before standing straight to remove his boxers. Her eyes burned a hole in him as she watched in anticipation, her breasts rising and falling steadily. When he popped free of the confining cotton, her stunned gasp filled the room.

"You're beautiful," she said in a seductive, tone. *Beautiful?* He wasn't sure if a woman had ever called him beautiful before. And even if a woman had called him that, he was sure they never looked as sexy as Lex did stretched out naked awaiting his arrival.

Slowly, Micah eased himself onto the bed, bringing his lips to her face as he did. In gradual, circular movements, his tongue traveled across her neck, branding her caramel skin in a way he knew no man had ever done before. When he hit a tender part of her neck, her body lifted off the bed in response to the pleasure.

"Told you I'd have you spread-eagle style on my bed," he whispered in her ear.

"You're so cocky."

"And you like that about me," he said, rewarded by her passionate smile.

"Please don't make me wait, Micah," she begged.

Not one to be told twice, he reached down on the side of the bed and pulled a condom out of his wallet. After protecting them both, he hovered over her and resumed the journey his lips had started moments prior.

When both their moans increased to a level of pure euphoria, he joined them in the most intimate way possible in one provocative thrust.

"Ah," he groaned in satisfaction, already warning himself to hold on for as long as he could. She was wet. Tight. Slick. His mouth was already well acquainted with her taste, and now his cock was getting familiar with her inner walls.

He threw his head to the ceiling as he rhythmically pumped in and out of her. She placed her hands on his butt cheeks, sucking him in even deeper as she met him thrust for thrust.

"What are you doing to me," she said breathlessly. Earlier that morning he'd heard her say those same words to herself when she hadn't known he was in the bathroom. Now, hearing her say them for him to hear caused him to swell even more inside her.

"Oh, my…" she screamed, evidently feeling him getting bigger…thicker. "I'm close, Micah. Real close…"

"Me, too," he said, concluding that sex with Lex was different than any women he'd ever had intercourse with. That fact made him increase his pumps, needing to relieve them both of the tension building in their bodies.

He kneeled on the bed, never disconnecting them and placed both palms on each of her thighs. "Wrap your legs around my waist," he instructed her as he pulled her thighs onto his so that she was sitting on his lap. Lex obeyed, and when she was securely in place, he grabbed her by her hips and began lifting her up and down, quickly sliding her in and out. It took him a few seconds to register the animal-like growl that escaped his own mouth. Soon, his growl was joined by her feline purr as both sounds mingled in the air resulting in the sweetest love music that Micah had ever heard.

Without further warning, his body jerked in release at the same time he felt her convulse uncontrollably in his arms. Completely and utterly spent, they both collapsed on the bed, only gathering enough strength to look at one another and smile. The satisfaction was evident on both of their faces, neither able to formulate any words. *Words aren't necessary,* he thought as he pulled her into his arms and continued to soak in the moment.

You've got to think of a better lie, Lex thought to herself as she wobbled from one food table to the next. Being a foodie, Lex had been really excited to help Micah's family pass out chili dishes and taste all the different Southern cuisines that had entered the Warm Your Soul food competition. Now that she was here, she really wished she would have listened to Micah and soaked in the tub before they left.

She glanced across the room at Micah and his mom

as they passed out bowls of her famous white bean and turkey chili. He caught her eye and winked before greeting some more customers. Lex was initially helping them pass out the chili, but her legs had started cramping up, so Micah had advised her to walk around and try to stretch.

Last night, they'd made love more times than she could count and Lex hadn't really thought about the fact that she hadn't had sex in over six years. She'd been too wrapped up in the moment to think about the sad sex life she'd subjected herself to after her divorce. She also hadn't gotten a chance to tell Micah how long it had been since she was sexually active. She had a feeling he knew it had been a while, but she was sure that if he'd known she'd been celibate for over 2,190 days, it would have ruined the moment.

"Hi, miss," said a cheerful lady with a Southern drawl and a bright red Christmas sweater on. "Want to try some of my famous five-layer mac and cheese?" she asked, handing Lex a plate.

"Thank you," she responded, taking the dish from the lady. *So much for my winter diet,* she thought as she took a bite of the deliciously cheesy pasta. There wasn't one dish that she'd tasted that she didn't like, with the exception of a chitlins-and-rice dish that she couldn't stomach after one whiff.

"This is delicious," she told the woman as she turned to walk to another table.

"Are you okay," the lady asked Lex. "You're walking mighty funny."

"I guess yoga isn't for everyone," Lex responded with a laugh, sticking with her original lie. Anything was better than saying she had the best sex of her life last night, and now she couldn't walk straight.

"Oh, I agree," the mac-and-cheese lady said, clasping her hands together. "I once went to a yoga class they had in the high school gym, and by the time we got to the downward dog, I prepared to do the move and couldn't get up. Is that what happened to you?"

"Um," Lex said, trying to come up with a response. "Yeah. The downward dog is the same move that put me in this position." When she thought about all the different ways Micah had bent her legs, they'd definitely done something similar to the downward dog, so she was at least telling the woman part of the truth.

"Well, when you get home. Take a nice bath," the lady suggested.

"Thanks! I'll do that," Lex said before making her way back to Micah and Cynthia. When she got to the table, she placed the remaining mac and cheese on the table and took a picture of it so she could upload the image on her Instagram account along with the picture she'd taken of herself eating a bowl of Cynthia's chili earlier.

"Are you enjoying yourself?" Cynthia asked.

"I'm having a great time," Lex responded with a smile. She glanced over in time to see Micah take a swig of his water, looking at her over the bottle. She tried to will her eyes away, but she couldn't, mesmerized by the way his throat constricted when he swallowed.

"Sweetie," Cynthia said after she passed a dish to another customer. "Are you okay? I noticed you've been limping all morning."

She pulled her eyes away from Micah. "I hurt myself practicing a yoga move last—I mean, this morning."

Micah slightly choked on his water, but she refused to look at him.

Cynthia lifted an eyebrow. "You did all that," she said,

pointing a finger at Lex's legs. "What type of pose did this to you?"

"Ummm…the downward dog," she replied, saying the first thing that came to mind. In her peripheral view, she saw Micah turn away, probably to keep himself from laughing in front of his mother. *Stay calm,* Lex warned herself, knowing that if she got flustered, she would blush. And Micah's mom was already paying close attention to her.

Lex looked to the floor before stealing a peek at Micah, who was still turned away from them.

"Oh, I see," Cynthia said, looking from Lex to Micah. "Downward dog, huh? That must have been some yoga move." With that, she smiled at Lex before assisting more customers.

"How embarrassing. Way to help me out," Lex whispered as she punched Micah in the arm when his mom wasn't looking.

"Yoga?" Micah said with a laugh. "LG, I couldn't help you with that one. And I told you to take a bath this morning when we snuck back into the manor."

"I know," she said with a pout. "And now I'm paying the price. My thighs are killing me."

"Well," he said, wrapping his arms around her waist. "How about we leave here in thirty minutes, I run you a nice hot bath and then we head back downtown for a couple night festivities."

"Hmm…like an official date?" she said, wrapping her arms around his neck.

"Yes, an official date," he answered. "Plus, I need you good to go for the Snowlympics the day after tomorrow since you're my partner for the events."

She looked at him inquisitively. "Do I even want to know what Snowlympics is? It sounds intense."

"You'll find out soon enough," he replied. "I'm just helping you fulfill my proposition to be more spontaneous."

"I assume that's what last night was about, too, right?" she responded, placing a quick kiss on his mouth. "And the night before?"

"Now you're getting it," he said before giving her a kiss that caught the eyes of a few onlookers.

Chapter 15

He was falling for her. Hard. Quick. And although he knew she was different from the moment he met her, the feeling was still something he wasn't used to. Their date last night had been perfect, and now all he could think about was a life filled with plenty more moments like that one.

"Earth to Micah," Lex said, snapping her fingers in front of his face. "Did you hear what I said?"

No...I was too busy looking at your face...lips... breasts...eyes. "Micah," she said again when he'd dazed back off. "Since the Snowlympics is tomorrow and the Christmas party at the B and B is after that, I need you to focus. Here are the plans I have for your parents' 35th anniversary party so far." She slid her notebook to him.

The current mayor had let them utilize the town hall. They'd been sitting in an unoccupied conference room for two hours as he handled some necessary M&M Security paperwork, while she made calls to the Elite Events office and other vendors she needed to assist with the party. Micah had also called his brothers and his cousins and learned that a couple of them couldn't make it to Arkansas for New Year. They had then decided to plan the surprise anniversary party in early February instead, so that everyone could make it.

"Okay," Lex said, pointing to one of the items on her list. "I'll talk to Mr. Grudy to make sure he is okay with us throwing the anniversary party at his barn house. It's the only place large enough to hold 300 to 400 people, so I think it will be perfect."

"Sounds good. He'll be fine with it and the more I think about it, maybe I should tell my parents that Mr. Grudy is throwing a Cranberry Heights Founder's Day party since the town was founded in February. That way they won't suspect anything if word gets around town."

"That would be great," she agreed. "Also, here is a list of the food dishes and desserts that will be available, all being supplied by shops here in town. We are outsourcing the cake and having it brought here from a bakery in Little Rock, a suggestion from the bakery here since this event is so special."

"I'm fine with that. What about the decorations?"

"All under control," she said, taking out her laptop. She typed in a few keys and turned her computer toward Micah. "Here are some images of the decor I have in mind after really studying your parents and taking note of their individual styles."

Micah liked the decoration ideas immediately. Victorian lace and old-world embellishments representing his mom, combined with charming rustic designs themed around nature that represented his dad.

"I love it," he said with a smile. "What website is this?"

She lifted her eyebrows. "You've never been on Pinterest?"

"Um, what exactly is Pinterest?"

"Oh, man," she said as she hit the backspace button on her computer. "Here's my Pinterest homepage. It's basically a site that allows you to electronically pin things you love to themed user boards. That way, all your likes are in one place in whatever category you want."

He laughed at the excited look on her face. "So I guess it's the same as cutting out pics from magazines, right?"

"True," she said turning the computer back to her and scrolling to another page. "But it's way more effective. I created a secret board for your parents' anniversary party that only my partners and I have access to. That's the electronic board I was in when I showed you the decor images."

"Pinterest. Instagram. I'm learning a lot about you Lex."

"Like what?" she asked.

"Like the fact that you're a visualizer and you need to visualize things to see the bigger picture. You probably react better to people and places after you do a little research through a website or social media," he said. "Am I right?"

"You don't know me," she said with a giggle that let him know he was right. "I'm just glad you like my ideas so far."

"I do. And I know my mom will be so surprised.

There's no way she'd think her sons or even her nieces came up with this decor."

"What about your dad?" Lex asked, gathering her notes to stack them in a neat pile.

"He'll probably be excited until he realizes that it was my idea to throw them a surprise anniversary party."

"Have you ever talked to your dad about how he makes you feel?"

"I gave up trying to talk to him," he huffed. "Years ago, after that college incident, my dad decided that I wasn't worth his time."

"I don't think that's true," Lex chimed in. "Every time I see you and your dad together, you both look like you want to say more, but don't."

"If he wanted to say something to me, he would."

"Or," Lex said gently, rubbing his hand, "like you, your father is stubborn and doesn't know how to right a wrong. I'm sure he was mad at you back then, but I bet he got over it and was just too proud to apologize."

Long ago, Micah had decided that he couldn't care about his dad's opinion of him. "When I needed a father most, he turned his back on me. If it weren't for my uncle Barry, who knows how I would have turned out."

"Son," Cynthia Madden said, entering the conference room, "I didn't know you felt this way and I probably should have had this conversation with you years ago."

Micah's head shot over to Lex, and he was glad to see that she had closed her laptop and placed all of the party planning documents back in her bag.

"What are you doing here?" he asked.

"I had to drop off some papers for the town-hall council meeting tonight. I didn't know you two were here."

"We're catching up on work," Micah said. "What conversation should you have had with me?"

Cynthia took a seat next to Micah. "Growing up, your father was constantly in trouble. It seemed he couldn't stay out of it. Even when he met me, he was still running up and down the streets of Arkansas. Believe it or not, what you went through was nothing compared to the things your father did."

Micah shook his head in disbelief. "Naw, I don't believe that. Dad has always been big in the community and into doing the right thing. Cranberry even chose him as mayor."

"But he wasn't always like that," Cynthia said. "I loved him and tried to convince him to give up a life in the streets when we met, but eventually I had to accept him for the man he was and I couldn't change that. Your uncle even tried convincing us to move to Cranberry Heights years before we actually did. But Mason chose to change his ways when he found out I was pregnant with Malik. The day we found out, your dad drove out here to Cranberry and told your uncle that he was going to stop being reckless and start a better life for his family. Luckily, people in Little Rock believed in him and he was given that community director job."

What? Micah couldn't believe what his mom was telling him. For years, he'd assumed that his father didn't understand what he went through back in Little Rock when, actually, he understood all too well.

"You know what I think," Lex said, still rubbing her hands against his, "I think that before our trip is over, you should have a conversation with your dad. A real conversation."

"I agree," Cynthia said giving her son a soft smile.

Micah looked from one woman to the other, trying to push aside years of anger and resentment to focus on the overall picture. Life was too short. If the streets had taught him anything, that was definitely it.

"Okay," Micah finally stated. "Before we leave, I'll talk to Dad."

"Great," Lex said with a gleeful smile. "I think the conversation will go well."

Micah smiled but kept the rest of his thoughts to himself. Conversations with his dad never went well.

"I can't believe we were in the town hall for four hours," Micah said, running his long fingers over his face. Although it was chilly outside and the first December snow had fallen, Lex had suggested that they take the thirty-minute walk back to Madden Manor instead of waiting for the local bus to arrive, which they'd taken to get into town.

"The life of an event planner," she said with a laugh. "Plus, we hadn't planned on running into your mom. On a positive note, I shouldn't have to bug you with any more details. I can handle everything from this point on, now that I have all your family's contact info. Patty in the library said she can print off the invites for all the towns-folk tonight so I can hand those out tomorrow since you aren't limiting who can come from here."

"That's good to know," he replied as they walked side by side down the long road to the house. "I don't know how I let you talk me into taking the bus this morning instead of driving. And now we're walking home in the cold," he said with a chuckle.

"I want to soak in as much of Cranberry as I can before we leave," she said, no longer surprised that she'd grown to love the town. "Besides. It's not that cold and I love looking at the fresh-fallen snow blanketed over the hills."

She could feel Micah's eyes on her, so she turned to look back at him. "What?" she asked.

"This doesn't have to be a one-time trip," he said to her. "Even though we head back to Chicago soon, I'd like to bring you back here sometime."

"I'd like that," she said, slipping her hand in his. The gesture had become natural to them, and when they weren't holding hands, Lex felt like something was missing. Looking back at him, she thought about how different he was from what she'd originally thought.

"Can we stop here?" she said as she pointed to a bench underneath a large hickory tree that was covered in frost.

"Sure," he said, walking over to the bench and brushing off the white flakes. Lex had never really cared for the cold even though she was born and raised in a cold city. But with Micah, here in Cranberry Heights, everything felt different.

"You're nothing like Evan," she said as they sat on the bench. She didn't really want to bring him up, but she felt inclined to share more about her past since he'd been so open with her.

"When I first met Evan, I was in high school," she said, curling one leg underneath her and turning to her side to face him. "I was on the cheerleading team and he was a football player."

"A cheerleader, huh," he said as his goatee curled to the side at his cunning smirk.

"Yeah, a cheerleader," she said with a laugh. "Back then, it seemed natural for us to be together. You never saw one of us without the other. We were both popular, although I never understood how I'd gotten so popular. I've always been a little different. A little clumsy… awkward at times."

"You may be all those things, but that's what's so attractive about you," he chimed in. "Plus, you have a great personality and you're extremely beautiful, although you have no idea how striking you are."

Her heart beat faster at his words. She supposed men had been calling her beautiful her entire life, but every time she heard Micah say the words, it had a different effect on her.

"I'll be the first to admit that I need to work on my insecurities. I know I'm beautiful, intelligent, driven. I just forget sometimes," she said softly before continuing. "When Evan met me, I had all the confidence in the world, but somewhere along the line, I lost a part of that confidence."

"You mean, he made you lose it," he said protectively.

"He definitely played a large part in it. But I let him. He wanted a trophy wife. Someone who looked good on his arm and did what he said. And as much as I hate to admit it, I fell into the role all too easily. I had convinced myself that being with a man like him was what I wanted."

"What did your family think about him?"

"They couldn't stand him. But while we dated, and even when we got married, no one had really told me how much they hated him. But, in their defense, I wasn't being honest about how controlling he was. They saw a few signs when we would attend family events, but whenever they asked me if I was happy, I would lie and tell them that I was."

"I bet it was hard keeping how you really felt to yourself," Micah said as he began rubbing her knee.

"It was," Lex said, shaking her head. "Especially the brief time we were married. There were many times I thought about telling the girls, but decided against it. Looking back, I realize that I never told anyone anything because I was embarrassed."

"What for?"

"Well, for starters, I was the one who chose to be with a person like that. Guaranteed, he wasn't always like that. But the signs were there in college. We were talking on the phone one day and he heard my roommate's boyfriend in the background and demanded to know who it was. I explained to him who the voice belonged to, but he didn't care. He went to college an hour from where I attended school and he drove down to mine right after our call. That's when his craziness started. We broke up for a while because I couldn't handle how needy he was, and during that time he would leave me messages saying how much he loved me and couldn't live without me. It wasn't the messages themselves that were strange, but rather the amount of calls I received."

"That's insane," Micah said, shaking his head.

"Tell me about it." She shifted in her seat when the brisk wind slashed across her face. "One day, he left me over twenty voice mails."

"Dude clearly had psychological issues," Micah said in irritation. "How did you end up getting back together with him?"

"His parents had moved to New Orleans once Evan went to college and were killed during Hurricane Katrina. He was devastated, and when he told me he couldn't live without me, I felt bad for him and we got back together. We got married right before I graduated, despite my parents' warnings to wait. Almost instantly, Evan started acting crazy again. Screening my calls, placing hidden cameras in our house, watching me while I slept... He claimed he was just protecting me from the dangerous world, but I still didn't feel safe. When I complained about him doing something, he would tell me I was lucky to have him and wasn't that attractive anyway. Then he'd claim I was bad in bed among other things and this was all within our first month of marriage."

"You can't be serious," Micah said as he outstretched her leg over his lap. "I hope you didn't take any of that nonsense to heart."

"At this point, I knew marrying him was a mistake. When I say he broke my confidence and made me more insecure, it wasn't because I believed what he said. It was because I couldn't believe that I had spent so many years of my life with such a jerk. I lost trust in myself and my ability to make the right decision. When Imani, Cyd, Mya and I decided to create Elite Events Incorporated, he found out and had a fit. And then my grandmother, Gamine, passed away, and he starting arguing with me because he felt I was spending so much time with my family. When I got the letter with the story that my grandmother left me, I told him it was over and that all the begging and pleading in the world couldn't convince me to stay. He finally left Chicago and became a financial advisor in New York."

"I'm glad you finally stood up for yourself."

"Me, too," she said with a sigh. "And you know the rest of the story... Him staging the robbery...stealing everything I loved, including my grandmother's brooches."

Micah reached out and gently rubbed his hand on her cheek. She shivered under his soft touch. "Are you ready

to head back, superwoman?" he asked with an endearing smile.

"Superwoman? Hardly," she said, standing up from
the bench.

"When faced with adversity, you overcame a huge
obstacle and re-created yourself into a better person by
learning from your experience. Sounds pretty heroic to
me."

She looked over at him and reached out for his hand as
they began walking. "Thank you for saying that, Micah."

"Anytime," he said, pulling her to him and kissing
her forehead.

Chapter 16

Forget falling, Micah thought when they were almost to Madden Manor. *I'm in love with her.* The entire time he listened to her story, one thing became completely evident in his mind. He was going to marry this woman. His mom had always told him and his brothers that when they found the one, they would know. Micah had known that he wanted to date her. He even knew he wanted a committed relationship with her. But now, he knew that neither of the first two options would suffice. She was the one he couldn't live without.

She looked over at him and flashed a smile. He smiled back thinking she had no idea just how much Cranberry Heights would become a part of her life. His mind ventured to the future as he imagined them bringing their kids to Cranberry Heights to stay with his parents. Or Lex's dad, Ethan, telling their kids all his cooking secrets before they could even cook. But he couldn't tell Lex yet. She wasn't ready.

"By the way," Micah said, breaking the silence, "what was the story that your grandmother gave you?"

"I love this story," she said with a grin. "The story was handwritten in a vintage journal about the size of the palm of my hand. It's about a woman who dedicated her entire life to meeting new people in hopes of taking a bit of every person she met to mold herself into the person she wanted to be. In the beginning of the story, the woman has a problem with change and as a result, she has a period in her life when she remains stagnant...not really living to her fullest ability. So for two years, she decides to journey outside of her comfort zone to find herself...to find her purpose by trying new things, visiting new people, eating new foods, learning about different religions. She meets some very impactful people on her journey, including her husband. Each encounter is detailed, along with the quality she chose to remember of that person. After two years, she finally realizes that life is what you make it. Her decisions and the people she met are all a part of her and her story. But she held the power to her life. Not anyone else..."

She leaned her head against Micah's shoulder as they walked.

"The story changed my perspective on life. When I reached the end of the journal, I realized that the narrator of the story was my grandmother and the man she refers to that she met on her journey is my grandfather, Ed Burrstone. The three brooches were a gift from my grandmother's friend, who was born in India and moved to the United States as a teenager with her family. She was the last person she met on her journey. Turns out, the woman was only given a month to live and in her last days, my grandmother happened to volunteer at the senior home where the lady lived. She had conversations with her every day and learned about her life and how she'd never married or had children. She was the last of her United States relatives and she told my grandmother that meeting her had made her last days joyful. A month after the woman passed, my grandmother received a letter from the woman's lawyer stating that the woman had left her three golden brooches that were made in India."

"Wow," Micah exclaimed, wrapping an arm around her shoulders. "That's an amazing story. And it's even more remarkable that your grandmother knew you'd need to hear that story one day."

"Gamine was intuitive that way," Lex said, looking up at Micah. He wiped away a fallen tear from her face.

"Although Imani, Cyd and I haven't discussed it, we each knew that she left us something when she passed. Gamine had a way of communicating with us in a way that our parents couldn't. If I had to guess, I would assume that she left handwritten items for me, Imani and Cyd. We're the three oldest grandchildren and she would always leave us little notes growing up."

When they arrived at the house, they said hello to the guests that were still up before they headed to their own guestroom. "Gamine seems special. I wish I could have met her," Micah said after shutting the bedroom door.

"Me, too," Lex said, placing a soft kiss on his lips before removing her shoes. "But she knows you."

"You think so?" he asked, removing his shoes.

"Yup, because at the end of the story, when she tells me it's about her journey, she also states that one day I will meet someone who will take one look at me and know my self-worth," she said bashfully. "And she said when that happens, I should embrace the feeling…and the person."

As Micah stood there watching emotions cross Lex's face, he was tempted to say the hell with keeping his thoughts to himself and tell her his plan to one day soon make her his. But he was more forthcoming with his feelings and she was just beginning to get accustomed to the idea.

"Thank you for telling me that," he said, crossing the room to her with one goal in mind—getting her out her clothes.

When he reached her, she was already tugging on her shirt, clearly recognizing his intent. He helped her remove her clothes in record speed. Once they had removed her last stitch of clothing, Micah grabbed her arm and walked to the bathroom.

"What about your clothes?" she asked.

"I'll take them off in a minute."

"Why are we in the bathroom?"

Instead of responding to her, Micah plugged the whirlpool tub and began running the hot water.

"Why, Mr. Madden," she said with a devilish smirk, "I think it's only fitting that I tell you that I've never made love in the tub before."

"Then I'm glad I can be your first," he said as he tugged on her ponytail holder to release her hair. Brown waves fell about her shoulders while loose strands teased her cheeks. Pushing the strands out of her face, he thought he'd never seen her look so beautiful. And he was so glad she wasn't hiding her body from him, because if he had his way, she'd never wear another piece of clothing again.

He lifted her onto the marble countertop and brought

his face closer to hers, wondering if she could feel how hard his heart was pounding. She did that to him…made his heart beat uncontrollably just by being near. He'd told her things that he was sure would run some women away, but not Lex. She understood him and, in turn, she trusted him with her own story of her past. Love was never something that he thought was in his future, but he guessed that's what people meant when they said love had a way of sneaking up on you when you least expected it. Lex had come along before he even had a chance to realize what had hit him.

She looked at him with her adorable brown eyes and winked before giggling. Needing to feel her lips, he leaned down and kissed her with all the love he felt.

When a man truly kisses the woman he knows he wants to spend the rest of his life with, that kiss will touch the depths of her soul and build a permanent home right on top of her heart. Mrs. Madden's words echoed in her mind as Lex sat there kissing Micah as if her life depended on it.

To the outside eye, it may appear to be just like any kiss like they'd shared many times before. But internally, Lex's stomach felt like she was riding a never-ending roller coaster. This kiss felt different… He felt different… The air that crackled around them felt different. By now, she knew Micah's lips and how he used them on her. The way he was kissing and suckling her now was definitely not the way he'd kissed her before.

She opened her legs wider and encircled his head with her hands. *What is going on?* she thought, unable to get enough of his taste. Her heartbeat quickened as reality hit her. The emotions in this kiss had surpassed the feelings a man had for a woman he was interested in dating, but instead, embodied the feelings that a man had for a woman he planned on spending the rest of his life with.

He nibbled her lips once more before releasing her lips and resting his forehead on hers. Both of them panted heavily, waiting for oxygen to seep into their lungs. Lex felt like the next minutes moved in slow motion as they struggled to get their breathing under control. Micah lifted his head, his eyes caressing her chin before moving to her lips and nose, settling on her eyes. His penetrating stare made her breathing falter as he gazed into her soul, displaying his emotions for her to interpret as she deemed fit.

In that moment, she fully understood what Mrs. Madden and her grandmother had tried to explain to her. *I fell in love with him*...she thought, her eyes searching his at her internal admission. *I fell,* she thought again. *Hard.* And it wasn't that she fell for him because of attraction or lust. She fell for the man he was in the past, the man he was now and the man he would be in the future. And after a kiss like that, she knew in her heart that Micah Madden wasn't going anywhere...and she loved that feeling.

He glanced over his shoulder at the tub and ran over to turn off the water. "Are you ready to get in?" he asked, testing the water.

"Yes," she said as she slid off the marble top. Even in clothes with his back turned to her, he looked good enough to eat. His hands grasped the bottom of his shirt as he lifted the fabric over his head.

Lex gasped louder than she'd intended at the sight of his full, muscular back. *How did I not notice this before?* she thought as she made her way to him and lightly touched the inked detail permanently splashed across his shoulders. The design of his tattoo made her mouth water to the point that she ran her lips across the edges, not caring if Micah thought she was crazy.

"Be careful," he warned. "I'm letting you do as you please, but if you keep putting your lips on me, I'm turning around to finish the job."

"Okay," she whispered, running her hands over the parts she'd kissed instead. Every woman had a list of qualities that made her weak in the knees. For Lex, muscular arms, nice teeth, a good cook, sexy dimples and tattoos were her top five. The fact that Micah had all five of her drop-your-panties-on-the-spot attributes made it hard for her to stand there without stripping off the rest of his clothes. So she did just that.

"I can't believe I missed this tattoo," she said as she bent down to tug his jeans off.

"The lighting has been really dim when we've been naked," he replied, undoing his belt when he realized what she was doing. "Plus I've kept you occupied in the bedroom so you haven't had a chance to study my body like I have yours."

Well, that's changing tonight, she thought after she got his pants off and went for his boxers. Once his boxers were halfway down his thighs, she let out another squeal. Tattoo number two was located on his left calf and somehow, she'd missed it when she had taken off his pants. Her hands moved to his calf, lightly caressing the design.

"Lex?" Micah's voice interrupted her observation.

"Sorry," she said, removing his boxers and then immediately becoming distracted by his butt. *Tight. Round. Kissable.* Never had Lex wanted to kiss a butt before, but Micah had the type of butt that begged to be kissed. Better yet, it begged to be bitten…so she bit it.

"Um, that's a first," Micah said apprehensively. "Not sure how I feel about you biting my ass."

"I had to," she said as she stood back to view his entire backside. "You are an incredibly tasty-looking man."

"Thanks," he said, glancing over his shoulder. "I'm guessing you have a fascination with tattoos?"

"You have no idea," she said, bringing one hand to her mouth as her eyes continued to roam over him.

"I think I do," he said with a laugh. "I'm turning around now."

Lex should have held on to the towel rack because she hadn't prepared herself for the complete view of his stark naked and very aroused, athletic body. Once again, she'd missed a tattoo on his right arm since she'd been so focused on his back. He also had a tattoo on his left pectoral muscle that flexed under her gaze. She wanted to run her tongue across the ink and pull one of his dark nipples in between her teeth. Her nipples began to harden at the thought. She didn't want to be cliché and bite her fingers to keep from screaming, but she had to. Temptation was too high and the way he was looking at her gave her goose bumps. *The body of a god.* Muscles. Abs. Tats. White teeth. Dimples. Mohawk. Dark eyes.

"Damn," she exhaled aloud as she closed the distance between them.

"You said the *D* word," he said, taunting her. But that wasn't the only curse word floating through her mind at the moment.

"Get in the water," she told him as she pointed to the tub and clicked on the jets.

"Whatever you say, boss," he said with a smirk. "You seem really dominatrix right now."

She was feeling that way, too. But she was tired of

talking. Tired of thinking. And quite frankly, she couldn't think around Micah anyway, with him looking this scrumptious. He sat in the tub with his legs open wide, awaiting her body. She followed him into the tub, immediately getting on her knees the moment her body hit the water. Micah looked at her inquisitively, probably trying to figure out why she was kneeling in front of him. She was nervous to do what her mind was telling her she had to do, so she leaned in to place a seductive kiss on his lips before her hands trailed down his chest and landed on his thighs.

Once at his inner thighs, she twirled her fingers in small circles until she reached the object of her pursuit. She glinted her eyes at him as she wrapped her hand around his shaft and began rotating her hand up and down.

His hands flew to each side of the tub as he slowly let his head fall back in enjoyment. She looked down at the piece in her hand, loving how the tip disappeared when she reached the top. The muffled sounds coming from Micah's mouth were giving her the encouragement she needed to move her hands faster, quicker, making sure she fondled his balls as she did.

"Lex," he blew in a rushed breath as he tilted his head back up to look at her.

"Can you do me a favor?" she asked. Instead of responding he just nodded his head in agreement.

"Scoot up a little so you're on the higher part of the tub."

She really appreciated the different levels that offered seating in the whirlpool tub because she definitely needed him elevated for what she planned to do next. Once he was on the highest level, as she'd predicted, his lower half sprang above the water. She submerged him in her mouth, taking the tip first before pulling him in as deeply as she could.

He jerked at the contact, his eyes widening in awe as she relaxed her throat and deep throated him like she'd never done before.

"Another first," she said in between sucks, wanting him to know she'd never taken another man in her mouth before. Not even her ex-husband.

"For real," he wheezed in a forced voice. She didn't have time to respond. Her mouth was too occupied and her mind was too fascinated by the way he felt sliding in and out of her throat.

"You should stop," he said on the brink. "I'm coming."

Duh, she thought. *That's exactly what I wanted to happen.* So instead of slowing her movements, she went faster, water swishing around them and splashing on the floor. In one sudden spasm, he shuddered irrepressibly, giving Lex the pleasure of knowing she'd been the cause of his satisfaction.

Chapter 17

"Shh," Micah said to Lex as they hid behind a large pine tree in the park, trying not to move as they heard the sound of snow crunching around them. From the anxious look on her face, he could tell that Lex had really enjoyed the different Snowlympics' contests.

Micah felt like a new man after such an exhilarating night with Lex. They'd gotten more snow overnight, making for a perfect day of winter festivities. The morning had begun with the sledding competition that required teams to sled down the biggest hill in town six times. The fastest ten teams moved on to the next round. Lex had been great at that, developing a technique that caused her to fly down the hill past other contestants. Next, there was a snow-ice-cream eating challenge in which one of two team members had to finish an entire oversize bowl of ice cream made of snow. The top seven teams moved on to the next round and Micah had nailed it and finished in second place.

After that, teams competed to see who could build the most unique snowman and Lex had the idea to build a beach snowman laying in a reclining lawn chair wearing sunglasses, a large summer hat, a bikini and holding a beer in one twigged hand. The judges had loved their idea, landing them one of five spots in the final round... a snowball fight.

But this wasn't just any snowball fight. Each team had a safe zone where they could reload on snowballs but other teams couldn't hit them while there. Each snowball had a paintball inside, five colors for five teams, and both team members had to remain within the war zone or else that team would be eliminated. When they had originally begun putting on their winter snowball-fight gear, Lex had looked hesitant after sizing up the other groups competing.

"Are you ready?" he asked her quietly, making sure her helmet was secure before they left the tree they were hiding behind.

"I think so," she said, taking a lipstick tube out her pocket to reapply a fresh pink coat.

"Are you serious right now," Micah said in disbelief. "We're in the middle of war and you're putting on lipstick."

"I'm nervous," she said in a frustrated whisper as she rubbed the color across her lips. "Leave me alone."

Her mouth opened and parted to make sure it was applied perfectly. The gesture reminded Micah of where her mouth had been placed the night before and how she'd used it to seduce him into submission. He looked down at his pants. *Great...a hard-on in the middle of a war zone.*

She then pulled out another tube of clear gloss to apply to her lips on top of the color.

"I wouldn't put on that lip gloss if I were you," he said firmly. "Unless you want me to take you on this tree and say to hell with winning."

Her eyes grew big in surprise at his comment, but she ignored his warning and began applying the gloss extra slowly. *Fine, have it your way,* he thought, inching toward her. The move caught her off guard and she fumbled with her lip gloss, which eventually fell into the snow.

"Shiitake mushrooms," Micah said, beating Lex to the punch while snapping his fingers for affect.

Lex shot him a harsh stare. "You must think you're so cute," she said with irritation before bending down to try and find her lip gloss.

Micah returned to the game as she searched. "We have to move from this tree," he said after she'd located her lip gloss. She nodded her head and followed his movements as they left behind the large tree. From what he could tell, two other teams were still in this. He motioned for Lex to go left, while he went right. She obeyed and they went in opposite directions. Unlike some competitions, if one team member was out, the other could still participate and take the win. So even if Lex got taken out, he planned on winning Snowlympics.

He crept behind another tree and counted to three before he nailed an opposing team member. Moving with ease through the trees, he reached the partner, eliminating a complete team. *Only one team left,* he thought, creeping behind a large bush. Out of the corner of his eye, he saw movement and noticed it was Lex. *Damn!* What was she doing out in the open? He waved one arm to try and get her attention. No use.

Micah eased from behind the bush just in time to see an opposing member headed toward her with a snowball. Moving swiftly, he tossed his snowball toward the individual, making contact on his shoulder, getting him out.

"Lex, let's go," Micah yelled as he was almost near her. Suddenly, a snowball whipped in his direction, hitting him right in the chest.

"Son of a—" his voice trailed upon realization that he was out of the competition. Even worse, he'd lost sight of Lex. He wanted to try and find her, but a referee was already directing him to leave the war zone. As he was walking from the area, his steps faltered when he heard screams that he knew belonged to Lex even though he couldn't see her. "Damn," he grumbled aloud. Micah hated losing, and the only thing that irritated him more than losing was coming in second place.

"I'm so proud of you," Micah told her for the fifth time since she'd come running from the war zone screaming in joy. Lex couldn't believe that she had won the snowball fight after being scared out her mind most of the duration of the snowball fight. Once she'd seen Micah get hit, she knew there was only one other person in the competition along with her. And since the other person was a high school football player, the odds were against her.

Once the football player had finally cornered her, she'd done the only thing she could think about doing in an uncomfortable situation…run like crazy. But he'd been right on her tail and just when he'd chucked his snowball in her direction, she'd tripped over a large branch that had been buried in the snow. Thinking as quickly as she could on the ground, she turned on her back and swung her snowball in his direction and hit him right in the leg. When the ref announced that the football player was out, Lex had jumped off the ground and screamed at the top of her lungs in excitement.

Now they were in Madden Manor enjoying the Christmas party with all the guests at the B and B, who were discussing how great the winter festival was and congratulating her and Micah on winning Snowlympics. Dessert was being served soon, but Lex had gotten a text from Cyd asking if she and Micah could call them.

"Is this regarding more wedding plans?" Micah asked Lex when they arrived at the bedroom.

"Cyd didn't say, but I think so," she said as she dialed Cyd's number. Cyd picked up on the third ring.

"Hey, guys," Cyd said cheerfully. "Just so you know, the whole gang is together right now and we have you on speakerphone."

After Lex and Micah exchanged hellos to the group, it was Imani who spoke next.

"Well, I know Cyd may have sent out the text to get you all here, but the news we wanted to share is actually about Daman and I." The other line grew silent. "We're having a baby," Imani and Daman said in unison. "We wanted to wait until after the first trimester before we said anything," Imani continued.

"Ahhhh," Lex screamed in the phone as she jumped up and down. "We're so happy for you guys."

"Congrats," Micah added after Lex. Imani and Daman thanked them both before Cyd got back on the phone.

"I wanted to make sure you heard the news," Cyd said. "I suspected that's what they had to share because I caught Daman swapping out the liquor in Imani's cup for apple juice during the Friends-giving drinking game. And my parents have been way too happy lately."

Lex laughed into the phone. "I bet! Thanks for calling, Cyd. We'll see you all soon."

"Wow," Lex said, looking to Micah after ending the call. "The first baby in our generation. I can't wait to spoil him or her."

Her thoughts wandered as she imagined her and Micah walking down Lake Michigan in Chicago with her belly as big as a watermelon.

"What are you thinking about?" Micah asked.

"Nothing," she said, pulling him by his arm. "Let's rejoin the party."

Once they reached the living room, Lex spotted a cozy seat right in front of the fireplace.

"Hey, Dad," Micah said when Mr. Madden walked past them, just as Lex and Micah were sitting down. "Can I talk to you for a second?"

Mr. Madden stopped in his tracks and looked at his son in surprise. Lex glanced over at Mrs. Madden just in time to see her clutch her hand to her heart.

"Sure, son," Mr. Madden finally said before the two walked into the kitchen.

Lex desperately wished she were a fly on the wall for their conversation. Micah had promised her he would have a conversation with his father before they went back to Chicago, but she hadn't known when.

Mrs. Madden glanced over at Lex and angled her head toward the door as she stood from her seat and walked toward the kitchen. Mrs. Madden gently cracked the door so that her husband and son wouldn't hear it creak.

"How do they sound?" Lex whispered when she reached Mrs. Madden.

Mrs. Madden smiled as she let the door softly close. "There voices don't sound tense like they usually do when they talk. I don't know what you said to my son, but my husband has been waiting years to have this conversation."

Lex just smiled as she linked arms with Mrs. Madden and they returned to the guests who were diving into another lip-smacking holiday pie.

"Let me start by saying that I am truly sorry for everything I put you through when I was younger," Micah said, taking a seat opposite his dad.

At his dad's silence, he continued. "I never thought about how my actions would affect you and Mom and at the time. It was hard for me to discontinue relationships that I had in Little Rock."

Mason creased an eyebrow before responding. "I wasn't disappointed in the fact that you maintained unhealthy relationships with men I felt you should ignore. It was more the fact that you let that nonsense follow you to college. I never wanted any of my sons to go down the same path that I went down."

"But dad, sometimes you have to learn lessons the hard way."

"I know that," Mason interjected, "but no matter what I said to you, you never seemed to listen."

"You were a great father. But not once did we have a conversation about your past and the things you went through growing up in Little Rock."

Mason shook his head. "That's because I knew you were my spontaneous son. The one who would push his limit just like I did. I didn't want to give you any ideas."

"Letting me know that you understood what I was going through at the time would have worked better than pushing me off for Mom and Uncle Barry to deal with."

"You only listened to the two of them, Micah. You never listened to what I told you."

"Only because I didn't know you were speaking from experience. It always came across as judgment and disappointment that I couldn't be more like Malik."

Mason squinted his eyes before clasping his hands together on the table. "I never wanted you to be more like Malik or any of your brothers and I'm sorry if I didn't make that clear. What I should have told you back then was that I knew that out of all my sons, you were a force to be reckoned with. All my sons are amazing men, but you had that extra something… You still do. I've always been proud of you, and now that you've started your security company with Shawn, you seem to have truly found your purpose, I couldn't be prouder."

Micah let out a breath he hadn't known he'd been holding as he stared at a man he felt like he was meeting for the first time. *He's proud of me.* He'd heard his dad tell his brothers that, but the words had never been directed at him. A man and his pride was something Micah knew all too well, and it seemed his dad had written the book on it. He leaned back in his chair and dragged his fingers over his face.

"To think of all the years we wasted avoiding this conversation," Micah said, annoyed at himself for not telling his dad how he felt sooner. And frustrated at his dad for never understanding that of all the people in his life, he was the one person he needed approval from. Finally having that approval was slowly filling a void he had in his heart.

"Hold on to Lex," his dad said, breaking his thoughts.

"That came out of nowhere," Micah said with a laugh. Mason joined in the laughter before his face grew serious.

"You and I are a lot alike, and men like us could search our entire lives to find a woman who truly understands us. When I found your mother, I honestly had no idea what she saw in me, but through her love, I was able to find my way and truly become a man. She saw in me what I was trying to see in myself and she didn't care that I didn't have a penny to my name or that our dinner the first few months of our marriage consisted of canned beans and bread. She loved me anyway because she saw the man I was growing to be. She knew we had all this in our future," he added, waving his hands around. "You found your path in life a lot quicker than I did, Micah, but that doesn't mean you don't need a woman who gets you now, accepts where you came from and sees where you're headed in the future."

"I agree," Micah said as he looked at his dad through a new set of eyes. "I haven't told her how I feel yet, but I plan to tell her soon. Even though she's her own woman, the way she understands me reminds me so much of Mom." Micah studied the worry lines permanently etched on his dad's face. Mason was still a healthy and handsome man, but in that moment, Micah realized how much time they'd lost on nonsense.

"So," Micah said, smiling at his dad in a way he couldn't remember smiling in years, "according to mom, you were a troublemaker back in the day. What did you do?"

Mason laughed and shook his head. "What didn't I do," he said as he proceeded to tell Micah stories about the antics he had caused when he was younger.

Chapter 18

Lex looked around her apartment for the tenth time trying to make sure everything was perfect. Although she'd shared many nights with Micah in Cranberry Heights, it was their fourth night being together in Chicago, but the first night they were having dinner at her place instead of his.

She grinned as she lit scented candles throughout her home and thought about the way Micah had acted when they had arrived back in Chicago. The plane had barely landed before he was hightailing it out of O'Hare airport, grabbing their bags and telling the cab to go directly to his condo. They had agreed on a committed relationship before they had left Arkansas, although Micah had admitted he hadn't dated or had sex with anyone since he met her in the lingerie boutique. Lex hadn't either, concluding that they had been acting like an exclusive couple anyway.

She heard a firm knock on the door and checked her clock. *Right on time.* Giving herself another once-over in the mirror, she smoothed out her navy blue cotton dress, fluffed her curls and reapplied a quick coat of Burberry lipstick. She briefly contemplated sliding on some slippers, but she opted to show off her freshly pedicured toes.

The moment she opened the door, her breath caught and her lips parted. When he'd asked her how he should dress, she'd told him to dress comfortably, and she figured she would surprise him and wear a cute dress in hopes of catching him off guard. Standing in the doorway with him in his heather-gray jogging outfit, white tee, basketball shoes and baseball cap, she was the one who was caught off guard by how sexy he looked. She couldn't recall ever seeing him look this casual and it was causing her insides to twist and turn wildly.

"Are you going to invite me in?" Micah asked.

"Sorry," she said, stepping aside. The minute she shut the door, Micah pulled her to him for an explosive kiss, giving her a chance to get reacquainted with his addicting taste. His mouth consumed hers in such an erotic way; she felt it all the way to the tips of her toes. She moaned into his mouth when his hands found their way to her behind and gripped her dress, sliding the material up past her waist.

When his palms met her flesh, she opened her eyes just in time to catch the inquisitive look in his eyes. He lifted her dress even more and glanced over her shoulder to her butt.

"You must not want us to eat dinner," he said upon realizing she wasn't wearing any panties.

"You weren't supposed to figure that part out yet," she

said, gently pulling the back of her dress down. "Come on. I'll give you a tour."

She led him through her condo and informed him that she wasn't showing him her bedroom until after dinner. Luckily, he didn't put up much of a fuss.

"What's for dinner?" he asked when they'd arrived at the dining room table.

"I'm so glad you asked," she said as she motioned for him to take a seat. "As you can see, we have a fresh salad and dinner rolls."

"Both look great."

"Thank you! And for the main entrée, we have green beans that I personally picked from my dad's garden and..." Her voice trailed off as she rounded the table to lift the cover that was concealing the main dish. "We have filet mignon and lobster tail with my special butter, garlic and herb sauce."

"Damn, girl," Micah exclaimed, looking over the entire spread. "I didn't know you were throwing down dinner like this."

"Told ya I'm good," she said with a laugh. "I also have a red wine that goes great with the filet mignon."

"I must admit," he said, shaking his head, "I was all set to take you to your bedroom first and eat dinner after, but this looks too good to ignore right now."

"Then let's eat," she said, pouring him a glass of wine and taking a seat across from him. "Besides, you'll need to keep up your strength for what I have planned later."

He didn't say anything, but the intense way he watched her told her all she needed to know. He was ready for whatever she had in store.

An hour and a half later, they'd finished dinner and washed the dishes. Micah was placing the packaged left-

overs in the refrigerator and Lex knew this was her time
to set the mood.

"Micah, when you finish, can you meet me in the living room?"

"Sure," he said, glancing at her with excitement in
his eyes.

After he agreed, Lex went into the living room and
dimmed the lighting before turning on her electric fireplace. All the candles that were burning in the living
room and bedroom were a jasmine and lavender mix—
scents that were proven to heighten a man's desires.

She glanced around the room making sure nothing
would get in the way of what she had planned next. She
didn't hear Micah come into the room, but her nipples
hardened the minute the stimulating scent of musk and
man oozed into her nostrils, taking over her senses. She
found comfort in knowing she didn't have to see him to
know he was in close proximity to her.

"I'll be right back," she said, discreetly grabbing the
remote to the iPod docking station. She pointed to the
couch, indicating for him to sit before leaving the room.
Once she was in the confines of her bedroom with the
door locked, she walked over to her iPhone and popped
in her headphones before scrolling through her audio-
books and pressing play.

"Congratulations on completing your journey to self-
discovery," the voice said through her headphones. "Now
that you have realized your self-worth, you can conquer
anything you want in life. Maybe take a chance on a new
relationship with that special person you've had your
eye on."

As the voice spoke to her, Lex stepped out of her dress
and dabbed some jasmine and lavender body oil on the in-

timate parts of her body before changing into something she was sure would bring Micah to his knees.

"Show that person that you can take charge and be the aggressor."

Lex added silver glitter pumps to her sexy outfit before running her fingers through her hair and throwing some gloss on her lips.

"Okay," she said, standing in front of her full-length mirror before she resumed listening to her audiobook. "The time is now! Don't keep your future waiting."

Lex cut off the audiobook and tossed her phone in a drawer before retuning to the mirror. "Tonight, you aren't Lex Turner, the woman who plays it safe," she said firmly. "Tonight, you're a woman whose ultimate goal is to seduce the man you fell in love with and prove that you're not the shy girl he met months ago." She really didn't need a pep talk, but she gave herself one anyway. She'd already stepped outside her comfort zone with Micah and she felt like she was gaining back the confidence that she'd lost after her relationship with Evan.

She stepped out into the hallway and angled her hand so that she could click on the music without Micah seeing her. The minute she heard Beyoncé's latest hit, she had immediately made a mental note to keep the song in the back of her mind. She'd been practicing her striptease all day, and now she was ready for Micah to see what loving him was doing to her.

Micah glanced around when the music suddenly came through the speakers. He didn't see Lex, but the hairs on the back of his neck stood on alert. He removed his jacket, too overcome with heat to sit on the couch fully clothed.

As soon as Beyoncé's voice started singing, Lex's leg

appeared from the side of the wall. Long. Sexy. Enclosed in a sexy silver heel. Micah leaned up in his seat, anticipating what would happen next.

When she turned the corner, his breath caught when he realized she was wearing the pleated lilac babydoll and silky lace boyshort that she'd purchased at Bare Sophistication lingerie boutique. *Oh, my damn,* he thought when he realized the scene that was unfolding in front of him. *A striptease…in my outfit no less.* He knew it wasn't really his outfit, but it felt like it was. Since the moment he'd rung it up for her, he'd wished he could see it on her.

Deciding he needed to enjoy this moment, he leaned back on the sofa and linked his hands behind his head. When she finally stood completely in front of him, he realized she was singing along to the song and her voice was amazing. She even harmonized, going low when Beyoncé sang high and vice versa.

She danced in front of him dipping her butt just to bring it back again and tossing her legs around as if she danced professionally every day. When she walked to the wall and did a quick in and out hip movement, he almost lost it finding it hard to enjoy the dance in it's entirety when he was hung up on the way her fingers slid down the wall and her back curved to make her butt pop out more.

After a couple minutes, she began making her way to the sofa. *Oh, shit,* he thought when she stopped within inches of his grasp, turned her back to him and eased all the way down to the floor before bringing herself back up. When she bent over, giving him an exposed view of her behind covered in the racy lace material, he lost it. His hands gripped her before she had a chance to turn around.

"Micah," she said with a giggle as she glanced over her shoulder. "I'm not finished yet."

"Oh, you're done," he said, standing up and throwing her over his shoulders. She yelped at the sudden overtaking.

He scanned the rooms until he located her bedroom and tossed her on the bed. "You couldn't honestly think I could make it through that entire dance without touching you, did you?"

Instead of answering him, she flashed him a look of innocence, but there was nothing innocent about that dance she'd just given him. He could hear another slow song starting to play and although the sound was faint, he decided to leave the bedroom door open so that they could make love to the music.

"I've been thinking about seeing you in this lingerie outfit since you bought it," he said as he watched her play with the edges of the babydoll. He took a mental picture, wanting to always remember how free and uninhibited she looked in this moment. Unable to hold back any longer, he quickly removed all his clothes and covered himself before joining her on the bed kissing every part of her body that wasn't hidden underneath material.

"Aren't you going to take off my heels and clothes?" she asked.

"Hell, no," he said loudly. "I'm making love to you in this babydoll with those sexy shoes on. And," he said as his fingers went in between her thighs, "since these panties have a slit in the center, we're definitely keeping these on."

He began massaging her clit with his fingers, gradually dipping in two fingers when he felt her getting hotter and wetter.

"Micah," she breathed as she began rotating her hips to the movement of his hand. When he felt her on the edge, he increased the pace of his fingers until his hand was soaking wet from her juices.

Her eyes grew dark and her breathing became labored...signs of a strong orgasm. He opened her legs and eased himself inside of her, loving the fact that he could make love to her at the same time he admired her in her underwear.

Her sweet moans filled the room and were quickly joined by his intense groans. She felt so good. Too good. He wanted to make this last for as long as he could, but sexing her in lingerie was becoming a new fetish of his and the fact that she looked so damn sexy was making it harder for him to refrain from coming.

"I want to flip on all fours," she said between pumps. *All fours? Ah, hell...* There was no way he could last long if she wanted him to hit it from the back.

He obliged her request and re-entered her from the back, the lacy material floating about her body with each thrust of his hips. She met him pump for pump, rotating her hips as she did so. Through pure miracle, he managed to push aside his growing need to release his juices and was able to add two additional sexual positions to their sensual rendezvous.

"I'm coming," she said in the sexiest voice he'd ever heard from her. Her words were music to his ears, since he was once again on the brink of exploding. With two more thrusts, they both released orgasms so powerful that they succumbed to fatigue.

"Wow," Micah said, heaving on the bed with Lex right by his side.

"Tell me about it," she said, leaning up to lightly kiss

him. They locked eyes and kissed once more with more hunger and potency than their prior kiss.

"I want to tell you something," he said after a few moments of silence. Lex gazed up to him, waiting to hear what he had to say.

"I love you," he stated as he watched her eyes fill with emotion.

"I love you, too," she said with a smile as she scooted closer to him.

She loves me, he thought as he smiled back and kissed her hard.

He loves me, she thought as she sat near her bay window drinking a much-needed cup of coffee. After their admission last night, they'd made love several more times before falling asleep. Micah had awakened her after only three hours of sleep for a quickie, and to let her know he had to run home to change for a meeting, promising to be back soon.

She already couldn't wait for him to hurry back. She was in her prime and was finally living her life, not dwelling on bad decisions she'd made in the past that had led to her biggest failed relationship. *Maybe I had to go through that to find and appreciate a man like Micah.*

When she heard the knock on her door, she secured her robe, although she briefly considered answering the door for Micah naked. She couldn't wait to tell him about all her revelations since they hadn't gotten a chance to talk last night after her striptease.

She swung open the door. "Hello, sweetheart," said a repulsive voice that had only appeared in her nightmares. *Please tell me I'm still sleeping.*

She'd often heard people say that you can't outrun

your past. As she stood there staring at the person on the other side of her door, it seemed the past she'd been running from and trying to forget had just popped up on her doorstep.

Chapter 19

"What are you doing here and how did you get past security?" she asked the man, demanding an answer. "And you're supposed to be in New York."

"I can't come visit my hometown and see my wife," Evan Gilmore said with a devious smile.

"Ex-wife," she replied quickly.

"Details, details," he said, trying to push his way through the door. "Security was busy so I decided to let myself up."

"I didn't invite you in," she said, pushing him back through the door. "And I'm calling security to escort you back out."

"Speaking of security, you may want to hear what I have to say before you kick me out," Evan said firmly.

"I'm not interested in anything you have to say."

"Even if it's about your little boy toy, Micah Madden?" Evan said, succeeding in getting her interest.

"He's none of your concern."

"He is when he puts the woman I used to love in danger."

"Love? Is that what you tell yourself every night?" Lex said, her voice getting higher.

"I did love you," Evan argued. "Besides, I may have been a lot of things, but I never forced myself on another woman."

"Excuse me," Lex said in irritation. "I don't know what the hell you're talking about and I need you to leave." She started to close the door on him.

"At least look at this file," Evan said, stopping the door with his arm. "Micah isn't the man you think he is. I don't have to come in, but at least meet with me before I go back to New York. After being together for so long you at least owe me that."

Lex opened the door back up. "Let's get one thing straight. I don't owe you one damn second of my time, nor do I care what you're up to. Once I shut this door on you, I plan to forget that your sorry ass ever existed, and I suggest you stay away from me unless you want me to get a restraining order."

Evan laughed maliciously and started clapping his hands together. "Bravo, Lex, bravo. Seems you gave up that stupid no-cursing rule."

"I only curse when I need to, and when it comes to scum like you, I have to stoop to your level to get my point across."

"Oh, I see," Evan said, leaning against the doorjamb. "You must think this guy Micah actually loves you and wants to be with you. I heard about him and trust me, you aren't the type of woman he's into. You're the girl next door...the nice girl...the *basic* girl. When he's done playing it safe with you he'll go back to the type of women he prefers dating. The kind of independent and feisty woman you'll never be."

"Go to hell," she said, balling her hand in a fist to refrain from slapping him.

"Already headed there," he said, holding the file out again. "And it seems your boy will be joining me there." He tossed the file through the door onto the floor.

"Read the file," Evan said. "Because if I have my way, I'll tell the press who the true Micah Madden is and dash any hopes of him really getting that stupid security company off the ground. And what's the name of their biggest recent investor? Grant & Parker Inc. is it? Did I forget to mention that I'm the financial advisor for Ben Grant and Liam Parker? Oh, yeah, I have clients all over the United States, not just Chicago and New York. Imagine my surprise when I was on a conference call with them and they mentioned having a great dinner with a new company they are investing in. What a shame that Shawn Miles will go down because he partnered with a shady guy like Madden."

"I've heard enough," Lex said as she shut the door again. "Don't ever come here again."

"I won't have to," he said behind the slammed door. "After you read what's in the file you'll be calling me."

She looked through her peephole to make sure he was gone. Usually she always checked the peephole before answering the door, but her mind had been elsewhere.

"He's gone," she said to herself as she tried to slow her heartbeat. She hadn't seen him in over six years and she'd hoped she went the rest of her life without seeing him again. As she got up from the door, she glanced at the file before picking it up off the floor and going to her desk.

Once she was seated, she opened the file and began reading the contents inside. She didn't really know what she was looking for until she got to a document from Fisk University. Micah's freshman year transcript was included. *He is smart,* she thought, taking note of all the A's and B's. During his first year, he'd even joined a business fraternity on campus that was really hard for freshman students to enter.

Lex was still wearing a smile when she got to one of two police reports, one from the campus police and one from the Nashville, Tennessee, police. Her smile dropped instantly.

"What the…" She scanned both documents, reading a detailed account about Micah's arrest in college. One of the statements in the report momentarily stopped her breathing.

"Micah Madden and Neil Timmons took turns sexually assaulting me against my will," Lex read aloud, quoted from a woman named Ashley Anderson. Lex sat there and read both police reports from top to bottom before looking at the final document that was a picture of Ashley after the attack. The image made Lex drop the entire file out of her hands.

One hand flew to her mouth and she leaned back in her desk chair. She couldn't believe what she was reading, and as she recalled all the details of her conversations with Micah, she remembered that he never told her what he had been arrested for.

The case was dropped based off of false evidence… His words swirled around in her mind. As she sat there, recounting everything that Micah had ever told her, she knew what was in the file couldn't be true. But still, there was a little voice inside her head that wondered how big of a role he actually played. She was aggravated that he hadn't come right out and told her what had happened.

She ran and got her work cell phone, which would allow her number to appear unknown to whomever she called, and dialed Evan's number. He answered on the second ring.

"These accusations are false," she said as soon as he answered.

"You're smarter than you look," Evan stated. "Even so, the info is still out there. If I have a friend who was able to dig it up, so are many others."

"What's your point, Evan?" she yelled. "Micah was cleared of all charges so whatever you're thinking about doing would be pointless."

"Think again, sweetheart," he said in a tone that made her want to throw up. "You met Ben Grant's wife at dinner, right? Denise Grant?"

"Yes, and...?"

"Did you know they have a daughter named Monica Grant?"

"They mentioned that's their only daughter. What's your point?"

"My point, Lex, is that dear sweet Monica didn't have the best experience at Arkansas State University. You see, Monica had an off-campus job and decided to help out a friend and take an overnight shift. She should have returned to campus before it got dark because she was waiting for the bus when she was sexually assaulted by a man who dragged her away from the bus and into an alley where there were more men waiting to sexually assault her. The entire ordeal was so devastating that Monica never fully recovered, and although the men were brought to justice, it wasn't enough to make Monica feel safe again."

"That is heart-wrenching" Lex exclaimed as she wiped a tear from her eye and placed her hand over her heart. "My heart aches for them, but I'm still not understanding. I met them and there is no way Ben and Denise Grant would hold it against Micah that he was falsely accused of something he didn't do."

"You may be right," Evan responded. "But they would if they knew Micah used to hang out in the same crowd as Neil Timmons, Monica's main attacker."

Oh, goodness, no... She tried to comprehend what Evan was telling her, but one thing still wasn't adding up. "Why are you involving yourself in this? What do you want?"

"Isn't it obvious," he said deceitfully. "The only thing that will stop me from informing Ben and Denise Grant about Micah is you. I want you back Lex. I want you back and I want us to get remarried."

Blackmail. Lex dropped the phone, refusing to listen to anything else Evan had to say. She went to the couch and lay down before she picked up her personal cell and told Micah she wasn't feeling well and needed some time to herself.

She knew he didn't deserve to be ignored and quite frankly, all she wanted to do was tell him everything she'd just found out. But a part of her didn't understand how Micah could be friends with a man like Neil Timmons. An even larger part was worried that Evan's accusations were true. Lex wasn't the type of woman Micah usually dated. *Could he have pursued me because he thought I was easily influenced?* She rubbed her forehead. *How much do I actually know about Micah?*

Guaranteed, she'd spent the past few weeks getting to know him and his family, so her heart was telling her to trust her gut and believe that there was nothing Micah would have in common with a man like Neil. Micah loved her...the real her. Unlike Evan, he didn't have any ulterior motives in dating her.

Lex stood and began pacing the floor. She'd been wrong in the past. Evan was proof of that. Even so, Evan Gilmore had ruined her life years ago, and she'd promised when she divorced him that she would never give him that power again. Micah was finally in a place that he wanted to be in with the type of job he'd always dreamed of having.

As soon as she figured out how to make Evan back off without getting Micah involved, she would talk to Micah about the entire situation and handle her relationship without Evan's interference. Until then, she would not do anything to jeopardize the rise of M&M Security.

"Hey, Malik," Micah said when his brother, who was also a private investigator, walked into the conference room at M&M Security. When his brother had asked to meet with him and Shawn, Micah knew it had to be important if he was driving from Detroit to Chicago.

He wanted to know what was up with his brother, but right now, he wanted to know what was going on with Lex more. He had no idea what was bothering her and she hadn't returned any of his calls in three days, only text messages. With Christmas approaching in two days he had hoped they would have made plans to spend the holiday together. *She probably got cold feet after I told her I loved her.* But she said she loved him, too, so he didn't understand the problem.

"Micah, are you listening," Malik said, interrupting his thoughts.

"Sorry, bro, what's up?"

"We have a problem," Malik said as he placed his black bag on the mahogany conference table before removing his black winter coat and taking a seat near Shawn and Micah.

"You know how I often run a background check on you to make sure there are no red flags?"

"I thought you ran a background check on me to make sure I wasn't doing something I shouldn't be doing," Micah replied with a sarcastic laugh.

"I'm being serious," Malik said as he took a couple pieces of paper out of his bag and slid them over to Shawn and Micah.

"It looks like somebody on the inside released information on your case from college," Malik said to Micah. "From what I can tell, the hacking took place in the New York City FBI office. Upon further digging, I uncovered the name Ralph Peters as the FBI agent who was investigating you."

"I've never heard of him," Micah said, shuffling through the papers.

"Neither have I," Shawn added.

"I hadn't either so I investigated some more and looked into the people he was associated with. For the most part, the people he hangs out with are clean. But one name stood out."

Malik slipped another paper on the table. "Evan Gilmore is his financial advisor, and according to the background check I did, he was married to—"

"Lexus Turner," Micah interrupted, having permanently etched the name in his mind the minute Lex had told him about Evan. "If he thinks he can get to me to get to Lex, he better think again," he continued, taking a swig from his water bottle to calm his nerves.

"I don't think that's all," Malik added. "Gilmore is the financial advisor for Grant & Parker Incorporated."

"Shit," Micah voiced. "Gilmore handles their finances. So this is more about bringing me down than getting back at Lex."

"I think it's about both," Malik said. "There were quite a few complaints filed against Gilmore from old clients who said he was manipulative, irresponsible and a snake in the grass. Most of the cases were dropped."

"Did you uncover why?" Shawn asked. "I can't imagine most of the cases being dropped when money is involved."

"You're exactly right," Malik stated as he pulled out yet another file that contained a list of names. "Gentlemen, if you look at the first page you will notice all the names of the accounts that Gilmore embezzled money from, and if you look at the second page of names you will find all of the people who he is currently working with or paid off for silence."

"This asshole," Micah stated, pushing all the paper away from him in frustration.

"I also found out that he's in Chicago right now," Malik added. "He's been here for about three days."

"That's right around the time Lex stopped talking to me. I wonder if he contacted her."

"Did you tell her about Fisk University?" Malik asked.

"She knows the story about my past and the trouble I used to get into. And she knows I was arrested and had to transfer schools, but she doesn't know the entire story about Ashley Anderson's accusations."

"If he contacted her, that explains why she hasn't spoken to you," Shawn said. "He could have told her the entire story and she could have been caught off guard because she didn't know."

"Maybe," Micah said, clasping his hands together on the table. "Okay, so what does Grant & Parker Inc. have to do with all this? They aren't on either of Gilmore's list."

Malik opened his mouth to speak and then hesitated.

"What is it?" Micah asked.

"Well," Malik said as he flipped through a couple pages of the file in his hand before slipping it to Micah, "if you read that, you'll see a detailed description of what happened to Ben and Denise Grant's daughter, Monica Grant."

Micah began reading the police report and the statement from Monica, growing angrier with every sentence he read about the sexual assault. No woman should ever have to go through what she went through, and no parent should ever have to watch his or her daughter go through that. It was amazing that she survived the ordeal, but the physical and mental damage that was done was just as devastating to read. Micah had done a good job at keeping his anger under control until he got to the last sentence of the report. *Sexual Offender—Neil Timmons.*

"Damn," Micah yelled as he threw the paper across the table and firmly hit the desk before he stood up to stand by the window.

"Oh, man," he heard Shawn say aloud after reading the document.

"I get it," Micah said, turning from the window to face Malik and Shawn. "Gilmore plans to tell Ben and Denise Grant that I used to hang out in the same circle as Timmons. Am I right? A sure way for M&M Security to lose our biggest investor yet."

"That's my guess," Malik said, walking to Micah and clasping a hand on his shoulder. "But you never know what could happen. I think a better question would be what bug did Evan Gilmore place in Lex's ear. You couldn't have known that Neil would turn out to be the type of man he did. We knew he was bad news, but most the guys in the neighborhood were into the same stuff he was, only he turned into a sexual offender. Plus, I'm sure Grant & Parker would be interested to learn this information about their financial advisor. We need to figure out what we're going to do next."

"I have to talk to Lex," Micah said. "You can work out a plan with Shawn while I'm gone. But first, I think I need to talk to Evan Gilmore."

"That's not a good idea," Shawn said. "I think we should both go."

"I'm going, too," Malik added, packing up his papers. "I figured you would want to talk to him after we uncovered this information, so I found out what hotel he's staying at."

"Great, let's go."

Chapter 20

"Let's sit over there," Lex said to Mya as they made their way to the corner of the sandwich shop attached to the hotel where Evan had asked her to meet him. After days of avoiding Micah and trying to keep everything that was happening to herself, she had finally decided that she needed to open up and talk to someone. She'd debriefed Mya on the situation and asked her to accompany her to the meeting with Evan. After spending thirty minutes trying to convince her to call Micah and ignore Evan's warning altogether, Mya had finally caved in and decided to come with her.

"This is a bad idea," Mya said as they sat at the table.

"Relax," Lex said as she removed her coat and draped it over the back of the chair. "I refuse to give Evan any power over me and I do plan on talking to Micah about this, but only after I give Evan a piece of my mind."

"Look, honey," Mya said, rubbing her hand, "I love this new fierce and fabulous you, but Evan isn't worth the air you breathe. He's lower than the scum on the bottom of your pumps. He's a jerk. He's a scummy jerk. He's a scummy, manipulating, evil, malicious jerk who should pay for the crap he put you through. My only hope is that when Micah finds out, Evan will curse the day he ever coerced you into saying I do."

Lex looked at her partner who was also one of her best friends. "Are you done?"

"Um, yeah, I think so," Mya said, taking a sip from the glass of water that had been brought to the table.

"Do you feel better now?" Lex asked.

"I do," Mya said, giving a quick smile. "But he better not say anything stupid because if he does, I may stab him with my fork."

Lex laughed although nothing about the situation was funny. Mya had always been her ride-or-die friend and she loved that about her. Many people knew that Mya's words were lethal. If she loved you, then you would always have a fierce and loyal friend in Mya, but if you crossed her, or someone she loved, Mya was a force to be reckoned with.

"Oh, great," Mya said, glancing into the lobby of the hotel. "There goes that son-of-a-bitch now."

"Mya," Lex exclaimed. "Can we try to refrain from all the name-calling when he actually gets here? Anger won't resolve this. I need to be able to vocalize what I'm feeling once and for all."

Mya was about to say something else, when Lex cut her off.

"Is that Shawn?" Lex asked when she noticed Evan had stopped walking.

"Uh, I think so," Mya said, peering out of the restaurant.

"Oh, no," Lex stated. "That's definitely Micah and Malik behind him."

"That's what I'm talking about, where are they walking to?"

"I don't know."

"Let's go see what's going on."

Lex barely had time to react because Mya was already halfway out the door.

"I could have you guys arrested for threatening me," Evan yelled. "You don't have a case here."

"I think you may want to lower your voice," Malik said as they walked to a part of the lobby that was somewhat empty.

"I'll tell you what's going to happen," Micah said, done with trying to play nice. "Either you keep my name and Lex's name out of your mouth, or we'll expose you for the embezzling bastard you really are." Micah was trying to calm his nerves, but he had been anxious ever since Malik had told him the information about Evan and Neil Timmons. He was trying to be the bigger person. Be a man about the situation. But his body wasn't listening to his mind, so all Micah wanted to do was knock Evan out cold.

"Your case wouldn't go far," Evan rebuked. "I know people in high places."

"I guarantee we know people in higher places," Shawn said, standing closer to Evan and looking him up and down.

"We'll see," Evan said before he looked past the men to something that had caught his eye. Never one to take their eyes off a target, none of the men turned to see what Evan was looking at.

"You know what," Evan said, shrugging his shoulders, "I can tell you like leftovers so you can have her." He looked straight in Micah's eyes before he continued. "The sex was never that good anyway. And once you get tired of playing with her, you'll throw her away just like I did."

"Be careful, Gilmore," Micah warned as he took two steps toward him.

"What are you going to do?" Evan egged on. "Hit me? Do it! I dare you! You can have that sorry excuse for a woman. I only married her because I felt sorry for her. I—"

Lex's fist connected with Evan's face, catching Evan off guard as well as everyone else. His hand shot up to his chin to cover where she had hit him.

"I know you didn't just hit me b—" Lex's fist connected with Evan's face again, halting whatever he'd been about to say. Her second punch knocked him out cold. Shawn caught Evan before he fell to the ground and sat him in a nearby chair so that it would appear as if he was asleep.

"Oh, man, that felt good," Lex said as she shook her hand in pain.

"What happened to vocalizing your words?" Mya asked Lex with a smirk as she gave her a high five.

"The moment called for hand-to-face contact," Lex said with a laugh.

"What are you doing here?" Micah asked, realizing that she was the trigger that made Evan start talking so much crap.

"I was supposed to be meeting with Evan and I brought Mya with me. He came to my house the other day and had an entire file on you. Although, I'm guessing you already know."

"Malik told me this morning," he said. "But I don't understand why you didn't talk to me."

"Because I wanted to stand up for myself once and for all. Evan had threatened me enough in my lifetime, and I wasn't going to let him dictate who I love or worry you."

Micah had a feeling she'd felt that way, which was why he didn't step in. Lex needed to finally feel in control. But that didn't mean he liked the fact she was going to meet him by herself.

"But Evan is too dangerous for you to deal with on your own."

"I tried to tell her to let you handle it," Mya chimed in, standing off to the side. Micah turned to tell Mya thanks, taking note of the way his brother was glancing at her when he thought she wasn't looking. He would have felt sorry for Malik if he hadn't noticed Mya trying just as hard not to look at him.

"Based off what I heard," Lex said, breaking his observation of his brother and Mya, "I understand that now. And you said something about embezzlement? What did he do?"

"We can talk about all that later," Micah said, picking up her hand and kissing her swollen knuckles. "All I want to do now is take care of your hand and make sure that we're okay."

She smiled as she raised her hand to his cheek. "We're okay," she said, lightly kissing his lips. "I know the type of man you are so I knew there was more to the story than what Evan told me. I just needed some time to myself to figure out how I was going to handle the situation."

"Thanks for believing in me," he said, pulling her

closer. "But please promise me that you will talk to me if you ever have a question about my past, instead of keeping things to yourself."

"Deal," she said as she pulled him closer to her for a kiss. The minute he heard her moan, he deepened their kiss, his tongue frolicking with hers, igniting all his senses in a way only she knew how to do.

The next night, Lex snuggled in Micah's arms on her couch as they watched a romantic comedy on Netflix. Micah had tried to convince her to watch an action movie, but once she told him that she'd had enough action for one holiday, he'd obliged her request to watch a romance.

After the incident with Evan, her and Micah had a long conversation about everything that they'd uncovered. She had already concluded that the situation with Neil had been something that Micah wasn't involved with, but she was glad to know what role Micah had played in the situation.

Ashley Anderson had had a huge crush on Micah in college and had followed him around for months. Although he constantly told her he wasn't interested, she hadn't listened and still tried to pursue him. When Neil Timmons had visited Micah in college, Ashley flirted with him to make Micah jealous. She even went so far as to ask Micah if she could come to his room to see Neil. Micah knew she was trying to make him jealous, but he didn't care, so he agreed.

Once Neil and Ashley started making out in his dorm room, Micah left, having better things to do than watch them make out. He was halfway out his dorm when he realized he forgot his book bag. When he went back to his room, Neil was forcing himself on Ashley and she fought back and begged him to stop. Micah acted quickly on his feet and attacked Neil, knocking him to the ground. His dorm neighbors had heard the screams and had called the police. But by the time the police arrived, Ashley had told the cops that both of them had forced themselves on her and they were both arrested. Micah tried telling the officers he didn't do it, but there was no use.

From what Micah was told, when Ashley's parents arrived, her mom was able to figure out the truth and Ashley finally told the police officers the true story about what had happened. She then apologized to Micah. Her parents removed her from the school and Neil was released because Ashley dropped the charges. By that time, the damage to Micah's reputation on campus was already done and his parents had been notified. The entire time Micah had retold the story, Lex's love for him grew deeper.

"I'll be right back," Micah said, getting up from the couch before returning with his bag.

"I was going to wait for Christmas," he said as he pulled out a red box with a green ribbon tied around it, "but I think tonight is a perfect time to give this to you."

Lex squinted her eyes at him before she untied the ribbon and opened the box. Her eyes softened and her voice briefly caught in her throat.

"Micah, it can't be," she said as her fingers glazed over the delicate item in the box. "How did you find another brooch?"

"After your dad said he found one in Michigan, I figured I would take a chance and have Malik check a few places in the Detroit area. He found this one in a more upscale area while we were in Arkansas. The owner of an antique shop had decided to keep it for herself, but Malik told her the story and she decided that it belonged to you."

"It must have cost so much money," she said.

"It did," he replied. "But she didn't charge anywhere near what I bet she paid for it."

"Wow," Lex said as she twisted the brooch so that the gems and diamonds sparkled in the light. "It's nice to know there are still good people out there."

"It is," he agreed.

"How did you know what the other two brooches looked like?"

"When I was at your parents' house, I asked them if they had a picture of all three brooches and they did."

She leaned in to kiss him before returning her eyes to the brooch. "Having two of the three brooches means the world to me."

"And I'm confident we'll find the third one," Micah said with a smile. She returned his smile, allowing his optimism to flow threw her. Even if they weren't able to locate the third brooch, Lex felt extremely lucky to have a man who cared so much about her happiness.

"I love the man you are Micah Madden," she said, cupping his face in her hands. "I love your strength," she said placing a kiss on his forehead. "I love your loyalty." She placed a kiss on his cheek. "I love your confidence." She placed a kiss on his other cheek. "I love your drive and determination." She kissed his neck. "I love everything about you and being with you makes me a better woman. Thanks for loving me for who I am."

With that, she leaned in for another kiss, this time making sure that it represented all the love and admiration she felt in the depths of her heart.

Epilogue

6 weeks later...

It seemed most of the townspeople of Cranberry Heights were in attendance for the 35th anniversary party of Mason and Cynthia Madden. The look on the couple's faces when they walked into the barn house and realized it wasn't a Founder's Day party, but their anniversary party, had been priceless. Cynthia began shedding happy tears almost immediately, and most of the women at the party had cried right along with her.

Lex glanced around at the beautifully decorated barn and soaked in the feeling of accomplishment. The combination of rustic decor with a vibrant old-world color scheme gave the event a very classy ambiance while maintaining the overall atmosphere of Cranberry Heights. It felt good to be back in Cranberry Heights and she was glad she finally got to meet all of Micah's brothers and cousins. The group had met for dinner in Little Rock a couple days prior so that Mason and Cynthia wouldn't know they were in town. They'd been all too willing to share embarrassing stories about Micah and even though Lex had been the only nonrelative in attendance, she'd felt like she'd grown up with Micah's family.

She got a chill when she thought about how miserable her life would have been had she remained married to Evan. His insolent words no longer affected her and she was done punishing herself for ever being with a man like him. Evan's trial was starting in a few weeks and new victims of his embezzlement were popping up in the news every day. Lex didn't have any sympathy for him and had even learned that he'd had two failed relationships after her and had stolen much more than brooches and pride from the other women. Lex was finally able to put the situation entirely behind her, but she hoped the other women he wronged sued him for all he was worth, even though that wasn't much.

Although Micah and Shawn had originally lost the support of Grant & Parker Inc. after Micah informed them of his prior acquaintance with Neil Timmons, they'd recently called Micah and Shawn to set up a business dinner. They also asked that they bring their significant others, so Lex had prepped Cyd and the two were prepared to support their men and prove to Grant & Parker that M&M Security was a company they could trust.

"Oh, Lex, sweetie," Cynthia said, breaking her thoughts as she pulled her into a warm hug, "Micah told me that Elite Events planned this party. You did such a fantastic job and I absolutely love everything!"

"It was my pleasure," she replied, returning her embrace.

"Come with me," Cynthia said as she linked arms with Lex. "There's something I want to show you."

"Sure," Lex responded. Since returning to Chicago, Lex and Micah's relationship had been on a complete upswing. No matter what she did, she just couldn't seem to get enough of him. Had Micah not been so persistent on having a relationship with her, Lex would have missed out on the love of a lifetime.

"Please wait here," Cynthia told Lex as she unlinked their arms and walked away.

"Um, okay," Lex said, although Cynthia had already dipped through the crowd and was out of earshot.

Lex stood in the middle section of the barn that had been set up for dancing. There were a few groups of people standing near her chatting, but she felt awkward standing there by herself when most of the attendees were sitting at the tables that surrounded the dance floor.

Lex turned around to find out where Cynthia had run off to when suddenly a song by Bruno Mars filled the speakers and one of the groups near her started dancing.

Man they're good, she thought, bopping her head to the song as she watched them dance together in unison. She was so wrapped up in the people who were twirling to the music that she didn't notice ten more people had joined the dance until she felt all eyes on her.

Lex did a 360-degree turn as she whipped her head around the room. *It can't be...* she thought when she realized that she was the only person standing on the dance floor who wasn't dancing. Her heart began beating profusely, and she finally began listening to the upbeat words in the song, which spoke of love, spontaneity and *marriage*.

Lex placed both her hands on her cheeks as she watched the people dance around her, making it unmistakably clear that she was the main attraction. Suddenly, out the corner of her eye, she saw Micah's brothers and cousins make their way onto the dance floor, each one of them swaying to the beat of the music and joining the others in harmony.

Her eyes began filling with tears and she briefly glanced at Cynthia and Mason Madden who were standing on the sidelines wrapped in each other's arms. *Don't cry, Lex...hold it together.* Her heart swelled at the possibility that Micah would go through all this trouble to propose and she wanted to enjoy every second of this precious moment.

Just when she'd calmed her nerves and had gotten her *almost* tears under control, Imani, Cyd and Mya entered the dance floor followed by Daman and Shawn.

"Oh, my goodness," she said aloud as her hand flew to her mouth in astonishment. Never in her entire life had she felt so adored...so cherished...so wanted. She clutched her heart and released the tears she'd been trying to hold in. By the time her parents, Linda and Ethan Turner, had made their way to the dance floor, Lex was an emotional wreck. She wasn't just crying because people who barely knew her were participating in the moment or because people she loved had taken time out their busy lives to be a part of it. She cried because she felt loved...truly and unconditionally loved by Micah Madden.

As the song reached the last couple bars, everyone who was dancing split as they continued moving in a type of soul-train line. Her parents stepped out of the line to escort her in between the two lines of dancers before they joined Micah's parents on the sidelines.

Suddenly, everyone stopped dancing and began clapping to the beat of the music. Lex wiped her tears as she glanced around the crowd, already knowing that Micah was somewhere in the room, based on the way her body was reacting. When he finally came into vision at the front of the dance line, he wasn't moving to the beat as everyone else had been. He was walking purposefully, his eyes locked to hers as he strolled past all the smiling people.

He was wearing black slacks and a deep maroon button-up that matched her burgundy dress perfectly. Even though they'd purposely chosen to dress in similar colors, he looked so different in that moment. So vibrant. And she noticed a small microphone attached to his shirt. She knew what was happening, but she was still nervous, although excitement quickly overtook her nervousness. When he finally reached her, he seized both her hands in his. The DJ turned the music lower and everyone in the dance floor began clapping softer.

"Lexus Tuner," Micah said before he cleared his throat. "When I first met you, I immediately knew that you were the type of woman I could spend the rest of my life with. You understand me, you love me for who I am and, more importantly, you make me strive to be a better person... a better man. You are such an amazing and beautiful woman and I love your strength, your compassion and your willingness to be there for others. But my love for you goes beyond the obvious. I love the faces you make when you get serious or uptight, I adore your clumsiness and the way you make me laugh, too. And I love the crazy words you say to keep yourself from cursing. You may have run into me and fallen the first couple times we met," he said with a chuckle as others joined in the laughter, "but I've been the one falling for you ever since."

He nodded at Shawn, who walked over holding a bright white box. "So, what do you say," Micah said as he got down on one knee and opened a box that contained a gorgeous princess-cut diamond ring sitting on top of a red velvet cupcake. "Will you marry me, Lex?"

Tears filled her eyes and she grinned from ear to ear, still in shock that he'd managed to plan the entire elaborate proposal using a flash mob of their closest family, friends and Cranberry Heights residents. "Of course I'll marry you," she said into the mic loud enough for everyone to hear.

The crowd erupted in applause and the DJ turned the music back up as everyone started dancing to the end of the song. Micah rubbed off a little of the cream cheese frosting that had gotten on the ring before he placed the ring on her finger. He gave her a soft kiss right before the sea of guests came to congratulate them.

"Just so you know," Micah said as he took the red velvet cupcake out of the box and held it to her mouth. "I personally made this cupcake."

She gave him a soft smile. "I can't believe you remembered I love red velvet dessert," she said as she took a bite of the delicious treat.

"This is amazing," she said, savoring the tasty mouthful. She put the dessert back in the box before placing it on a nearby table. "You know what this means."

He laughed as he encircled his arms around her waist. "What does this mean?"

"I've been cooking a lot lately and if you can cook

dessert this well, I think you owe me a few more cooked meals before we solidify this union," she said jokingly.

"Baby, you can have any meal you desire," he said with a laugh as he pulled her even closer to him. "In the meantime, how about you give me what I desire." He glanced down at her lips before licking his own.

She enclosed her arms around his neck. "And what might that be?" she asked, although she had a pretty good idea.

Instead of answering her question, he dipped his head to hers as he captured her lips in the sweetest red velvet kiss.

* * * * *

LET'S TALK
Romance

For exclusive extracts, competitions
and special offers, find us online:

[f] facebook.com/millsandboon

[twitter] @MillsandBoon

[instagram] @MillsandBoonUK

Get in touch on 01413 063232

For all the latest titles coming soon, visit

millsandboon.co.uk/nextmonth

MILLS & BOON
MODERN
Power and Passion

Prepare to be swept off your feet by sophisticated, sexy and seductive heroes, in some of the world's most glamourous and romantic locations, where power and passion collide.

MILLS & BOON
True Love
Romance from the Heart

Celebrate true love with tender stories of
heartfelt romance, from the rush of falling in
love to the joy a new baby can bring, and a
focus on the emotional heart of a relationship.

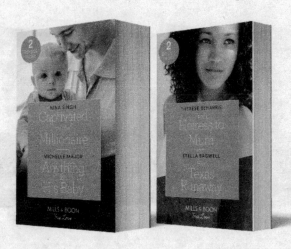